Trouble in Paradise

Also by Pip Granger

Not All Tarts are Apple
The Widow Ginger

Trouble in Paradise

Pip Granger

Poisoned Pen Press

Poisoned Pen Press
6962 E. First Ave., Ste. 103
Scottsdale, AZ 85251
www.poisonedpenpress.com
info@poisonedpenpress.com

Printed in the United States of America

*This one is in loving memory of my mother Joan,
my brother Pots and my half-sister Valerie*

Acknowledgments

Many thanks to Ray for all his help, support and forebearance. Also thanks to Selina Walker and Jane Conway-Gordon for not losing their patience or their grip when things looked hairy. Last, but by no means least, thanks to everyone at Transworld who work so hard behind the scenes to bring us books—you know who you are…

Chapter 1

'Zeld! Zeld! *Zelda!* Have you heard? It's over, it's finally bloody over. Answer the door, there's a love. I feel a right prune standing here, yelling myself hoarse.'

It was my friend Dilly's voice, husky with excitement. It was late Monday afternoon; I'd just finished my shift at the canteen, or British Restaurant as it patriotically called itself, and was up to my eyebrows in cold, scummy water at home. I was wrestling with a greasy frying pan without benefit of either soap or a shilling for the gas, so it was a relief to drop the thing and hurry downstairs to the street door. Dilly's lovely face, normally pale, was glowing with joy under her blue headscarf, and her brown eyes glittered with tears. Dilly was always inclined to blub when she was happy; and when she wasn't.

'Oh, Zeld!' she yelled, then threw her arms around me, yanked me into the street and hurled me up the road to Hobbs the butcher's and back again in a mad polka. It took a fair amount of navigational skill to dodge the broken paving stones and pot-holes that still littered our East London streets despite the best efforts of the authorities.

It was a good half an hour before we were free of the small crowd we'd collected and had settled at my kitchen table, toasting the great news in weak tea with no sugar. The war in Europe was over! Hitler had chucked in the towel. Of course, we'd been hearing rumours for days and our harkers had been glued to the wireless at the canteen, but there'd been no official announcement, so we'd hardly dared to believe it until we heard it from Mr. Churchill's own lips. The buzz around London would not be denied a second longer, though. We had won at last, announcement or no announcement!

We were ready to let our corsets out and our hair down and to throw caution to the wind. We were sick of it, heartily sick of it, and we wanted our proper lives back. Of course, some of us didn't really know what our adult lives were supposed to be like, having been young when the war started, but we were willing to find out. Most of us were, anyway. I had a horrible feeling I knew what my real life with Charlie was going to be like, and I was sure I wasn't going to like it. Still, the time to worry about that was when I heard the bleeder's hobnails on the stairs. Until then, I could join in the merriment along with everybody else.

'Some Yank told me that Hitler blew his own brains out,' Dilly told me. Her face split in an evil grin as she lit up a Chesterfield. American servicemen kept her supplied with life's luxuries like cigarettes, stockings and, God bless 'em, chocolate. Which was very handy indeed, what with the black market not being cheap and us being broke most of the time.

'Ma Hole says he swallowed poison and Hobbs the butcher says he's been hanged, drawn and quartered by his own bodyguard, but I reckon that's wishful thinking myself. Nobody's found the body yet, so it's all guesswork. He's always been bloodthirsty, that Lenny Hobbs. He was like it when he was at school, you remember.' Dilly's face was getting pinker by the second.

Lenny Hobbs had indeed been a bloodthirsty kid. A picture of his large, red face when he was a schoolboy floated across my mind. We were all huddled behind the toilets staring at a pair of sheep's eyeballs in the palm of his grubby hand. There was no telling what Lenny Hobbs was likely to whip out of his pocket next—once it had been a pig's trotter—and we girls learned to scuttle to the toilet at top speed when he and his pals were on the loose. But he didn't matter at that moment, and neither did Hitler. The main thing was that the war in our neck of the woods was over.

'Your mum says to come round to the Gardens tonight,' Dilly continued, still breathless with it all. 'I bumped into her and she says there's going to be a knees-up to end all knees-ups. They've decided the weekend for the street party, but there'll be a bit of a do tonight.'

And Mum should know, because she could drum up a party in an empty house. She just loved to celebrate. Any old excuse would do. She'd been known to bung a candle in our bread and dripping and call it a 'Bloody Monday party' because she hated bloody Mondays with the mountains of wet, smelly washing hanging all over the place, and would do anything to put a shine on things. Added to her natural inclination towards jollity, she dearly loved to organize anything with a heartbeat, which was handy because she'd had six kids and a husband to care for on a very few quid most weeks. She always said that Winnie, Mr. Churchill, should have had some mums in his war cabinet; they would have shown him a thing or two about getting the right bodies in the right place at the right time, fully clothed and with bellies suitably filled.

Paradise Gardens was a miracle, or so everybody said. Somehow, throughout the war, it had remained more or less intact, although large chunks of the surrounding area had been flattened by doodlebugs or burned to blackened stumps by incendiary bombs. The only things missing from Paradise Gardens were the railings, and the men from the Ministry had had those away at the beginning of the war, along with our pots and pans, to churn out ammunition and to build ships, tanks and Spitfires. I often wondered if Grandpa's tin chamber-pot had wound up landing on some Nazi's nut, but of course, there was no way of finding out. I simply had to hope.

Apart from the ironwork, though, there had been very little damage to the Gardens. The odd roof tile had been shifted by the shock waves from nights of particularly heavy bombing in our bit of Hackney, and Zinnia Makepeace's shed window was blown in at number 23, but that was about it. As people said, it was a miracle, especially with the Gardens being so near the railway line and presenting such a beautiful sitting target.

Mum and Dad had lived at 3 Arcadia Buildings ever since they'd married and moved in with Gran and Grandpa. All six of us had been born in that narrow, three-storey terraced house. We had the top two floors, four rooms in all. One doubled up as kitchen, living room, and bathroom on bath nights. Mum and Dad slept in one room, us girls were in the one next to them and the boys had the room next to the kitchen. Gran and Grandpa lived on the ground floor and had their kitchen in the basement, with a window overlooking the area and the dustbins. We all shared the one toilet, which was at the end of the garden by the back gate on to Paradise Alley. The Alley ran behind our rank of buildings, snaked behind Zinnia's place and joined the narrow path that hugged the far side of number 23 and led from the Gardens out on to Paradise Gardens allotments and the railway just beyond. The line was so close that Zinnia's house shook whenever the heavy coal and munitions trains went by, while our carrots, onions and King Edwards got liberal doses of soot from the belching engines.

Grandpa was long dead. My sister Vi lived with Gran now, along with her son Tony and, when he was on leave from the army, her husband, Fred. But Fred hadn't been home in some considerable time. He had gone missing in action and nothing had been heard of him. Fred was Dilly's older brother, so the pain of losing him had spread through my family and my best mate's family as well. He was a good bloke, was Fred; kind, funny and solid.

Tony missed him more than any of us; he idolized his dad and they had been very close. Like all the kids around our way, Tony had been evacuated, but like a good many others, he was soon back. The phony war and homesickness saw to that. Once the Blitz started in earnest, it was clear that he, his cousin Reggie and a lot of their friends wouldn't be wrenched away to the sticks again, bombs or no bombs. I think that later Tony believed that, if he took his eye off of us, we'd disappear the way his dad had done when he marched off to war, and he simply couldn't bear it.

Upstairs, Mum and Dad rattled about in their four rooms, mostly empty now, with their chicks scattered to the four winds. Well, littered about the surrounding houses, streets and the army and navy, to be exact. Except for Albert, the oldest: he'd bought it early on in France, and nobody liked to talk about him for fear of setting Mum off again. The telegram from the War Office had sent Mum spiralling into one of the darkest moods we had ever seen. If Winston Churchill was stalked by a 'black dog,' then our mum had the whole bleeding pack baying at her heels. It took her ages to come out of it. As she said, losing her eldest boy and a much loved son-in-law to a bloody madman wasn't something a body's quick to forget. And she never, ever did: nor forgave it either.

Chapter 2

Although there still hadn't been an official announcement that
the war in Europe was over, London heaved that night. Everywhere you went, men, women and children were delirious with
joy. People were hanging off the lampposts in Trafalgar Square,
there being no room to stand, and the Palace was besieged by
a mass of loyal subjects, hell-bent on sharing their ecstasy with
the Royal Household, even if a lot of them were away at Windsor. Every pub in London, and probably the whole country,
was stuffed to the rafters with happy punters. Bomb sites were
raided to provide the wherewithal to build victory bonfires that
twinkled like millions of giant fireflies. And the fire in Paradise
Gardens outshone them all.

Unless you knew your way around our bit of Hackney, you'd
never find Paradise Gardens. It was tucked away down a narrow
alley—Paradise Row—that led from one of the maze of little side
streets that huddled behind the bustling main road. Most of the
Gardens was made up of terraces of tall brick houses shoe-horned
into the meanest possible space. Those Georgian speculators
knew a thing or twenty about squeezing the last farthing from
their investment. Some things never change.

However, they hadn't managed to get their greedy hands on
the narrow end—the bit with the footpath that led out on to the
allotments. Number 23 Paradise Gardens hogged that, sprawl-
ing untidily, like an ancient mongrel, over the whole plot. Our

mum's good friend, Zinnia Makepeace, lived there alone, apart from a motley crew of cats and dogs that came daily to be fed and her own pair of tabbies, Hepzibah and Hallelujah. Makepeaces had lived at number 23 as far back as anyone could remember. They were a funny lot. Everybody said so. Our dad swore they were witches, and that the presence of Zinnia in the Gardens explained its amazing escape from Hitler's evil intentions.

'Let's face it, would you take the old battle-axe on?' he'd ask, then plough ahead, without waiting for a reply. Our dad didn't usually need replies, being certain in his own mind about what was what. 'I know I wouldn't, and 'Itler wouldn't neither, not if he wanted to hang on to that last bollock of his, that is. One look from her and it'd shrivel to a sultana, only smaller.'

There was no love lost between Zinnia and our dad. He thought she was a bossy old boot and too lippy by half. According to him, that was why she was still a spinster. I always thought the word 'spinster' was a terrible insult, like 'bastard,' until I married Charlie. During the reading out of the banns, I was referred to as 'a spinster of this parish' and as I couldn't imagine dear old Reverend Cattermole swearing, especially in church, I worked out it couldn't be rude.

Our mum liked Zinnia, though, and had been her friend since her arrival in the Gardens more than thirty years before. That was another thing about Zinnia: she was mysterious, like Primrose Makepeace had been before her. According to our mum, Zinnia arrived one day, hat skew-whiff and scarf stuffed into a lumpy tweed coat that was the colour of peat and heather and smelt strongly of sheep (or what our mum imagined was sheep; if it wasn't, she shuddered to think what it was).

Anyway, Zinnia arrived carrying a very small suitcase and said she'd come to nurse Primrose. This was the first anyone knew about old Prim being ill, apparently, but sure enough, she died three years later. She lasted just long enough to teach Zinnia everything she knew about the people in and around Paradise Gardens, which came in handy as she was called upon to help us into and out of this world. Zinnia, like Primrose and the other Makepeaces before her, was the local midwife, layer-out of bodies and unofficial first port of call when there was sickness in the house. Before you flashed out your hard-earned cash for the doctor, it was a good idea to find out if it was necessary, or whether a little something from Zinnia's garden or allotment, mixed with a drop of brandy or, more boringly, a slosh of boiling water, would do the trick. Either way, Zinnia was asked to make the judgement. If a doctor *was* needed, she'd even lend you the money if your old man's suit had already been pawned. By the end of the war, I think even our dad had a sneaking respect for her, despite her ways.

Old Primrose may have told Zinnia all about us and our doings, but even after all those years, we still knew bugger all about her. Well, about her past, anyway. As far as our mum could gather, she was an obscure cousin of Primrose and was brought up on some island called Harris, where the tweed comes from, and it was way up north. And that was it.

That, and the fact that she was a good friend, an excellent gardener, the soul of discretion when the need arose and a wonderful gossip when it didn't. There wasn't a lot that Zinnia didn't see or hear. She had seen four of our mum's six kids into the world, had seen Grandpa out of it and was busy keeping Gran's knees in working order and young Reggie's chest clear in winter. Reggie was one of my older sister Doris' brood, a pale, skinny scrap of a lad who was inclined to be chesty.

On top of all that, Zinnia Makepeace kept my poor old feet in mid-season form, and for that I will love her until the day I die. I've always been a martyr to my feet, ever since I was knee-high to something small with knees. She produced a cream every winter that kept the chilblains at bay and some concoction that I swallowed that kept my joints from swelling and aching too badly. According to Zinnia, it wasn't just old people who got painful feet, and judging by my poor plates, she was right; even my bunions had bunions.

Number 23 took up the whole of the narrow end of the Gardens: Arcadia Buildings formed the left-hand side, Paradise

Buildings were on the right and at the wide part, opposite Zinnia's place, were Utopia Buildings. In the middle was the garden itself, now filled with vegetables and soft fruit, the smutty laurels and sooty privet having been dug up for victory long before.

As Zinnia said, 'The man who had the job of naming this place allowed religious zeal or brainless optimism to cloud his judgement just a wee bit. It's hard to imagine a spot further from the Promised Land.' And then she'd added, graciously, 'I like it fine, though.'

She was never one to over-egg the pudding. The truth was, it was hard to imagine the Gardens without Zinnia or Zinnia without the Gardens, despite the tiny trace of haggis-noshing accent she still had after all her years in the East End.

That Monday night, the people in Paradise Gardens went completely off their trolleys. Although there was a proper 'do'—a street party—scheduled for the following Saturday, there was no holding us back. We danced, sang and drank the night away. Lenny Hobbs found a fistful of rockets, God knows where, so we even had fireworks. The King's Head rolled its piano into the street and I took my turn to bash out 'Roll Out The Barrel,' 'Pack Up Your Troubles,' 'Knees Up Mother Brown,' 'The Lambeth Walk,' and one or two other favourites.

The Gardens was a sea of heaving bodies as we twirled and danced our joy. Black, brown, green and blue skirts flashed their stripes or flowers among the sombre shades of khaki and navy blue uniforms as they waltzed, tangoed or jitterbugged by. The pigeons roosting in the plane trees almost dropped off their twigs, stunned by the deafening racket of 'Rule Britannia' being belted out by so many happy, drunken sets of vocal cords.

We kept the party going well into the next day, and some folk started all over again once Winnie had made his official broadcast. That famous voice drifted out over the Gardens from a hundred wirelesses. You could have heard a feather drop right up until the last full stop and then a roar went up that shook the sparrows out of the eaves and the knees-up started all over again.

Well, it was more of a knee-wobble really, everyone being half-cut and knackered already. Some braver souls managed to line up behind their eyes just enough to totter into work, only to be sent home again: it was a holiday. Let's face it, most of us wouldn't have been much use, so they might as well make it official.

For me, the best bit of Monday's celebrations was when the men had repaired to the boozer and the women and children settled down for a good old natter over the teacups and the crumbs of the Victory cake Dilly and I had knocked up. We had made it mostly from this and that scrounged from Terry Rainbird, the grocer with the corner shop next to Hobbs the butcher. Dilly had worked for Terry ever since we'd left school at fifteen. He was a bit sweet on her, I reckon, but she wouldn't have it.

'Don't be daft, Zeld, he's old enough to be my dad. You're disgusting, you are. Now then, as all your stockings are so full of darns you'll look like a two-legged Dalmatian, we'll have to do a paint job. I brought my eyebrow pencil just in case. Stand still and stop your rabbiting or your seams'll be all over your legs and you don't want that. Your Vi'll be on about 'em all night.'

She licked the precious stub of eyebrow pencil and screwed her forehead up in concentration, desperately trying to get the fake seams to look straight and real. I swear that girl was as blind as a blindfolded bat, but she was too vain to wear specs.

I wore the rose print frock I'd made up out of half of some old curtains from Zinnia's front parlour. The other half went to make skirts for my sister Doris' twins and a blouse for my other sister, Vi. Very fetching we looked, too, even if I do say so myself. Naturally, all of us turned up at the party in the same curtains, not having discussed what we were wearing beforehand, but I think we carried it off. As long as we made sure we didn't stand too close together when we were indoors, in case some drunk mistook us for the furniture and sat on us, we were all right.

Most of the women present had set my old Singer humming at one time or another. I knew for a fact that at least half a dozen of us were wearing silk knickers knocked up from a parachute donated by one of Dilly's many admirers. She was a stunner, was Dilly, a natural blonde with surprising brown eyes, soft like a cow's, and a curvaceous figure, topped off with a cheerful and generous disposition when you got past the shyness.

Once we were dolled up to the nines we made our way, with the cake—which was *meant* to be a Victoria sponge, but was more municipal manhole cover—round to the Gardens, which were already heaving with merriment. The walk there had been a strange one. At least, it seemed so to me. The deliriously happy people, the women in their very best clothes and full, red-lipped make-up and the men spruce in uniform or their Civvy Street suits, contrasted sharply with the narrow, dark streets around them. These were littered with the twisted, broken remains of houses, shops, factories and warehouses that had been caught up in the fury and shattered, their insides gaping for all the world to see, like open wounds. Which I suppose they were.

Even among all that joy, I was aware of the people whose lives would never, ever be the same again, in my own family and the families of friends, neighbours, countrymen, allies and foe alike. Each ruin of a familiar house reminded me of who was missing. And despite all the happiness around me, I was immensely sad.

As soon as we arrived in the Gardens, Dilly disappeared into a group of merchant seamen, who were pouring out of the King's Head, led by our friend Ronnie. They'd come straight from the docks and were eager to get started. I made my way to 3 Arcadia Buildings to dump the cake in the familiar kitchen. Mum, Gran and Zinnia were there. Dad had disappeared to the pub with Lenny Hobbs and his dad, Leonard.

'Zelda, love, you're here, and about time too,' Mum greeted me. 'Vi's somewhere around with your cousins and Doris will be back soon.'

'Aye, I saw her chasing Vi's Tony and that Brian Hole off the bomb site opposite the church,' said Zinnia. 'They were collecting for the bonfire but those stairs weren't a bit safe.'

She turned to me. 'How are you, hen? You're looking a wee bit peely-wally if you ask me. I see my curtains are holding up.'

I never got to answer, because my sister Doris turned up, breathing like an old traction engine, and sank into a chair, large face creased in concern. 'You know, I don't like our Tony hanging around with that Brian Hole. He's trouble, just like the rest of that family. Where's Vi? And why ain't she keeping an eye on her son and heir, that's what I want to know?'

Vi and Doris were so different, it was hard to imagine that they came out of the same stable. Doris had taken to marriage and motherhood as if born to it, which I suppose she was, being a woman and all. Most women got married, and those that didn't were pitied by the rest, which always seemed a bit hard to me. But that's the way it was—and always had been, as far as I knew.

Zinnia once told me a story about how a woman saddled with a work-shy, drunken husband and twelve ragged, snotty-nosed children, asked her what it was like being a spinster. Zinnia had told her about her own beloved home, her satisfying job and her annual holiday in Scotland. The mother, looking green with envy, said, 'Ooh, it sounds lovely; I'd like that—if it wasn't for the shame.' Which just about summed it up, really.

Vi liked being a wife all right, but she was nowhere near as keen on being a mum. She had hated being pregnant, had referred to her growing lump as 'the parasite' almost as soon as she knew it was there. Mind you, she had been horribly sick for most of the pregnancy, which was enough to try the patience of a saint. Even Zinnia's herbs seemed to be failing, until we found out Vi wasn't taking them, preferring a Woodbine, weak tea and a biscuit.

When baby Tony finally struggled out a month premature, we all heaved a sigh of relief, thinking things would improve—but they didn't. Vi wouldn't put him to the breast. She refused point blank, despite the pleadings of Mum and Zinnia, to part with a single drop of mother's milk. I know they were very worried about her then, but all she'd do was stare out of her parlour window, hour after hour, looking for God knows what or who. Every time I walked past in the street, there'd be the glimmer of her round, plain, pale face, behind the nets, staring. I'd wave, but she wouldn't wave back. I'd knock on the door, but she wouldn't answer. In the end, Fred gave us a key to let ourselves in while he was at work to make sure poor little Tony was still alive at least. Luckily, Doris was still feeding her Reggie at the time, so she had plenty left for Tony and he began to thrive, but it was touch and go there for a bit.

Zinnia said she'd seen it before: it was a kind of melancholia brought on by childbirth and that it would eventually go away. And it did, but Vi never really took to her Tony, or him to her. He preferred going to Doris or our mum for comfort when he was little, and he hung about with his dad a lot as he got older. But then Fred went off to war, and Tony, well, he had to shift for himself, poor little mite. When he came back from being evacuated to Wales, he began to go about with Brian Hole, or 'Bung'ole' as we called him.

Even moving in with our Gran, a year or so after his return, when it was obvious things weren't too clever between mother and son, hadn't improved things that much. Vi was less lonely, perhaps, but Tony was still far too friendly with Bung'ole for anybody's comfort. Then, just to make things a million times worse, another telegram had come, saying that Fred had gone missing. And later, a letter from his commanding officer saying he'd been brave and had disappeared in the thick of the fighting.

'Aye, well.' Zinnia sighed and stood up. 'I'm away home. Zelda, why don't you keep me company?' Zinnia had a way of putting things that made it quite clear this was more than a suggestion.

'You'll be back later, for the real party?' It was still early in the evening and Mum was amazed that anyone would leave a party before the very last knockings. 'The men'll be back from the pub later and the kids'll be tucked up in bed and we can let our hair down. What do you say, Zin, Zelda?'

'Aye. We'll be back. Keep a wee dram for me. I'm just going to find some food. That Victory cake barely touched the sides before it crashed to the pit of my poor stomach. I can take a look at Zelda's feet while I'm at it.' And Zinnia swept out, with me in tow and wondering why she was so keen to get me on my own.

It took quite a while to find out, because we were stopped every few yards by our happy neighbours, singing and dancing, staggering and falling, depending on how far gone they were. It seemed like hours before we fell through Zinnia's front door and the thick walls reduced the singing to a distant hum.

Chapter 3

I don't know how long we were holed up in Zinnia's kitchen, but it felt like ages. I loved that kitchen. In fact, I loved the whole house. It was different from anybody else's place that I'd ever been to.

The basic house wasn't very big: two up, two down, with a scullery tacked on the back. But over the years—centuries, Zinnia said—various Makepeaces had added bits, so that it was a jumble of rooms, one of them made almost entirely of glass that the bombs failed to shatter. Maybe Dad was right: perhaps Zinnia had cast a spell to save her windows.

Out the back was a wooden workshop and storage sheds. There was even an old railway carriage, complete with window-boxes and curtains, at the end of the garden, nestled under some of the few apple and plum trees to be found in Hackney. As kids, we played for hours in that walled garden. It was always a magical place.

The kitchen was low and dark, with a small pine table, scrubbed almost white over the years, in the centre. A pine dresser took up the whole of one wall and china twinkled from its shelves in the lamplight. The gleaming butler's sink, with its brass tap jutting above it like a big, hooked nose, was under the window that faced on to the garden. There was a large, black range along the third wall, while the fourth held a door into the parlour and the stairs to the rooms above.

Nothing on this earth would get Zinnia to trade in her range for a proper cooker. She said she'd been brought up with one that burned peat, and although coal and coke weren't the same, they'd do. Every now and then, out would come the Zebra black leading and the monster would get a good seeing-to, brush and cloth seeking out every little cranny—and there were hundreds of them. I should know; I had helped with the ritual more than once.

Luckily, the coalie, Mr. Whitelock, had a brood of thirteen kids that Zinnia had birthed and treated for measles, chickenpox, whooping cough and mumps as those childhood lurgies had run through the lot of them like the dreaded cascara. She'd saved young Ivy from diphtheria and nursed her in her own home to stop the other twelve from getting it, so she had plenty of goodwill stored up round at the Whitelocks'. This meant that when there was coal to be had, Mr. Whitelock made absolutely certain that Zinnia got some, and the range rarely went out, war or no war.

When there was no coal, the Whitelock tribe collected wood from the bomb sites and delivered that on their old cart drawn by Dobbin the Third, a huge dappled grey with shaggy hooves. While they were at it, they supplied manure for Zinnia's garden and allotments, too. It was what Zinnia called 'a happy arrangement'; she had loads of those with the people round and about.

'So, hen, the war's over. Have you given any thought to your future at all?' That was typical of Zinnia, dismissing six years of world war as if it was just a bit of a squabble. There she was, ready to move on to the next thing the second that particular unpleasantness was over.

'Give me a chance, Auntie Zin, I haven't taken it all in yet. Nobody has.' Truth to tell, I had been avoiding thinking about the future, it being a bit bleak, as far as I could figure it.

'Aye, well, to my mind it's time you *did* give it some thought. That Charlie of yours is no good. You don't need me to tell you that. I didn't believe you when you said that you fell when you lost the baby, and I don't believe it now. You were pushed down those stairs when Charlie was in drink. You know it and so do I.'

Zinnia held up her hand to shut me up when she saw my mouth open to protest. I snapped it shut. There was no point; I could see it in her shrewd, grey, far-seeing eyes. Zinnia always looked as if she was scanning some distant horizon, even when she was staring right into your face from not five feet away. It made you feel as if you were there, but not there, as far as she was concerned. It was very odd, until you got used to it. I knew I could argue till I was blue in the face; nothing would change her mind, because she was right. I had been pushed.

'We'll not waste time examining the point,' she told me, 'we'll just concentrate on what comes next. Unlike your revered father, I don't take the view that, having made your bed, you should be made to lie on it. We all make mistakes, especially the young. Some folk forget that.'

My eyes filled with tears. Zinnia always seemed to be able to see right into my mind to the things that worried or frightened me the most. Sometimes she caught on before I realized I was upset at all. But then, I *had* trailed around after her almost since I could walk, fascinated by her knowledge of herbs, gardening, birds, bugs and bees, and her brisk common sense with her patients, so I suppose she knew me well.

'Hold your water, young Zelda. We don't have time for your tears,' she said firmly. 'We've a party to attend and you'll ruin your mascara. All I'm saying is this: should you ever need to run away from it all, you have a sanctuary here with me. Your mother and I have talked it over and we're agreed. Your dad won't abide the shame if you walk out on your wedding vows, but that's no reason for you to stay where you're not safe. He wouldn't have you home; you know it and so do we. So, if ever you need to run, run here. Charlie'll not interfere with me. And if he does, he'll regret it.'

Sympathy always undoes me. All that time I'd thought that terrifying night when Charlie had gone berserk and bounced me off the walls before slinging me down the stairs had been my secret. Bearing my mascara in mind, I made a big effort not to cry, but the expression on Zinnia's face finished me off. Every inch of its hard, angular lines was softened by tenderness and understanding, and her eyes told me there wasn't a lot she hadn't seen and there was even less she couldn't imagine. I cried for what seemed like hours, but felt better at the end of it. I hadn't realized, until that moment, just how afraid I had been of my future with Charlie. It was a relief to know that Zinnia and my mum knew, even if I hadn't had the nerve to tell them.

The whole thing was such an awful mess. I'd thrown my life away at seventeen on one stupid act of defiance that had wound up in a tipsy and sweaty struggle on a grave behind St Mary's. Next thing I knew, I was dragging myself up the aisle of the selfsame church, three months gone and desperate to get away. That was just after Charlie had joined up, early on in the war, and I'd barely seen him since. Chucking me down the stairs had been the last thing he'd done before he rejoined his regiment at Catterick after his first leave. All those years I'd kept the secret, and it turned out to be hardly any secret at all.

In the end, Zinnia became businesslike. 'Aye, well, here's a hanky, have a good blow.' She gave me a little shove towards the sink. 'Wash your face—you look like a tabby cat with all those black streaks. Let's get away to that party before all the whisky I know your dad's been hoarding is drunk. Just remember what I say, lassie, you've a home here if you've a mind. Any time.' She collected up our cups and saucers, ran them under the tap, absentmindedly dried them and put them away in the cupboard before turning back to me, smiling.

'Now, where's that wee dram I was promised? I'll not get it standing here blethering with you, that's for sure.'

As we walked back to Arcadia Buildings arm in arm, I wondered, not for the first time—nor the last—how Zinnia and my mum seemed to know *everything*.

Chapter 4

The piano was going like the clappers and voices were raised in song, telling us how Hitler only had one ball, to the tune of 'Colonel Bogey.' A good time was being had by all. Mum and Dad were by the bonfire fishing out hot spuds from the cinders with long toasting forks. Their faces glowed with happiness, booze and firelight as Zinnia and I wound our way through the crowd to join them.

I had two choices that night. I could worry myself to death about what life was going to be like in the future or I could let my hair down and enjoy the moment that every person I knew had been waiting for for six long years. It took just an instant to make up my mind. I was going to enjoy the moment, because it was one that would never come again.

The whole thing was a blur of singing, dancing and drinking. Lots and lots of drinking. God knows where all the drink came from. It'd been so long since spirits had been freely available, us younger ones thought they were something to do with ghosts. We knew little about the sort that came in bottles. Things had been very tight for the previous six years. What little there was around certainly wasn't wasted too freely on the young, who hadn't had the chance to develop a taste for it. So, inexperience might explain why, for only the third time in my life, I got myself stupid giggling drunk.

The very first time I was the worse for wear, the giggling had stopped abruptly on that grave in St Mary's churchyard. I remember looking, when Charlie'd finished, at that grave, to see who had been my silent witness. Her name was Emily Alice Davies, 1821–1838, Beloved Daughter of Ezekiel and Eliza. She was seventeen, the same age as me at the time. It seemed important, that, to hang on to the fact that poor Emily Alice had died, which was a fate *worse* than a fate worse than death, in my opinion. I often took flowers and chatted to Emily Alice. I still do now and then.

The second time was a lot more fun; the bits I can remember were, at least. I was up West with a whole load of pals. Charlie was already at Catterick, so wasn't there to spoil everything like he always did when he'd had a few. This third time, the night war ended, was the very best time of all. I danced with Terry Rainbird, Ronnie Rigby and Lenny Hobbs in the flickering light of the bonfire until I thought my feet would drop off, closely followed by my legs.

I went into the house to rest and collapsed at last next to my gran, who was three sheets to the wind, singing 'Danny Boy' in a quavering soprano and waving a large glass of stout about in the most alarming fashion, stopping just short of slopping it on the lino. Every now and then she'd break off singing, cackle, tap her feet as if she was dancing and chant, 'We won the war! We won the war!' at the top of her lungs.

She was having a fine old time until Ma Hole, Bung'ole's mum, stumped into the kitchen. 'Bleeding 'ell, Ida Smallbone,' she said, 'why don't you shut your tuneless trap and offer a body a drink?'

Gran stopped abruptly and eyed Ma Hole as if she'd come in on someone's shoe. 'Because, Gladys Hole, I normally choose only to drink with my friends, and you ain't no friend of mine. However'—she paused as she gathered herself up for a big effort—'as it is such a wonderful occasion, I'll overlook past trouble between our families and give you a convivial glass of stout. Zelda, pour the woman a drink.' So I did. Then I went outdoors again to carry on dancing.

The last thing I remember of that night was my nephew Tony, standing in the dying light of the bonfire as dawn was just beginning to glow red in the east, looking like a fallen angel, but sounding like one that was soaring to the sky, as he sang 'Oh for the wings, for the wings of a dove' in a voice so pure it broke every heart within hearing distance.

The next thing I knew, I was being gently woken by Gran. I had been put to bed in my old room in Arcadia Buildings sometime after dawn.

A hair of the dog, a cup of tea and two aspirin—Dad's remedy for hangovers—was waiting for me on the bedside table. Along with the cure came instructions to proceed downstairs to Gran's to calm Vi down. Dad had nipped round to the police station to pick up Tony and Mum had gone round to the baker's before the bread ran out.

I couldn't get my brain working enough to instruct my mouth to ask what had happened before Gran disappeared as well. I was left wondering what on earth our Tony was doing at the nick. I was pretty sure the little bugger wasn't signing up to join the police, on account of him being a good bit too young and far too short. That meant he was in trouble, but the last time I'd seen him, he'd been singing his heart out to a rapt audience.

I tottered downstairs, clutching my cup of tea like it was the Holy Grail, and walked into a storm of weeping, wailing and gnashing of teeth. When our Vi wasn't staring out of windows, as if in another world, she could get into such a state and make such a bloody racket that you wished she *was* in another world, preferably one a good long way away from this one. Another universe would be nice, and you were half inclined to help her into it as well. It wasn't hard to see where Tony had picked up a talent for being heard.

It took me ages to get Vi to stop crying long enough to tell me what had happened. Tony'd been seen, apparently, loitering watchfully outside a warehouse just off Homerton High Street in the early hours when there was a break-in going on. The thief or thieves had got away with two pounds, seven and sixpence three-farthings from the petty cash, and three and a half feet of rubber hose.

Neither money nor rubber goods had been found on Tony when he'd been picked up, which was why he hadn't yet been accused of being involved. He was simply at the police station to answer some rather pointed questions. But according to PC George 'Nosher' Grubb, who'd come to pick him up only half an hour after the poor kid had finally got to bed, there were suspicions, serious suspicions. Just to add to the general joys, the lad had been found to be drunk when he was woken up and had put up a token struggle as he was marched away, which meant that he'd got a clip around the ear for being drunk and disorderly while he was at it.

Maybe I was being unusually dim, being hungover and all, but I couldn't work out when Tony'd had time to get himself into trouble. I asked Vi.

'According to George Grubb,' she said, 'he was seen at least a couple of hours before he sang for us, and it's true, I did lose sight of him for a while round about then. I thought he'd put himself to bed,' Vi wailed, working up to a new storm of weeping. I was beginning to be afraid we'd both drown.

I was just thinking that if Tony had been involved in some skulduggery, then he had to have some nerve to stand there singing like an innocent choirboy, when the door burst open. Ma Hole stumped into the room, face red with fury. There were times when I wished we locked our doors round our way, and this was one of them. Nobody in their right mind wanted Ma Hole cluttering up their kitchen, but there she was, standing in the middle of the room like a malevolent toad, all saggy, swarthy and warty.

'What the bloody hell are you carrying on about?' demanded Ma, glaring at the sodden Vi. I have to admit, it was a good question, and one I'd been thinking of asking myself. True, it was not good that Tony was suspected of a crime, but on the other hand, it looked as if nobody had proved anything, so shouldn't we be giving him the benefit of any doubt there might be? And as for being drunk and disorderly—well, it was far from ideal behaviour in one so young, but then, everybody had been the worse for wear ever since peace had broken out. And his family didn't seem to have set much of an example.

'Belt up, Vi Gunn, or I'll make you,' said Ma Hole, but the warning fell on deaf ears, so she stepped forward and slapped Vi's face hard. 'I said belt up, you stupid mare.'

'Now,' she demanded, 'where's your Tony?' She rested her fat hands on her large hips. Her eyes bulged like organ stops and her mouth was set in a thin line. Poor Vi went white and seemed to be struck dumb; her mouth opened and closed, but no sound came.

I stepped in and replied for her. 'What's that got to do with you?'

'My Brian said he saw him being taken away by George Grubb this morning. What do the rozzers want with him?'

'I'd have thought that was our business, Mrs. Hole. What's it got to do with you?' At a guess, I'd say Brian was worried our Tony'd blab and drop him in it. Whatever her interest was, we never got to hear about it, because a commotion at the door told us that Dad and Tony were back, along with Gran and Mum. They'd met in the High Street and had come home mob-handed.

All hell broke loose as soon as Gran spotted Ma Hole in her kitchen. She wouldn't wait for an explanation, just launched straight into a tirade. 'Oy, you. Out!' Gran glared, grabbed her broom from the corner and made sweeping motions as if to brush her away. 'I don't recall asking you in and I'm damned sure my granddaughters didn't. They've got more sense. So, out with you!'

'I just came to…' Ma began.

'Save that for someone who cares. Me, I don't give a tinker's curse what you're here for. We're in the middle of private family business and you're not family, so OUT!' Gran turned to Dad.

'Harry, sling her out if she won't go voluntary,' she ordered, puffing up to her full four foot eleven and three-quarter inches tall and three and a half feet wide. Her dander was well and truly up.

It suddenly seemed to dawn on Ma Hole that she was all alone in extremely hostile territory. None of her 'boys' were around to provide muscle and she was far too fat to fight or to dodge or to stand her ground against determined opposition. She normally relied on an assortment of spivs to impose her will on the unwilling, but she must have charged over to us before she'd had time to think properly.

Her eyes glittered as she headed for the door. 'Just you keep your gob shut, Tony Gunn, if you know what's good for you.'

'Are you threatening my great-grandson, Mrs. Hole?' Fury shook Gran's body as if it was jelly.

'Just a word to the wise, Mrs. Smallbone,' Ma spat back, and was gone.

We all heaved a sigh of relief. But we never did get young Tony to tell us what he was doing outside that warehouse, or who he was with, either, because in the kerfuffle of getting Ma Hole out of the basement door the little blighter had slipped out of the room, and we heard the front door slam upstairs.

You didn't need to be a genius to work it out, though. The appearance of Ma told us everything. Tony had been at the warehouse with Bung'ole, or Brian Dudley Hole, as the Clerk of the Court would address him each time the magistrates had the pleasure of telling him what an incorrigible little villain they thought he was, even if they couldn't prove it.

Chapter 5

There were three distinct physical types in our family. Doris and Vi were typical of the majority of Marriotts: mops of mid-brown hair, grey/blue eyes, sturdy figures on average-sized frames and rather round faces. There was no mistaking who they belonged to, because it had been the Marriott look for generations. You only had to scrutinize the family photographs to see it. Even in the olden days, when the poor souls had had to stand or sit for ages, holding the pose, and their faces had set in concrete, they were still obviously Marriott faces.

The Smallbone element made itself obvious too. They were on the short side, with little pointed, pinched, pixie-like faces, fair, thin hair and pale blue, squinty eyes. Some were shortsighted as well and wore specs, like Reggie, who was a Smallbone down to his socks. Mum had the blue eyes and pixie face but had run to plump in middle age.

Every now and then, though, a cuckoo would appear in the nest. I'm one, with my black hair, dark brown eyes, pale skin and pink cheeks. I can be half dead, yet my cheeks still have a healthy glow. It's just the way they're made. It can be a bloody nuisance, in fact; I have to be covered in spots or chucking my boots up before people believe I'm poorly.

According to the photographs, Great-Aunt Zelda was another cuckoo, her flashing black eyes and dark ringlets sticking out like a sore thumb in a sea of pudding faces at Great-Uncle Harry's wedding. Because of the sepia, I couldn't vouch for her cheeks, but I'd put a pound to a penny they were a cheery and healthy red. Which would have been ironic really, because she died of consumption at the age of twenty-one. I bet nobody believed her, either, until she coughed her last, poor girl.

I was christened Enid Zelda, after my dad's mum and his aunt. Everyone called me 'Enie' for the first fifteen years of my life, but when I left school and started work, I chose to be called Zelda. I hated the name Enie, and anyway, I had a soft spot for my namesake and a previous generation's cuckoo and I wanted to remember her. It was something to do with her not having had a decent innings, as well as the fact that we looked so much alike. Only my dad and Charlie called me 'Enie' after that, and they only did it to annoy; they succeeded, too.

Nephew Tony was yet another cuckoo. There were the huge dark soulful eyes—his fringed with black lashes about a yard long, I swear—the milky white skin and flaming cheeks. And like Great-Aunt Zelda and me, he's a little on the small side, with narrow shoulders that make him look frailer and younger than he actually is. Unlike me and Great-Aunt Zelda, he's not endowed with the large bosom that made us both look a tad top-heavy; which is just as well I suppose, him being a lad.

Some said that the dark thread that ran through our generally mousy lot was due to gypsy blood way back. Others said it was Italians, from Naples. Dad favoured the Italian theory, despite them being foreigners, because according to him, anything was better than 'gyppos,' but I secretly disagreed. I rather fancied a gypsy connection, though I have to admit our Tony looked like one of those angels in Italian paintings you get on jigsaw puzzles and posh cake tins. Funny thing, he sang like an angel, too, and I played the piano, but the rest of the clan could barely carry a tune in a bucket. Maybe the first cuckoo was a singing Italian gypsy pianist; that would explain everything.

By the time we saw Tony again, some hours after he'd legged it, he looked anything but angelic. I eyed him as he sat there, still hungover but looking defiant despite the hint of green around the gills and a room full of angry relatives. He was a spunky little devil, I had to give him that. He didn't look even remotely cowed, despite his mum's hysteria and the formidable rage of his grandfather.

He wouldn't say where he'd disappeared to or who he'd been with at the warehouse the night before. In fact, he'd barely speak at all. He just sat there, looking scruffy and faintly grubby, until I thought Dad would blow a gasket. Dad always had a terrible temper, and didn't believe in sparing the rod to spoil any brat who broke his rigid rules. Girl or boy, it made no difference. Off would come the belt and it wouldn't go on again until the buttocks of the guilty party glowed in the dark and gave off enough warmth to heat a small room. Spittle had begun to form at the corners of Dad's mouth and his red eyes bulged as he roared his questions at a silent Tony.

Dad's stubby, freckled fingers began to fumble with his belt buckle—a move that always made me cringe, even when I wasn't the object of his wrath. Then the door flew open and Gran marched in. She took in the situation immediately but started to chatter as if she hadn't noticed anything. 'I've just seen Mabel Cattermole talking to Ruby Whitelock outside the church. You'll never guess'—she didn't wait for us to try—'It's about Ruby's sister, Iris' youngest girl, Joan. Well, they just found out the poor girl was born without a womb. They've been waiting and waiting for her monthlies to show, poor little mite…'

Her voice trailed away as Dad grabbed his cap from beside the door and left. All Gran had to do was start talking about 'women's troubles' and Dad would almost break a leg in his haste to get away. She'd saved many a kid's hide in much the same way over the years; it never failed!

The look of relief that flashed across Tony's face was the only sign of how scared he'd been. He might have been reprieved that time, but what worried me and the rest of the women in his family was what he was going to get up to next. I couldn't help feeling that the boy was heading for big trouble, in bad company, unless we could find him something else to do. Beating him was all very well, but it didn't seem to be working. Doses of Dad's belt had become more and more frequent recently, and so had Tony's spots of bother.

I'd talked it over with Zinnia and my mum many times and we were all agreed: the lad needed a healthier direction to head in than Ma Hole's boarding-house. The trouble was, the war and having little money limited the options.

Chapter 6

It was Friday, just one day away from the kids' street party, and there was a lot to do. Zinnia was going to make jelly from a stockpile Terry had hidden at the very back of his storeroom at the grocery, ready for just this occasion. I was helping her with the bulging oilcloth bags filled from Terry's secret stock—elderly packets of Rowntrees Jelly, flour, marge, cocoa powder, two small tins of Carnation Milk, one large tin of sliced peaches and a whole packet of dried eggs—when we literally bumped into Bung'ole. We'd just turned into Paradise Row as he was leaving. Our Tony was close behind him.

My voice could have cut bacon as I grabbed Tony by the scruff of the neck and demanded to know what he was doing hanging about with Brian when his mum and grandfather had expressly forbidden it. The trouble was, our Tony wasn't a little kid any more, he was twelve and getting to be a strong lad despite his size. He'd soon wriggled out of my grasp and legged it to catch up with Brian. I could've sworn I heard him tell me to 'Sod off' under his breath, but he was gone before I could make his ear glow.

I sighed. Rumours about Ma being stinking rich might have been true, but it didn't mean her darling Brian wasn't the brains behind the theft of that rotten two pounds seven and sixpence three-farthings, and the three and half feet of rubber hose. Bung'ole couldn't resist the opportunity for thievery or villainy any kind. It just wasn't in his nature to pass it up; his mum and dad had seen to that. They'd taught him never to enter even their own house by the front door, but had him shinning up drainpipes and breaking open windows almost as soon as he could walk without help, just for practice. At the age of barely fifteen, he was an old hand at burglary.

Air raids had presented the perfect opportunity for a bent boy to hone his breaking and entering skills. All that was needed was a jemmy, the nerve not to jump into the nearest shelter at the blast of an air raid siren, and a sack to carry away the haul. When that eerie wailing started, people would often just belt for the nearest shelter and count themselves lucky to have made it. They didn't stop to grab their valuables and lock their doors and windows. Bung'ole and his pals were free to stroll around helping themselves. The little toe-rags didn't restrict themselves to money. During the war it wasn't unusual to find yourself buying your own half-pound of mince or onions or margarine or soap back, at hugely inflated prices, from the black market spivs that Bung'ole's mum organized, supplied, housed and ran.

The trouble was that, although we all knew what Ma, her mob and her precious boy were up to, nobody was ever able to prove it. Ma saw to that. Wonderful what a broken limb can do for the memory, especially if you really need it to earn another crust to replace the one Brian has just nicked. You could trip over the little rat coming out of your house as you went in, but if you knew what was good for you, you never actually *saw* him.

Zinnia looked at Bung'ole swaggering down the road, our Tony trailing him like a puppy, and shook her head. 'I knew when I delivered that laddie that I'd live to regret it, but what could I do? I couldn't just walk away. The woman was in labour in my own kitchen.'

'You could've smothered the little bastard—and the sow that spawned him, while you were at it,' suggested Dad as he appeared—just too late to grab Tony—from the King's Head in a cloud of baccy smoke and brown ale fumes.

'Sows don't spawn. That's fish, you ignorant wee man,' Zinnia explained, none too patiently. 'I should make allowances, I suppose. The nearest you've ever been to a pig is a bacon sandwich, I'll be bound, and your fish always comes in batter and surrounded by chips, so how would you know? Pigs have litters. Thank the good Lord, Gladys restricted herself to just the one. Can you imagine a dozen like Brian Hole? It brings on the palsy simply to contemplate it. They wouldn't leave a one-legged sailor with a leg to stand on, that lot.' We might have laughed, but all three of us stared at Tony's retreating back with worried frowns ruining our looks.

As everyone said later, at the noisy family conference, it was bad enough that I had married into the Flucks—the disgrace still hung over us all like smog, and they were only relatives of the Holes—but to be involved with someone as close to Ma as Bung'ole was definitely asking for trouble, and plenty of it.

I had news for them; even being involved with a rotten Fluck brought trouble enough. They could take my word for it. However, I wasn't the problem this time. Tony was. And although I was relieved to have Dad's attention diverted for a change—he never really forgave me for Charlie—I was very worried about Tony. He was a good lad underneath it all and I didn't want to see him sliding into trouble. It was all too easy to keep on sliding until you never found your way back out again.

'The shame of it, the shame of it!' wailed Vi. 'We've never had nothing to do with the law, unless you count Charlie, and he only married in.' She dabbed at her tears with a sodden, mascara-grey hanky.

It was wonderful how Vi could work Charlie into any conversation where she might be shown up to disadvantage. It was as if she was reminding Mum and Dad that I was the one who had first connected our family with that particular barrel of rotten apples, not her Tony. I was the one who had brought a double dose of shame, first for not keeping my knickers on and secondly for having to marry Charlie Fluck of all people, one of the enemy. Everything paled before that; well, it did with Dad and Vi anyway. The rest of us had almost learned to live with it. There were times when my sister Vi got right up my nose, and this was one of them.

'Give it a rest Vi, do,' I told her. 'Just this once, leave Charlie out of it. He isn't the one leading your Tony astray. What are you doing to stop it, eh? That's what I'd like to know. As far as I can see, it's bugger all. As usual.' I was red in the face, I could tell.

Mum tried to be soothing. 'Now, now, girls, no point in getting at each other's throats. That sorts nothing. What we've got to think about is how to make young Tony see the error of his ways. I was hoping it'd wait till his dad got home...' She trailed off. Everyone knew Fred wasn't coming home any more. Well, everyone except me, that is. I had a funny feeling about Fred. I'd had dreams on and off, ever since we'd got the telegram saying he was missing. Once I saw him in what looked like a barn, another time he was in some sort of compound, wire all around, like a giant chicken run, and just like chickens, men seemed to be scratching at the ground, leaving pockmarks in the dust. I couldn't make out any individual faces, but one of the men felt familiar to me and deep down I just knew he was Fred. I'd once tried to comfort Vi by telling her I didn't believe that Fred was really dead, but Mum and Dad were furious with me for getting her hopes up, when they'd just persuaded her to accept the inevitable.

'If Fred was alive,' Dad had stormed, 'the bleeding War Office or the Red Cross would have told her so. If his commanding officer even thought it was a possibility, he would have said so in his letter. Or there would have been a whisper among his mates in the regiment, and one of 'em would've said. And they haven't! So don't go filling the girl's head with your bloody dreams, Enie.' You can get a good sneer into 'Enie.' It sort of lends itself to the curled lip and the whine, whereas 'Zelda' doesn't. But Dad was right: all anyone would say about Fred was that he had almost certainly been killed in action and his body lost when his comrades had been forced to retreat.

Dad's grating voice brought me back to the kitchen and the business at hand—Fred's wayward son. 'I'll give Tony another bloody good hiding when he gets in.' Dad had a theory that there wasn't much in a kid's life that couldn't be put right by a clip round the ear as a first resort and a hefty session with his belt as a last. His father had taught him that way, and what was good enough for him was good enough for his children and his grandchildren.

Dad could be a very hard man when he was crossed. He believed in King and Country, or better still, old Queen Victoria and Country; her portrait still had pride of place over his mantelpiece. He demanded hard graft and rigid honesty from all of his descendants and, with the possible exception of Tony, he got it. We were all too much in awe of him to stray far from the straight and narrow, and he never forgot it if you did. I could testify to that.

I couldn't help thinking, though, that the belt wouldn't work any better than it had the times before. Tony was trailing around after Bung'ole before the welts from his last beating had lost their glow. Even a night in the cells hadn't put him off. Punishment wasn't making a dent on the boy. In fact, it was just driving him further and further away from us. It was time to find another way to reach him, and I made up my mind to give it some serious thought. I also decided that it might be an idea to talk to his cousin, Reggie, who probably knew Tony better than anyone.

Chapter 7

Mum's and Zinnia's allotments were directly behind Zinnia's house and garden, which was handy for sharing cups of tea in the privacy of the railway carriage. I'd loved that railway carriage from the first moment I clapped eyes on it. Being allowed to play in it as a child had been my idea of heaven. And every other kid's as well. It felt safe and, of course, it was exciting. A real, live railway carriage could be so many things in the imagination. It could be thundering across the plains of the Wild West, chased by howling savages or gun-toting outlaws. Or it might be crawling through the lower slopes of the Hindu Kush, puffing and belching with the effort, while dark men with white turbans and unfriendly intentions bore down on it on the backs of wild stallions. Or it might simply be a railway carriage taking soldiers to war, evacuated children to the sticks or a family to Southend for a day at the seaside. Nestled quietly under the protection of the garden wall and the fruit trees, the carriage remained an enchanted place for me. In spring it had a halo of blossom. I spent hours there with Mum and Zinnia, drinking tea and chatting away about everything from the price of knicker elastic to the best way to grow runner beans, and the state of the war.

Zinnia had furnished the carriage with an assortment of battered Lloyd Loom chairs in a variety of pastel shades of green, pink, blue and white. There was a table under one set of windows, which looked out on the rest of the garden. A primus stove heated the water for tea and a selection of cups hung from hooks above a washstand complete with a large bowl and jug. Zinnia would fill the jug with water from the house, and that supplied the tea and the washing-up water for the cups. Above the cups was a small shelf with an old Petticoat Tails shortcake tin that occasionally even held biscuits, a Coronation tea caddy and a small pile of tea plates. Sometimes, when the weather was warm enough, the chairs were pulled out on to the lawn, under the plum and apple trees, and we had picnics between our labours on the allotments.

I had a day off, and I was beavering away on the allotment by early morning. I'd started a few runner beans on my bathroom windowsill in some tubes I'd made out of salvaged cardboard, mainly old fag and tea packets, but anything would do. Several thicknesses of newspaper served the purpose at a pinch, but they tended to get too soggy; as newsprint got scarcer, it was better to save them for use in the toilet when the Izal ran out, which was often. Whatever they were made of, the tubes saved disturbing the roots too much, which all plants appreciate, according to Zinnia. Some mind more than others. Beans have strong views on the subject, apparently, as do peas, sweet peas and of course all root vegetables, which is why they are normally planted in the ground and then thinned out.

Whether it was the tubes or not, Zinnia's beans were always first when it came to judging time in the allotments' annual competition for the best crops. The competition was eagerly looked forward to by all the allotmenteers and their families. The picnic afterwards was one of the high spots of our year, with everyone doing their bit by providing food. It brightened up the whole Digging for Victory idea, especially for the reluctant gardener, because the prizes were well worth getting your hands on.

Mr. Whitelock usually donated a cart full of horse manure for the first prize for the best overall allotment. As we all knew Zinnia got manure anyway, it was silently agreed that she never won that, although her patches were usually by far and away the best. However, there were prizes for the best individual vegetables and it was Zinnia's beans that walked away with first prize in that category every single year. The prizes included such luxuries as a bar of Sunlight Soap, courtesy of Terry Rainbird, a ball of garden twine from Flowerdew's Ironmongers, or a jar of the Reverend Cattermole's honey, produced in hives that he kept on the verge of the allotments, so that his bees could feed with ease. One year, there was even a small bale of chicken wire. Such richness! No wonder everyone took it all so seriously.

It was a toss-up between the manure and the honey for the most desired prize. The dung appealed to the serious gardener and the dedicated nosher, the allotment produce being a valuable addition to the table of many a household, but the honey was prized by everyone with a sweet tooth and was fiercely competed for.

Gladys Hole would enter each year. God knows why. She had Brian working like a Singapore coolie on her patch in the season, but try as she might, she could never win best beans, or best anything else for that matter. It drove her bonkers, especially the beans. I often wondered why the Holes troubled at all, being as how Ma ran the local black market and could normally get first dibs on anything worth having, but there's no accounting for greed, or the deadly rivalry Ma had with Zinnia.

Nobody could fully explain that, either, but it was there all right. Mum said she thought it was down to the fact that they were both powerful women in their way. Which was true, but they weren't in the same line of business, so it was difficult to make sense of it. But as Mum said, Zinnia was freely respected for her skills as healer whereas Ma had to rely on fear of pain and retribution to gain grudging respect from the locals. If Ma could compete with Zinnia, then she would.

Zinnia would never divulge the secret of her great success with runner beans. When asked, she would say, 'Well, there's the root run, that helps. Then of course, there's the sweet peas that pull in the wee beasties to pollinate and then finally, there's my recipe for the trench.' Here she would grin her secret grin. All the serious vegetable growers on the allotments were itching to know the exact ingredients that went into her trench mixture. We all knew that Mr. Whitelock's Dobbin made his contribution, often in nice steaming piles outside our houses, but there was more to it than lashings of well-rotted manure. All her kitchen peelings went in, eggshells if she had had any actual eggs and bits of newspaper, shredded to make a little go a long way. I'd even seen a motheaten garment or two dropped in before now.

But there was still something else, and it was this that Zinnia point blank refused to reveal to the hopefuls that hung about chatting and eyeing her trench as she shovelled the earth back over her mixture. She said it helped if it all cooked down nicely over the winter months. Some sneak had even had the gall to dig up her trench in the dead of night once, to get a sample, but to no avail, because all they found was rich, crumbly earth; the winter frosts and the 'even wee-er beasties, awfy small, too wee to see with your own eyeballs' that lived in the soil, had seen to that.

Anyway, there I was, bum stuck up in the air as I carefully lowered the beans' long roots into equally long holes, when I became aware of a pair of feet, attached to a pair of grubby knees, topped off with a pair of grey flannel shorts.

'What're you doing, Auntie Zelda?' Tony asked.

'Knitting socks for sailors. What's it look like I'm doing?'

'Am I supposed to say "Ha, ha, very funny," or something? 'Cause I've got to tell you, it wasn't that good, Auntie Zelda.'

'You are a cheeky little so-and-so, Tony Gunn. Now what do you want? Unless of course you've come to help? Nip over to the standpipe and fill this watering can, will you?'

We worked away quietly together for a bit, Tony schlepping the watering can back and forth to give the beans a really good drink to start them off in their new surroundings. Once the beans were settled, Tony and I took a well-earned rest in the sunshine and drank a companionable cup of tea under one of Zinnia's apple trees. Bees were humming gently on the breeze and all was peaceful apart from a robin swearing at a rival for daring to check the newly turned soil for grubs, slugs' eggs and eelworms.

'Auntie Zelda?' Tony said, to see if he had my attention. He did. I knew he hadn't just happened to drop by.

'Yes, Tony,' I answered, to let him know that just because my eyes were closed, it didn't mean I was snoozing.

'Do you think my dad's dead?' There was going to be no tarting it up, then. I opened my eyes and looked at his rosy-cheeked face, great brown eyes pleading for me to tell him everything was going to be all right. But I couldn't. My dreams were just that: dreams. They weren't certainties, and that's what the boy needed.

'I don't know, Tony. I really don't.' I couldn't tell him that there were times when I could have sworn that I felt his dad drawing nearer. It would have given him a hope that I wasn't at all sure wouldn't be shattered. His grandad was right. It was best not to build up anyone's hopes. It was hard enough as it was.

'I miss him, Auntie Zelda.' Tony's voice cracked slightly and his eyes took on the glassy sheen of unshed tears. Poor little blighter, he couldn't even have a cry in peace, because strong men did not cry, even before their voices broke and they were still budding, as it were. I had to strain not to gather the poor little sod to my bosom and comfort him, but I knew that if I did, he'd be off like a halfpenny rocket on Guy Fawkes Night.

'I know you do, love, I know you do. You were close, you and your dad.' It was all I could think of to say. We sat quietly for a moment, then I added: 'I know one thing, though. If your dad is still alive, he'll crawl over broken glass and walk through fire to get home to you and your mum. That's certain sure, that is.'

I heard a quiet sob beside me, but pretended I hadn't noticed. I gazed up at the bees buzzing around the apple blossom, and listened to their gentle hum. It was soothing, and it seemed to do the trick for Tony, too, because a mighty sniff told me he was pulling himself together. My heart bled for him.

Still, it didn't bleed so much that I didn't exploit the moment. It was time for a little heart-to-heart. 'Tony, why do you hang around with Brian Hole when it gets you into so much hot water? I've often wondered. You know he's a bad lot, and I know that you're not, underneath it all.' I ruffled his hair in a friendly fashion and he batted my hand away with a watery grin.

'Geroff!' he growled, and pulled his head away.

'I mean it, Tony. Why do you hang around the Holes? You'll wind up in serious trouble one of these days. Is that what you want?'

'Course not! Don't be daft! Nobody goes around looking for trouble. Trouble just happens.' He shrugged and avoided my eyes: he knew he was talking rubbish.

'You know that's not entirely true, Tony,' I told him. 'Sometimes it just happens and there's nothing you can do about it, like your dad going to war. And sometimes you make it happen by mixing with wrong'uns like Brian Hole, who will drag you into bad situations that will, eventually, get you banged up in jail. Is that really what you want to do with your life? Drift in and out of the nick?'

'Well, it's better than being blown up or shot by Germans, ain't it?' Tony asked.

'I suppose you've got a point there,' I said, 'but at least your dad was a hero, fighting for you and your mum and everyone he knew and loved and millions that he didn't. That's something to be proud of, that is. Spending your life in and out of prison is nothing to boast about, now is it? It's more of a waste, if you look at it in a certain way. And anyway,' I said, shoving the barb in under the ribs, 'I'm sure your dad would be very sorry if you did that with your life. He'd expect better from you.'

Tony thought about that for a minute or two, realized he couldn't really argue the point and then changed the subject slightly. 'What am I s'posed to do, then? I'm not clever like Reggie; he's brainy, but I'm not good at anything. I can't even do woodwork. My toast-rack looks like a chimp made it.'

'Well, I'm not surprised. It's scrap wood, you need the proper materials to do a proper job. You'll get better at it when the supply of decent wood starts again.' It was true; before it was a toast rack, it'd been part of a small bookshelf, and before that, a crate for oranges from Seville—the inky stamp had shown through the watered-down woodstain someone had used to try to disguise it.

'They could give me bloody oak and I'd still make a balls of it,' Tony said.

'Watch your language,' I answered automatically.

'Sorry. But it's true. I'm not good at anything, I told you. I'm as dim as a Toc H Lamp. Mr. Sneddon at school told me.'

I know I was prejudiced, but that simply was not true! Tony was a bright little spark, quick on the uptake and funny with it—when he put his mind to it, he could make me weep with laughter.

'The very idea! The man doesn't know what he's talking about. You, a fool? No you're bloody not!' I said, forgetting myself in the heat of the moment. Who was this moron to call my nephew dim? 'You run rings round this family, and there are not too many half-wits in our clan!' I assured him. 'You have to be up fairly early in the morning to pull one over on your gran, your great-gran, your mum, Reggie, Auntie Doris and even me, and yet you manage it, you little toe-rag, and that, my boy, is not the sign of a raving idiot.'

I ranted on for a bit more, until I ran out of steam and Tony was rolling around in his Lloyd Loom, clutching his sides with laughter. Then I got serious. 'And anyway, you *are* good at something. As it happens, you're bloody wonderful at it,' I said, forgetting myself again. 'You can sing. In fact, you sing like an angel. Everybody says so.'

'Oh very handy that is,' he sneered. '"You can't eat singing and it doesn't put clothes on your back or shoes on your feet." That's what Mum says when I tell her I want to be like Bing Crosby or Frank Sinatra when I grow up.'

Good old Vi, always there with the encouragement, I thought. 'Ah well, your mum misses your dad too, remember. It makes it hard for her to look on the bright side.' It was true, it did. 'But I don't suppose for one minute that either Bing or Frankie got where they are today by hanging around with sneak thieves. I expect they practised their singing and looked for ways to get where they wanted to go, don't you?' I asked, all innocence. 'Don't give up on dreams, Tony, because if you work hard enough at them, they could just come true.'

'Oh yeah?' he asked, eyebrows raised. 'Then how come you're married to Charlie and working in that rotten canteen? It can't be what you dreamed about, surely?' See, not stupid, not stupid at all.

I didn't answer straight away. I could feel my eyes filling. 'No, Tony, it wasn't what I dreamed of. But you see, I hung about in bad company and in the end I got myself a prison sentence, or as good as. So what I'm saying to you is, don't make the same mistakes as me. Choose a different way and make a better life for yourself. What's wrong with that?'

Tony dropped his eyes, along with the sneering defiance, and had the grace to look ashamed of himself. At last he managed to look up again and meet my eyes. 'I'm sorry, Auntie Zelda,' he whispered.

'So am I, sweetheart, so am I. But that's not your responsibility. What you do about yourself is,' I told him.

We washed and dried our cups carefully and put them back on their hooks. Tony emptied the teapot on the roots of the apple tree. It was time to go home. After I'd dropped Tony off at his house, I walked on towards home alone, deep in thought. Tony had given me a lot to think about and I made up my mind to do what I could to help him. He was a nice boy, I liked him and I wanted him to have his chance. What he did with it after that would be entirely up to him.

Chapter 8

'All that snot and red eyes does nothing for her looks,' said Dilly in a withering tone.

She and my sister Vi had never been what you might call close. The trouble between them began when Vi and Fred started courting. Fred was very fond of his baby sister, and she of him. He just laughed when she popped up, often with me in close attendance, to play gooseberry and ruin their courting moments. It was our sisterly duty to put the dampers on snogging and close clinches if we could. It was a younger sister's revenge for all the bullying that had gone on before romance took over.

Well, it was in my case. In Dilly's? She wasn't bullied by Fred, she just never thought much of Vi. She considered her to be too wet for her beloved brother. Fred was Dilly's hero; he had been since she was a scrap and he used to carry her on his wide shoulders or plonk her on the crossbar of his bike and whizz her down the hill at dizzying speed. She'd loved that. We all had.

'I mean, I know the truancy man coming round about Tony was tricky for her,' Dilly grumbled, unwilling to let it go, 'but really, must she carry on so? You'd think she was the only one with troubles.' Bumping into Vi outside Dean's the bakers had upset Dilly and her mum, who were, after all, Tony's auntie and gran.

I nodded sympathetically. With my mouth full of pins it was impossible to do anything else.

'I miss Fred too, you know. We all do. Mum hasn't been the same since he went, and when the telegram came, she seemed to sort of crumple from the inside and she suddenly got ever so old. It happened almost overnight. One minute she was the old Mum and the next, she was this little grey shell.

'Everyone's lost someone, Zeld, it's not just Vi. I know it's wicked to say it, but she always has it worse than everybody else, somehow. It's always "Poor Vi." It has been all her life.'

I couldn't really argue, because Dilly was right in a way. But on the other hand, not knowing whether she was a widow or not was a really difficult one for Vi—or anyone else, for that matter. If she gave up hope and accepted that Fred was not coming back it was as if she was betraying him in some way, wishing him dead. But if she kept hope alive, how long could a body go on without looking a damned fool about it? Then there was the question of getting on with life; that wasn't easy if you were constantly marking time and waiting, endlessly waiting.

Poor Tony was the living proof of that. He seemed to be stuck in a groove. It suddenly occurred to me that the excitement of climbing through windows not his own might be the only thing that really took his mind off the enormous hole that Fred had left in his young life. Maybe running the risk of being caught made him feel closer to his dad in some peculiar way. I decided that my thoughts were getting too deep for me and it was politic to change the subject.

'So, tell me about this Yank, then. What's his name? Where's he from? Where's he stationed?' I grinned as my friend went pink and became a bit flustered. Dilly had come to my place to take in a frock she'd inherited from one of her sisters-in-law. It was nothing fancy, a navy blue cotton with wide shoulders and a narrow belt, but it was smart enough. Or it would be, once she'd altered it. It had crisp, white piping around its collar and its short sleeves.

'His name's Chester. He's from somewhere called Memphis, Tennessee. He's stationed on the coast—in Suffolk, I think. And he mends cars and lorries and things like that; he was a mechanic in Civvy Street. When he's not doing that, he sings sometimes, but mostly he plays the trumpet in his own band. I haven't heard him yet. He calls his band Chester Field's GI Jivers,' she told me proudly, her face aglow over my trusty Singer sewing machine. Good old Chester had hit the spot all right.

'He looks lovely in his uniform,' she added shyly. 'Really lovely. He's so handsome, Zelda. I've never seen anyone as handsome in my whole life, not even at the pictures.'

That was saying something, because according to Dilly, Clark Gable was the most handsome man in the entire world—until she met Chester, that is. Personally, I always thought Humphrey Bogart was a bit of all right. Vi and Doris had a thing for Robert Taylor, but I couldn't see it myself; too much of a lounge lizard for my taste. Doris went all soppy if you mentioned his name, even in front of her Ernest, who looked nothing like him. The fact that Dilly thought Chester outshone even her beloved Clark Gable, though, really impressed me.

'It must be love,' I said, and she didn't deny it. 'Why don't you tell him about the dance Al and his mob are planning? Maybe he'll buy tickets for the pair of you, you never know.'

'It's an idea, Zeld. I'll bring it up next time I see him. I told Al I'd flog some tickets when they're ready. How about you? You could get rid of a fair few down at the canteen. So could Molly Squires at the boozer. It's for a good cause—Dr Barnardo's.'

We chatted on for a while about nothing in particular and then we rummaged through my wardrobe looking for some bits to complete her outfit. We topped the dress off with my thin, navy serge coat and her own hat, shoes and gloves. She looked a picture! But then Dilly would have looked a picture in a khaki trench coat and a pair of wellies. She was just made that way. It was something else poor Vi held against her. She yearned to be like Priscilla Lane or Veronica Lake and spent hours working on it when she went out, but somehow she always wound up looking like pudding-faced Vi, pleasant but plain. Whereas her sister-in-law would have shone in sack-cloth and ashes.

I never minded being slightly in Dilly's shadow. It suited me. It could be a bloody nuisance being too good-looking. Dilly was often pestered, and although she always tried to be nice, some blokes just didn't take the hint. Don't get me wrong, I wasn't hideous or anything, and I got my share of attention from the blokes all right. Most people reckoned my eyes to be my best feature, although some men's attention was riveted by two spots lower down, the filthy beasts!

Chapter 9

Dad was not a happy man. Tony's continued bad behaviour was making sure of that. Dad set great store by respectability. Said the old Queen had laid down certain standards of behaviour that he, for one, was happy to live by. One of those standards was that nice gels didn't get up the duff before they were safely married, and another was that good boys stayed on the right side of Lily Law. I'd erred in one department and young Tony had erred in the other, which made us stablemates in a funny kind of a way. The trouble was, when someone new managed to get on Dad's top note, it reminded him of all the others that had annoyed him over the years. As he said, 'I don't give a monkey's what other people's families get up to, but I expect mine to behave themselves and abide by *my* rules or they can do the other thing.' And off would come the belt and someone's backside would glow for a week.

He never did explain what 'the other thing' was, because up until then, nobody had opted for it. And it wasn't true that he didn't mind what other people's children did, either. He did mind. He minded quite a lot, because he liked to compare his with theirs, and God help us if he decided that his were wanting. He never forgave anyone who let him down in any department. And Tony's spot of bother had reminded him of my wicked ways.

I knew the minute I walked in for Sunday dinner. Everyone was unnaturally quiet and I noticed Tony wasn't very comfortable resting both cheeks on his hard kitchen chair at the same time. He fidgeted from one buttock to the other and tried to keep his head down while he was about it. I sat down opposite him and gave his knee a gentle nudge under the table. He raised his beautiful eyes, with their great, long lashes, and we exchanged small, sad smiles. Message understood!

'Oh, so her ladyship has finally arrived, has she?' Dad's tone had that edge that said he had a grievance, a belly full of beer and plenty to say. My heart bled for Tony; his poor bum must have been raw, with Dad half-cut *and* with a strop on.

'Not too busy dropping your drawers to get a decent night's kip in, I trust?' God, I hated the old man when he was on one! I kept my head down and didn't even dare smile when I felt another tiny nudge, this time from Tony to me.

Vi's voice cut in, slimy with innuendo. 'She *said* she was going to the pictures with Dilly, but mind, she's said *that* before.' And I had, the night I'd sneaked off to the Palais de Dance with Charlie. I had wanted to go to a grown-up dance so badly. Charlie had had tickets, he wasn't a bad-looking bloke and he could be such a laugh when he felt like it, so I went. I wondered whether I'd live long enough to stop regretting that act of defiance, and if my bloody father and sister would ever let me.

Mum's voice was sharp as she carried the chicken to the table. It was one of Mr. Whitelock's finest, kept in his yard with Dobbin and swapped for Tony's cast-off school uniform, with a pair of stout boots thrown in for good measure. The boots were hardly worn, on account of Tony having had a growth spurt shortly after they'd been bought. They didn't fit his cousin Reggie, who had big feet. Mr. Whitelock always had a child or two in need of clothes, even third-hand ones.

'You can keep your opinions to yourself, Violet Gunn. I seem to remember you've had one or two moments that you needn't be proud of yourself. And you, Dad. Let it be, for God's sake! Tony's had his thrashing; you've had your say; and our

Zelda's paid her dues, with knobs on. It can't be any picnic to be married to Charlie Fluck, now can it?' Mum's voice was rising dangerously.

'That's the trouble with going to the pub of a Sunday dinnertime. It gets you moody. Let's just have a nice, family dinner for a change.' Mum's cheeks were burning cherry red and her hair was standing up in a harassed halo around her head. At that moment, I loved my plucky little mum so much, I thought my heart would burst.

Dad's tone would have soured lemons. 'What is this with the "Zelda this" and "Zelda that" cobblers? I named her Enid, and if the name is good enough for my mother, then it's bloody well good enough for my daughter!'

'It's what she prefers to be called, Harry. I see no harm in it. Anyway, *we* also called her Zelda, remember, after *your* bloody aunt! So what difference does it make? Except you're a stubborn old git who is hell bent on ruining my Sunday dinner!'

Mum stood up, hands planted firmly on her hips. Her chest heaved indignantly and her glittering eyes dared him to make something of it. Every inch of her said that if he did, he'd wind up *wearing* his chicken, roast potatoes, two veg and gravy, and possibly his blancmange as well.

I jumped to my feet and stood beside her, just in case Dad decided to make something of it anyway. I noticed that Doris slid in on the other side and, after a moment's hesitation, Tony joined us. Vi stayed put and Doris' Reggie struggled to decide what to do. The twins, bless them, looked interested, in a nervous and thoroughly bewildered sort of way. They were only little.

A long silence followed, with Dad's face growing more purple by the second. Then Reggie nodded slightly to himself, stood up slowly and placed himself firmly beside his cousin. Reggie always liked to think before doing anything. Zinnia said it came of being hard of breathing; he liked to work out if the effort and the breath was worth it.

It was only when Gran came in and broke the tension with a rude remark about Mrs. Cattermole's church hat that I realized we'd all been rigid, waiting for the explosion. It felt like the 'all clear' after a night's heavy bombing. 'I swear it's that same old brown felt that that woman has under all that green-grocery,' Gran was saying. 'If she shoves another cherry on it, she'll be pecked to death by the bleedin' starlings.' Nine sets of lungs expelled stale air as we exploded into hysterical laughter. Well, nine breathed and seven laughed while the twins looked on, to be exact.

'Well, what's got into you lot?' Gran demanded, looking from one to another. 'It weren't *that* funny.' But the moment had passed, and Dad decided to give it up. While the rest of us chatted uneasily, he ate in sullen silence. He didn't like it when Mum stood up on her hind legs, but he knew that she meant it, because she didn't do it often.

'I saw Molly Squires in Mare Street this morning,' Doris told me quietly over the washing-up. Dad had retired to bed to sleep it off. Mum and Gran had nipped round to Zinnia's for a chinwag and to get out of Dad's way for a bit, the twins were playing quietly and the boys had disappeared—God knew where. 'She says that she could've sworn she saw Ma Hole with your Charlie last night. She caught a glimpse of them, she says, in the snug of the Star and Garter. The place was packed and she was run off her feet, so she can't be sure. But she said if it wasn't Charlie, then he's got a double.'

Doris must have noticed the colour drain from my face because she patted my shoulder reassuringly. 'I told her she was probably seeing things. She did say it was only a glimpse.'

The damage was done, though. The merest hint of Charlie was enough to make my heart turn to lead and sink rapidly to my footwear. Even the sunlight seemed to dim. I walked home very slowly that afternoon, dreading what I might find there.

Chapter 10

Charlie wasn't home when I got in, but I knew he'd been there because he'd cut a hunk of bread and slathered three-quarters of my margarine ration on it—and on to the table as well. More evidence came in the crumbs that had mingled with the dirty washing spewing from his kitbag, which he'd dumped in the middle of the kitchen table. I salvaged the bread from the grip of a sweaty sock and glared at the unsavoury pile, then found the bucket in its place under the sink and dropped socks and underwear into it with some small bits of old soap. After boiling a kettle and pouring the water into the bucket, I topped it up with a spot of cold and refilled the kettle ready to tackle the shirts.

I sighed heavily, thinking it was a pity he hadn't left his dirty washing wherever it was that he had spent the night. It was even more of a pity he hadn't thought to let me know he was coming back. But that was Charlie for you, never one to let a little common courtesy stand in the way of his natural born selfishness. I blamed his mum for not introducing him to the idea of manners, but then I blamed his mum for a lot of things; taking up with his dad being one, and giving in to the natural urges that had led to her dropping Charlie on an unsuspecting world being another.

I'll say one thing for getting stuck into that washing: even though it was on a Sunday when I ought to have been dwelling on holier things, it helped me not to worry about what might happen. I just concentrated on rubbing the collars, cuffs and stubborn stains up and down on the washboard in the sort of mindless rhythm that numbs the brain and allows it to drift off to God knows where for a while.

Before the war I'd rarely been on my own with peace enough to simply waft away. I'd always been in the middle of family life, even sharing a bed with my sisters until they married, then I was wed as well and had a husband to look after and to sleep with. As luck would have it, Hitler hadn't heard about our nuptials and so Charlie's leave had been mercifully brief; he was soon back in his barracks at Catterick, a good long way away in the north. It was only then that I found myself living alone for the first time in my whole life. And I loved it!

I didn't sit and mope, not knowing what to do with myself, the way some girls did. I made the most of it. I didn't want to go out on the town, I wanted to stay home and wallow in the luxury of doing things that I wanted to do, when I wanted to do them. I got the flat just the way I liked it, making do with what came to hand. It was wonderful what a lick of paint or a bit of fabric could do to cheer up clapped-out fourth-hand furniture, old orange boxes and bare floorboards. Before long, there were cheerful rag rugs scattered throughout the flat to make it cosy.

I even had some second-hand lace curtains, from Terry Rainbird's gran's parlour after she passed away, to hide the crisscrossed tape stuck on the window panes to prevent flying glass and to give daylight relief from the drab blackout curtains. The lace was really pretty, with flowers and butterflies worked into the design. Terry said his gran had made them herself when she was in service. I was amazed she found the time, knowing just how hard domestic work could be. My own gran had stories about being 'a tweenie,' which was a maid of all work apparently, before the Great War. She'd flogged herself half to death as she worked her way upstairs and down, with mop, bucket, duster, polish and broom, when she wasn't humping coal to the many fires or rushing about with jugs of hot water for the washstands in the bedrooms.

Once Charlie was back at his camp, I was in heaven. I'd swanned around that flat like Lady La-Di-Dah, with all that elbow room and no-one else to please and no-one else to clear up after, for most of the war—apart from Charlie's leaves that is. Now Hitler had chucked in the towel, all that lovely freedom would be over. I would have to get used to the idea that I was married to Charlie and I'd better get on with it.

I was brooding deeply over the scummy sink full of tepid water when I heard the downstairs door slam and the clatter of Charlie's hobnails on the stairs. I braced myself as I pulled the plug and listened to the grey, soapy water gurgle away, taking what was left of my spirits with it. The flat door was thrown open and a familiar voice said, 'Come in, come in, do. Zelda, there you are love, get the kettle on, we're parched.'

I turned round and there was Charlie. His funny, odd-coloured eyes, one blue, one brown, were glittering the way they did when he had a pint or two on board, or was in the mood for a fight, or both. My cousin Mavis stood sheepishly in front of him, grinning toothily, and beside her were Lenny Hobbs and Percy Robinson. My heart gave a relieved lurch. I wouldn't be alone with Charlie for an hour or two if I played my cards right! I smiled back at Mavis and Lenny and then, more reluctantly, at Charlie and Percy. The relief of seeing the others with Charlie was so great that everything went wobbly for a moment or two, even my voice.

'Hello, Charlie,' I said. 'Hello, you lot. Take a seat, do. I'll have the kettle on in a jiffy.' I turned to get on with it. 'Did you have a good trip down, Charlie?'

'The usual, love. Stop start, stop start all the way. Had to change in the middle of bleeding nowhere because the engine conked out. We was stuck there for ages before they found another one. Still, I won ten bob in a game of brag with some squaddies from Crewe, so it weren't a total waste of time.' He grinned. 'It paid for a bevvy or two at the King's Head.'

'That's good,' I murmured, my mind on pouring the tea and not slopping it in the saucers as I passed the cups round. 'How long are you home for, Charlie? Have you been demobbed?' I tried hard to make the question sound hopeful. It wouldn't do to show the dread I felt at the answer.

'Can't wait to get on with married life, eh?' Charlie winked at our guests and slapped my bum playfully as I walked past him to join them at the table.

I didn't know what to say to that, so I smiled weakly and turned to my cousin. 'And how are you, Mavis?' I asked politely, heartily grateful that she was in my kitchen on that Sunday afternoon, which was not something I'd normally be able to say. We weren't close. I didn't dislike her or anything, it was just that she was one of Vi's cronies really, and we'd had little to do with each other over the years.

'Not bad, thanks. And you, Zeld, keeping well are you?'

'Fine, ta,' I answered. I didn't seem to be able to think of anything else to say. I turned to Lenny. 'All right are you, Len?'

'I'm always all right, thanks, Zelda. I'm pretty much the same as when you saw me last week.'

'And your mum? Did her hair ever grow back after that peroxide? It was nasty that, the poor thing.' It had been, too; she'd lost it in great, brittle clumps. All Zinnia could do for her was give her soothing scalp washes made from chamomile and suggest she prayed it would grow back, while wearing a bad wig in the meantime.

'It's much better, ta. She's got a bit of hair now and her head ain't red and peeling any more.' Lenny grinned his amiable grin. 'Nip down the shop with me after this tea, Zeld. I've got some dripping and a couple of marrow bones put by for you. I was hoping to see you yesterday, but I didn't, so you'd better pick up the bones at least, while they're fresh.'

The late afternoon was warm and the scent of Mavis' Evening in Paris seemed to take up all the available air in the little kitchen. My head was throbbing. It was a relief when Lenny swallowed the last of his tea with a smack of his lips and suggested I went to the shop with him to pick up my bones. I could hardly wait to get down the stairs and into the air.

'So, where did you pick Charlie up?' I asked once we were in the street. 'And what's Mavis doing tagging along? She with

Percy?' She obviously wasn't with Lenny, seeing as he'd left her behind at the flat.

'I bumped into him at the King's Head. He was having a jar with Percy and some of Ma Hole's lodgers and insisted on strolling home with me when I left. Mavis sort of appeared out of the Ladies and joined us. Whether she'd been with them before I turned up, I couldn't say. But it looked like it. I s'pose she dropped in for a quick one with one of the lads. Hang about, let me find me key. I'll soon get this door open, then you can get back to your old man.' I didn't like to tell Lenny that there was no rush.

The whole of the tiny flat still reeked of Evening in Paris when I got in. Mavis could certainly slosh it on. It made my head ache again, but Mavis and Percy had gone and Charlie was in a good mood, so I tried to relax my hunched shoulders a bit. Perhaps it wouldn't be so bad, if Charlie was happy. I just wished I knew how long he was stopping this time. I decided to try to get a straight answer to a straight question. It wasn't easy to do with Charlie, because sometimes the bugger was so twisted that he could hide behind a corkscrew. Other times, he could be good company and a great laugh, charming the old ladies at church teas into giving him extra dollops of jam on his bread or a second rock cake. Unless, of course, the old lady in question was my gran, who saw straight through him.

'Never trust a charmer, they'll nick your purse before you've got your drawers back on, that sort,' she warned. 'You mark my words, girl, you mark my words.' And I did, but much too late.

'Come over here, love, and give your old man a little cuddle,' Charlie said as I came through the door with my bag of bones and dripping.

I tried really hard to smile and look enthusiastic but I knew what 'a little cuddle' meant and my stomach turned over at the prospect. I was absolutely terrified of getting pregnant again. My knees turned to jelly and Charlie virtually had to carry me to our bed in the cramped bedroom.

Chapter 11

Charlie's leave lasted a whole week, and gave me a taste of what my life was likely to be like once he was demobbed and home for good. It wasn't all bad. True, I really missed pleasing myself and had to remember the way Charlie liked things done, and that was hard, because he was touchy about mistakes. But his friends were in and out all the time, not having seen him for a while, and Charlie was nearly always in a good mood when we had company, so I managed to relax a bit at first.

We even had some laughs, especially when Dilly and Ronnie came round with some GI-issue V discs Chester had lent her. The music was fabulous and we danced and laughed the night away. Woody Herman, Fats Waller, Lester Young, Tommy Dorsey, Peggy Lee, Lena Horne, Count Basie, Louis Armstrong, Hot Lips Page and the rest seemed to knock Vera Lynn and our other home-grown favourites like Billy Cotton into a cocked hat somehow. They seemed too homely to have any glamour at all. A bit like Jack Warner versus Humphrey Bogart at the pictures. I mean, there was no contest there either.

Charlie had been really good company that night, telling jokes, serving drinks and dancing with me and Dilly by turns. He was a good dancer; being neat and small, he could move well. He was strong, too, and had no trouble hurling us around in the more lively numbers.

So, the first part of the week went smoothly enough. Of course, I was more tired than usual because I was cooking, cleaning and performing my wifely duties half the night, then lying awake worrying about getting in the pudding club for the other half. Needless to say, Charlie snored contentedly, with no apparent care in the world. The war was over, and as he was one of the first into the army, he'd be one of the first to be demobbed. Most nights, he went out with his mates until closing time and he visited friends and family during the day while I was at work. So we muddled along; I was jumpy, but tried hard not to show it because that only irritated him, especially in company.

In a way, work at the canteen was a relief; even though you could say it was more of the same—waiting on men hand, foot and bloody finger—it kept me out of Charlie's way. I didn't want to push things while his good mood lasted, but there was no telling what would set him off, so out of the way was a good place to be. It also gave me time to think if I wanted to, over vast sinks full of washing-up.

I reckoned that if Charlie stayed the way he was, I could manage to rub along all right with him. But in my heart, I knew that was about as likely as Brian Hole becoming a vicar. I tried not to think too hard along those lines. Luckily, if I wanted to take my mind off my troubles, there was enough company for me to chat to and not think too much about anything. After all, all the brooding in the world wasn't going to change things one tiny little bit. Only action could do that, and I was blowed if I could think of a single thing to do. I was a married woman, and unless a handy number 8 bus widowed me, I was stuck with it. In that way, I managed to get through almost the whole week without anything or anyone blowing up in my face. The nights were the hardest part, but I found if I gritted my teeth and thought of England, it was soon over.

—❀❀—

On Friday I had a rotten day at work. The chip pan caught fire, which was no joke because there was not enough fat to refill it. This set the punters to grumbling and moaning all day. They liked their chips. As if I didn't know! I told them they had to make do with bubble and squeak, and think themselves lucky to get that. I was just about to add, 'There's a war on, you know!' in that snotty, self-righteous tone of the seriously hard-done-by doing their best under Blitz conditions, when I realized that there wasn't a war on any more. That cheered me up for a minute, until Mrs. Dunmore set me to cleaning up the greasy scorch marks left by the 'conflagration,' as she called it. Mrs. Dunmore was new and reckoned she was a cut above. At least one.

Then there was a power cut for over three hours. The canteen was gloomy at the best of times, what with the windows being filthy, still blacked out and way up near the roof—which was why the blackout hadn't come down. The original owners of the warehouse hadn't seen a lot of need for light. So there we were, charging about by candlelight and tilley lamp, trying hard not to drop anything or crash into each other. It turned out there was an unexploded bomb a few streets away; they'd gone through the cables trying to get at it. We heard a dull 'whump' and the china rattled when they exploded it.

By the time I dropped into the Lloyd Loom next to my mum in Zinnia's garden, my dogs were howling and my nerves were in tatters. My dear old mother looked at me hard and said, 'Gordon Bennett, gel, what happened to you? You look like you've done a couple of rounds with Genghis Khan *and* his heathen hordes. You all right?'

'Nothing a cup of rosie won't cure, and a bit of a sit. My poor feet weren't built for days like today, that's all,' I told her, rubbing my aching, throbbing feet in turn to ease the pain.

That wasn't the whole story of course. I didn't tell her I was dodging Charlie. I just needed half an hour's peace and quiet before I faced the barrage of 'Enie, get this' and 'Enie, get that' from the moment I got through the door until he buggered off out at opening time. I now knew why Mum had never complained when Dad went out boozing, even though it often left her short of money to feed and clothe us: if he was in the pub, he wasn't at home bothering her. Judging by the number of kids she'd had, that had come later, after chucking-out time. It seemed best not to mention all that, though.

I was so tired I could have wept. The flat had always been my refuge until Charlie came home. After that it wasn't. My eyes filled with tears of self-pity. I blinked rapidly and had a furtive sniff. Best not to dwell, it did no good.

'Aye, well. You rest a wee while there and I'll get the primus on. I see you've been busy with your sewing machine again. Is that a new skirt?'

As Zinnia puttered about making the cup that cheers, I explained that three of us at work—cook, Beryl and me—had brought in the clothes we were fed up with and swapped. A few minor alterations and we were all happy.

It was a real challenge to ring the changes to your wardrobe. Even those of us who hadn't been that bothered by clothes and fashion became obsessed with the whole thing once rationing, coupons and austerity took a grip. We were sick to death of khaki, brown, black, grey, and even navy blue. We longed for fine fabrics in pretty colours. I, for one, would have given one of Charlie's arms to have enough silk chiffon to make a garment that would allow me to waft about the way they did in the Hollywood pictures. A hemline to the ground would have been something. Even civilian clothes had more than a touch of the armed forces about them, which was a novelty to begin with, but wore thin as the years dragged on. Skirts were short to save fabric; the cut was usually tailored for the same reason.

Those Hollywood girls had a lot to answer for. There was a whole nation of women who were green with envy. Oh for decent wedding dresses, evening frocks and stockings! An endless supply of stockings. Those of us who were on the brink of womanhood when the war broke out had rarely, if ever, experienced such luxuries and we were absolutely certain it was our turn.

Sadly, the authorities didn't agree. It was beginning to dawn on us that even with the war over, shortages would continue for quite a while yet. I think if we'd realized just how long they were to go on, some of us would have rioted, but luckily, we didn't. Instead—at the canteen at least—there was an orgy of swapping, unpicking and remaking. Some garments had been unpicked and resewn so often, the poor things were limp with exhaustion. Not unlike me that day.

I had something else on my mind too. I was really worried that Charlie's fumblings would lead to another baby, however quick he was about it. He said he knew what he was doing, but I didn't think that he did, even when he was stone cold sober; being fuddled with beer made the whole thing even more hit-and-miss. The funny thing was, everyone seemed to take it for granted that I would be bursting to have another baby, to 'replace' the one I'd lost, as if that was possible. But I wasn't. I never had been keen on the idea, and time had made no difference. I realized very quickly that Charlie was not the kind of bloke to change his habits and that I would have to earn any money I needed.

That wasn't easy for married women before the war started. Kids or no kids, married women didn't work. A working wife was considered shameful, a sign that her husband wasn't man enough to support her. Once children came along, finding paid work became even harder. I didn't want to depend on Charlie for a crust, because I knew the bugger would either squander it or eat it, but he wouldn't hand it over. I'd seen children bought up in homes like that, and I'd never wish that on any kid of mine.

I shook myself out of that miserable daydream to find Zinnia and Mum looking at me in a faintly worried sort of way. 'What?' I asked. 'What's the matter?'

'Nothing, love,' Mum answered. 'I was just wondering what the matter was with *you*. You were miles away, then, and you looked so sad. Charlie giving you a hard time, is he?'

'No, Mum, no. He's not being too bad at all. Of course he's a lazy sod, expects to be waited on, but don't they all?' I asked, with what I'm sure was a rather weedy smile.

'So what *were* you thinking about, hen,' Zinnia asked gently, 'to make you look such a sorry wee scrap?'

'Babies.' I blurted it out before I could use my brains. Luckily, Mum grasped the wrong end of the stick and Zinnia just smiled sadly but kept quiet. I'm pretty sure she knew exactly what I was thinking.

'Don't you worry, love. You're young, you're healthy, there'll be more babies. You just be patient and do what comes naturally,' she chuckled, with a wicked twinkle.

As I was leaving, Zinnia hurried out of her gate after me with a jar of chutney she'd made the previous autumn. 'Here, hen, take this. It'll stretch some cold meat a bit further.' She caught my arm and pulled me a bit closer, so that only I could hear her when she whispered, 'Don't worry, hen, there'll be no baby this time. It'll be all right, I know it.' And she was gone, back to my mother. I can't explain why, but I believed her, and I fair skipped down the road, all tiredness gone.

Chapter 12

Charlie started hollering as soon as I walked in the door. 'Where the bleeding hell have you been? My belly thinks me throat's been cut, and I want my tea. I'm off out in about half an hour.'

I eyed my husband with distaste: he hadn't washed, he hadn't shaved and he was lounging about in his vest, khaki braces, uniform trousers and slippers. His eyes looked damp and red, as if he'd just woken from a deep sleep, which he probably had. During his leaves, Charlie rose in the afternoon and had a swig of something alcoholic to settle the beer he'd swilled before bedtime. After his tea, he'd wash, shave and dress properly for a night on the town. The routine didn't vary much until he ran out of cash, when he was forced to stay in or cadge. That evening, though, it looked as if he'd taken more than a swig of the medicinal booze, judging by his foul temper and the empty half-bottle of whisky that lay on the kitchen table.

'I'm supposed to be meeting me mates at seven, and it's half-six now,' he grumbled. 'So you'd better get your skates on. What's for tea?'

'Not a lot. I haven't been shopping today. I think I can rustle up some macaroni cheese,' I said, almost running to get the water in the pan and on to the gas. The sooner he was fed and out the better, I reckoned.

'I can't stand fucking macaroni cheese, and you bloody well know it. I'm a bloke. I need meat and two veg, not bleeding cheese and that Eyetie muck,' he said, an edge creeping into his voice.

'I'm sorry, Charlie, but the meat ration's all used up this week. I suppose I can see what Lenny's got tomorrow, for your dinner, but it's too late tonight. It's macaroni cheese or there's bread and dripping. Which would you like?' I'd been saving the small, hard lump of cheese for the end of the week, when things were tight. Now I grated it for all I was worth. I just had to get him fed. It'd soak up some of the booze for starters, it might soften his mood, but best of all, it'd get him out of the flat that little bit faster. My fingers trembled so badly, I grated the tip off of one of them and had to rush for a tea towel so as not to bleed any more into the precious cheese.

'Fucking hell, can't you watch what you're doing? I don't want your claret all over me grub.' The louder Charlie's voice got, the more I seemed to fumble and the more furious he became.

'Seeing you've fucking bled all over the Eyetie muck, and time's passing while you fall over yourself, I'll have the bread and dripping, or I'll never get out of here. Make us a cup of tea to go with it,' he instructed, and I leapt to it.

I set to work and Charlie went off to get washed and dressed. I had a steaming cup of tea and a plate of bread and dripping on the table by the time he got back. I carried on making the macaroni cheese: it gave me something to do while I waited, hardly daring to breathe, for Charlie to finish his tea and go. Anyway, I could have it for my own tea once he'd gone. I *liked* macaroni cheese. I jumped when he spoke from just behind me.

'Where's your purse? I need some readies, I've run out.' He reached for my oilskin shopping bag and fished about until he found it. Before I could think, my hand shot out to take it from him—Friday was pay day, and he'd have the lot. But he was too quick for me, and he held it way out of my reach.

I didn't see it coming, but I certainly felt it. The back of his hand met the side of my head in a thump so hard it rocked me on my feet and for a moment, I saw stars. His face was purple with rage and a vein throbbed in his forehead. 'If you'd come straight home from work, you useless mare, you could've nipped into Lenny's on the way, but no, you pissed off to God knows where and left me here to starve to bleeding death.' He was panting, and spittle had collected at the corner of his mouth, like a mad and particularly spiteful dog.

'And I get fucking bread and dripping for my tea. How the hell I got saddled with a dead weight like you is beyond me. Just because you got yourself in the pudding club, I'm stuck with you and your bleeding macaroni cheese for the rest of my fucking life.' He raised his fist and punched me in the mouth, while I just stood there, too frightened to move, duck or do anything. Then he really let rip.

I managed to protect my head with my arms as the blows rained down on my back and sides. He kicked the back of my left knee so that I crumpled sideways in a heap on the floor and he drew his boot far back, ready to kick me into kingdom come.

For a second, I could see my wide-eyed, terrified face reflected in Charlie's brilliantly polished toecap and the next, when I thought I must surely die, I heard hammering on the front door and someone calling.

'Zeld! Zeld! *Zelda!* Are you there? Come on, open up.' It was my sister Vi's voice. I don't think I've ever been so glad to hear it in my life.

It seemed to bring Charlie round, and he lowered his boot. He stared at me huddled on the floor for a moment, as if he'd never seen me in his life before, then picked up my purse that he'd dropped and emptied it of every brass farthing. When he left, he slammed the flat door behind him.

Chapter 13

Terry Rainbird was a bit older than Dilly and me, but contrary to what Dilly said, he was not old enough to be her dad, not unless he'd started really, really young. And he hadn't. He was only a year or so older than Vi. Scarlet fever had left him with what he called 'a dodgy strawberry.' He made jokes about never starting any long serials on the radio and watching out for circling vultures overhead, but despite the jokes, his heart condition was serious. That's why none of the Services would have him at the start of hostilities, and he'd tried 'em all. Army, navy and air force were united, apparently, in deciding he was unfit for duty, any kind of duty, even shuffling bits of paper.

I think the quiet depression he suffered following their decision was the only time in my entire life that I saw Terry anything less than fairly chirpy. Even the torch he carried for the uncaring Dilly was carried with good humour as well as resignation. So it came as a shock when, on seeing me and putting two and two together, his dear face twisted into something resembling fury.

'Did Charlie do this to you?' he demanded as he, Vi and I stood on my doorstep. He'd caught us on the way out.

'No,' I said.

'Yes,' said Vi.

Terry looked from me to Vi and back again and sighed when I dropped my eyes, too ashamed to meet his honest blue ones. 'The bastard!' he muttered. 'Look, you two hang on here a mo and I'll nip round the garage and get the motor. I'll drive you to where you're going. You won't want to be seen, I expect. If I can put two and two together, you can be sure every other bugger can. I'll be back in a tick.'

The short trip to Zinnia's was made in style in the front of Terry's van, which was normally used for journeys to the wholesalers and back and that was about it. Terry was not one for gadding about much, despite the little extra petrol ration he got for his heart trouble.

To be honest, it was a relief to be driven to Zinnia's, because everything hurt. Any movement sent agonizing pain through my side, where my ribs had taken a kicking. My head ached for the same reason. In fact I was beginning to ache all over, and I couldn't stop the odd shudder running through my body, jerking muscles that really didn't want to be jerked. I could almost feel the bruises on my face turning purple and black as I sat there, trying to be invisible as well as absolutely still.

If I hadn't been so sore and scared, I'd have found our arrival at Zinnia's funny. First Vi got out, had a good look around and scurried up to the front door to make sure that Zinnia was in. Then, with Terry on one side and Vi on the other, I was hustled up the garden path like a criminal on the way to the gallows. That's how I felt, anyway.

Zinnia didn't say a word at first. She just looked me up and down, thinned her lips and put the kettle on. She told Vi and Terry to 'Bide here a wee while, while I look at her. Make a cup of tea, why don't you? I'm sure we could all do with a drop.' And she ushered me out of the kitchen and into a room that I had known since childhood and that had always fascinated me.

It was where she stored her supplies of herbs, dried and bottled, in a dresser that took up a whole wall, end to end, floor to ceiling. It looked as if it had been specially made for the job a few hundred years before. There were drawers, cupboards and shelves, big ones and small ones, each with a purpose. The small drawers, a hundred in all, housed dried herbs arranged in alphabetical order. Yellowing labels, in small brass holders, announced the drawers' contents: *Adder's tongue, Eyebright,*

Feverfew, Lungwort, Meadowsweet, Motherwort, Plantain and good old *Yarrow*—if not a cure for all ills, then damned close to it, according to Zinnia. Sometimes there was the Latin name as well. One of the Makepeace women had been something of a scholar, way back in the distant past.

The larger drawers held bandages, forceps, scissors and stuff like that and some of the shelves held row upon row of labelled brown bottles. Many simply had the name of a herb on them—*Thyme, Sweet cicely* and *Horehound*—while others said things like *Bronchial mixture, Kidneys* or *Liver tonic* in Zinnia's distinctive copperplate handwriting.

The rest of the shelf space held an assortment of jars, tins and several large, leather-bound books which Zinnia called 'Herbals,' or sometimes 'Materia medica,' depending on the tome. It seemed to me that the ancient Makepeace hadn't been the only scholar in the family: they appeared to have made quite a habit of it.

Zinnia was brisk about looking at my injuries and careful not to ask any questions, other than 'Does that hurt?' as she prodded gently in the areas where my bruises were already beginning to show. She pronounced the injuries to be not too bad, considering the beating I had taken. My ribs weren't broken, just badly bruised.

She asked me how many fingers she was holding up, then whether I had had any double vision, or had lost consciousness at any point, and did I feel sick? I answered 'No' to them all except the sick one. Zinnia said that I was probably free from concussion as well, but she'd like to keep an eye on me. Which was dead handy, really, because I wanted to stay, badly. We went back to the kitchen together to join the others since I was too afraid to be left by myself. I just couldn't stop shaking and my teeth chattered.

We spent the rest of the evening together. I dozed in and out of an exhausted—and, I suspect, drugged—sleep on the sofa in the parlour. Zinnia had given me a small glass of something foul with brandy and told me to drink it, that it'd help me relax. I drank, and it did the trick. Pretty soon I was very relaxed, to the point of bonelessness, but also blessed painlessness; and I was snoring on and off, according to Vi and Terry.

The others drank tea and ate slivers of a fruit cake donated by a grateful patient who had contact with the royal kitchens. That explained why each sliver was almost black with dried fruit, rather than the token sultana, currant and half a morello cherry floating in an otherwise barren slab that the rest of us could get hold of. It showed how poorly I felt that I didn't fancy cake that night, but, bless her, Zinnia saved me a piece.

I listened to the murmur of voices and, for the first time in a week, I felt safe. Even when Charlie wasn't in a bad mood, I had been tense, waiting for the change to come over him. Sometimes, you could almost put money on it, if he'd been on a bender or a visit to his mum. He always came back from her place in a filthy mood. God knows what she said to him. I heard Vi's voice get a little louder and a bit squeaky, like it did when she was getting cross or worried.

'She can't go to church on Sunday, the whole neighbourhood will be talking by dinnertime. And work on Monday's out, I should think. Anyone got any bright ideas about excuses? I don't know what to say to Dad.' Which is where the squeak came in. I didn't know what to say to Dad either.

'Don't say anything, hen,' Zinnia suggested. 'I'll say she fell down my cellar steps in the dark. It's probably best if you say she was fine when you saw her. Then you'll not get the thumbscrews from your father.'

Vi agreed rapidly. It made good sense, given her terror of Dad's interrogations. She'd always blabbed immediately, even after she was married and Dad gave up the right to use his belt on her. He believed that disciplining his daughters became their husbands' prerogative, along with their 'conjugals,' on their wedding day. He gave up beating his sons on the day they looked as if they could fight back and win.

Zinnia's voice floated around me. 'We'll tell that to everyone but your mother and grandmother, agreed?'

Terry and Vi murmured that they did, then Vi's voice came again, sounding sad. 'Ain't life a bugger?' she asked, continuing before Terry could agree or Zinnia could object to her language, 'There's poor Zelda, stuck with a bullying bastard of a husband, who, God help me, few of us would miss if he was killed in action. I know as I shouldn't say it, but if you'd seen him when he shot past me…' Vi's voice caught slightly.

'If you'd found her lying there, all curled up in terror, then you'd say it too. And then there's me with dear old Fred, who wouldn't hurt a fly, not really, not given a choice. I'd give anything to have him safe home again.' Her voice cracked. 'Anything.' Then she sniffed once, hard, and added, 'Still, this isn't about my troubles, it's about our Zelda's, poor little thing. What *is* she going to do? I never realized it was so bad. She never said and I never noticed any bruises or anything. Did either of you?'

'No. Not a thing. He always seemed quite fond of her when I saw them together. Quite the loving hubby, in fact,' Terry said quietly.

But I noticed that Zinnia said nothing.

Terry and Vi must have left when I was snoozing, because the next thing I knew, Zinnia gently woke me, led me upstairs to her spare bedroom, tucked me in and said, 'Goodnight, hen. Call if you need anything. I'll look in on you before I go to bed myself. Sleep now, Zelda.' And I did.

It took most of Saturday for Charlie to track me down. Vi kept her mouth shut and point-blank refused to tell him anything when he saw her in the street. Luckily, there were loads of people about, the King's Head having just chucked out, so he didn't dare risk slapping it out of her. In the end, he had to rely on a process of elimination. If I wasn't at my mum's, my gran's or my sister Doris', then Zinnia's was the next logical place. It was teatime before he finally worked it out and came hammering on Zinnia's door.

The moment I heard him talking to Zinnia at the front door, I began to shake and shiver like a Chivers jelly, even though I was cowering in her kitchen. I was certain she'd not let him in voluntarily; and if he managed to get past her, he'd think twice about another beating in front of a witness. He'd more likely try charm, which, in a way, was worse, because most people were taken in, even me. I always hoped that he meant the apologies and promises never to hit me again, what Zinnia called the triumph of optimism over experience. I suppose I wanted to believe because then the future didn't look quite so bleak.

This time, however, charm didn't work. Zinnia kept her bony frame firmly planted in the doorway. I couldn't hear what they were saying to begin with, but then Charlie began to get louder as it became clear that Zinnia would not be moved. I crept closer to the kitchen door.

'What d'you mean, I can't see my own wife?' he demanded. 'I'll see what the police have to say about that. She's my wife and I can do what I like with her, including taking her to her rightful home if I want to.'

'I think you'll find, Charlie, that the police will be none too keen on giving you a hand. They don't like interfering with what they call "domestics"; it's usually messy. And do you really want the whole neighbourhood to know that you're a coward who beats his wife?'

I heard Charlie splutter and his voice got louder still. 'What do you mean, I beat 'er? She fell down the stairs. If she says any different, then she's bloody lying.'

'If she fell, Charlie, then her sister Vi would have found her at the bottom of the stairs. Instead she found her semi-conscious in the flat. I think it is you who is lying, Charlie Fluck. In fact, I *know* it is. I've known you both all your lives. There's only one lying, spiteful wee bully in your house, and it isn't your wife.

'Now get away from my door, before I see you off myself. It shouldn't present much of a challenge, you being the runt of your mother's litter. Now away with you before I chase you.'

I heard the door slam with a resounding thud that shook the house and then Charlie's voice bellowing from outside. 'You wait, Zinnia fucking Makepeace! I'll get you for this if it's the last thing I do.'

Zinnia opened a window and roared back, 'And it will be, Charlie Fluck, it will be. Now away with you, before I set my pussycats on you. Only they'd spit you out, you scrawny wee man.'

I didn't see Charlie again on that leave, but the neighbourhood was buzzing by nightfall about the flea Zinnia had shoved in his ear. I don't suppose the ragging he took for being sent packing by a middle-aged woman improved his attitude one little bit. He'd never liked Zinnia much, but after that afternoon he must have fair hated her. I was worried about the threat he'd made, but Zinnia wasn't.

'Ach, hen, he was talking through his beer as usual. It's one thing to beat up your wife—there's a school of thought that would see nothing wrong in that—but a helpless old spinster is a different matter entirely.'

I just hoped she was right.

Chapter 14

I was confined to Zinnia's house and garden on Sunday, partly from embarrassment, partly to dodge Dad, but mostly to make sure Charlie was safely on his way north before I set foot outside my sanctuary.

It was peaceful there and I loved it. Zinnia had set up breakfast in her glass room, so we ate our toast with honey donated by a grateful Reverend Cattermole, whose chilblains had been held at bay by Zinnia's magic hawthorn ointment and a brew laced heavily with ginger. Zinnia did not believe in rushing meals, and so we were on our third cup of tea before we got on to the subject of what I should do next. 'You'll have to make a plan, hen, as to how to proceed. It is one thing to be castigated in a foul tongue, and it is quite another to be beaten and kicked.'

I almost choked. There were times when you could really tell that Zinnia wasn't from around Hackney way, especially when she talked like the Bible. 'What can I do, though, Zin?' I asked. I couldn't see a way out.

'You could leave him,' she said, shaking me to the core and showing that she didn't *think* like the Bible, where that kind of thing was expressly forbidden, as far as I understood it. We all knew that respectable women didn't leave their wedded husbands, and if they did, they were shunned by everyone. So they lost everything: their children, home, friends, family and even familiar streets, because they would be forced to move a good long way away if they wanted any kind of life at all.

'I'm not sure I'm up to it,' I wailed. 'It would mean starting again from scratch.' It was like a bloody great yawning crater opening up at my feet, and I was terrified to take another step because the hole had no bottom that I could see.

'What would I do? Where would I live?' Everyone knew the housing situation was desperate, what with all the bombing and blokes coming home hell-bent on indulging in the kind of activity that founded dynasties. It stood to reason, them being starved of their women for long stretches of time. More kids would mean that the call for homes would become even more urgent. What chance did some lone female stand of getting a place, especially one on the run from her husband?

'Well, be that as it may, you never really know when an opportunity may present itself. Meanwhile, lassie, it behoves you to make a plan, and to start saving your money. You'll need it.' Zinnia had a good point, but the fly in that particular ointment was that Charlie had already cleaned me out. I'd have to borrow left, right and centre just to get through the week, and then I'd be paying everyone back for months.

'Aye, well, start as soon as you can and make sure you keep it in a safe place, where Charlie can't get his unscrupulous hands on it.'

I found the whole subject so frightening, I decided to head off on another tack altogether. It felt safer. 'I had a natter with Tony the other day and it gave me an idea,' I said, thinking aloud, really—I hadn't realized I'd had an idea until that very moment, when I really wanted a diversion. 'You know we said he needed a direction, rather than more punishment, to mend his wicked ways?'

'Aye, I remember fine,' Zinnia assured me. 'I'm not senile yet, thank the Lord.'

'Well, I had a thought. How about his singing? Why don't we try to do something with his singing? He *is* good.'

'It's an idea, Zelda. Funny thing, I know a singing teacher. Maybe he can help.' Zinnia sounded thoughtful and miles away from Hackney in 1945. 'I'll write to him and ask how we should proceed. He may be able to make some useful suggestions.'

—❀❀—

There was no question of dodging work the next day, fat lips and sore ribs or not. I needed the money, and I wouldn't earn it sitting around on my bum at Zinnia's. We also decided that Zinnia would make sure Charlie had returned to Catterick, and if it was safe, I'd go home on Monday night, after tea at her place.

Sunday wasn't a quiet day. First Mum and Vi came to have a look at me after church and to cluck over the damage. Mum slipped me ten bob, bless her, with the instruction that I wasn't to dream of paying it back. I almost cried. Vi stuffed a packet of ten Woodbines in my bag when I wasn't looking. I knew how much her fags meant to her and to part with a packet was a sacrifice indeed.

They'd just left, to get the Sunday dinner sorted at Arcadia Buildings, when Doris turned up, twins in tow, with a brown paper bag containing a twist of tea and another of sugar, 'to tide you over.' She'd heard about Charlie and my purse. News could travel in the air, like smoke, in our family. It wouldn't have surprised me if Bill and Jimmy, our surviving brothers, knew all about Charlie as well, and one of them was in a submarine. I was touched all the same.

We'd just settled down again, with a view to getting our dinner down us while the getting was good, when Tony and Reggie turned up. I sighed. So much for blaming the cellar stairs and keeping my secret.

'Uncle Charlie was round at Brian's this morning, before church. He must've stayed over. He was doing his nut over Auntie Zinnia and you, Auntie Zelda. The trouble is,' Tony said ruefully, 'things were just getting interesting when Ma saw me and slung me out.'

'What were you doing round at the Holes' so early anyway?' I demanded. First things first.

Tony rolled his eyes at me. 'Nothing.'

'Don't give me that, Tony Gunn. Nobody goes round to Ma Hole's for nothing.' I glared at him as best I could with a black eye and fat lips.

'Don't keep on, Auntie Zelda,' Reggie advised. 'He ain't going to tell you. He won't even tell me, so you might as well save your breath. The point is, Uncle Charlie had the right hump, according to Tone. Tell her, Tony.'

'I don't know what he'd had to say about you, Auntie Zinnia, but whatever it was, it wasn't good. Ma was ranting on about how you'd interfered in her family business once too often and how you had no right to keep a man away from his wife. Uncle Charlie was fit to be tied and Ma was winding him up something rotten. Kept on about him getting some control over his wife and keeping her away from the influence of Scottish hags. I'm sorry, Auntie Zinnia, but that's what she said. She don't like you much.' Tony's eyes were enormous as he relayed his information and, for once, he was pale. 'Then she threw me out and I didn't hear no more.'

Zinnia and I looked at each other solemnly for a moment, and then she smiled rather a thin smile. 'It looks as if Mrs. Hole is about to declare a war in Paradise Gardens,' she said mildly. 'A pity. I thought we'd have a little peace for a while.'

Chapter 15

It was a peculiar week altogether. On the Monday I went to work as usual. Mrs. Dunmore was horrified by the state of me. I don't think she believed for one minute that I'd fallen downstairs, but there wasn't a lot she could do about it, except keep me in the kitchens where I couldn't put the punters off their grub.

If she'd sent me home, she would have had to graft herself, and despite her name, Mrs. Dunmore did considerably less of that than the rest of us. She preferred to stick to the office work, of which there was plenty. Virtually every crumb, saucepan, spoon, dishcloth or mop needed at least two forms, done in triplicate, to ensure supply—except it did no such thing. Having submitted the half-ton of paperwork, another half-ton came back saying why they'd sent a bucket and a box of soda instead of the mop requested. Then we were told that we couldn't have any toilet paper, as paper was in such short supply.

Because Mrs. D. had stuck me in the kitchens to pearl dive (or wash up, to the uninitiated), scrub down the cookers and generally act as skivvy, she had to wait on tables herself, which is how she came to meet Charlie's pal, Percy Robinson. Everyone knew Octopus Robinson, he of the desert disease—wandering palms—except Mrs. Dunmore, but then she *was* new to the area. He was a right con artist, could charm your granny out of her own dentures and then flog 'em back to her, no trouble at all.

The regular waitresses ignored the Robinson smarm, knowing, as we did, that he was very much married to the dockyard boss' daughter. However, that little consideration never stopped Percy from trying it on as a matter of course with any female between the ages of nineteen and ninety. My mate Ronnie said the sheer weight of numbers ensured he got lucky sometimes, a bit like blanket bombing. Rumour had it that he had several kids, but none of them by Mrs. Robinson.

Nobody really understood how old Perce managed it. He was no looker, having ears like jug handles and hair so thin on top that he had to grow some side bits long so that he could comb a few strands over his shiny dome. It fooled no-one, except perhaps Percy. But charm, however transparent, evidently works on some people, judging by all those rumoured kids and the way Mrs. D. fell for it.

Watching Mrs. D. fall for Percy Robinson was the first peculiar thing that week, but it didn't stop there. On Wednesday, I went to the allotments to do a bit of watering after work and perhaps a bit of hoeing if I could stand it after spending a hard day on my feet. Zinnia showed up looking a bit bewildered, slightly amused and perhaps a tad worried, but not very. I asked her what was up.

'Come and look at this,' she said. We walked into her house and she led me round the ground floor. It took me a moment or two to cotton on and then it hit me: she'd swapped the parlour with her workroom. Her sofa, armchairs and stuff now sat in the room where her desk and her enormous dresser used to sit, and vice versa. I was nonplussed, because I couldn't see why she'd gone to the trouble after all those years of having it the same way. Or, indeed, how she'd managed to move that damned great dresser. Perhaps she *really, really* wanted a change of scene, I thought.

'Er, very nice, Zinnia. Felt like a change, did you?' Then I noticed something: she hadn't cleaned where the dresser used to be. It had stood in that very spot for many, many years; surely she'd at least give the area a dust, if not a damned good brush and scrub with hot water and plenty of soda and soap, which is what it needed. All she'd done was put the sofa where the dresser had been, and the dirt showed up clearly. Also, the wallpaper was different from the rest of the room, but perhaps she was going to decorate. However, it wasn't like her not to clean up as she went along.

'Do you want a hand with the scrubbing?' I asked, my heart sinking. I seemed to have been scrubbing all my life and it wasn't as if I liked it.

'No, hen, you don't understand. I didn't do this. I went out this morning and I've just got back and I found it like this.' She seemed more mystified than anything.

'Is any stuff missing?' Not that it sounded like your usual robbery. As a rule, if thieves were going in for furniture moving, they *removed* it good and proper, and flogged it to a dodgy dealer quick. They didn't just shunt it from room to room and leave it at that. It was very odd.

Zinnia shook her head. 'Not a thing, as far as I can tell. I suppose it must be some kind of practical joke. They've even changed the curtains and the pictures around. But who'd do such a thing?'

I really couldn't say who or, indeed, why.

'Ach, well. I'd better round up some strong lads to help me put it back again. One thing's certain: it has nothing to do with Brian Hole and his pals, they'd have cleaned me out. Maybe I'll have a wee scrub first, before I put things back, as it seems I've been pushed into yet more spring-cleaning.

'Do you want a cup of tea, Zelda? I have something to tell you.'

'I always have time for a cuppa, Zin, you know that.' I could see she was still rattled by the idea that strangers had wandered into her house for a spot of furniture shifting. I'd have been rattled too.

'It's about my friend, Digby Burlap,' Zinnia began, surprising me.

'Who is this man, Zin? How come I've never heard of him before?'

I swear Zinnia blushed to the roots of her hair. 'He's an old friend, that's all. I met him when I first came to London and we keep in touch.' And that's all she would say about her friendship with him.

'I see,' I said, but I didn't, not really. Fancy old Zin having a secret male friend. It was very odd and quite out of character. Zinnia had never shown the slightest interest in men. Well, not in the secret admirer kind of way. I was willing to bet that even my mum didn't know about this chap.

'He teaches singing, stagecraft, that kind of thing. He's the singing teacher to a lot of the West End show people. He's been at it for years. He does a lot for radio too.

'The point is, he's agreed to see Tony on Saturday and to see what he thinks of his voice and his chances for making a career in music. If he thinks that Tony has promise, he'll advise us on what can be done for the boy. Anyway, hen, I thought perhaps you could come, too, and we could make a little outing of it. You could do with a wee trip, it'll perk you up.'

'I'd love to, Zin.' Try and stop me, is what I thought. I just had to see this Burlap person, now that he had surfaced.

'Good, then present yourself with Tony prompt at ten. We'll have our meal in town. My treat.' And she wouldn't take no for an answer.

Dilly presented the week's last little mystery. She'd told Chester all about Al's dance for the Yanks returning to America and he hadn't said a word, just changed the subject. 'I thought he hadn't taken it in at first, Zeld, so I brought it up later and he changed the subject again. He started talking about some singer called Billie Holiday. Anyway, Chester ignored it again just as we were saying good night. Instead of saying anything about the dance, he kept on about how I had to hear this Billie person. Funny thing, this Billie Holiday's a girl, not a chap like you'd imagine. What do you think, Zeld?'

'Well, I suppose if you want to call your daughter by a bloke's name, it's up to you,' I answered.

'No, silly, not about her name, about the fact that Chester keeps changing the subject when I talk about the dance.'

I didn't know what to think, so we carried on mending her summer coat instead. It had ripped under the arm, and the lining was a mess as well.

'Zelda…' Dilly began, trying hard not to look at my bruises, which were fading. 'What are you going to do about Charlie? You can't let him go on hitting you. He'll do for you one of these days, then where will you be?'

'The cemetery?' I suggested.

'Don't even joke about it, Zeld. It ain't funny.'

'I know, Dills. But if I don't joke, I'll cry, and what good will that do? The truth is, I don't know what to do. Zinnia reckons I should think about leaving him, but I don't know. Where would I go? How could I leave all my family and friends? What would I do for money? It all needs a lot of thinking about. The trouble is, the minute I start thinking, the worse I feel. It all seems so hopeless.'

I snivelled a bit there and stopped talking. I only got upset if I talked about it. What's more, I couldn't get used to all these people in the know. Up until the last beating, Charlie's temper had been our little secret. If you can call it little.

I did try telling another of my friends early on, but all she said was, 'What, Charlie? Don't be daft. He's a laugh, is Charlie, and underneath it all, he's a right old softy.' Which showed what she knew. 'You can't be treating him right. Try and spice up you-know-what.' She winked. 'You know, the *bedroom*,' she mouthed, thinking I might be too stupid to understand. I understood all right. I understood that, despite being pals all our lives, she didn't want to know my troubles. The minute I told her about Charlie, she started cutting me dead in the street. I never really knew why, exactly, except perhaps that I reminded her of her own situation in some way. Her marriage can't have been a happy one. She was stuck with a man a good bit older than her, who had a nasty squint and managed to dodge the army and any other paid work. He spent a lot of time whining about his lot in life and hardly any time at all trying to do anything about it. Maybe he hit her as well; he certainly called the shots in every other department. She made me realize, though, that Charlie losing his rag and beating me was not the sort of thing most people wanted to hear about. Worse, they were likely to think it was all my fault, that I was a lousy wife.

I had never talked about it again, not until Charlie's last leave, and even then only reluctantly. Looking back, I can't for the life of me think why I felt so ashamed. I only know that I did. By rights, it should have been Charlie who felt shame, but he always maintained that I asked for it. But he never told me how, so that I could stop.

Chapter 16

Mrs. Dunmore was unusually scratchy on Friday morning. Nothing and nobody pleased her. She kept us hard at work for every second; we didn't even have time for the usual fag break. Mrs. D. was a nervy sort, thin with sharp features. Her movements were fast and jerky, but often appeared to be without much of a purpose—besides checking up on the rest of us and cracking the whip, that is; she excelled at that.

At dinnertime our canteen was a sea of dark, rough clothing, with just a hint of blue or khaki here and there, where the odd off-duty sailor or soldier shovelled down toad-in-the-hole or a sausage, with a large helping of bubble and squeak made from left-over cabbage and spuds. We'd managed to get hold of a consignment of bangers that very morning, so that dictated the menu. The beauty of toad-in-the-hole was that you could chop each sausage up into several bits to give the illusion of more banger per customer. It made a little stretch a long way, especially if you were generous with the batter. There was bread pudding for afters, using up the leftover loaves. Mrs. Dunmore dared not waste crust or crumb, because she had the Ministry to answer to. They were incredibly strict about their paperwork, were the Ministry.

However, even the Ministry knew dockers and sailors must be fed, and with grub that stuck to the ribs. Solid food fuelled their labours, and formed insulation against the rawest of days or a thorough-going wetting when the briny was kicking up

in socking great waves out in the Atlantic. So, it did its best
to see that our canteen was amply supplied with stodge, and
plenty of it, with a little protein thrown in now and then for
good measure. The ships and docks were our lifeline and the
men who worked them were vital. They still got leftovers, but
they got more of them.

Our establishment looked like what it was—a hastily transformed ex-warehouse. The walls were painted a dark green at
the bottom and the colour of elderly mashed potatoes above, but
the paint stopped at around fourteen feet, there being no point
in going right up to the rafters—according to the providers of
the paint, that is. Dim lights dangled by long chains from the
ceiling and stopped just above some of the scrubbed pine tables.
The naked bulbs added to the sad, dingy feeling. It was a place
to fill your face, but not a place to tarry.

It was difficult to know why Mrs. D. was so het up. She
wouldn't have dreamed of confiding in her staff, us being lower
orders in her book. So we fell to speculating, naturally. There was
no doubt that something 'had stuck a wasp up her jacksie,' as Cook
so delicately put it. The general opinion was that it had to have
something to do with Percy 'Drop your drawers' Robinson.

'Surely he can't have got into her knickers already,' Beryl said.
'I mean, I know he's a fast worker, but they only really met on
Monday, surely?'

'Yes, dear, that's true,' said Cook, 'but I heard that his missus
is away this week, nursing her mum, who's poorly again. That
woman don't half suffer from her innards.'

'What's her mum's innards got to do with anything?' Beryl
was mystified and, I have to confess, so was I. We turned as one
to Cook for an explanation.

'Well, his coast is clear, innit?' she said, raising her eyes to
heaven as if she was talking to idiots. 'It'll spur him on to get
his leg over while all's quiet, won't it?'

She had a point, and we discussed it for a while until Mrs. D.
appeared in the kitchen with instructions for us to stop gossiping

and get on with our work. We waited until she'd bustled back to her office, then carried on with our conversation.

'Yes. But if she's being serviced already,' I pointed out, 'she should be full of the joys of spring, not steaming around having a go at everybody. She ought to be full of the milk of human kindness, now shouldn't she?'

'True, Zelda, true,' Cook agreed. 'But since when has the course of true love, or true lust even, ever run smooth? I mean, it doesn't, does it? And if Percy's managed to meet and bed her in less than a week, then sure as anything, he can piss her off in double-quick time an' all.' Once again she had a point. 'Maybe someone's told her what a womanizer he is. She wouldn't want to hear that if she's just dropped 'em for him, now would she? Nobody likes to think they're one of a crowd.'

Beryl and I had to agree. It wasn't good to be one of many in romantic situations.

'Do you reckon their bones'd crash together,' Beryl asked, 'looking like a pair of stick insects the way they do? I mean, they're no advert for the grub here, are they? Surely banging away must hurt when you're that skinny.' She started to giggle.

I tried hard not to imagine the clatter of bones, but a giggle escaped me, too, at the thought, which was unfortunate because I was overheard by a small group of sea queens from one of the merchant ships that had docked in the early hours. They were at the table nearest the serving hatch and had caught the hint of rude talk. Now, there is nothing like a sea queen for spotting a grubby thought at 5,000 paces with his eyes shut. And the queen of the salty thought, my mate Ronnie—Rita to his close pals—Rigby, son of Mrs. Rigby of the junk shop opposite the King's Head, had joined them for his dinner.

He was a favourite of mine, as it happens, because he and his friends never stared at my main assets, or pinched my bum. He wasn't interested in asking me out, and treated us waitresses as ladies. He shared the best jokes and the hottest gossip with me as well, and had done so since I'd become old enough to understand them.

He knew just how important cosmetics, clothes, fabric and stockings were to us poor, deprived females and bought us the odd yard of cloth or pair of fully fashioned nylons, smuggled in among cases of canned corned beef, luncheon meat or peas, bales of jute, tons of wood or metal or mountains of dried goods in sacks. Whatever the cargo was, Ronnie and his pals managed to smuggle in some little luxuries if they'd been allowed to even sniff a foreign port. There was a very lively black market trade going on behind Mrs. Dunmore's back. The sea queens would always bring something that us ladies actually wanted for ourselves, rather than odds and sods we could trade on.

'What's oiled your giggling gear, may I ask?' Ronnie flashed his eyes at me. I swear he had more mascara on than I did, and the rouge—well, a girl could go too far! Especially in daylight. Luckily, as Ronnie was a local, he and his friends were safe enough in dockland where they were well known and liked. Anyway, just because they liked to dress up as ladies at the drop of a sequin didn't mean they weren't well muscled and used to defending themselves. Being a sea queen had its dangers in the wider world, and it was just as well to wear regular mufti in the hopes of passing unmolested among the throng. Or so Ronnie had told me once when we were half-cut in an air raid shelter up West, a Christmas or two before.

'Speak, Zelda,' he demanded, 'or I won't show you the nice bit of cloth I found for you. Swapped it for a third of a bottle of gin I got off a Dutchman. I'd swigged the other two-thirds, so it was a bargain. Yours, Zelda my flower, for half a dozen small bangers to take home to my old mum and for spilling the beans about what is so bloody funny. What do you say?'

I stopped my giggling. This was business. I needed a change, and a new garment, made with previously unused fabric, could be just the thing. 'I'll have to have a dekko first, Ronnie, but it sounds interesting. Meet you at the Star and Garter later. I'll tell you then what is so funny. It's a bit public at the moment.' I leaned over and whispered, 'Rumour is that our Percy is seeing to La Dunmore.' That had him gasping for the whole story, I could tell. You could always rely on Ronnie to enjoy the local scandals right up to the hilt.

All I had to do was to work out how to liberate a few sausages from the big, but virtually empty, meat safe in the kitchen. I looked around. Mrs. D. was waiting on Percy personally. She looked much more cheerful; perhaps she'd been in a bad mood simply because she couldn't wait to see him again. While she was preoccupied, it was the perfect time for a little creative thievery. All in a good cause, naturally. Cook was no problem; all I had to do was promise her a pair of nylons and pray like mad I could lay my hands on some. I was pretty sure that Dilly had a spare pair, thanks to the Yanks. The promise of a new blouse should secure them. Sometimes all the haggling, bargaining and swapping made your head spin.

I had those bangers stuffed into the bottom of my oilcloth bag quicker than blinking. If I didn't like the swap, I could always have sausages for my tea. Meanwhile, Mrs. D. was still fluttering around Percy Robinson and missed the whole thing. For the umpteenth time, I wondered just what it was about the man that got certain women to abandon their brains and hurl themselves on to their backs. True, he scrubbed up all right, but he was also married and no Clark Gable, except perhaps for the ears. His pale eyes watered all the time, as if he had a permanent cold, and they stuck out like dogs' bollocks, as my dear old ma would say after a stout or two. Then there was the comb-over hairstyle. I mean, talk about looking a prat. Mrs. D. must have been blinded by desperation or something.

I muttered my confusion to Ronnie and the others as I delivered their bread puddings and the news that the sausages had been liberated. 'What does she see in him? Tell me that. You lot are supposed to be experts on men after all. What *does* she see in him?' A lively discussion followed but no definite conclusions were drawn.

Later, having met outside the canteen, Ronnie and I repaired to the snug of the Star and Garter to swap goods, gossip, and

Guinness if available. To my surprise, Dilly was already sitting in there, chatting to Molly Squires. Everyone greeted each other and we settled down with our drinks. 'What are you doing here?' I asked Dilly. 'I wasn't expecting to see you tonight. I thought you had a date with Chester.'

'That's tomorrow, Zelda. Molly's been showing me her posh frock, in case I want to borrow it for the dance,' she explained. We spent a happy half-hour or so talking about our possible outfits. Half the fun of going anywhere special was working out what we were going to wear and tracking down bits and pieces to complete the ensemble. Mostly we searched through our friends' wardrobes; clothes coupons, and anything decent to get with them, were in chronically short supply. Still, the triumph you felt when you'd hunted down everything you needed was pretty good, and almost made up for the sense of deprivation. Almost, but not quite.

'Molly, guess who came into the canteen this dinnertime?' I asked, after a while.

Molly gave me a sour look. 'The King and Queen,' she said, without much conviction. 'How the devil should I know? Spit it out if it's good.'

'It was Percy Robinson!' I couldn't help the note of triumph. 'He's an ugly sod. Can't see what all these women see in him, honest I can't. You could hang a coat on his Adam's apple. And several on each ear, along with a couple of scarves and a hat,' I added as an afterthought.

'I've always wondered what he's got myself,' Molly said.

'Ah, well, I can help you there, ladies. I took the liberty of trolling into the cottage after our fascinating omie. I was intrigued after our little chat.' Ronnie gave us a big smile and took another swig from his glass, smacked his lips and continued in a conspiratorial whisper. Not that just anyone would have understood him if he'd been yelling from the rooftops. He was parleying in Polari and even Dilly didn't understand him.

'What's he on about?' she asked me, mystified.

'He says he followed our Percy into the gentlemen's toilets, Dill. Shush, I want to hear this. I'll explain later.' I found I was whispering too.

Ronnie continued with indecent relish. He did *so* enjoy dishing the scandal. 'Well, dollies, when he whipped his bingey out of his lally drags I am here to tell you it was fantabulosa!' Ronnie's eyes sparkled at the memory and he threw his hands up to his face in illicit delight. 'Gigantic, huge! You catch my meaning, young Zelda?'

I did. 'Percy Robinson's a big boy in the underwear department,' I whispered to Dilly.

But Ronnie had not finished praising the man's sole attribute: you could hardly call it a virtue, seeing how he spread it about. 'The omie was a veritable donkey beneath the waistband, darlings. A donkey! No wonder your boss-palone is so smitten. I've seen my share, dollies, but this old omiepalone was shaken to the core. Such a terrible waste on a naff bloke.'

'OK, you've lost me again. Translate, will you?' Dilly pleaded.

'I ought to get translator's fee. How about a Woodbine for my trouble? He says Mrs. D. is hooked on the size of Mr. Robinson's John Thomas.' She'd handed over the precious cigarette before I added, 'But a naff bloke's new to me.'

'Let's just say it means a straight man, one who saves himself solely for the pleasure of you ladies. A direct translation, my little innocents, is far too disgusting for your ears, dears.'

So that was the secret of Percy Robinson's success with Mrs. Dunmore: bulging trousers! Surely that wasn't enough, though. No wonder the man had developed his charm muscle. After all, he had to get himself in the position to show off his main asset. He didn't just drop his trousers and say, 'Cop a butcher's at this,' now did he? I said as much to Ronnie and we decided that, unlike sea queens, who thought nothing of eyeing a bloke's basket to assess the possibilities, most women wouldn't dream of doing such a thing, and needed to be persuaded into the boudoir.

Once we'd finished dishing the dirt on Mrs. Dunmore and her paramour we moved on to the important business. Ronnie had done me proud: the fabric was five yards, no less, of cotton in a creamy colour with poppies, cornflowers and daisies scattered about. Enough to make a brand new, never-worn-before, and definitely *not* unpicked-and-resewn-for-the-umpteenth-time, summer frock. I could have kissed him. I handed over the bangers wrapped in a nearly new bit of greaseproof paper and the deal was done.

We drank up and Dilly, Ronnie and I strolled towards home arm in arm in the gathering dusk. It had been a good night, full of merriment. I loved old Ronnie.

Chapter 17

Saturday dawned fair, and Tony, Reggie and I duly presented ourselves at Zinnia's kitchen door. Tony hadn't needed much persuasion once he'd heard that Digby Burlap had dealings with stars of stage, screen and radio and had his studio in Soho. However, his mother was much more dubious.

'Who is this bloke? And what's more important, how much is he going to charge? I don't have any spare cash, as you well know. Certainly not spare enough to throw away on singing lessons. I mean, I ask you, whoever heard of such a thing?' Vi looked at her son, then at me and back to Tony. 'And anyway, he won't keep it up. It'll be good money after bad, you both know it will. He can't even get to school on a weekday; what makes you think he'll give up his Saturdays for more bloody lessons?' She had a point there.

'Nothing's set yet, Vi. This Burlap bloke's got to listen to him first, and see what he thinks. If he reckons Tony's got talent and a chance to make something of it, we can worry about the lolly then. Let's wait and see, eh?' I suggested.

Vi reluctantly agreed. The look of relief and delight on Tony's face was a picture. He'd obviously set his heart on having a go. Or at least, I thought he had, but as Saturday approached he'd become more and more nervous until finally, I thought he was going to bolt in sheer terror. That's when having a cousin came in very handy.

'Don't be weedy, Tone. I wish I could sing. I'd go like a shot. Trouble is, I'd wheeze at the bloke and he'd sling me out. But you *can* sing, everybody says so. I reckon you'd be a real prat—sorry Auntie Zelda—' I shrugged and let it go: apart from the language, the boy was doing good—'if you missed your chance.' Reggie's argument swung it. Tony took a deep breath and said he was ready.

'Lucky you're coming with us, Reggie,' I said. 'You can keep Tony from getting too nervy.' Also, he could supply the necessary scorn if his cousin balked at the last hurdle. Reggie's sneers would drive Tony on far more effectively than all the well-intentioned praise of any two women. Blokes quite often work like this. The opinion of men and other lads is far more important than that of a mere female; even when the chaps are obviously wrong.

The bus dropped us in Oxford Street, but we didn't waste much time looking at the shops. The war had ended so recently, the supplies of clothes and fancy goods hadn't got going again. Other things, like building materials, coal, petrol and basic foodstuffs, were needed more urgently, and they had priority when the supply lines finally opened up again.

Posh frocks and decent furniture would just have to wait a while; a good long while as it turned out. It didn't occur to the powers that be that in order to rebuild our country, a spot of morale boosting might not go amiss. Well, not immediately anyway. It did cross their minds later, when it came to the Coronation, but not much changed straight away. Even then we were supposed to get our jollies out of the fact that it was the Queen and other women in the Royal Family who got the posh, brand new frocks.

To my utter astonishment, Zinnia seemed to know her way around Soho like a native. 'Follow me,' she cried, setting off at a fair old clip. The two boys and I had to gallop to keep up with her. She dived down a narrow side street lined on both sides with tall, sooty buildings, with flats above and small shops below. Several were boarded up, supplies of whatever it was they had sold having dried up. However, a tobacconist, a baker, a butcher and a hardware store still struggled on. I was so busy looking at a shop window that had bunches of weird sausages hanging from cruel hooks in the ceiling and a large mound of something that looked suspiciously like string in a huge bowl, that I missed one of Zinnia's turns and found myself alone for a moment.

Then Tony's head popped out of a nearby alley and yelled, 'This way, Auntie Zelda!' and I scurried along the narrow foot-way to catch up. I noticed the alley still had gas lamps, and wondered if they worked. I liked gaslight. It had a more mellow atmosphere than the brash electric jobs.

Eventually, we wound up outside a place called the Old Compton Cafe. Two large, steamy windows flanked the central door, through which Zinnia swept as if to the manner born. Tony, Reggie and I were nowhere near as confident. I had eaten out once or twice, but the boys never had, and their eyes were like saucers.

It was fairly crowded already, although it was barely noon, but we managed to find a table for four next to one of the windows. It was a far cry from the canteen I was used to. With its rows and rows of tables crammed into a lofty, dingy space, that was more like a mess hall in a run-down barracks. The cafe was cosy in comparison.

The ceiling was lower, for starters, so you didn't get the feeling that there were bats in the rafters way above your head. Although there were plenty of tables, it didn't feel like an institutional canteen. There was no dark green and mashed potato paint on the walls either; the plaster beneath the dado rail was white, and above it was panelled in pine, also painted white, with shelves and mirrors fixed to it. The shelves held china, spare cups, saucers and plates. Every now and then, a spider plant or wandering Jew hung over the edge and was reflected in a glittering mirror. The whole effect was light and airy, and a far cry from the dark cavern I worked in.

There was a counter at the back of the shop, with an urn and a display cabinet with rock cakes, scones and teacakes tastefully arranged on plates, complete with sparkling white, lace-edged doilies. A large, ornate till stood at the other end of the counter and behind, on each side of the door leading to the kitchen, were more shelves. The woman who appeared to be running the show couldn't have been more different from Mrs. Dunmore. She was younger for starters, and a good deal bigger. She looked as if she actually *enjoyed* her food, whereas Mrs. D. looked as if she never touched the stuff. Maggie, as she was called, was what you might call a real advert for the delights on offer.

'Hello, Miss Makepeace, how nice to see you again. It's been a while,' said Maggie, little realizing that she could have knocked me down with a feather as she said it. How did *she* know our Zinnia? 'What can I get you? The special today is liver and bacon, mashed spuds and gravy. Oh yes, and some cabbage and carrots to go with it. Or we've got cauliflower cheese or sausage dish, take your pick.'

The boys were struck dumb and could only stare, open-mouthed, looking around the place and at the other customers; anywhere except at Maggie, poised with her pad and pencil. In the end, I chose liver and bacon on their behalf, when it looked as if their voices had deserted them for ever. Once the food was delivered, however, they tucked in quietly. They even used the table manners their mums had tried so hard to teach them. There were no elbows on the table, they chewed with their mouths closed and took small mouthfuls, instead of stuffing their cheeks like hamsters, the way they did at home. Their mums would have been puffed with pride and I was quite pleased myself. As Zinnia said, the boys were a credit to us. They were too over-whelmed by their new surroundings to be anything else, but nobody mentioned that.

We even had a pudding—apple crumble and custard—and I was in heaven. I wasn't expecting a pudding. Neither were the boys, and they wolfed theirs down in double-quick time as if they thought some bugger might nick it from under their noses. Zinnia ate hers in a more leisurely manner and chatted quietly with Maggie.

'And how's your husband, Maggie?' she asked politely.

'Lovely, thanks, Miss Makepeace. His trouble's a lot better since you gave him that jar of ointment.'

'I'm glad you reminded me.' Zinnia stuck her head into her enormous bag and came out waving a large jar. It wouldn't have surprised me if she'd whipped out her range, the butler's sink and her two cats while she was at it. It seemed to be bottomless, that bag of hers. 'Here's some more. Do give it to him with my compliments, hen.'

Maggie smiled. 'I will. He'll be pleased. He's been eking the last lot out.

'Are you here to see Mr. Burlap? He was in just the other day. He came in with Mademoiselle Hortense and some of her dancers.'

'Aye, hen. We've brought young Tony here for an audition,' Zinnia explained.

'Good luck then, Tony. Mr. Burlap's a poppet, you needn't worry about him. We all think the world of him round here. He put on some lovely carol singing last Christmas, right in the middle of Soho Square. Cheered us all up no end. He's a good teacher too, or so the show people say, and they should know. Right, I'll leave you to finish your pudding. Would you like some tea?'

By the time we'd finished our dinner and taken a stroll up Shaftesbury Avenue and back again, it was time to go to see Mr. Burlap. I noticed that as well as being quiet, Tony had also managed to lose some of the blush from his normally rosy cheeks. He must have been afraid, poor lad. I would have been, too, in his position. It was scary to have to perform all on your own, for a complete stranger who knew his stuff.

Chapter 18

There was nothing to show that Digby Burlap's music studio was above the violin shop called *Fishbein's Strings*, except a small sign that simply said *Digby Burlap* and nothing else. Below it was another plate that read *Mademoiselle Hortense, Ecole De Dance* in the same fancy writing as Mr. Burlap's and Mr. Fishbein's signs, so I figured they must have got a job-lot price from the signwriter, who went the whole hog once he'd got his eye in. Zinnia applied a large, capable finger to the brass bell push and we waited and we waited and we waited.

I was just wondering if we'd arrived at the wrong time, or on the wrong day, when I heard a sound like a runaway horse clattering down the stairs. The brown door crashed open and a tiny figure in black chirruped, 'Zinnia, *ma chère,* 'e is up the stairs in 'is studio, waiting for you. I must fly. I 'ave a re'earsal with a 'erd of buffalo that I must turn into swans before ze month is out.' Then the wispy little figure flitted down the area steps and disappeared into the basement, where she could faintly be heard yelling, 'Come, *mes petites* pachyderms. Places, places and one and two and…' A piano started up a shade before what sounded like a dozen sets of hobnailed boots began to thunder a syncopated rhythm on wooden floorboards. '*Non, non, non*—glide like the swan, not thump like the kangaroo! *Alors*! It is 'opeless, 'opeless…'

I was beginning to think that Mademoiselle Hortense might've been better off keeping a zoo, when Zinnia led the way up the narrow stairway. The boys were in the middle and

I brought up the rear, ready to field Tony if he made a last-minute dash for it. The poor lad looked as if he was mounting the scaffold.

At last Zinnia arrived on a small landing. A panelled door flew open and a huge, indistinct figure swept her up into the most enormous bear hug, swung her off her feet and round so that she landed inside the room before turning to greet us in a voice that could clearly be heard in Slough. 'Welcome, welcome! Come in, do. Zinnia, my flower, so good to see you.'

I just had time to think 'Zinnia, a flower? A thistle perhaps,' when my hand was grabbed in a giant paw and raised to a pair of full lips. 'Enchanted, my dear lady. And the boys? Not yours, surely, you're far too young, far too young! Nothing but a spring sapling yourself.'

Once the introductions were made and I had got over some of the shock of seeing Zinnia manhandled by this giant of a man and apparently loving it, we settled down to business. 'Which one of you likely looking lads is the singer?' Mr. Burlap asked, turning first to Tony and then to Reggie, shaggy eyebrows raised in enquiry.

Mr. Burlap had a huge head to go with his body, and thick, black hair that seemed to writhe with a life of its own. He wore a rusty brown velvet jacket, with tarnished gold braid around the lapels and cuffs. More gold braid made elaborate patterns around the buttonholes that strained across a large chest and an even larger belly. Mr. Burlap was definitely built for comfort, and speed was not an option. What I liked most about him were his eyes, which were large, brown and very kind.

'Zinnia, my queen, sit, sit, do. And you, dear lady, and the spare boy, sit and we will proceed.' So we sat. Tony, Reggie and I were too overawed and dumbstruck to say anything, but Zinnia chatted away comfortably about Tony's singing as if she was in Rainbird's grocery buying tea and a bag of flour and discussing the state of the Empire with Terry. She seemed oblivious to our astonishment at her being addressed by Mr. Burlap as a 'flower' and his 'queen.'

'I see. Right you are. You, Tony, come and stand by me and we'll run you through a few things. See how we do. Hmm?' Up went the caterpillar eyebrows again and Tony followed him over to the piano. Mr. Burlap sat down on the piano stool and ran his fingers over the keys in an absentminded sort of way. He looked Tony up and down, nodded once and played his little tune for a moment longer. Then he asked Tony about his experience of singing with the Reverend Cattermole's choir at St Mary's. Tony told him about being the main soloist and singing at all the important church events.

'Enjoy it, do you?' Mr. Burlap asked, when Tony had run out of steam. Tony nodded. 'Good!' Another tinkle or two on the piano and then he said, 'Right you are. Your scales now: run up and down for me, will you?'

Tony obliged and was rewarded with a nod and an 'Again.' Tony's voice sang out in the silence. 'Hmm,' was Mr. Burlap's only comment.

Then, out of the blue, he asked, 'Can you sing the tune I've just been playing, dear boy? In your own time.' And without hesitation Tony's voice soared over our heads, chiming out the intricate tune in a voice as clear as the waterfalls Zinnia talked about when she fell to pining for her Highland home.

'Hmm, I see,' said Mr. Burlap again after another moment or two. He fumbled on a shelf and found some sheet music. He began to play the piano again, then asked Tony to hum what he'd just heard and follow it up with the first piece again. He did that once more, with a different piece of music. Then he took a funny fork thing out of an otherwise empty milk bottle that stood on the shelf next to the piano stool, gave it a resounding whack on the edge of his stool and said, 'Can you hum that note and hold it?' Tony did as he was asked. After another half an hour of similar exercises Mr. Burlap turned to Zinnia with a smile that matched the rest of him. Big, in other words.

'The boy has perfect pitch.' Another smile, this one so wide that you could've posted parcels in it. 'Absolutely perfect pitch.

That's a rare gift. And a good musical memory. He'll do. I'll teach him.'

'Oh Digby, dear, I am delighted,' Zinnia said, and she looked it too.

I was sorry to spoil the mood, but I had to be practical. Apart from anything else, Vi would expect it of me. 'Can I ask about cost?' I said in a small voice. 'You see, his mum doesn't have a lot of spare money. So it's something we have to consider. Sorry,' I finished lamely.

'Oh don't trouble yourself too greatly about that, dear lady. Zinnia and I have already made an amicable arrangement. A donation of a pound a week to my poor box should do nicely. Or less, if you find that troublesome. Dear Zinnia will arrange everything to everyone's satisfaction I am sure.'

I wondered what 'amicable arrangement' he and Zinnia had come to, but realized I'd never find out unless she chose to tell me. I was determined to try, though. You never knew, she might come over all communicative. And pigs might square-dance, I thought to myself. Still, I reckoned that between me and Vi, we'd manage a quid a week, just. I might even be able to tap Dilly for a few bob, and her mum too, I thought. They were, after all, Tony's relatives just as much as we were. One way or another, Tony was going to get his lessons, if I had anything to do with it. That's if he wanted them, of course. It'd be a waste of money otherwise.

I turned to him. 'What do you think, Tone? Fancy giving it a go, do you?'

Tony nodded, his face aglow with achievement. 'Yes, Auntie Zelda, I'd like to give it a try.'

'Good!' boomed Mr. Burlap, and it was arranged we'd present ourselves the following week.

Tony was very quiet on the way home as he thought about Mr. Burlap and the new direction he was taking. It was certainly a lot for the lad to get his brains around. We had never seen anyone even remotely like Mr. Burlap in our entire lives before.

Which had me thinking about what I had learned about our old friend Zinnia. She was pretty eccentric herself, in her own quiet way, but seeing her being treated to hugs, kisses and extravagant endearments by someone so much bigger than life was a bit of a facer. We were all too much in awe of Zinnia to take personal, physical liberties like grabbing her and hurling her around, but she did seem to love it, so may be she missed it when we kept our distance. Or possibly it was only Mr. Burlap who was encouraged to take such liberties. In which case, why was he the exception?

Then, on top of all that, Soho's apparent familiarity with our Zinnia suggested she was a fairly frequent presence in their midst, which made the whole thing even more of a mystery. She really was a much darker horse than I'd ever given her credit for being. She'd have made an ace spy or member of the Resistance. She had never, ever given us the slightest hint that she'd even stopped in Soho for a cup of tea, let alone long enough to be well known and held in obvious affection by quite a few of the locals.

I couldn't guess what Reggie was thinking about, but he too was silent on the way home. He simply gazed out of the bus window, taking in the passing scene. Like Zinnia, our Reggie was a deep one. In the end I asked him, 'A penny for 'em, Reggie.'

'They're not worth it, Auntie. I was just thinking what a nice afternoon we had, what a funny lot they are in Soho, 'specially that Mr. Burlap, and what a lucky bug…bloke Tony is to have a talent, and that I wished I had one too,' he said, rather sadly I thought.

'But you have got a talent, Reggie, lots of them in fact. You're clever for one thing. You always do well at school in most of your subjects,' I pointed out.

'That's because I work hard at it, not because I'm clever,' Reggie answered me glumly. 'Being a swot is nothing to write home about.'

'But you *are* clever, Reggie,' I argued. 'You have the sense to work hard, make the most of your talents and best of all, you have the sense to keep out of trouble, which is more than can be said of your cousin.'

Tony came round at that and grinned at me cheekily. 'Thanks a lot for nothing, Auntie.'

'Oh it ain't *nothing*, Tony, to get singing lessons. Anybody'd think you was being rewarded for being a tearaway,' Reggie told his cousin bitterly. Tony did have the grace to look a bit ashamed and he looked away, blushing.

Reggie had made a good point. It did look that way. I made up my mind there and then to make sure Reggie had his turn one day.

Chapter 19

It was Sunday. Charlie had been safely back in Catterick for only a week, but my bruises were fading and the aches and pains were getting better already. Having missed church the previous week, I was about to give official thanks to the Lord for Charlie's blessed absence and my healing powers. I also thought I'd offer up a prayer that I wouldn't have to put up with Charlie around the flat again until he was demobbed.

Charlie had been one of the first into the army when the call came, not from choice but because getting away had seemed like a very good idea at the time. He'd had a spot of bother with Lily Law over some boxes of fags found in his cousin's possession. They had been ambushed somewhere between a bonded warehouse at the docks and a posh tobacconist's in South Kensington. The law couldn't prove Charlie was actually *there*, but on the other hand, Charlie couldn't prove that he wasn't. After all, Lily Law reasoned, his cousin had possession of the swag and had been seen hanging around the bonded warehouse along with Charlie's older brother, Sid. The chances were, therefore, that Charlie boy was busy close by.

So, with his relatives tucked up in custody awaiting trial, hostilities with Hitler had come to the boil and call-up seemed inevitable, so Charlie thought, why not volunteer? That way, he could get away in a reasonable and orderly fashion *and* be thought to be a gung-ho hero ready to serve King and Country, while he was at it. He'd also just discovered he was going to be a father and strongly suspected a shotgun wedding was in the offing. He felt that great distance would definitely lend enchantment to *that* particular domestic view. He was right, too.

Anyway, the upshot of all that was, the first men and women into the forces were likely to be the first out again. So I was going to pray hard for an administrative cock-up that would keep Charlie in service until the very last knockings. Otherwise, it wouldn't be that long before he was home for good. It didn't bear thinking about, so a fervent knee job was definitely called for. God might be listening. A body never knew for sure, even if He had been cocking a deaf 'un from the very start of my married life. Let's face it, if He'd been listening, there never would have been that grapple on Emily Alice Davies' grave, there'd have been no wedding and my whole life would have been different.

I was just getting my hat and gloves on, ready for church, followed by dinner at Mum's along with the rest of the family, when a loud hammering on the street door made me jump. I snatched up my handbag and the oilcloth shopping bag with my meat ration in it. I had worked out that there was just enough time to drop in at Arcadia Buildings to put it on to cook in the huge stew pot before we made our way to St Mary's church. We often pooled our meat rations on a Sunday. It made a morsel go a long way and every little helped. This week we had a minuscule, tough and stringy mutton chop each and a few spuds, onions and carrots too. So stew it was.

The Sunday routine in our family rarely varied. Mum and the rest of us girls were expected to attend the nine o'clock service while Dad had a lie-in. He attended the eleven o'clock, which was done and dusted in time for a swift pint at the King's Head and then home for his Sunday dinner, cooked by his women. Any men at home went to church and, if old enough, to the pub with Dad, except poor Tony who had to be at all the services because he was in the choir.

The Reverend Cattermole loved music. He always had Mrs. Cattermole pounding her heart out on the organ and had the choir in attendance as often as humanly possible, war or no war. 'Music lifts the spirits,' he'd say, 'far better than any sermon I could preach. This is especially true if young Tony's singing a solo, because his voice is so beautiful, so strong, so sure and so pure.'

Which left me thinking it was a pity the boy didn't measure up to his voice in the purity stakes, but I never said so. However, the family chests swelled with pride to hear that glorious voice soaring effortlessly up to the rafters. Except it wasn't effortless. Tony's beautiful rendition of 'Once in Royal David's City' the Christmas before had been the result of many hours at choir practice. He sang all the time at home, too. He only had to hear a song on the wireless once and he could hum the tune; give him a couple more hearings and he'd have the words, as well.

It was the one thing he stuck to, despite serious ragging from his mates. I'd heard him being taunted for being 'a holy Joe' and one of 'Jesus' little sunbeams.' But it seemed not to touch him at all; he'd just grin, shrug, roll his eyes and say it kept him off the streets. Which it did—sometimes. It also made him a favourite with Reverend Cattermole, which came in handy at church teas when Tony always got a slightly larger slab of cake or an extra sandwich, and these were not to be sneezed at during hard times. The Reverend's precious choir members had always been first into the crypt for shelter when the air raid sirens sounded. Of course, they *were* mainly women and children, and the Reverend insisted this was the reason, not favouritism for his precious choir at all.

'Think of the Devil and he shall appear,' as my old gran would say, and sure enough, it was Tony hammering on my door. Eyes huge and sticking out like organ stops, he panted, 'Can I come in, Auntie Zelda? Good!' and barged past me without ceremony, bounding up the stairs to the flat door. I followed after him with my keys. Once we were safely inside the flat I turned to him and had a good look. He definitely looked scared.

'What or who has rattled your cage?' I demanded, thinking it best to get straight to the point. Time was passing and the service would be in full swing when we got there if we didn't get our skates on.

Tony looked furtive and desperate by turns. His eyes kept darting around the room and then settling briefly on his boots, then back searching the corners, like a hunted, but hugely embarrassed animal. What on earth was the matter with the boy? 'Spit it out, Tony, there's a love. Your grandad'll have my guts for garters if I don't show my face at church this week. Your mum or someone's bound to tell him if I don't make the early service. Which is where you're supposed to be, I might add!'

There was a bit more eye sliding and then he finally blurted it out. 'I think something's wrong at Auntie Zinnia's,' he said.

My voice was sharp. 'What makes you think that?'

'I saw some smoke coming over her garden wall,' he answered.

'It could be a bonfire,' I suggested. It seemed reasonable.

'Not on a Sunday, Auntie. Auntie Zinnia would never have a bonfire on a Sunday.' Tony sounded shocked.

He was right. Zinnia wouldn't dream of lighting a bonfire on the sabbath. It would have been sacrilege where she came from and considered none too clever in Paradise Gardens either. Sunday was supposed to be special, a day of rest and worship and not a day for gardening chores.

Which was how I came to miss the service for the second week in a row. I sent Tony packing: he had to sing in church, and anyway, there was no reason for both of us to land in hot water. I told him to tell everyone that I'd heard a rumour about trouble at Zinnia's and that I had gone to warn her. No point in dragging Tony into it, even though I was convinced that the little toe-rag knew a whole lot more than he was letting on. If fire was involved though, it was not the time to give the little bugger the third degree; Zinnia could be burned to a crisp before I got the first thumbscrew on.

It made sense to keep schtum as far as his grandad and mother were concerned, as well. No point in prompting them to ask questions until I was sure the answers would be satisfactory. I had high hopes of Tony and Mr. Burlap and I didn't want the boy to be put off by a huge family row if it could be avoided.

I arrived at number 23 and saw smoke drifting over the garden wall just as Tony had said. I went through the front gate, followed my nose to the source and found that Zinnia's wooden tool shed was smouldering. Someone had a lit a fire underneath it with petrol-soaked rags and garden rubbish, and it was beginning to catch. I could smell petrol fumes clearly. The problem was, the shed nestled up snugly to the glassed-in room, which in turn was right up against the house. I had to get a move on!

I pounded on Zinnia's back door but got no reply, so I looked frantically around for something to carry water from the outdoor tap to the shed. Zinnia's hose and watering can were *in* the shed, so they were no help. Then I noticed a mound of earth with a spade sticking out of it and a wheelbarrow nearby. It looked as if Zinnia had been using one of her many compost heaps to feed the garden. I shovelled like a demon until the wheelbarrow was half full then trundled it along the path to the shed at a gallop, narrowly avoiding dumping my load before I got to the fire.

I shovelled the contents under the shed, peering through the smoke until my eyes ran with tears and stung like mad, but I was pretty sure I'd dealt with the source. I needed water for the shed itself: the door was blackened at the bottom and glowing red further up. At any moment it would burst into flames, and if Zinnia kept any paraffin or paint in there, God help her poor house! I ran back to the tap with the wheelbarrow and filled it with water; it was all I had. Then I thundered back again and tipped my load on to the door, swamping my shoes, stockings, feet and the hem of my clothes in muddy water.

The shed door hissed and steam rose into the air but the glow from the timbers had died. I could have wept, partly in relief that I'd got the fire out and partly in abject misery because I'd had to ruin my Sunday best to do it.

And that's where Zinnia found me, sitting on her compost heap in my tattered finery, face streaked with black smuts and eyes red with smoke and tears. I had been thinking that it was ironic, really: not a spot of bother all through the Blitz and the moment peace was declared, some bugger was trying to burn down Zinnia's house!

Chapter 20

'How're things going with Chester?' I asked Dilly as we lay out in the sun the day after the fire. We'd strolled over to water the allotment after we'd had tea at my place and were sprawled on the grass verge staring up at fluffy white clouds. It still seemed strange to feel that you could do a little cloud watching without fear of a doodlebug appearing out of the wide blue and spluttering into that awful, eerie silence that came just before it dropped.

I remembered a time Dilly and I were baby-sitting the twins. They were in a playpen on the tiny patch of smutty green Doris called 'the garden,' and we were in the kitchen, making a drink, when we heard the distinctive sound of a doodlebug chugging towards us. For a moment we froze: doodlebugs did that to you. Our ears were out on stalks trying to catch that moment when the chugging stopped; you even postponed breathing while you waited.

Anyway, the engine cut out right overhead. Dilly and I rushed to the back door to get to the twins and became jammed fast in the doorway. We could not budge and had to wait, powerless, until the explosion came. Which it did—a few streets away, thank God. Once the tension left our bodies, we sagged with relief and were able to get to the twins at last. We had to hose them down gently, to get rid of the brick and plaster dust that had settled on them. It had been that close!

Our relief was short-lived, however. We may have escaped the blast, but a girl from our old school, Spotty Penn, hadn't.

She was blown sky high when it caught her running for the family's Anderson shelter in their back yard, or so her sister Rose reported after Spotty's funeral. The family were never quite sure whether or not they'd managed to bury all of her in St Mary's churchyard.

Dilly's voice brought me back and I had to think for a moment to remember what I'd asked her. Of course, it was about Chester.

'Not bad, Zeld. He took me to this club in Soho last night. There was a bunch of Yanks playing jazz and Chester was right up there with them. He's ever so good.'

'Any progress on the dance?' I asked. 'Has he taken the hint yet, or is he still being dim?' Dilly had gone quiet about the dance.

'He seems to go deaf every time I bring it up, Zeld. I don't understand it. It's not as if he can't dance, like some blokes, and doesn't want to say. We've *been* dancing. He's good at it.'

'So what are you going to do?'

'What do you mean, what am I going to do? There's nothing I *can* do. I can hardly ask him outright, now can I?'

It was true, she couldn't. No decent girl would, and our Dilly was thoroughly decent. We were quiet for a while. I was trying to think of ways round her problem. 'Do you know any of his mates?' I asked. 'Maybe one of them could help—or one of their girlfriends would be even better.'

'We don't go out in a gang,' explained Dilly. 'I met one of his friends once, a nice chap called Skinny—or was it Slim? I know he wasn't; he was a great, hulking fella, but I don't know if he has a girlfriend and I don't know if I'll meet him again. So I don't think that'll work.'

It was certainly a thorny one. There were times, lots of times, when being a girl was a nuisance, and the dance was one of them. It looked as if Dilly was going to have to find a substitute partner. Ronnie was taking me, so I was all right. I had a partner who was most unlikely to try to take any liberties. Now we needed one for Dilly. She wasn't worried about this, though. 'It's all right,' she sighed in resignation, 'Terry's agreed to escort me so that I won't look like a complete lemon.'

Poor old Terry. He seemed fated to be the escort but never the boyfriend. It was good of him, but then he was that kind of chap. Being a brick seemed to come naturally to the man. What's more, he'd do it with good grace, and wouldn't feel sorry for himself nor expect any reward for services rendered. Incredible, really; in my experience of men in general, and Charlie in particular, they expected to be rendered a service, or at least a hasty grope, in return for the purchase of a lousy cup of tea and a fish-paste sandwich. I'd obviously mixed with the wrong sort.

We were just gathering ourselves up to go when Zinnia arrived, looking fretful, with her hair all over the place. 'Have either of you seen Hepzibah and Hallelujah?' she asked, looking anxiously around the allotments then under the hedge for her cats. Dilly and I shook our heads as one.

'How long have they been missing?' I asked, catching her alarm.

'They didn't come in for their food last night, or this morning. And that's not like them,' she answered, peering under the shed belonging to Molly Squires' mum. 'Well, I can't spend too long here looking for them. I have to get to the Whitelocks' to see to their Eunice's eldest. Keep your eyes open, will you? And ask around?'

We said we would, and she was off at a gallop. Her hair made her look like a worried scouring pad on legs. I couldn't help remembering how upset she'd been the previous evening when she saw how badly her tool shed had been damaged. Poor old Zinn really was in the wars.

It was only when she was gone that I thought to wonder what was wrong with Eunice's eldest. Eunice had been at school with me and Dilly and the poor girl already had three children and was up the duff with her fourth. Eunice's old man had a bad back and couldn't do his stint in His Majesty's forces, but he obviously liked to keep himself busy. Everyone always muttered, 'Like mother, like daughter,' when another baby was born. Fertility was a Whitelock family trait, like the girls growing impressive moustaches as they grew older, while the boys only seemed to manage bumfluff.

I had promised to help Zinnia with the birth of Eunice's next one, if I could, as I had helped in a very modest way with the last. I had been visiting Zinnia when the call came that Eunice was in labour. It had been an easy birth and Eunice had said I was her good luck charm. She had even called the baby girl after me, which was a big thrill.

———※※———

At work, all was sweetness and light on the Mrs. Dunmore front. She was walking around with a soppy grin on her face most of the time. She and Percy Robinson had taken to having their lunch—among other things—in her office. Poor Beryl swanned in there once and caught them at it. Or at least it seemed that way, what with Mrs. D. lying across her desk and him having his trousers round his ankles. Beryl said that they were so involved in what they were doing, she was able to back out of the room completely unnoticed. However, she didn't leave before she was able to confirm Ronnie's assessment of Percy's assets.

'I've never seen anything like it,' she gasped. 'It looked like a bloody log from where I was standing. Gawd knows how Mrs. D. took it; I know I couldn't. But she was panting like a dog in a greenhouse and yelling, "Harder, harder," and Percy was thrusting so hard, the desk was skidding along the floor making this terrible screech.' Beryl giggled, her face far redder than your average beetroot. 'That's how I got out of there without them seeing me. They wouldn't have noticed if the Regimental Band of the Black Watch had marched through there blowing their bagpipes and banging their drums.'

Sure enough, when we checked later, we found long scratches on the lino, and judging by the marks, the desk hadn't been replaced in quite its original spot either.

With the boss lady being satisfactorily rogered on a regular basis, work was a dream for once. Mrs. D. was in such a good mood, I was able to flog her two tickets to the dance. I hesitated,

I must admit—who wants their boss cluttering up their free time?—but in the end, I decided it was for a good cause, and anyway, I'd be surprised if Mrs. D. actually put in an appearance. She seemed to have much better things to do with her time.

So, all in all, I was quite relaxed that week, what with Charlie being away and Mrs. Dunmore easy to get along with. I worried about her secretly, though, because she was heading for much misery. Old Percy had never left his wife for any of his bits of sly, even the ones who got pregnant, so I didn't see why Mrs. D. should fare any better. But none of us had the nerve to burst her bubble and tell her she was being had by a very married man. Anyway, perhaps she knew and didn't care. Percy did seem to have that effect on some people.

Ronnie was typically disgusting on the subject. 'She's being rogered rigid, dolly, with an enormous tool. Of course she doesn't care. Who would? Hmm? Answer me that.'

'I'd care. Big thingy, bingey or whatever you want to call it, or not, I'd not want to throw my cap at a married man.'

'Not even the Dutch one?' he asked innocently, at which point I clouted him playfully with my handbag and scattered its contents all over the Star and Garter's snug. Which, in turn, got Molly Squires involved in our conversation, as she helped pick up my bits and bobs. She could have knocked me down with one fingertip, I was so surprised by what she told us. It just showed how sneaky people could be.

'You've got it wrong, Zelda. Percy Robinson's been walking out with that snotty Mrs. Dunmore for a couple of months now, not a couple of weeks like you think. They was in here together as early as last March. The landlord's a mate of Percy's, and he often lets them have one of the rooms upstairs for an hour or so.'

'Are you sure, Molly? I thought they met at the canteen.'

'They did, but a while back.' She seemed quite certain.

'Of course, what Mr. Armstrong *doesn't* know is that Percy's knocking off his wife as well, on Thursday nights when he's at his meetings and sometimes a quick one early in the mornings when Percy's on his way to work and His Nibs ain't up yet. They've been at it for years. There's even rumours their Robert isn't his, but Percy's. It wouldn't surprise me. He's always been a little bastard, that one. And if you look at him from certain angles, you can see it. It's those ears of his, and his nose.' Molly grinned a knowing grin.

'Check in his nappy,' advised Ronnie with a filthy chuckle. 'That should give you a hint.'

Molly laughed. 'Her ladyship's fit to be tied when old Percy's upstairs giving it to Mrs. D. instead of to her,' she continued. 'But there's nothing she can do or say, is there?' And we agreed that there wasn't, but it made me feel worse about Mrs. Dunmore, somehow. She wasn't *that* bad an old stick.

'Do you reckon I should tell her?' I asked.

'Who?'

'Mrs. Dunmore,' I answered.

'No!' they barked in chorus.

'No, dolly. It never does to interfere with the free expression of lust. Mrs. Dunmore won't thank you; she'll hate you for it. Keep schtum is my advice.'

'I agree,' said Molly. 'I told Mrs. Armstrong, and she sacked me. Then Mr. A. rehired me, because she couldn't come up with a decent excuse and I'm a good barmaid. So I'd keep your mouth shut, unless you've got another job to go to. They always shoot the messenger.'

'Oh do listen to the girl, dolly,' Ronnie said firmly. 'Mrs. Dunmore is old enough and ugly enough to look after herself.' So I left it there. They were probably right.

———※※———

Whether it was the cheese and gherkins I ate for my tea I don't know, but I had a lot of bad dreams that night. I woke up several times, thinking I could hear the pitiful wailing of a cat, and then, worse, it turned into the howls of a person in pain. Extreme pain. But when my eyes flew open, the noises stopped, and I lay there in silence, drenched in sweat. Dreams that vivid and that bad always left me with a kind of hangover. I was like a wet rag when I went to work the next day.

Then, just to add to the general joys, Mrs. Dunmore went to the bank and while she was gone, Cook nagged me into reading hers and Beryl's tea leaves. I told them the usual stuff: Cook was going to be surprised by a new grandchild—which, seeing she was Eunice's mother-in-law, came as no surprise to anyone, except Cook. She managed to work up astonished delight every time, bless her.

And of course, I told Beryl she was going to meet a new man in the very near future. Which was highly likely as she worked in a canteen full of them. Whether or not she would strike it lucky with this new man I didn't say, largely because I didn't know. When I gazed into those two cups that day, I saw nothing but tea leaves. Still, I had two satisfied customers, and that was the main thing.

Cook heaved a sigh and stood up slowly. 'Beryl, go get her ladyship's cup from her office, there's a good girl. She'll be back directly, and she'll only moan that you're slacking if it isn't cleared away.'

When Beryl trotted back with Mrs. Dunmore's special cup, saucer and side plate—in bone china with fat red roses as decoration—I took them from her to plunge into the washing-up water while it was still hot. As I did so, I glanced into the cup. According to Beryl and Cook, I went as white as a sheet, which wasn't easy for me, as they well knew, then fainted. Beryl just managed to grab the precious cup before I hit the deck. When I came to, I was choking on the fumes of the smelling salts Mrs. Dunmore kept for such moments. I opened my eyes, stared into her thin, sharp face and saw the tea leaves once again.

I saw death in those leaves, and in her eyes. I saw it as clear as anything.

Chapter 21

Tony and I presented ourselves at Digby Burlap's front door smack on time the following Saturday.

'Ah, dear lady! Young sir! Enter, enter, do.' We did. Once we settled down, Mr. Burlap joined us, placed his hands together as if in prayer, and looked hard at Tony and then at me and back again. At last he spoke, his eyes having finally settled on Tony.

'Young man, if you wish to take the opportunity of learning to sing to your full potential—which I believe is considerable—then we must have a serious talk now.'

Tony opened his mouth, but Digby held his hand up imperiously. 'I am doing the talking, Tony. When I am finished, I'll indicate as much, and you may then ask questions.'

He thought for a few moments before continuing. 'Firstly, you must think about, but not necessarily decide upon immediately, what kind of singer you would like to be. There are many kinds, from operatic, through choral, classical and modern. There is holy music and jazz...' Mr. Burlap's eyes misted over and his face gained a faraway, rapt expression. 'Personally, I think that jazz *is* holy music, but perhaps I am being just a tad profane. Don't tell your nice Reverend Cattermole I said it, there's a dear chap. Zinnia tells me he is a fine fellow who has encouraged you in your love of music. What a delightful name Cattermole is...'

He was away with his thoughts. When he'd been gone a while, I coughed politely and brought him back to us, and to the point.

'Harrumph!' he spluttered. 'Where was I? Ah yes, you may wish to be a crooner, or perhaps you'd like to be in musicals. The thing to do at this stage is to listen to as many kinds of music as you can. The radio has a lot to offer, as you doubtless know. When the opportunity arises, I shall expect you to attend various musical events with me: rehearsals, shows, wireless broadcasts and so on. Do you have any questions?'

Tony and I looked at each other and then shook our heads. It all seemed perfectly straightforward so far. Tony plucked up his courage and started to raise his hand, as if he was in school, then suddenly realized he wasn't, and dropped it hastily. Flushing scarlet, he said, in a nervous, wobbly voice, 'I know what kind of singer I want to be, Mr. Burlap sir. I want to be a singer like Frank Sinatra.'

'Ah!' Mr. Burlap beamed. 'A fine choice, dear boy, a fine choice. The man can sing. His phrasing is second to none already, and will only improve with time. I can't promise you'll be exactly like the sublime Mr. Sinatra, because he is, of course, his own man. However, I think if we give you plenty of exposure to jazz and popular music in its many forms, that would count as a thorough grounding.

'What you do with it later on will, of course, depend upon you and the whim of the gods. Simply keep your ears and your mind open for the moment, dear boy; no decisions need be set in stone. With a gift like yours, many musical avenues will be open to you.

'The next thing I wish to discuss with you is that I think it would be a good idea, given that you have perfect pitch, to learn an instrument. It never does any harm to have another string to one's bow, as it were. The musical world can be difficult. There are many more aspirants than there are positions, so it behoves you to be flexible, and if you can play an instrument well, it will help enormously when it comes to finding work. I want you to think about it and decide which instrument appeals to you most. Then we shall see.

'Right, dear lady! Tony and I must get to work. Please feel free to stay if you so desire, but it may be as well if you go off for a cup of tea and leave us to it for an hour. Lessons can be tedious for onlookers and onlookers can be off-putting to the student. We'll only be doing scales and breathing exercises—essential if the phrasing's to be right.' Mr. Burlap waggled his eyebrows at me. I took the hint, arranged to meet Tony at the cafe in Old Compton Street when he'd finished, and scarpered.

I went to the cafe straight away. It was raining steadily and it was as good a place as any to wait. Anyway, I liked it there. It was so much more cheerful than the canteen, and I liked being waited on. It made a nice change. The dinnertime rush hadn't started, but a few people were in for their elevenses.

Maggie smiled a big smile at me as I came in the door. 'Hello again, dear. What can I get you? We've got a nice sliver of chocolate sponge left, I think. Or there's some Rich Tea biscuits if you'd prefer.' Naturally, I plumped for the chocolate sponge. I was almost drooling at the thought.

A few minutes later Maggie brought a tray laden with two cups and saucers, teapot, strainer, milk jug, sugar bowl, cake and two plates. 'I thought I'd join you if you don't mind,' she said. 'I can always do with a little something around now, to keep me on my feet through the dinnertime rush. I don't get a minute to put a crumb to my lips until it's almost over, at around two.'

We'd been chatting for a while when a very attractive young couple came in and looked around. The blonde woman's face lit up as she saw Maggie. She came over to our table saying, 'See you, Frankie,' over her shoulder.

'Yeah, see you, Cass,' the dark young man answered. He walked towards another table where two blokes were already sitting and talking over brimming ashtrays and several empty cups.

'Hello, Maggie. Is there any chance of a cup of tea?' Cass asked. 'I'm parched.'

'Course there is, love. Park yourself and I'll get another cup.' Maggie stood up and smiled at the newcomer. 'Cassie, this is

Zelda. And Zelda, this is Cassie.' She walked over to the table with the newcomer at it. 'Wotcha Frankie, what can I get you? You two want another cup each?' The two men nodded and Frankie ordered what his friends were having. Maggie smiled, said, 'Right you are,' and went to her counter to fill the orders.

'How's Bert?' Cassie asked as soon as Maggie returned with another cup and saucer.

'He's fine love, ta. You can nip out the back and see him when you've revived yourself. How are you? You look a bit peaky to me. Too many late nights I expect,' Maggie said comfortably.

'Actually, I haven't been too well,' Cassie said quietly. 'I've just got back from the doctor.'

'Oh love, I *am* sorry. Nothing too serious, I hope?' Maggie asked, sympathetically.

Cassie began to laugh, then her voice caught in something that sounded suspiciously like a sob. I looked at her more closely. Sure enough, there were tears in her eyes.

Oh Gawd! I thought. I'd better leave and let them talk. But my heart was heavy. I'd really been enjoying the tea, the cake and the chat. I had started to put on my coat when Cassie's voice cut into my thoughts.

'Oh please don't let me drive you away. I promise not to cry. It'll be no secret soon anyway. Apparently I'm pregnant, Maggie. My life of sin has caught up with me.' Her voice wobbled dangerously and I looked across the table at Maggie, who shrugged and looked serious.

'I don't know what to say, Cassie. Honest I don't,' was all Maggie could come up with. It occurred to me then that something was wrong. Usually a cry of 'Congratulations!' would be a good starting point, but not this time, apparently. My eyes shot to Cassie's left hand. No rings on her fingers. That explained everything. We all sat quietly for a long time.

'I don't suppose you know…?' Maggie asked eventually.

'Not for sure, no. But the doctor thinks I am at least six months along, far too late for an abortion.' The awful word hung in the air, bringing up pictures of dingy basements with seedy men and women wielding awful metal instruments. It was terrifying, the number of women who died from abortions. And it was highly illegal as well, so you could wind up in court if you lived through the experience.

'Six months! And you didn't notice?' said Maggie and I almost in the same breath.

Cassie looked embarrassed. 'I just thought it had something to do with my change in circumstances. Leaving home, it makes a person nervous, you know,' she said, slightly haughtily. 'And bad nerves can delay things. It's happened to me loads of times.'

'Of course they can, love,' said Maggie soothingly, 'I can see that.'

Cassie took a long drag on her fag and carried on. 'And then, you know, all those men. It's been a hell of a year.' Maggie nodded. She seemed to know what Cassie was talking about, but I was blowed if I did. I was too busy getting over the fact that a girl with such a cut-glass accent could find herself in the family way with no husband to show for it.

'I've had to go to the pox doctor, too. That could hold things up as well. And what with one thing and another, I didn't notice. Until my gowns became too tight, that is. Even then, I put it down to over-eating or constipation at first. Even wind can do it, if the gown's a snug fit to begin with.'

'So, you've no idea who the father is?' Maggie got back to the point.

'No, not really…' Cassie stared vacantly at the glowing tip of her cigarette, took another long drag and then stubbed it out.

'So there's no question of marriage or maintenance?' Maggie wouldn't let it go, and I could see why not. *Somebody* had to take Cassie's situation seriously. The girl herself seemed to be away with the fairies; or in her case, spirits, judging by the smell on her breath—pure juniper berry. And it was before noon, too!

'But Cassie,' said Maggie, 'don't you realize that your…er… friend isn't likely to want you in his Mayfair flat if you're expecting a child that isn't his?'

I was agog. What friend? What Mayfair flat? This girl's life read like one of those stories in the scandal sheets about posh men and women carrying on in country houses, where they seemed to swap husbands, wives and lovers all the time. But in those stories, people rarely wound up in the pudding club, and if they did, they had a husband to blame it on.

'I suppose you're right. Jeremy's never been keen to share,' Cassie said vaguely. 'I had better think of finding a place of my own…' Her voice kept trailing off into nothing, as if it was a wisp of smoke floating off into the ether.

'I think you'd better, dear. And start putting some money aside for bills and so on. I expect you'll have some lean times and you'll need money for the baby. They're not cheap, everyone says that.' Maggie sounded rather sad. The thought popped into my head that Maggie would give almost anything to be Cassie at that moment—or at least, to be expecting. She probably wouldn't have troubled with the unmarried, drunk-before-dinner side of things.

'And you must eat properly, dear,' she insisted. 'Everyone knows that's important. You mustn't go hungry, so if money's a problem, you just come here for your dinners. Promise me you'll do that.'

'I'll second that,' said a man's voice from behind us. I looked up and, for a moment, I thought my hero Humphrey Bogart was standing there. Then the man moved slightly, and the resemblance faded.

'Hello, Bert,' said Cassie. 'Thank you both. I'll remember that if it comes to it.' She sighed. 'I suppose I'd better get home soon. Jeremy's free this evening and he's taking me to some club or other and I could do with a long bath, I feel ragged. I wonder how much longer it will be before he notices that I'm in what I cannot imagine why any sane person would call an "interesting condition." Frankly, I find it immensely boring. It's going to mean no end of upheaval, and I thought I was just getting settled nicely too.'

The tears welled up again and Cassie sniffed, fished into her handbag for a hanky and dabbed at them with a tiny square of white linen and lace. There was no question of giving her nose a hefty blow, not into that thing. I rootled in my bag and came up with a freshly ironed job that looked like a tablecloth next to hers.

'Here,' I said, 'have a good blow, you'll feel better.' I handed my hanky over. 'You can hang on to it, if you like.'

She smiled wanly. 'Thank you, you're very kind. You see, I kept my promise. I haven't cried, not quite. Now I really must go. Bye-bye, all of you. Thank you for putting up with me.' And she was gone.

Maggie looked at Cassie's retreating back and sighed. 'That girl worries me, she does really. No sense of self-preservation, none at all.'

'Oh, I dunno, Maggie love. She does all right most of the time. But I know what you mean. You always think it wouldn't take much for her to fall to bits.'

Bert turned to me, his hand out to shake mine. 'Hello. I'm Bert, Maggie's other half. And you are?'

Maggie introduced us, we shook hands and Bert sat down in Cassie's empty chair. 'So, did I gather that our Cassie's got one in the oven, then?' he asked. Maggie nodded. 'Not much of a surprise, really, the way she carries on. A shame, though. Unwanted kids are always a shame.'

That's when I had one of my funny turns. Zinnia told me once that 'mystic experiences' happened most often at times when people were deeply unhappy and had what she called 'a psychic wound.' This tended to make a person more likely to pick up signals from others, apparently, especially distress signals. Whatever the reason, I was having more strange dreams, feelings and sightings of death, mayhem and destruction in this period of my life than ever before.

True, I was deeply unhappy and afraid about my marriage to Charlie. He scared me as much, if not a bloody sight more, than Herr Hitler had. Perhaps that was because I was going to have to live with Charlie, whereas Hitler was good and dead at last. I tried hard not to think about it most of the time, as there was nothing I could do about it. I shivered.

'Are you all right, love?' a man's voice said from a long way away.

Then Tony's voice piped up. His lesson must have ended. 'Don't worry. She'll come back to us in a minute. She's always done this,' he explained. 'She has these funny dreams and visions. If she's in the right mood, she can read palms, cards and tea leaves an' all. Everyone says she's ever so good. Gran says it's the gypsy blood running in her veins, but Grandad says we don't have any, it's Italian and Gran shouldn't forget it.'

Tony laughed. 'He hates the thought of being part gyppo, but Auntie Zelda loves it.

There was a murmur of other voices. As I struggled to open my eyes, I heard Tony again. 'I told you she'd be back. See, she's blinking fast—that's always the sign.'

I looked around and saw two slightly anxious faces and Tony, who was looking very pleased with himself. While I was away, I had seen this couple and sensed a terrible sadness centred on children and babies. They wanted one so badly, but if my vision, dream or whatever you could call it was right, then it was quite clear that Maggie was never going to know the feelings of pregnancy or the pain of childbirth. She was barren. I could have wept for her, but I didn't. I pulled myself together and smiled at her and Bert.

'Do you feel OK?' Maggie asked. 'Would you like a cup of tea?'

I nodded.

'I'd better get back to my kitchen, I suppose,' said Bert, looking like Bogart again; it was unnerving the way he did that. 'Nice meeting you two. See you again, I hope. Do you want anything to eat, son?'

Tony glanced at me. I nodded slightly. I could probably run to egg and chips or something.

'So, is it true that can you read fortunes?' asked Maggie, eyes wide.

'Right, that's definitely it! I'm off to my kitchen. I'll leave you to your horoscopes and fortune telling, ladies. Don't hang about though, Maggie, the rush is starting.' And sure enough, two parties came in the door and settled themselves at their tables. Maggie heaved a sigh and got to her feet.

'P'raps if you're in next week, you could take a look at my leaves or something?' she asked as she made her way back to the counter.

Chapter 22

Tony looked sullen, Dad looked furious, Vi was tearful and, for once, Mum was silent.

I knew what it was about of course. Tony had been missing from church and Dad was taking a dim view. Between church and dinner, I'd nipped round to Zinnia's to see how she was coping. The news wasn't good. She was still a bit shaken about the fire and there was still no sign of her cats. They had been missing for several days and I knew that she was more upset than she let on. Hepzibah and Hallelujah were company for her and she loved them in her own, no-nonsense sort of way, although she *said* she only kept them as ratters, and that it was being so close to the railway line and the allotments that was the problem. Rats love such places but they don't just stick to them, they soon find their way into gardens, cellars and, if not stopped, larders.

To cheer Zinnia up, I'd suggested she tagged along with me for Sunday dinner. Mum was magic at making grub stretch. The trouble was, we walked straight into another Marriott family 'chat.'

'What do you mean, "I dunno"? You ain't blind, deaf or stupid as far as I've heard, so you must know where you was when you wasn't at church singing your bleeding heart out.' Dad was roaring at Tony, his red, spittle-flecked lips not five inches from the poor lad's ear.

Zinnia and I stopped dead in the kitchen doorway, took in the scene and decided to back out again to make another entrance at a quieter time. Then a bony elbow jammed into my ribs, while its partner connected with Zinnia's, judging by the sharp intake of breath on my left.

'Shift 'em, gels. I want me dinner. I'm starving to death here, and at my age, I ain't got that far to go.' The cackle would have told me Gran had arrived, even if her elbow hadn't. Zinnia and I parted and let Gran go in first. 'Oh Gawd, not again! Can't you two try to get along? It's Sunday, the Sabbath Day, you bleeding heathens! It's the day to worship, eat and spend the afternoon digesting. How the hell are we supposed to do that with you two tom-cats going at it hammer and tongs?' Gran demanded, glaring at Dad and Tony in turn.

'You could try eating in your own home!' Dad shouted back.

'Don't you talk to my mum like that, Harry Marriott,' yelled Mum.

'Don't you worry, petal, I'll deal with him,' said Gran, menacingly, and advanced on Dad. 'Now you stop bullying that lad this minute, Harry. I mean it, or I'll make you pay.'

'And how are you going to do that?' Dad sneered.

Gran picked up a chair. I thought she was going to hit him with it, and took a step forward, ready to grab it before it landed, but Gran simply sat on it. Slowly, very slowly, she removed her long hat pins from her hat and laid them on the table, then took off her hat and smoothed her hair. Next, she removed her Sunday gloves and carefully placed them together on her lap, before undoing the buttons of her coat. 'I've never told you about the time when Florence was born, have I? Awful it was, the blood clots kept coming liked chopped liver…'

We heard a thud. When we peeled our eyes away from Gran and looked down, there was Dad, out cold.

Gran smiled her slow, sweet smile. 'It never fails,' she said. 'Even when he knows what's coming and braces himself. Thank Gawd he never had the babies, eh?'

She turned to Tony and fixed him with a gimlet eye. 'So what have you done this time, to get on your grandfather's top note?' she asked. All the sweetness was gone from her face.

Tony shrugged and looked down. 'I missed church,' he muttered.

'We all know that, on account that *we* didn't miss church. What we want to know is, why did you?'

'I dunno, do I?'

'For once, I agree with your grandfather, and we can't often say that, now can we? Of course you know. Where were you?'

'Down the market,' Tony mumbled.

'It's closed on Sundays. What did you want with the market?'

'To see me mates.'

'Which mates?'

There was a long pause. 'Brian and them,' he finally admitted.

'How many times have you been told about Brian Hole and his gang?'

Tony kept his eyes firmly on the floor. Gran leaned forward, lifted his chin and stared into his eyes, voice very quiet now. 'How many times? A dozen? Two? When will you learn that we mean it?'

There was another long silence, then Tony shrugged again.

'Right then, go to your room and stay there. There'll be no dinner for you today.' Gran's voice was firm.

Tony trailed towards the door, head down. I knew what a blow this was for him. Sunday was the best dinner of the week.

'Oh, and Tony, you'd better be there when I come to see you after dinner.'

'Yes, Granny Ida,' he whispered.

'What?' Gran asked.

'I said, yes, Granny Ida,' he said louder.

'Good. Time for grub, I think. Serve it up, Florence. It's handy, Zinnia being here. She can have Tony's and, by the looks of it, Harry's as well.' Dad had got up from the floor and was staggering towards the door in Tony's wake, still green behind the gills. He didn't trust Gran not to go 'all gynaecological' on him again. Judging by the sound of springs creaking a few moments later, he'd gone to lie down. Peace reigned at last.

But not for long. A few minutes later, Doris, Reggie and the twins arrived. 'Sorry I'm late,' said Doris. 'We just got in from church when Lenny Hobbs dropped by on his way to the King's Head. He had a knitting pattern his mum sent round for me. Anyway, he was saying that our Mavis was in the King's Head last night, waving this engagement ring, or something very like it, at anybody with a heartbeat and a pair of eyes. She says—wait for this—that it was "from a secret admirer," but then she won't say any more. Lenny reckons she's walking out with some married bloke, from something one of her brothers said later on, when he'd had a few.' She turned to Vi. 'She's your mate. What do you know about it?'

All eyes turned towards Vi as if she was the goal at a football match. But as so often happens in life, and at football matches, we were disappointed. 'I know about as much as you do,' she replied. 'The ring turned up on her finger at the beginning of the week, but she's not telling anyone who gave it to her, not even me.'

'Do you reckon the geezer's married?' Mum asked.

'Well…' Vi hesitated. She'd obviously been told to keep her lip buttoned, but on the other hand, she was the keeper of a bit of gossip that wasn't about her Tony. 'Mavis did say she was sworn to secrecy until he's free,' she told us. 'I took that to mean he had a wife somewhere that he had to get shot of before he could make it official with Mavis.'

'It's not going to be easy,' said Mum. 'And if she ain't careful she'll wind up being named as "the other woman" in court. It could be very nasty, that, for her mum and everyone else. Can you imagine trying to hold your head up at church if your daughter was involved in a divorce case?'

'No,' said Gran drily, looking at Dad's empty chair, 'but I'd like to give it a try. I expect I'd manage, and so would Mavis' mum—probably will too, if it comes to it.'

I looked at Mum. She had the grace to blush. Zinnia noticed, too, and decided to bail her friend out.

'Has anyone heard the rumour about Brian Hole?' All heads turned to Zinnia, just in time for the goal. 'He's been seen siphoning off petrol down at the lorry depot near the station. George Grubb says his informant definitely identified Brian, saw him as clear as anything in a street light, but doesn't want to give a formal statement. The usual story. There were two other lads with him, but they were not known to the man. As George said, now we know what the three and a half feet of rubber hose from the warehouse was for, if only he could prove it.'

'When was this?' asked Gran.

'Early hours of this morning, I believe,' Zinnia answered.

'Ah!' somebody said. It didn't take all three guesses to know why Tony had missed church; he was busy helping stash jerry cans of petrol somewhere. Probably in a lock-up at the market, seeing that's where he admitted to being. There was money to be made in stolen petrol, as there was still so little of it about.

Gran nodded grimly and we finished our dinner in silence. Well, near silence; nothing really shut the twins up, especially talk that they were too small to understand.

The washing up was done in very short order, as there were many hands available to do it, and then we all went our separate ways. Mum took Dad his dinner on a tray—she'd kept it warm on a saucepan of hot water—and Vi went down to the basement with Gran to confront Tony.

Zinnia and I were not invited, thank God. I'd had enough family life for one day. I was looking forward to going home, putting my feet up and listening to the wireless, or maybe the gramophone. Or perhaps I'd just listen to my hair grow in the peace and quiet of my own home.

Chapter 23

Mrs. Dunmore was still in a good mood at the beginning of the following week, so all was quiet on the work front. Which was just as well, because my nights were bloody awful. I kept tossing and turning and waking up in either a hot or a cold sweat depending on which of two dreams was plaguing me that particular night. They kept playing over and over like a double feature at the Odeon.

The trouble was, I couldn't remember either of them in enough detail to know what was going on. They got jumbled up. In one dream, there were cries coming from deep in the earth, and a feeling of sadness. The other dream was far worse; it involved fear, pure and simple. I seemed to be in a dark, cold, clammy place, like a cave or possibly a cellar. I was in a cold sweat when I woke up and the awful sense of dread that had filled the dream filled my mornings as well.

By Wednesday, I was so fed up I decided to nip around to Zinnia's to see if she could give me something to help me sleep a dreamless sleep for a night or two. I was feeling ragged, and she wasn't much better. Her cats had been missing for a week now and I could tell she was worrying herself out of sleep over them as well.

'Why do you suppose you're having these nightmares, hen?' she asked, brow wrinkled in concern. 'Is it anxiety about Charlie and yourself, do you think?'

'I expect that's what's putting me in the right frame of mind. I'm really afraid of him, Zinnia, terrified. I thought he was going to kill me last time, honest I did.' I was getting upset and tears were beginning to well up.

Zinnia patted my hand comfortingly. 'I know, hen, I know,' she sighed.

'But I'm not dreaming about that. I may be dreaming up all this fear, but it's not mine, I'm sure it's not. It feels separate, different.' I shrugged, really near to tears. It was so frustrating, because I just couldn't explain.

'Perhaps the very fact that you are fearful yourself has made you sensitive to the same thing in others, hen. Like tuning in on the wireless. It happens, I'm sure. It will pass. Meanwhile, I'm sorry dear, I'm not certain we should interfere with the dreaming. I can only smother it, anyhow. I can't make the feelings go away.'

'Are you sure?' I said lightly. 'Dad says you're a witch, that's why we never got a direct hit in the war. He reckons you were protecting your precious house, garden and allotments.'

'It's true that the Makepeaces do have special talents,' said Zinnia, 'but I'm not sure they run to making the Luftwaffe do as they're bid. How am I supposed to issue my instructions to the pilots—thought waves?' She laughed a shade too heartily at her own joke.

'No, I think he was thinking more along the lines of a spell, complete with cauldron and eye of newt, testicle of toad, that kind of thing.'

'Aye, I see. Well, it's nothing like that at all. Sheer luck, I'm afraid. Do you think that if I could weave spells, I'd've not woven one to stop Hitler in his tracks? And I'd certainly weave one now, to turn my tormentors into the rats they so richly resemble,' she concluded—with some venom, I thought. Poor old Zinnia was pretty shaken by the turn of events and she was missing her cats very badly.

'No, hen, the Makepeaces aren't witches in any sense that your father would recognize. We're healers. We're chosen and trained for the purpose and have been for hundreds of years.'

'Who chooses you?' I asked, intrigued.

'A committee,' she answered, surprisingly. 'They choose the candidates, then the final selection is made by the resident Makepeace, who is also the one who does the training.'

I wasn't enlightened. What *was* she talking about? 'Zinnia, start from the beginning,' I begged her. 'I have no idea what you mean.'

Zinnia sighed, and settled back into her chair. 'Very well, hen,' she said. 'There has always been a Makepeace living in this house ever since the Great Plague.' She shuddered as if she'd been there and remembered it all too well. 'A wise woman saved the precious son and heir to the local Laird, or Lord of the Manor, with a combination of herbs and good nursing. Also, despite nursing and treating many, many victims, she did not succumb herself. Perhaps your dad is right,' Zinnia chuckled. 'Perhaps the first Makepeace *was* a witch.'

'So what happened then?' It was like listening to a fairy story. Zinnia's voice had even taken on the singsong rhythm of a teller of tales.

'Ach well, it was a toss-up whether to burn her as a witch or reward her for her endeavours. At the last, they decided on gratitude and the Laird gave over a house and some land to the old lady. She was a spinster with no child of her own to leave it to, but she was clever. She built more houses on the land and rented them out so that the rents paid her way, while she concentrated on healing the poor who could not pay her. When she felt the end drawing nigh, she chose a likely lass to succeed her. And we've been chosen ever since.

'The only requirements for the post are that we remain unmarried, so that our energies may be used for the folk who need us—the puir, the ones who suffered so badly in all the epidemics because their living conditions were so bad; that we take training in herbalism, midwifery and the particular care of children and women; and finally'—she smiled gently—'we must take the name of Makepeace in memory of Flora Makepeace, the lady who saved the boy and so many others. Usually we take the name of a flower as well, to do it properly. As you know, it was Primrose before me.'

I was fascinated. I could tell that my jaw had dropped open and my eyes were wide. 'What's your real name, then?'

'Well, hen, it's Zinnia Makepeace, of course.' She laughed again. 'But before that it was Ishbel Macleod, or Isabel to you.'

I tried them on my tongue; 'Ishbel Macleod,' then 'Zinnia Makepeace.' 'They're both nice,' I concluded, 'but I prefer Zinnia Makepeace, perhaps because I'm used to it. And it runs off the tongue better.' Then it occurred to me that that might be tactless; maybe she was very fond of her given name. 'Do you mind? I mean, did you mind having to change your name?' I asked her.

'No. Not at all. I'd've changed it if I'd married. I see no real difference.'

'But you only have to change the one when you marry,' I argued, 'not your first name as well.'

'Aye well, I never was that struck on Ishbel. The original was my grandmother, and an awful old besom she was. She used to delight in frightening us wee 'uns with dreadful stories at bedtime. Which reminds me, isn't it about time we turned in?'

'I s'pose so,' I said vaguely, unwilling to leave the story there. 'So, what's in it for you?'

'I don't understand, hen.'

'Why would you give up marriage, children, your name, your homeland, everything, to become a Makepeace?' I asked.

Zinnia chuckled. 'Well, I'd already come to London to learn nursing and to see a little something of the world, the Hebrides not being in the centre of things, you ken. So I didn't give up my homeland to be a Makepeace. And there's never any guarantees about marriage and children, as you well know, and so did I, from my own home life. But what I gained was a rewarding career in helping folk, which is what I trained for anyway, at the hospital, and a home for my lifetime with no rent to pay and a good income.

'The committee of the Makepeace Trust administer the estate. Over the centuries they've built new houses to fund the enterprise, and they pay me well, better than a nurse's pay. So there was no heroic sacrifice on my part, hen.

'Now, I'm tired and I can see that you are too; your eyelids are drooping. Why don't you try sleeping here tonight?' Zinnia suggested kindly. 'There's a bed already made up in the spare room. You may feel more secure there, and that could give you a quieter night.'

I yawned mightily and nodded blearily. She was right, it was time for bed. I could barely drag myself upstairs to her spare room, and was snoring almost before my body landed on the mattress.

Chapter 24

Zinnia's spare room was at the back of the house, overlooking her garden, the railway carriage, the allotments and the railway line. Apart from the trains, it was a quiet room. The narrow single bed was neatly made, with the sheets, blankets and bedspread tucked in with hospital corners, thanks to Zinnia's early training. The bedspread was almost white; it had been washed so often that the pattern of roses had faded to ghostly shadows. The bed linen smelt of lavender from Zinnia's garden, dried and sewn into the muslin bags that nestled among the piles of sheets and pillowcases in her linen cupboard.

Beside the bed was a small chest of drawers that gleamed with polish and elbow grease. On top was a mirror stand. A chair, with a ladder back and a rush seat, stood in the corner and a small vase of freshly picked buttercups on the windowsill. And that was it. It was one of the calmest and most peaceful rooms I had ever been in. No wonder I went out like a light.

It should have guaranteed a deep and dreamless sleep, but it didn't. At two o'clock in the morning I was pounding on Zinnia's bedroom door. 'Zinnia, wake up. I know where the cats are. Bring a torch.' I'd had the crying dream again, and finally I knew who was doing the wailing and where it was coming from. It was Hepzibah, and the noise was coming from the bombed-out cellar of the old dairy.

Zinnia appeared at her bedroom door in her nightie and a surprising pink hairnet. The net was surprising because Zinnia's hair never gave the slightest sign that it had ever been restricted by anything. It made me wonder how wild her barnet would have been without its nightly straitjacket. As it was, it could have had things nesting in it.

'What did you say, hen?' she asked, yawning wide but covering it politely with her large right hand.

'I said I know where the cats are. Get dressed and meet me in the kitchen. I've had a dream. Where do you keep your torch?'

Ten minutes later we were ready to set off. Zinnia was wearing sturdy brogues and tweeds, but I had to make do with my work clothes, which was all I had with me. The night was dark, with clouds covering any moon there might have been. It was the kind of weather that had been a relief to see during the Blitz, because you knew there would be no bombing that night. It was less of a boon and a blessing in peacetime when trying to get around the bombed-out streets on foot.

We spoke very little because we needed every ounce of concentration just to pick our way across the bomb sites. Although we had a torch each, there were muffled curses as we ricked ankles, stumbled against piles of rubble and splashed into water-filled craters of a variety of sizes. Twisted pipes and sharp nails made grabs for our clothing; I heard the ominous rip of material more than once, but tried hard to ignore it. Broken glass crunched underfoot.

Finally, we arrived at the sheets of rusty corrugated iron surrounding the site of the dairy that had once stood proudly at the junction of Tennyson Road and Wordsworth Street, known to everyone locally as 'Poets' Corner.' We walked round it, looking for a way in, and eventually found a sheet of iron that had been twisted back on itself, allowing us to clamber over broken bricks, tiles and cobblestones into the dairy yard.

We stopped and listened. I thought I heard a faint mewing above the sound of the wind sighing through gaping windows and the shattered roof. There was also the tap, tap, tap of something banging against a pane of glass and the rustle of rodents running through the piles of dead leaves caught in corners. It was eerie standing there in the dark, remembering how the bustling dairy had been before the war, full of the clatter of horses' hooves and clanking milk churns, and straining to follow that one tiny thread of sound to its source.

We followed it to the edge of the dark, dank hole which opened beneath the pile of rubble that had once been the white-tiled shop and head offices of the Morning Dew Dairy, and shone in a torch. Sure enough, two sets of frightened, golden eyes shone back at us. I heard again the cry from my dreams, but this time Zinnia could hear it, too.

We explored carefully. There was only one obvious way down. The entrance to the cellar steps had been blocked with masonry but the stairs—most of them, anyway—still clung to the wall. The once-sturdy set of wooden steps had been exposed to the weather for years, and rot had made it treacherous.

'What do you think?' I asked Zinnia.

'It looks tricky, hen. I don't think we can trust those steps without a rope for safety,' Zinnia replied, between the comforting murmurs and kissy noises she was directing towards her beloved cats, who, sensing relief was in sight, were kicking up a racket.

'Let's look and see if there's anything handy for the job,' I suggested. It was a good idea in theory, but a disaster in practice, because I dropped my torch, which went out and refused to come on again, and we never did find any rope.

'I think you'll have to go and get help, Zin, or at least some rope and a basket or something to carry them home in. You'll be quicker, seeing you know where you keep it all,' I told her. 'I'll stay put and keep the moggies company.'

'Don't you think it'd be better to wait for daylight?' Zinnia asked.

'No, I think we'd better hurry. One of the cats is dying. I feel it.'

Zinnia nodded and didn't even try to argue. 'I'll not be long if I can help it. I'll bring another torch, but I'm sorry, hen, I canna leave you this one, I'll break my neck. Don't you move either, in case you break yours.'

Good old Zin! Always level-headed in a crisis. I suppose that's what made her a suitable Makepeace. 'I'll be as quick as I can. And Zelda,' she paused, 'thank you for finding my wee cats for me.' She patted my arm in the dark and was gone. I saw her torch beam weaving about, rising and falling for a long time in the darkness, as she climbed over the piles of rubble to get home.

Once the sound of Zinnia's scrambling died away, the night was very quiet. Every now and then Hepzibah would mew, Hallelujah would whimper and I'd murmur encouragement to them. 'It's all right, pussies, nice pussies, just hang on.'

I remembered coming to the Morning Dew Dairy with my sisters or one of my brothers, to collect milk, butter and, sometimes, a small jug of thick, yellow cream. It was cheaper to collect your own; having the milko deliver it on his horse and cart cost money. The cobbled yard was always busy with horses, carts, milkmen and housewives, and the clang of the metal churns having their lids clamped down on the frothy, white milk ready for delivery on the carts. The shaggy hooves of the horses clattered against the cobbles and their leather harnesses creaked as the shafts of the carts were lowered into place. Milkos in blue-and-white striped coats and long pinnies coaxed the horses to stand patiently while their carts were loaded or unloaded, depending on which end of the day it was.

It was better to buy milk and cream at the tag end, when they were cheaper. The dairy would flog it cheap rather than risk it going off and spoiling. Still, nothing was wasted; pigs didn't mind a drop of curdled milk and it fattened them up a treat, so it was shipped out to them sharpish if it wasn't sold by teatime.

Regular as clockwork, Arthur Robinson, Percy's dim older brother, would go round the yard, sweeping up the piles of horse dung and carting it away to a neat heap behind the stables. Then he'd hose down the yard, and the water would run through little channels around the edges. Us kids would squat beside the channels, racing wisps of hay that had drifted from the horses' feed-bags. That yard was always immaculate. Arthur was dead now, killed somewhere in the North African desert, a long, long way from the Morning Dew Dairy on Poets' Corner.

I shuddered, brought back to the present by the pitiful mewing coming from the dark hole beside me. 'There, there, pussy, it won't be long now,' I murmured, trying hard not to hear the skitter of many tiny feet on broken white tiles.

At last I saw the beam of a torch wavering in the darkness. Zinnia was back!

'Sorry to be so long, hen. I tried to find help, but Ronnie wasn't home and I didn't like to bother Terry—we don't want him falling down holes with that heart of his.' Her voice was loud in the darkness. The cats heard her and stepped up their crying.

'I don't want to be falling down holes with this heart of mine, neither, or these kidneys, so I hope you brought a strong rope.' I was trying to make a joke of it, but I really didn't fancy the next bit. As the younger of the two of us, I thought I should be the one to go down to fetch the cats.

Zinnia was carrying a wicker basket stuffed with a spare torch, a washing line, a couple of soft towels and a bag containing two boiled fish heads, for use as bribes. Zinnia always had such tasty morsels about, for feeding the many stray cats and dogs that roamed the streets. The poor dears were lost for all sorts of reasons. The bombing sent many animals running in blind panic and some never found their way back home. Others survived a direct hit but their people didn't, or the people had been bombed out and forced to move and nobody had been able to find their pets before they left.

I tried really hard to forget I was terrified of rats and none too keen on pitch darkness either. And that the combination of the two had me quaking in my slippers. 'I reckon we should wind the rope round my waist and fix the other end to that beam there,' I suggested. 'With all the rubble on the other end of it, nothing's going to shift it. Certainly not my weight.' Zinnia nodded in agreement.

Gingerly I put my left foot over the edge. Hanging on to the rope with one hand and a torch with the other, I felt about the yawning gap for the first available step. My toes touched something and I took a deep breath and pushed off with my right foot. The rope stretched and the beam creaked as it shifted slightly—but it held, and the toes of my right foot found the step.

I put my weight on it and it cracked with a sound like a pistol shot. I dropped through the next two rotten steps, barking my shins on their jagged edges. It felt as if my stomach had lurched into my mouth by the time the rope stopped my fall. Warm blood trickled down my leg and into my shoe, and my heart hammered so hard I thought I was going to choke. I waited for it to slow a bit, and realized I was standing on a solid tread.

I took each of the next six steps with great caution. Finally my right foot hit solid ground—and something skittered across it. I screamed, a cat howled and Zinnia shouted, 'Are you all right, hen?'

'Yes,' I quavered, not at all sure that I was. I'd jumped about a foot in the air and tried to levitate, desperate to keep my feet off the ground, but I had to come down eventually, to deal with the cats.

I'd also dropped my torch, and had to will myself to feel about on the filthy floor for it.

I found it by instinct almost. Every nerve and fibre of my body were on full alert. I was drenched in a cold sweat, except for my left leg and foot, which were warm and sticky with blood. Weren't rats attracted by the smell of blood? Or was that crocodiles? Now I knew where the dreams about terror and cold, clammy darkness had come from.

An inner voice told me that it was not the time to dwell on the noshing habits of rats; better to find the cats and get the hell out of there. I tried the torch and, to my huge relief, a beam of light illuminated the scene around me.

One of the cats was lying on its side in a pile of litter, seemingly too weak to move much, and the other was standing protectively nearby.

'I've found them, Zinnia,' I shouted up to the blur that was her face peering at me from above. 'I'm going to fix the basket to the rope now. When I've done that I'll get the cats and pop them in. I'll give you a shout when I want you to pull them up.'

'Right you are, hen. I'm ready. Put a loop or two round the basket, so they can't force the lid open and get away,' Zinnia suggested. 'They'll be frightened.'

I distracted the guard cat with a fish head and gently wrapped the other cat in a towel, cooing reassurance all the time. 'There, there pussy, gooood pussy, there, there.' I stroked a set of claggy ears and placed the bundle in the basket.

I turned and found the other one ignoring its fish head and watching me and what I was doing to its mate very carefully. I made kissy noises and called encouragingly, 'Here, Hepzibah, come over here. There's a lovely girl, what a pretty puss, come on now.' She sidled towards me: instinct told her that I was the way out, but natural caution made her hesitate and weave and wave her tail about.

At last she came within reach and deigned to let me pick her up. I wrapped her in the other towel, cooing all the time and tickling her chin with a spare finger. I popped her in the basket next to her much quieter companion and closed the lid, which was secured by a bar running through wicker loops. I wound the rope around the basket several times to make sure the lid stayed closed.

'Haul away, Zinnia,' I shouted. 'And be quick about it. I want to get out of here.'

'Right you are, Zelda,' she called back and began to heave. Once the basket was safely beside her, she sent the rope down for me. I got up those steps a bloody sight faster than I got down; I fair flew up them, and have rarely been so relieved to be out in the air in my entire life. I hadn't dared look to the left or right while I was in that cellar, in case there were lots of little eyes looking back at me.

My lungs heaved on the dawn air. The sky was just beginning to lighten in the east and the birds were waking each other up.

The walk back to Zinnia's was far easier now that we could make out the narrow tracks made by children and animals between the piles of rubble and the puddles. At the end of it, we had two filthy, frightened tabbies nestled on hot water bottles in front of the range in Zinnia's kitchen, so I suppose it was worth it. Well, I know it was, by the look of relief and tenderness on Zinnia's normally somewhat stern face when she unpacked her cats.

She turned to me, eyes filled with tears. 'Thank you, Zelda, for everything you have done for me lately.' I opened my mouth to interrupt, but she held up a large hand and I shut it again. 'Thank you especially for restoring my moggies to me. I shan't forget it, hen, any of it.' And to my utter astonishment she gave me a swift cuddle before briskly getting on with the business of caring for her cats.

Hallelujah was in a bad way. His fur was matted with dried blood and he was very weak. Hepzibah was in much better condition. There had been no shortage of rats, mice and water to keep her going. 'I've a mind that she kept him in rodents too,' said Zinnia. 'After all, when they're home, they bring me my share because I'm too slow and stupid to catch my own.' Her fingers probed gently at Hallelujah's bloody flank. 'Ah! I see.' She stopped prodding and stroked his head instead. He tried a feeble purr, but soon gave it up.

'What do you see?' I asked once I could stop my teeth from chattering. I hadn't got over that cellar yet.

'He has an infected wound and there's something lodged in it. I'll have to get it out and clean things up a wee bit if he's to come around.'

She drugged him with a drop of whisky in warm milk, adding the tiniest dose of something from her shelves to help him relax. While she was at it, she gave a drop or two to Hepzibah, who could finally stand down from her long watch, and a rather larger splash for me. She cleaned and dressed my scrape and then started work on Hallelujah.

Half an hour later Zinnia and I were staring at a small pellet glinting in the first rays of the morning sun that was rising fierily over the railway tracks. Some bastard had shot Zinnia's cat with an airgun. How the cats came to be in the cellar was a mystery. It was possible that the same bastard had put them there, but we couldn't know for sure. Zinnia swabbed the wound with antiseptic, wrapped Hallelujah tenderly in a clean, white towel, then popped him in the smallest oven of her range.

'Zin!' I cried, appalled.

'Don't worry, hen. I'm not cooking the puir wee scrap. When I was a lassie we put our premature or orphaned lambs in the wee oven of the range. It keeps them warm and secure, because they can't move about much. He'll come to no harm in there. It may well be the saving of him.'

We sat quietly in front of the range for a while, sipping cups of Ovaltine and talking quietly about the events of the last few weeks. I felt we'd grown closer, somehow. I'd always felt like a child around Zinnia, the way I did with Mum and Dad, but now, in a funny sort of way, I felt I was coming of age and that Zinnia recognized the fact and treated me accordingly.

'Do you know, hen,' Zinnia confided in me, 'all this business with the furniture, the tool shed fire and now my dear cats makes me feel as if there's something really malevolent taking an interest in me, and I don't mind admitting that I don't like it, I don't like it at all. It's making me more nervous than Hitler ever did. I wonder why that is?'

I thought about it as I sipped my drink. 'Because this time it's personal?' I suggested.

Zinnia sighed deeply. 'Aye, that'll be it, hen, that'll be it. You're a good person, Zelda, and I am glad you're on my side.'

I'd never heard Zinnia talk that way before and I don't know whether it was because it moved me, or simply because I was exhausted, but for a minute there, I thought I was going to burst into tears.

Chapter 25

So much for a peaceful night at Zinnia's. The bags under my eyes were almost down to my knees, so I was in the wrong frame of mind for what faced me at work that Thursday morning. Mrs. Dunmore was a human tornado, whizzing around the place wiping her bony digit along this surface and that, finding fault wherever she turned. 'Just because the men eat like pigs at the trough, that's no reason to feed them in a sty. Get cracking with a scrubbing brush and plenty of soda,' she ordered. 'I want this dining hall spick and span by the time I return.'

'Get her!' Beryl mouthed behind Mrs. Dunmore's back. 'Dining hall? It's a bleeding canteen.'

Cook and Beryl were mystified. 'She arrived with a wasp up her jacksie,' Cook told me. 'It was nothing we done.' We agreed it was time to raid Mrs. D.'s secret hoard of Rich Tea biscuits and have a quiet cup of tea to soothe our jangled nerves. Mrs. Dunmore had a way of sharing her feelings with you, so you ended up wound tight, like a wet rag.

'It's gotta be her love life, now she's got one,' Beryl told us confidently. 'I mean, first it was because she was a frustrated, dried-up old bat, but now she isn't, Percy's got to be giving her trouble. Stands to reason.'

'Maybe she's found out about Mrs. Robinson,' I suggested: it was only a matter of time before some kind soul told her, after all. News, especially bad news, got around. It was a miracle that she had been in the dark for so long.

'I did hear that Mrs. Robinson was back from her sister's. P'raps that's it,' suggested Cook. 'Percy's having to stay closer to home.'

We agreed. It was probably that.

Whatever it was, it didn't improve as the day wore on, and I was virtually on my knees by the time I got home that evening. Dilly arrived with Terry just after I'd got in from work. I'd only had time to make a cup of tea and sit down by the window with my poor throbbing dogs resting on a pouffe—made, the man said, from camel hide. It was a shabby object in a deep, dark red with gold patterns dodging and weaving all over it. I'd bought it from a bloke in the market when I'd first married Charlie and it was still the only item of furniture I actually owned. The rest came with the flat, but of course I'd re-covered the chairs and painted the rest. There wasn't a lot.

Our landlord was not a generous man, whoever he was. I left the rent money at the greengrocer's downstairs on a Friday morning and the landlord's agent collected it, signed my rent book and buggered off. I'd only ever seen the agent once, when Charlie and me took the flat, and I hadn't been impressed then. As I remember, he was sweaty and had dandruff.

Dilly was in a bit of a state and Terry looked mournful.

'How's life treating you?' I asked, about as brightly as a Toc H lamp.

'Seldom,' said Terry as he marched in and nicked my comfy seat.

'Same here,' said Dilly, nicking the other one.

'Sit down, do,' I said, bitterly. 'I'll jump around making you two lazy swine some tea, shall I?' I already knew the answer. I whacked the kettle under the tap with undue force. Time I reread *How to Entertain Gracefully* by Lady Emmeline Snot.

'Sorry, Zelda, have I taken your pew?' asked Terry, eyeing my tea cooling beside him but not shifting his bum at all.

'Don't mind me,' I grumbled. 'I only live 'ere. So to what do I owe the pleasure of seeing your dolly old eeks, may I ask?'

'We were fed up,' said Dilly.

'So we thought we'd share it,' Terry added.

'Well, as it happens, laughing boy, I am way ahead of you. Mrs. Do-Bugger-All Dunmore has been a cow all day and I'm almost dead on my feet, so shift your arse to a kitchen chair, Rainbird. Here's your tea, but don't expect any sugar, I haven't got any.'

'Ah! But I have!' He grinned, producing it like a conjuror producing a rabbit. 'A bag split, and I couldn't waste it, could I?'

I grabbed the slightly scruffy white and blue Tate and Lyle paper bag and poured some into my empty sugar bowl. The remainder of the precious contents disappeared into a storage tin and was stuffed right at the back of the cupboard, out of harm's way. Suddenly, life had looked up considerably. 'Thanks, Terry. You can keep the comfy seat after all. I know what's the matter with Dilly—Chester! What's the matter with you?' I asked. 'As if I didn't know—Lily!'

None of us had met the mysterious Lily, but we'd heard about her. She had been widowed early in the war and Terry had been walking out with her for a few months in a low-key sort of a way. However, I'd heard via Dilly that Lily had suddenly cooled off and asked Terry to stop calling in to see her for a while. She hadn't explained why; privately, Dilly and I thought she had another bloke in tow and was trying to choose between them.

'I s'pose you could say that, Zelda. Although I wouldn't want you to run away with the idea I'm broken-hearted, because I'm not. A bit disappointed, maybe. I like Lily, she's a jolly sort and she'd make a good wife. What's more, she could have been a big help in the business. But it wasn't a grand romance. It's just time I settled down, is all. I've always wanted nippers, and so did Lily,' he said wistfully. 'It gets lonely on your own after you've sown your wild oats. To be honest, I never did have that many oats in me, wild or otherwise. I'm the sort of boring old fool who wants a quiet life, with a decent woman and a few kids.'

He brightened. 'No, it's not Lily. It's old Limp and Droopy here. She's been hanging about like a black cloud with an even blacker lining all week. I wish that bloody Yank would either declare himself or put the poor thing out of her misery. You wouldn't let a dog suffer like her, honest you wouldn't.'

'Oy you, don't talk about me as if I wasn't here. And who are you calling a dog?' Dilly forgot to droop for a moment, in her indignation. Then she remembered, and sighed. 'It's Chester, Zelda. He hasn't been in touch for ages. Not a dickie bird. What do you think it means?' Her face was pale and her eyes were set in dark blue circles, like bruises. Poor old Dill.

'Maybe he's busy,' I said hopefully. Too busy to see you even though he's going thousands of miles away very, very soon? It's not looking that good, gal, was what I thought—but I didn't say it.

'Molly Squires says I shouldn't look too desperate. That I should take another bloke to the dance, just in case Chester shows no interest. She says I wouldn't want to look a fool. What do you think?' Dilly's eyes were pleading, as if I was the fount of all wisdom in these matters. Which I wasn't.

'I suppose it couldn't do any harm to give the blighter something to think about. It's not as if he's the only man in the world, now is it? Then again, spare men ain't that thick on the ground right at the moment, Dill, are they? The dance is just over a week away. Where are you going to whistle up a spare geezer this late in the game?' I asked, carefully avoiding giving a solid opinion. A girl could lose friends by giving opinions about people's love lives.

'Oh that's all right,' she said, almost airily. 'I told you. Terry's offered.' I saw a spasm of pain flit across Terry's pleasant face and disappear into a sad little smile. Poor old Terry; he never gave up hope. I'd rather hoped he had when I heard he was walking out with Lily, but apparently not.

'The more the merrier, eh? We'll be quite a party by the time Saturday week gets here,' I said heartily.

Nobody said anything, so I thought I'd change the subject. 'Anyone fancy staying for devilled fish? I was just going to get it going, I reckon it'll stretch if I add another egg and put some spuds with it. Have you got an egg, Terry?'

'Not about my person, but I've got a few at the shop. I'll nip along and get 'em and anything else I can find.' He left rapidly. Terry liked to eat with company. Come to think of it, so did I—which was why I was being so free with my rations.

'Good, that's shot of him for a minute or two,' I said, looking hard at my friend. 'Are you sure you want to put the poor soul's hopes up like that? You know he fancies you like mad, Dilly.'

'Don't be daft, Zeld. He's too old. He's years older than us, practically dribbling. Anyway, he's interested in Lily. I don't know whether to hope he gets her or not. If he doesn't, he'll have to start looking round again. He really does want to get married and have kids.'

'Yes, but he's not that old. Why's he so keen now? What's the hurry?'

'I dunno. You'll have to ask him,' was the quiet reply.

Terry reappeared brandishing three real, whole, fresh eggs, an onion and two spuds from his own pantry. He also brought a drop of milk and a small, slightly grey slab of fish. It was probably snoek, but I didn't like to ask, in case it was. However, with nutmeg, cayenne pepper, curry powder, mustard and Worcester Sauce smothering the flavour, it could be old boot and nobody would know. He also brought a packet of margarine and a tin of cocoa. He had raided his own rations as well as the shop.

The evening went with a swing after its miserable start. We perked up with some nosh inside of us, a cup of cocoa each and several hands of whist. I finally got to tell them all about the cats, and why I was so tired, but I didn't go into much detail. I just wanted to forget that cellar. By the middle of the evening, we were laughing, joking and gossiping as if we hadn't a care in the world.

Then, when Dilly nipped to the khazi, one floor above, I asked Terry casually when he had got so keen on marriage.

'Most men are dead set on dodging matrimony for as long as they can. How come you've decided you've got to gallop up the dreaded aisle?' I really wanted to know because, at the back of my mind, it made me sad for him. I was very fond of Terry.

'It's not sudden, Zelda. I've wanted it for a while. The war, you know, all those people dead. It makes you think. Then, there's my dodgy ticker. It's not getting worse, but it's not getting any better neither. That makes a body stop to have a think as well, take my word. Course, I could go on for ever, but then again, I might not.'

As I heard him out, my stomach lurched slightly. I *knew* something was wrong.

'You might not what?' asked Dilly as she came back in. Terry and I exchanged glances and he shook his head very slightly. I kept schtum.

'Get a ticket to the dance,' Terry told her.

'Don't be daft,' she told him, sighing and rolling her tired, sad but still beautiful eyes at him. 'I *told* you I had a spare. In fact I've got two. Mavis is taking the other one in case she knows someone who might want it.'

'Yes,' mumbled Terry, looking at his knees carefully, 'I'd forgotten. Well, there you are then. I'm coming. Shall we all meet here, drop in for a drink at the Star and Garter then carry on from there?'

And so it was agreed that we'd meet up and go to the dance mob-handed.

Chapter 26

I had recovered enough to take Tony to Digby Burlap's on Saturday, but I didn't go in. I carried on to the cafe instead. I was looking forward to a bit of a sit and a think about the week.

Things at Paradise Gardens were getting out of hand; Tony still hadn't settled down and was worrying the life out of his already anxious mother, and, although I'd got shot of the pitiful wailing dream once the cats were found, the nameless dread was still with me in the mornings when I woke. To add to the general joys, I'd heard that Charlie expected to be demobbed in the next few weeks.

Meanwhile, I'd been in the wars far more than any ordinary mortal would expect. Hardly an inch of me hadn't taken some sort of battering. All the scrubbing at work had ruined my poor hands and I had a big dance coming up where I really wanted to look my best. I was beginning to wonder if the gods had it in for me.

I was sunk in a funk when Maggie brought my tea and another cup for herself. She also had a plate with four digestive biscuits arranged on it. Whoever supplied her seemed to have no trouble getting sugar, biscuits and some of the other finer things in life, like cocoa powder for making chocolate sponges.

'Wotcha, Zelda. You looked like you could get under a snake's belly with a top hat on just then. You all right, love?'

I outlined my week, although I didn't trouble to tell her about Charlie. A person had her pride.

'And they say it's dodgy round here!' she said. 'Have you got any ideas about who's got it in for Miss Makepeace?'

Bert's voice came from the kitchen: 'What? Is somebody troubling Miss Makepeace? What's the problem?' And he appeared, unshaven and looking even more like Bogey than usual.

I have to admit, my heart leapt at the sight of him; then I remembered, he was not Humphrey Bogart and he *was* a married man. Married, I might add, to a very nice woman. So I instructed myself to take a firm hold of all such ideas and banish the buggers. There's right, and there's not right, and lusting after somebody else's husband was not right in my book. So I took a mental cold shower and I explained it all again.

'Are you sure you're all right now, love?' Maggie asked, concerned. 'It all sounds very nasty.'

'I'll be fine,' I assured them.

'Still, we can't have Miss Makepeace being terrorized,' Bert said. 'She helps a lot of people, me included. That cream of hers works wonders when my lumbago's playing up. Who do you think's behind it?'

I said I had my suspicions about a certain mother and son, but couldn't prove anything, and when all was said and done, it could be anybody. 'Not that most people have anything to be snotty about. I mean, Zinnia can be a bit blunt sometimes, but there's hardly a soul in our neck of the woods who hasn't got reason to thank her.'

Just then, Cassie stuck her head round the door, said 'Hello' to us all and asked if anyone had seen someone called Sharky. Maggie and Bert said they hadn't. 'Never mind,' she said. 'Tell him I'm looking for him, will you?' And then she was gone again.

'How's she doing?' I asked.

'Not used to the idea of motherhood yet: nowhere near, I reckon, but becoming resigned to the fact that there's bugger all she can do about it.' Maggie smiled ruefully, then brightened. 'How about reading my tea leaves? While it's quiet.' This was Bert's cue to get back to his kitchen, and Maggie and I settled down for some fortune telling.

First I asked Maggie to swirl the dregs of her tea and the leaves around in her cup three times clockwise, three times widdershins and three times clockwise again. I'm never sure if all that twirling is necessary, but it helps to set the mood, and it's what you might call a spot of ritual. It never does any harm to set the scene, is what I always say. Then I gazed deep into the cup. To be honest, all I usually see when I do that is a load of soggy tea leaves and maybe, after sugar rationing was over, some sugary sludge. In the war, sugar was far too precious to waste, so people stirred thoroughly and there was never the slightest hint of sludge.

Sometimes, though, very, very occasionally, the leaves do seem to form patterns. I won't say I see a dog shape when some poor bugger's about to be bitten by a pooch, or anything like that. It's more that I sort of sink into the patterns and thoughts begin to form and words pop out of my mouth. I'm as surprised as anyone, take my word for it! Usually, though, I just tell people what I reckon they want to hear, and it seems to make 'em happy.

I have found, all my life, that my 'funny turns,' as the family used to call them, come in patches. I have periods when I am dreaming twice nightly and seeing things in the cards, tea leaves and palms that are thrust under my nose. Sometimes these periods go on for days, weeks, even months. Then they disappear as mysteriously as they arrive and my dreams become just dreams and palms are simply sweaty objects for fingers to be attached to. Two things I *have* noticed, though, are that these turns usually coincide with tricky periods in my own life, and that I am totally useless at predicting things for myself. If I try, I am usually completely and utterly wrong, so I gave it up as a bad job years ago.

So there I was, staring into Maggie's cup when the patterns began to form and my mind went to another place.

'Oh Maggie,' I said. 'I see a terrible sadness.' My voice seemed to be coming from far off. 'There's a big hole in your life, like a terrible wound that won't heal.' I paused for a while, feeling the yawning, painful gap as if it was at my own centre, then peered into the hole and saw a barren place. I waited for the pattern to re-form. Then I saw babies, loads of babies all floating about like so many little ghosts. But they weren't ghosts. Somehow I knew that they were sort of babies-in-waiting. A flickering movement made me turn my gaze away from them and towards a group of people standing around. Some were waiting hopefully, others had a sense of dread about them. And the rest? Well, they just seemed to be hanging about to see what was going to happen next.

One by one, the babies floated over to a couple, or occasionally to a lone woman, and then the little family would disappear silently, like a bubble that's burst. This happened until all the babies had gone. But not all the people had gone with them: some were left waiting. One couple didn't seem to belong in either group, but were stuck out on their own. I looked closer, knowing what I was going to see, and sure enough, the couple were Maggie and Bert.

I looked up to see Maggie's face looking concerned. 'Are you all right?' she asked. 'You went into a trance and I thought you was never coming back. Here, have a sip of tea. What on earth did you see?'

I thought about it for a good long time before I decided what to say and how to say it. In the end, I thought I owed the woman the truth: to tell her what I saw but not to pretend that I knew what it all meant. I felt my way gently, ready to back up if she looked as if she couldn't take it. 'I saw your great sadness, Maggie. You want a baby badly, you and Bert both.' I stopped as I saw tears well up and crumples appear on the sweet face opposite me. I reached out and patted her hand and her fingers closed round mine. We sat like that for a while.

Then she squeezed my hand hard, but didn't let go. 'And?'

'Are you sure, love?' I asked. She nodded and squeezed again. So I told her everything. 'I don't know what the last bit means, Maggie.' I paused, then stressed what I said next. 'I'm only guessing, mind. You must understand that.'

Once again she nodded.

'Well, what I think it *could* mean is that although you're not going to actually have a baby of your own, you will have a lot to do with them, or with one at least. I'm not sure which. What I *am* sure of is that you will never give birth.'

And then I burst into tears and Maggie joined in and pretty soon we were awash. I had no idea why I was crying, but I was heartbroken as I sat there sobbing. Maybe I was thinking about my own baby, the one that Charlie had hurt.

Finally, a new voice broke into our weeping and wailing. 'Come on, girls,' it said, 'it ain't that bad, surely.'

Bert's voice floated out from the kitchen. 'Wotcha, Sharky. Don't worry about the sob sisters too much. There are times when women enjoy a good cry. I've noticed that. A cup of tea will set 'em right.' And he appeared with a tray of fresh teas and some slices of Victoria sponge. Where did those buggers get their supplies from? That's what I wanted to know.

I dabbed with my hanky, Maggie did the same, and pretty soon we were more or less back to normal and I was able to take in the newcomer. I suppose he must have been in his thirties. He had thick blond hair, neatly cut, and was wearing a smart business suit. He smiled and held out his hand to me, but looked at Maggie. 'And whom do I have the pleasure of meeting?' he said.

'This is Zelda.' Maggie turned to me. 'This here is Sharky Finn. Watch him: he's a one for the ladies, a smooth talker, you see, on account of being a lawyer.'

'Yes,' said Bert. 'It ought to be on his name-plate: "Sharky Finn, Lawyer to the Bent and Scourge of the Ladies."'

'Cassie's looking for you. She stuck her head in earlier,' he said to Sharky.

'It's slander, Zelda, all of it.' He smiled a brilliant smile that could blind at a hundred paces. 'What did Cassie want, Bert? Did she say?'

'Nope.'

'Ah well, I dare say it can wait, then. So, Zelda. Tell me all about yourself. I bet you're a fascinating girl.'

'And a married one,' Maggie said heavily.

'Life's rarely perfect, Maggie dear. You know that. We simply have to make do with things as we find them. I am prepared to be bewitched, Zelda. Dazzle me.' He leaned back comfortably in his seat, smiled another wide smile and lit a huge cigar.

Luckily, just at that moment, Tony arrived and saved me from having to answer or be bewitching. After a bit of prompting he mumbled shyly that his lesson had been 'All right.' Which I suppose was the best I could hope for in front of so many strangers.

'Zelda here was telling us that Miss Makepeace is having trouble, Sharky,' Bert said. 'Someone seems to have it in for her.'

Sharky Finn stopped grinning immediately and a steely glint replaced the twinkle in his pale blue eyes.

'What do you mean by "trouble"?' he demanded, first looking at Bert then at me, all signs of the playful flirt gone.

I explained what had been happening, while trying to ignore Tony's fidgeting beside me.

'And you've no idea who is behind these things?' Mr. Finn asked. 'Or why the trouble has started up now?'

'No, not really. There's one or two who might hold a grudge but not enough of a grudge to turn nasty, as far as I know,' I explained. Why had Zinnia never mentioned her connection with these people until Tony had needed singing lessons? She obviously knew this strange lawyer, and he her, judging by his interest. But then, she'd only let on at all because she had to, and she'd hardly been what you might call forthcoming on the subject. She kept her secrets closer to her chest than her bleeding vest, that one.

I was lost in that particular thought when I felt Tony's bony elbow in my ribs, reminding me it was time to go. We said our goodbyes and spent a quiet hour on the bus heading towards home, both lost in our own thoughts.

Chapter 27

Sunday dinner passed, for once, with no family ding-dong.

Even Tony managed to stay out of scrapes—well, scrapes that anyone knew about, anyway. Doris, Reggie and the twins were in good form. Doris had heard from her Ernie a few days before. He'd written that he expected to be home in a couple of months. There was a glow on Doris' cheek that hadn't been there for a good while and it was cheering to see. There even seemed to be a special sparkle around Reggie's glasses and a twinkle of merriment in his eye. He was usually quite a serious lad. The twins, well, they didn't really know what was going on, but they had caught the mood and were being high spirited and jolly. Even Dad was full of the pale ale of human kindness, his usual brown having temporarily run out at the King's Head. Mum, bless her, was smiling because she felt the excuse for another party coming on and Gran was full of gossip from her cronies at church.

Only poor Vi had trouble getting into the spirit of the day, and nobody could really blame the poor dear for that. Fred must have been on her mind a good deal around that time, because everywhere she went—the shops, work, bus queues or the pub—there was talk of the men returning at last. All those sons, boyfriends and husbands coming home, but not hers. I mean, it'd make anybody down in the dumps.

I wasn't in the mood to join her, even though thoughts of Charlie were enough to send me dumpwards at any time, because I had made up my mind to try to enjoy my day off as much as possible. If Mrs. Dunmore's mood of the previous week and the alarums and scarums round at Zinnia's were anything to go by, I was going to need the recovery time to cope with the coming week. So I started my day in the way I liked the best. I had a long, hot bath with an elderly lavender bag thrown in to make use of the very last hint of pong.

I dressed carefully in my Sunday best, then dropped boiled egg down the bodice of my frock and had to change it for the second best. But I didn't spit or grumble about it, simply dabbed at it carefully until it looked clean and left it to dry up on the airer hanging from the kitchen ceiling.

I was feeling sunny because I'd had a decent night's sleep for a change. Just as suddenly as the dreams and strange trance-like goings-on had started, so they had stopped dead again on Saturday night. It was as if I'd shot my final bolt for a while when I'd read Maggie's leaves; I had slept like a baby that night. All my lumps, bumps, bruises and grazes were fading away at various rates, depending on when I got them, but the main thing was, I was on the mend. I was almost tickety-boo once again. The only flies in my particular ointment, apart from Charlie, were Mrs. Dunmore, driving her slaves with much more than her usual determination, and my worries about Zinnia.

Practical jokes were one thing, but the fire and the shooting of her cat were downright frightening. PC Grubb had been informed, and was on the case, but nobody suspended their breathing: they'd certainly have snuffed it before George 'Nosher' Grubb got even the hint of a culprit. He was not the brightest candle in the box, although he was steady and thorough.

When we got to the afters, baked apples and custard, talk turned to Tony's lessons. 'What's "phrasing" when it's at home?' demanded Gran through a red-hot mouthful of the dried fruit Mum had stuffed into the hole where the cores used to be, before putting the apples in the oven.

'Well, you sort of have to take a breath then let it out really carefully so that when you're singing, you don't have to breathe in the middle of a melody, or a word or even a sentence, when it would sound daft and ruin it.'

'So what sort of exercises do you have to do?' asked Reggie. That boy was interested in everything.

'I dunno yet, do I? We're doing it next week.' Tony turned his back on his cousin abruptly and looked at me and then his mother. 'I've been thinking about what instrument to try and learn, like Mr. Burlap said, and I thought the piano would be best, because we've got one and I can practise on that.'

I felt pleased. It was good to see the lad using his head for once. There was still the question of lessons, though. I just hoped Mr. Burlap would include a bit of joanna in the hour, because I couldn't see us finding any extra money for proper lessons. I played a bit, but I'd learned to play the tunes by ear. I didn't know anything at all about technique and I certainly couldn't teach Tony much.

'Does that mean you're going to be thumping and crashing about in our parlour, then?' asked Dad, none too thrilled at the prospect of another learner let loose on his piano. When Tony nodded hopefully, Dad just grunted and said, 'Well, either learn fast and get good at it, or do it when I'm out. I can't abide hearing music mangled by bleeding amateurs. It grates on me lug'oles something 'orrible.' For Dad, this passed as encouragement.

'Mrs. Cattermole learned the piano as well as the organ when she was a girl,' chipped in Gran. 'They've got one at the vicarage. I'm sure they'd let their favourite choirboy use it. I expect if you asked her right, she'd give you a few lessons as well. You could make yourself useful round the place. The Vicar, bless him, is all thumbs when it comes to handling tools or anything else—besides bibles, bees and Mrs. Cattermole.' Gran let out a faintly dirty chuckle that made Mum and Vi blush. I don't think the kids got it; at least, I hoped they didn't.

After dinner I strolled home, changed into my gardening togs and made my way to the allotments. It was time to earth up the first early spuds again. I'd been a bit tardy getting them in, and the flower buds were just forming. My mouth watered: new spuds straight from the earth and into the pot, via a brief stop to run them under a tap to get them clean. A sprig of mint in the water, then when cooked, a knob of butter, salt and pepper; there's nothing like it.

I also had to water generally. I'd planted out the last of the runner beans. The plan was to stagger planting. Some went in really early, risking late frosts, and the rest went in when the danger of frosts was almost certainly past, but in England nothing like that's ever certain. It's not unheard of to get a rogue frost in late May and even into June, but meanwhile the good, early start with some of them meant that they'd be on our plates all the sooner and it would prolong the cropping season. A mad dash with some net curtains to sling over the vines could save beans from a late frost, so it was worth risking some of them. Beans were thirsty buggers, though, which meant much toing and froing with cans of water.

I eyed the onions critically. The ones I'd pulled previously were drying nicely and it was time to pull the rest, so I could fork over the soil and use it for some salad crops. The gentle hum of the Reverend Cattermole's bees and the warmth of the afternoon sun on my back were really soothing as I worked away. I felt the tensions and worries of the previous weeks slacken still further, so that I was quite relaxed.

I should have known it couldn't last and, sure enough, it didn't. I became aware of a pair of scuffed black boots and long, grey knee socks that had slipped untidily from a pair of clean but grazed knees to a set of bony ankles—Reggie was waiting patiently for me to notice him. I sat back on my haunches and squinted up.

'Wotcha, Reggie,' I said.

Nephews coming for private chats with me were beginning to become a feature of my visits to the allotments. It hadn't been long since Tony had turned up in much the same way.

'Hello, Auntie Zelda.' There was a long silence as I waited for him to tell me what he wanted, while he examined the toecaps of his boots and shuffled a bit. The silence stretched until we were both uncomfortable. I decided to help him out.

'So, to what do I owe the pleasure? I don't suppose you're here to help with the watering, are you?' I asked hopefully.

'I'll give you a hand, Auntie,' Reggie answered, relieved at having something to do while he worked his way round to the point of his visit.

I tried to give him the small watering can, but manfully, he grabbed the bigger of the two. Reggie's dodgy chest had always made the poor little blighter even more determined to try to keep up with his more robust friends, and his cousin; on the occasions when he felt he had to, that is. He always gave it some thought first, naturally.

He managed to keep up for the most part, too, except when the smog or the pollen got to him. It depended on the time of year. June is pollen time and he was wheezing quite a bit, but we toiled away in amicable silence for a while. I nearly always enjoyed Reggie's company. He had a stillness about him that was easy to be with.

Once the beans were thoroughly watered, we took a breather. I put the kettle on in Zinnia's railway carriage and we sat under an apple tree to enjoy a well-earned cuppa. 'So,' I said, 'did you come for anything special, Reggie? Or was it simply the pleasure of your old aunt's company and humping water to the beans that drew you here?'

Reggie grinned. 'Hardly.'

'Well. Ta very much,' I answered, grinning back. 'How do you feel about the news from your dad?' I went on, taking a flyer.

'It's great news, Auntie.' He paused, brow creased above his specs. 'But I feel sorry for Tony. His dad isn't coming home and I know it...er...'—he searched for the right words, soppy talk about feelings not being easy for any male over the age of seven—'upsets him.'

I felt my way carefully. I didn't want Reggie to feel he had to betray any confidences. 'Has he said anything?' I remembered how Tony had virtually ignored his cousin at the dinner table.

'No-o-o, not really. It's more the way he isn't saying it. I know he wishes it was *his* dad coming home, and he's really spitting mad that it isn't. But it's not just that he's being a bit off. He'll get over it, he always does. He's a moody bloke, Auntie, you know that. It doesn't last. It's more the way he's carrying on.'

Reggie stopped abruptly and stared into the boughs of the apple tree. The glass in his specs reflected the light and made his eyes look blank. I waited for him to carry on, knowing there was no point in prompting him or trying to hurry him along; I'd only put the wind up him and he'd clam up. Talking about his cousin behind his back, and to a grown-up at that, didn't come naturally. It must have been serious for him to even attempt it. Finally, he gave a very small shrug, took a deep breath and launched into what was troubling him.

'You see, I think he's being bullied, and because he's cheesed off about his dad, he doesn't seem to care what happens to himself that much.'

'I thought his music lessons had perked him up a bit. He sounded quite interested in learning the piano at dinnertime,' I said, because he had. He'd seemed in a much better frame of mind.

'Yes, well, the lesson only really takes up a morning a week, dunnit? There's the rest of his spare time to worry about.' Poor Reggie looked far too serious for his age. He shouldn't be the one worrying about his cousin, he should be looking forward to his dad coming home. And it didn't sit easily with him to talk about 'stuff,' as he called it.

'It's just that I think he's being shoved into doing things he doesn't want to do,' Reggie said at last. He was busting to spit it out, but he didn't want to commit the deadly sin of grassing. Reggie's pinched and pointed face showed the struggle the poor lad was having with himself. To tell or not to tell, that was obviously the question. It was so ingrained in him not to breathe a word out of turn, when it came to family and friends, that Reggie was literally having trouble getting the air in and out. A wheeze rattled in his chest and he coughed a dry, nervous cough for a moment or two. I felt sorry for the boy, but it was probably better if he got it off his chest, so to speak.

'What sort of things?' I asked carefully.

It came out in a rush, as if the lad had closed his eyes and jumped. 'I think that Ma Hole is training him up the same way she did Brian,' Reggie gasped, his asthma getting worse from sheer tension. 'You know, breaking into places and that sort of thing. He can shin up a drainpipe quicker than Bung'ole, I've seen him do it. He's got this funny tool thing as well, that opens locks, and he knows how to use it. He opened the cash box Grandad keeps his money in to show me that he could.'

Reggie blinked worriedly and added hastily, 'He didn't steal nothing, he was just showing me. It's just that I'm worried, Auntie Zelda, because he's got so as he really doesn't seem to care any more. I saw him running along the top of Keyworth's roof the other night. If he'd slipped, he'd have been a goner.'

'I see.' It was all I could think of to say. I knew the feeling of well-being had been too good to last. It was a funny thing, but we'd had nothing but trouble and more trouble since peace had been declared.

I got up and poured myself another cup of tea. It may have been funny, but I certainly wasn't bloody laughing.

Chapter 28

The following Tuesday, I was picking my way carefully along the edge of a bomb site on the way from my flat to the Gardens. I was impatient to show off my new finery for the dance and to borrow the finishing touches, like Vi's blue glass necklace with the matching earrings and Mum's ancient rabbit fur cape that just covered the shoulders. The short-cut over the bomb site was a tricky manoeuvre even in broad daylight, and virtually impossible when it was getting dark; the street lights on that stretch of road had been shattered for ages. Just to add to the general joys, I was wearing my brand new frock, run up on two frenzied nights when I sat chained to my trusty Singer, and was desperate not to ruin my outfit by making a single careless move. There was also the pair of revamped, suede, peep-toed high heels to consider. They had once been a scuffed white but were now a rather patchy royal blue, thanks to a bottle of ink and a soft cloth made from a pair of drawers recently retired from active duty. But I loved them—the shoes that is, not the drawers.

I was concentrating so hard I didn't hear him coming. The first I knew that I had company was when a hand landed on my shouder. I almost fainted with the shock—my nerves were still jangling from rescuing the cats in the cellar—but self-preservation won, and I socked the bugger with my handbag. It was only as my assailant staggered backwards and landed knee deep in a hole filled with cold, muddy water that I realized that

I knew him. It was Percy Robinson, the dockside Lothario and Charlie's friend.

'You stupid sod!' I roared—at least, I tried to roar, but it came out more of a squeak.

It took him a good few moments to haul himself clear of the sucking, wet clay at the bottom of the puddle. He got no help from me—I was still shaking from the shock, and I was wearing my best outfit, after all—but he finally made it, and looked balefully down at his soaking, filthy shoes and trouser legs. Best to stay on the attack, under the circumstances. 'What the hell do you think you're doing, creeping up on a person like that? You scared the life out of me!'

Percy Robinson was bitter. 'Apparently not!' he said, glowering at me. He bent to pick up his hat, which had landed in the puddle beside him and was sinking steadily. A stream of yellowish water cascaded from it like a small waterfall. Percy tried to summon some dignity, while obviously struggling manfully not to clout me back. But he got his revenge accidentally as his hat splattered watery clay on to my newly blue, but sadly not waterproof, shoes. Ink ran all over my feet.

I looked down at them with horror. Not only had he given me a hell of a fright, he'd also ruined what were, in my mind, my best and what's more, *brand new* shoes, even though they weren't. I'd put a lot of effort into those shoes, so that I could attend the Yanks' farewell dance with Dilly and our friends. It was an important occasion, a chance for me and Dilly to dress up and swank for a change. Poor Dilly still hadn't managed to get any sense out of Chester. He point-blank refused to be drawn on the subject of the dance. Why he was so obstinate was a complete mystery, but Dilly couldn't keep on and on about it without looking desperate. So it was even more essential for us all to put our best foot forward, both for appearances' sake and to help cheer her up.

Now look what Percy Robinson had done! Resentment and fury welled up in me and I bashed him again. 'You swine! You've ruined my shoes.'

He staggered slightly. Even through the red mist, I could see I packed a fair old wallop when my dander was up. It must've been all that scrubbing and heaving around of stodgy dinners. It had built up my muscles nicely. 'I asked you a question. What are you doing creeping about in the dark after me?'

He pulled himself upright—he was a tall bugger. 'I was *not* creeping!' he said. 'I was just going to say wotcha and ask if you wanted to come for a drink. I want to talk to you about Sylvia—Mrs. Dunmore—and anyway, I've been watching you in the canteen and I've come to like the cut of your jib.' Then he lunged at me, taking me off guard. He was fumbling for my waist in an attempt to pull me towards him. 'We can always have a little cuddle here, it's nice and dark.'

I shoved him away, good and hard. No wonder Mrs. D. had been in a mood; she must've got wind that her Percy was wandering again. The bloody man was insatiable! And where was the legendary Robinson charm? Not that it would cut any ice with me—but still, just grabbing like that. What sort of a girl did he think I was? Blind, deaf, stupid and easy? Well, he had another think coming.

'Are you mad? My feet are wet through and covered in bloody ink and you're giving me the right hump. You're my husband's mate *and* you're walking out with Mrs. Dunmore—or had you forgotten her along with your missus? Funny how your womenfolk just seem to slip your mind.'

He was puffing himself up to answer me when a friendly voice boomed out of the darkness. 'Zelda, my flower, is good old Perce upsetting you in any way?' Ronnie strolled into view, with five large friends bringing up his rear, like a small flotilla of Thames barges.

Percy Robinson accurately assessed the situation. 'I was doing no such thing,' he blustered. 'It was just a misunderstanding, that's all.' He tried to look earnestly at my saviours but failed miserably, and appeared furtive instead. He knew it was time to squelch away as rapidly as his slippery shoes would take him over the rubble.

Hysteria overtook me. I almost split my sides laughing with relief. I hadn't realized just how frightening the strange hand in the dark had been.

When my escorts and I found a street lamp that was actually working, we surveyed the damage. Ronnie's hands flew to his face and he gasped: 'Oh sweetie, your poor batts! They're ruined.'

It was true: a vat of ink couldn't put my poor peep-toes right. They looked like clapped-out blotting paper—only worse. My eyes filled with tears as I explained about the farewell dance, and sympathy etched itself on Ronnie's homely mush. 'The drag looks tres, tres bona, dolly. It's just the batts.' He eyed my shoes for a moment, then said thoughtfully, 'Ma's got loads of shoes from the Twenties that'll never be worn again unless they're passed on. Troll round for a look, dolly, you might find something.'

He turned to his friends. 'I'll meet you lot in the pub later. I'm just going to nip home with Zelda for a minute.'

Poor Mrs. Rigby: the look of sheer joy when her beloved Ronnie walked in with a girl was a bit sad. Especially as the girl in question was only me, and she knew I was married. But any girl would do for Mrs. Rigby. It allowed her to carry on with the fiction that one day soon her Ronnie would make her a proud granny. Nobody liked to tell the poor old darling that Ronnie wasn't going to found any dynasty in this lifetime, on account of her being such a poppet we didn't want to disappoint her.

Mrs. Rigby's shop was a wonderful dark and dusty cave filled with teetering piles of mismatched china. More than a dozen old washboards stood propped against the wall, next to stacks of picture frames, some empty, some sporting elderly, spotted prints of *The Stag at Bay*, *Morecambe Bay by Moonlight* or *The Hay Wain*. A cardboard box of unmatched, blunt knitting needles—a good rootle about was necessary to find a pair—stood next to another, filled to the brim with odd buttons, on a table by the door. Nestled next to them was a third, crammed with cutlery, and a shoe box filled with nutcrackers. Other, larger boxes held second-hand overalls, work boots with strong toe-caps and a fine selection of string bags. Shelves were lined two deep with tatty old books; lampshades with fringes and bobbles hung from hooks. Children's clothes and footwear, too tired to be passed on or unpicked and resewn, were stuffed into two old prams. A fancy gazunder held dozens of zips torn from their garments and baring their often broken teeth. It'd take a while to find one that worked, but find one you would, if you didn't mind rummaging about in a chamber-pot, that is. I'm certain it would have been thoroughly scrubbed before the zips were dumped in it. Mrs. Rigby was thoughtful that way.

Several enamelled bowls were piled one inside the other in a corner; the top one was filled with enormous, wooden laundry tongs. Ornate Victorian vases and plant pots, along with dozens of glass oil lamps in all the colours of the rainbow, with or without their chimneys, cluttered a shelf above a huge, battered mangle that somehow completed the picture. The thing about Mrs. Rigby's was that you could find virtually anything you needed if you were prepared to delve deep enough. That shop proved an absolute godsend during all the years of rationing and was rarely empty of foraging females.

However, it wasn't the stock of shoes in the shop that Ronnie had been referring to when he suggested I might find a pair. It was his ma's own private collection, left over from her heyday as a flapper in the 1920s. She must have had almost a dozen pairs, each wrapped separately in a shoe bag or a length of soft cloth. Her dad had been a master cobbler at a posh bespoke shoemaker's in Bond Street and he'd made all her shoes from scraps right up until the day he died.

I was in ecstasy as I unwrapped each pair to reveal another beautiful silk or kid leather creation. The stitching was tiny and the colours were gorgeous. 'He made them to match my clothes,' Mrs. Rigby told me, eyes shining with pride. 'My mum was a seamstress, so I was always well turned out. I've never thrown any of my shoes away, even though my poor feet are too swollen to wear them now.'

I could quite see her point: the shoes were works of art and it seemed like sacrilege to wear them, let alone dump them. I was hesitant about borrowing a pair in case they were ruined, but Ronnie and his mum would have none of it.

'My dad would be thrilled to know his shoes were seeing a dance floor again after all these years. Choose a pair and wear them in good health.' There was a pause. 'But bring 'em back when you're done.'

In the end, I chose a navy blue kid leather pair, with a cross-bar and low, elegantly shaped heels. If I stuffed a hanky in each toe, they fitted me fine, and the bar across my instep helped to keep them on. I was in heaven and I couldn't thank the old lady enough. But I made up my mind to try, with a hefty sample of the very next meat delivery to the canteen and some vegetables from the allotment.

Chapter 29

On Friday, I hurried home after work for a soak in a tepid bath before Dilly and Ronnie came for our predance hairdressing session. As a bath required boiling up kettles of water on the gas hob and pouring it into a tin bath, it was a lengthy process. So was emptying the bathtub afterwards. If I didn't get a move on, all I'd get was a lick and a promise, not the relaxing soak I'd hoped for.

I was dressed and emptying my bathwater, a bucket at a time, down the kitchen sink, when Dilly turned up, closely followed by Ronnie. They grabbed a saucepan each and helped until it was shallow enough to lift up and tip. I mopped the lino while Ronnie took the bath downstairs into the yard and hung it on its hook by the back door. A small, makeshift porch put up by Charlie on one of his leaves saved it from the worst of the weather and serious rusting. Galvanized tin would only take so much punishment before the tell-tale orange rust started and, along with virtually everything else to do with cleanliness, tin baths had been hard to come by during the war. No wonder we'd hummed a bit at times. Even hot water was rationed.

'Tut, tut, dolly, you've been cheating and taking long, hot and, worse yet, solitary baths,' Ronnie said, wagging a large finger at me.

'I cannot tell a lie, governor!' I told him. 'I am almost guilty as charged, although it wasn't that hot. However, tomorrow I shall have one right up to me neck, piping hot and scented with a whole gardenia bath cube—so there!'

Dilly gasped. 'You jammy baggage! Just for that you can make me a cup of tea.'

'And me,' Ronnie said. 'And while you're at it, some water to wash our barnets. I certainly can't set yours without a shampoo first. And it just so happens, ladies, I have shampoo and setting lotion, thanks to the sainted Zinnia Makepeace. Plus she sent a chamomile rinse for the blonde and rosemary for the brunette. She says it will give a gloss to our locks and make us smell divine. She recommends the rosemary for me, despite the golden threads among the mouse, says it smells more butch. So, we'll do our riahs tonight, pop a hairnet on to sleep and all we'll have to do tomorrow is comb it through.'

Dilly laughed. 'And I didn't come empty-handed either. I've still got some of Chester's records. I thought we'd get in the mood for dancing by playing a few. You've still got Charlie's gramophone, haven't you?'

'Yes,' I told her, grinning. I was forbidden to use Charlie's gramophone when he wasn't there, on pain of death, so of course I used it all the time. I liked music. It cheered a body up, especially a drop of Swing. Once we'd heard Glenn Miller, Artie Shaw, Tommy Dorsey and Benny Goodman, our own home-grown music suddenly lost its shine—and how! Who wanted to polka when they could jitterbug? 'Show us what you got, Dill.'

I sorted through the modest pile carefully. It wouldn't do to break any. If Chester was going to do a runner, and his stubborn silence on all matters to do with the dance suggested he might be working up to it, they might be among the few things she'd have to remember him by.

'Any more news on the Chester front?' I asked as casually as I could.

Dilly shook her head, eyes filling up with tears. 'I haven't even *heard* from him in over a week. I think he must be ashamed to be seen with me among his mates or something,' she said sadly.

'If that's the case, then it's good riddance to bad rubbish, dolly,' Ronnie said firmly. 'You're certainly not the kind of girl to be ashamed of. You're good looking, well turned out and any bloke should be proud to have you on his arm—unless of course he prefers other blokes, in which case the cove should never have dallied with you in the first place. Mind you, he wouldn't be the first to use a pretty young girl as a camouflage…But still, it's never right. Feelings get hurt.'

Not for the first time, nor the last, I thought what a poppet Ronnie was. Being a sea queen wasn't easy, but the hardships never seemed to sour him, and I sincerely hoped that one day he'd meet the man of his dreams and settle down. He deserved to be happy. But then, so did we all.

We pored over Chester's records. Some were real treasures. Records, gramophones and gramophone needles weren't so thick on the ground, money being tight and the bombs being merciless, that we could afford to be careless with the few records that came our way. I looked at the familiar red, white and blue labels: Count Basie, Louis Armstrong, Jack Teagarden and the V-Disc All Stars. What wonderful, exotic names they all had. What's more, I knew for a fact that Count Basie, Nat King Cole and Duke Ellington weren't landed gentry at all. In fact, they didn't have a family seat between 'em, on account of being Americans. Dilly explained to me that a lot of American GI Joes thought these blokes were the aristocrats of the music world and when I'd heard them, I really couldn't argue with that. They were wonderful.

Chester's records were really something, too. He played the trumpet in his own band, according to Dilly. She said he was pretty good, but then, she'd have been impressed if he'd been cleaning his fingernails. Everything he did or said was impressive, or so she thought. I reserved judgement against the day I finally heard him, if it ever came.

I put Hot Lips Page and His Hot Seven on the gramophone and we listened to Mr. Page's strange but wonderful singing and velvet trumpet in 'Uncle Sam's Blues.' It was impossible to get excited about poor old George Formby's ukulele when you'd heard that trumpet! The saxophones, pianos and the fabulous rhythms of American bands completely bowled me and all my mates over. Even Vera Lynn's bluebirds paled to boring when you got earfuls of voices like Lena Horne, Ella Fitzgerald and that girl with a boy's name, Billie Holiday. It was a whole new world of sound and it brightened up grey old England no end.

The lazy melody of 'Uncle Sam's Blues' dragged me round in a slow, dreamy dance, and Dilly and Ronnie just had to join in. Then I noticed the time. If we didn't get a move on, we'd never get our hair done. Terry and Lenny Hobbs were dropping in to pick us up for a swift drink at the King's Head before closing time, and as Dilly worked all day Saturday, and I had to take Tony to Soho, if we didn't do our hair that evening, before the chaps turned up, we'd never get it ready for Saturday night.

Ronnie was all business. 'Right,' he said to me, 'let's get that riah of yours set toot sweet, ducky, while Dilly washes hers. Once I've crimped you both, I'll wash my own.'

The next couple of hours flew by in a haze of setting lotion, gossip and music. Well, Ronnie and I gossiped, while poor old Dilly grew ever more nervy and anxious. 'What if Chester brings another girl?' she asked for around the nine-thousand-and-twenty-third time as Ronnie pinned her curlers into place.

'You'll hold your head up, dolly, and dance the night away with the three handsome devils in your party. That's what you'll do,' Ronnie told her bracingly.

'I'm not sure I'll manage,' Dilly quavered.

'You'll manage, even if we have to hold you up in turns. Now, that's your riah shushed, let's get cracking on your make-up. Nothing like a practice run with a bit of slap, to see what suits. I'm all for putting a brave face on things, ducky. You often find you live up to it.'

By the time Ronnie'd finished with us we looked like film stars, faces and hair immaculate. The man was a genius! Our fingernails had been shaped too, and would be polished a vibrant red on the night. We couldn't risk doing it too soon then chipping it, because bottles of nail varnish did not grow on trees.

It was only when you saw some colour that you noticed how little there was in our everyday lives. We were even going to wear proper stockings on the night, and wouldn't have to resort to a covering of watered-down gravy powder and the stub of eyebrow pencil to draw in the seams. The trouble with gravy powder was that it was difficult to get a uniform tan colour. It tended to get blotchy unless applied by an expert with a steady hand and a precious lump of cotton wool. Ditto the seams; they could wobble disastrously if you tried to do 'em yourself, or had a shaky helper.

Dilly had given in to pressure and extreme shyness and decided against the revealing black dress that Molly Squires had offered on loan especially for the occasion. Instead she had finally chosen to wear a plain midnight blue, short-sleeved but higher-necked number she'd had for years. It had a neat, scooped, scalloped neckline, a self-coloured belt and a full skirt. Ronnie had, as promised, fished out a pearl choker and some long, pearl drop earrings and had brought along a pair of his mum's long, white evening gloves to perk it up a bit. Like mine, Dilly's blond tresses had been piled up high in large curls. She looked lovely.

I didn't look bad either, even if I say so myself. I had my dark hair piled up in a mass of curls on top and held up by combs and craftily hidden hair grips. Thanks to Zinnia's hair rinse, it glowed and smelt of rosemary. Vi's earrings and necklace were shown up a treat when my hair was out of the way, and my dress, although simple in style, looked crisp and fresh thanks to its obvious newness. Several petticoats made the skirt full and my cinched-in waist looked tiny. In the end, I'd cut the bodice like a sun dress. Mum's fur cape would see me all right if the night turned chilly.

I have to say, Ronnie was a handsome man when he scrubbed up. His shirt was blindingly white, his dark blue suit was immaculately pressed and his blue and red striped tie had a fat, neat Windsor knot. His black brogues glistened, his brown hair shone and the cowlick at the front made him look positively boyish. He was tall and well-built and it was hard at that precise moment to remember that he was a self-styled sea queen and proud of it. As he said, if he hadn't been running the risk of arrest or a severe beating, or probably both, he'd have indulged in a little slap himself. 'But I believe the butch look is the order of the day for this engagement, dollies. We don't want bloodshed. Claret might get on those lovely frocks, and we can't have that, can we, girls?'

We agreed that we certainly couldn't.

There was a knock on the street door: Terry and Lenny had arrived. Dilly and I changed back into our usual clothes as quickly as we could, while Ronnie entertained our guests. We'd had our dress rehearsal and were satisfied we would look our absolute best on the night. What's more, we'd had a nice evening giggling, playing with our hair, faces and clothes, just like when we were kids. It had made us forget our troubles almost completely, which was a boon and a blessing for all concerned. Even Dilly managed to have a good time, and that was saying something.

Chapter 30

The Yanks had really pushed the boat out for their last dance and several units had clubbed together to hire the local town hall. It was at some place almost in the sticks, a fair way out of town on the District Line as I recall, but to be honest, I was too excited to take much notice. I didn't get out much beyond East London as a rule.

We'd all met at my place, Dilly, Ronnie, Lenny, Vi, Terry and me. The only people missing were Molly Squires, Beryl from work, who had decided to join us at the last minute, and Mavis. We picked up Molly and Beryl at the Star and Garter; Mavis had told Vi to carry on without her, she'd catch up later. We had a convivial drink and then set out for the dance. It didn't do to arrive too early, before the thing had got going. We were all chattering like a flock of starlings as we made the long trip on the tube. All except poor Dilly, of course, who was very quiet.

'Why are you so worried that Chester'll come to the dance and bring another girl?' I asked. 'Has he said anything?'

Dilly shook her head. 'No,' she admitted. 'He never said a word about it, even though I hinted like mad.'

'So, why do you think he'll turn up? It doesn't make sense if he showed no interest at all.' To tell the truth, I was getting a bit irritated with her.

'I dunno; it's more what he didn't say and the way he didn't say it,' Dilly tried to explain.

'What do you mean, for goodness sake? You're not making a lot of sense, Dilly dear.'

'I see what she means,' Ronnie chipped in. 'Silences can be very informative. Just ask the Gestapo.'

We laughed nervously. The Gestapo had been operating far too recently to be seen as anything but terrifying, even by those of us who had never had anything to do with them and were never likely to now.

'Well…' Dilly hesitated. 'It's the way he ignored my hints, and just changed the subject or talked over me about something completely different. He kept doing that. When someone talks over awkward questions, you know they're being dodgy. Then, when I kept on, I stopped hearing from him altogether.' I thought Dilly was going to cry, which would have been terrible, on account of the lashings of mascara Ronnie had applied before we left my place. She'd have black streaks down to her knees. 'And if he wanted to give me the brush-off, what better way to do it than to bring another girl to the dance?' She had a point, but I didn't want to come out and say so.

'You've been trying to read between the lines,' I accused her. 'No good ever comes of that! You nearly always end up jumping to the wrong conclusions. I know, because I'm always doing it myself. The only thing to be found between the lines is sodding great gaps. Anyway, you're not trying to give him the elbow, but you *are* going to a dance with another bloke—several, in fact. So even if he does show up with someone else, it might mean nothing at all. Let's just wait and see, shall we? And meanwhile, do try to have a good time, there's a dear.'

To give Dilly her due, she did try. We chatted about work and how impossible Mrs. Dunmore was being. We bitched about how skinny she was and speculated about the state of her affair with Percy Robinson, given that he seemed to be casting his roving eye about again. Just thinking about how his roving eye fell on me made me feel a bit sick, and I was pleased when Dilly changed the subject to Zinnia's recent troubles.

'Who do you reckon's got it in for her, then?' she asked. 'I mean, Zinnia's so good to one and all; how could anyone have the needle to her?'

'Well, Ma Hole's always been jealous of her, as you well know. It's never been any kind of secret. She's got a real thing about Zinnia having that house and gardens, but why would she suddenly turn nasty now? I mean, she's been peculiar about Zinnia for donkey's years: why start any funny business at this particular time? It doesn't make any sense,' I said. 'I reckon it's someone else.'

'What doesn't make sense?' Terry asked, suddenly joining our conversation.

'Ma Hole being behind all the things that are going on with Zinnia,' explained Dilly. 'Zelda can't see why she'd start up now.'

'Funny, me and Lenny were just discussing the same thing. We can't think of another candidate, either. She doesn't really need a reason, that one. She likes being a dog in a manger for its own sake. It gives her a twisted kind of thrill, I suppose.'

We talked about it until we arrived at our stop and then route-marched up a long hill to the town hall. The Yanks had thoughtfully provided a venue right next to a pub, as the town hall itself was not licensed to sell alcoholic beverages and the Mayor had no plans to give it away to a load of foreigners and plebs. So we all piled in there for another pre-dance stiffener.

It was a nice pub with plenty of fancy glass and glowing woodwork. Hitler had managed to miss the place and the splendid town hall next door, which looked as if it had been built around the same time and by the same builder. No expense had been spared in its ballroom. The gorgeous wooden dance floor was properly sprung, so a body could trip the light fantastic for hours before the old feet and legs gave out. Golden cherubs clustered like naughty children around the pillars that held up a kind of gallery, way up near the ceilings. The plump cherubs played their harps, blew long, shapely horns and bowed golden fiddles for eternity, while chandeliers twinkled brightly, reflected in the long mirrors around the walls. It had been many years since anyone in our little party had seen such splendour.

Ronnie gasped as he walked through the huge doors. His hands flew to his mouth and he muttered, 'Fantabulosa, dollies, it's like fairyland.'

'Just the spot for you, then,' Molly laughed.

'Cheeky mare.' Ronnie grinned broadly. 'Just for that, you can ask me to dance.'

'Not on your nelly, iron man. I see a few dozen spare Yanks just yearning for my attention. I'm off to mingle—there's Arty over there. I'll go and thank him for putting some tickets our way. Coming, Beryl?'

Molly and Beryl disappeared into a sea of uniforms and party frocks, which left Ronnie, Lenny and Terry between Dilly, Vi and me, which was handy. We found the cloakroom and dumped our coats with an elderly lady who obviously came with the place. She was flushed with excitement and I guessed it had been a while since the town hall had seen such action. To be honest, I'd *never* seen anything like it. The only dances I'd been to—apart from that one with Charlie—had been held in dingy mess halls or Scouts' huts. The Palais de Dance, where Charlie had taken me, had been nowhere near as posh as this. The Yanks had done themselves, and us, proud.

We'd done several circuits of the dance floor, swapping partners and leaving the others to gossip and keep an eye on our table and handbags, when Ronnie, Dilly, Terry and I found ourselves sitting out a particularly strenuous number at the same time. Vi and Lenny were having a twirl, but if my experience of dancing with Lenny was anything to go by, they'd get back to the safety of their seats in very short order and Vi would be limping.

Ronnie had just asked us all if we fancied some lemonade to cool us down, when Dilly glanced towards the door and turned ashen. With the large, dark stains around her eyes she looked like a pasty panda, and her lipstick made her mouth look like an open wound against the awful pallor. The poor girl was stricken with terror. I thought she was going to faint.

Ronnie moved his chair slightly, so that he blocked her view and made her look at him, eventually. His dear face was deadly serious as he willed her gaze to focus on the new view. 'I take it Chester has arrived,' he said, and all eyes swivelled towards the door. Five men stood there. Several were carrying instruments. The men hesitated, had a swift discussion that we were far too far away to stand any chance of hearing, even if the band on stage hadn't been blaring away, then moved as one body around the outer edges of the packed dance floor until they reached the stage. Dilly's anxious eyes followed the group's every move.

'Which one's Chester?' I hissed—not that the group could possibly have heard me.

'The one standing on the left, a bit by himself. He's holding a trumpet,' Dilly whispered back.

'Dolly,' Ronnie said accusingly, 'you never said he was coloured.'

'I never thought,' answered Dilly, bewildered. 'What's that got to do with anything?'

'It's got everything to do with it,' Ronnie answered. 'That's why he couldn't come to the dance.'

'But he's *at* the dance!' I objected.

'Yes, but he's obviously going to play with his band. He's not here for the dancing,' said Terry, as if that explained everything.

It didn't to me. 'So?' I asked. Poor Dilly seemed to be struck dumb.

Ronnie was patient. 'Coloured soldiers have their own dances, their own pubs, everything. Americans call it "segregation." Haven't you noticed that the white GIs and the coloured blokes don't go to the same places? It's how they run things. The coloured geezers even have their own regiments. It's like down Poona way,' he explained. 'That's in India. You don't get the natives joining the same clubs as the sahibs, now do you?'

'But how are we supposed to know?' I asked reasonably. 'We've never been to Poona, or America. Down the docks, we just all muck in together.' It was true, too. Well, up to a point. Africans and West Indians were exotic to us, so people did tend to stare a bit at first, but they soon got over it if they worked or lived near the docks. Further afield, dark faces were a much rarer event.

'And the Gurkhas have their own regiments as well,' Terry pointed out. 'It's a bit like that with the Yanks. Allocating different watering holes is like having different messes for the officers and the men. Of course, if officers and men want to drink in the same pubs, they do, but I expect they choose different bars, saloon or public, depending.'

'But what's that got to do with Chester coming to the dance with me?' Dilly had come round and was following the discussion.

'How many coloured people do you see here, Dilly?' Terry asked.

Dilly looked around her and shook her head slightly.

'Right, the five waiting to play and they're it. And none of them is with a woman. Don't you see? Chester *couldn't* bring you to the dance—it's not allowed.'

'But why didn't he tell me?' Dilly asked. It seemed a good question to me.

'You'll have to ask him that, dolly. Maybe he was embarrassed and thought if he ignored the whole thing, it'd go away,' Ronnie suggested.

'But he must have known he was going to play here!'

'Not necessarily,' I said. 'Perhaps they were asked at the last minute. You won't know until you talk to him.'

Just then the music stopped and the MC announced, 'Ladies and gentlemen, while the orchestra takes a break, please welcome Chester Field and his GI Jivers.'

There was an outbreak of rapturous applause. Chester stepped up to the front of the stage, and when there was hush said, 'Thank you. We'd like to play a Louis Armstrong number called "Jodie Man."' And they were off.

Chester was every bit as good as Dilly had said he was, and as we settled down to listen and to watch, I could quite see why Dilly had fallen for him. He was gorgeous, exotic *and* gifted. It was certainly a heady mixture when you considered the kind of blokes she was used to—pasty, with bad teeth and about as exotic as suet pudding. Of course, we did have good-looking fellows—Maggie at the cafe in Soho had found herself one—but on the whole, the Americans were better. Most girls thought so, anyway. It was why our men got fed up with them and so many fights broke out between our Tommys and the Yanks when they met on the streets; they became more enemy than ally then.

Having had a good look at Chester, who was tall and slender, with skin the colour and glow of new conkers, I turned my attention to Dilly, who was transfixed, a look of absolute adoration on her face. Then I saw Terry looking at her, with an expression of such resigned sadness that I thought I'd cry.

It was Ronnie who saved the day, grabbing Dilly and yanking her to her feet. 'Time to put the best foot forward, dolly. We'll show them who can cut a rug round here.' And he spun her away into the dancing crowd.

'How're you doing?' I asked Terry.

'I'll survive,' was all he said.

'I certainly hope so.' We watched the dancers as they swayed to the rhythm of Chester's magical trumpet.

Chapter 31

Between them, Ronnie, Lenny and Terry managed to keep Dilly busy on the dance floor for the greater part of Chester's set. I was resting my poor feet for a while as I watched Chester and his band playing their hearts out for the dancers. I thought about what Ronnie and Terry had been trying to tell us about segregation in America and how difficult it must be for some of the people who lived there. After all, Dilly and Chester couldn't be the only mixed couple Americans had ever seen; it must have happened a lot over the years. It stood to reason. You can't have men and women living cheek-by-jowl and not have mingling, I thought. I mean, us and the Yanks mingled ourselves senseless, given half a chance, despite the disapproval of our families and British blokes. In fact, all disapproval did was make the minglers keener. It's human nature, that is.

I must have had a serious look on my face, because when Terry got back to the table he looked at me hard. 'A penny for 'em,' he said.

'I was just thinking…'

'I could see that. You could run trams along the think lines on your forehead. *What* were you thinking?'

'I was being deep, Terry. I was thinking that segregation must be a bit like Prohibition.'

He laughed. 'What's keeping the races separate got to do with banning booze, dare I ask?'

'Well, it's just that it seems to me that the best way to make people do the opposite of what you want them to do, is to forbid them to do something.' I was in a tangle that even I couldn't make sense of. I tried again. 'Prohibition didn't work, did it? People drank like fishes and made their own booze in the bath. And in India, they tried to stop British blokes from taking up with the local girls, but some of them wound up making their own babies, possibly also in the bath, who knows? The point is, there's loads of half-and-half kids dotted around over there and over here to prove it. Right?'

Terry nodded. 'Right. I'm following you so far.'

'Therefore, the best way to make people do what you don't want 'em to do, is to forbid them from doing it. It's human nature. Right?'

'Right. Well, some humans, anyway. Most like rules to follow but you'll always have your renegades, I suppose. But what I don't understand is why you're thinking about it in the first place.'

'Well, if they have segregation like you and Ronnie say, what will happen to our Dilly if she decides she wants to follow him to America? I know she's been hoping he'll ask her. She really wants to be this particular GI's bride, Terry. She really, really does.'

Terry looked at me sadly for a long moment, then said, 'I don't know what will happen to her, Zelda. I expect it'll be difficult for her—for both of them.'

Just then, Ronnie and Dilly twirled to a stop by the table and sat down. 'Can't we just find a corner somewhere?' said Dilly.

'What?' I was bewildered.

'I was talking to Ronnie, silly. He says that Chester and I need to have a serious talk and he was trying to think of how to arrange it and I said—'

Ronnie interrupted her. 'I don't think it'd be wise for you two to be seen together in here. Why don't I arrange for him to meet you outside the cinema we passed down the road? It's not far, but it's not under everyone's noses either.'

Dilly nodded vaguely. The lights may have been on, but there was no-one in. She hadn't taken in a word he'd said. 'I'm just so relieved that he hasn't brought another girl. I really thought he would. I mean,' Dilly turned first to me, then Vi and finally, Beryl, 'wouldn't you snap him up if you thought he was going spare?'

Beryl and I agreed enthusiastically. Vi said she was feeling a bit low and out of sorts and couldn't even think about it. She was missing Fred, of course, which made me feel guilty that I hadn't given Charlie a thought. Poor Vi had been trying hard, though; she'd even danced with Lenny more than once, and that really was heroic. He'd crippled virtually every girl there, and now they hobbled for the woodwork if they spotted him coming up for seconds.

'I don't think you really understand, Dilly,' Terry said gently. 'Some Americans take a very dim view of a coloured chap walking out with a white girl, a very dim view indeed, especially if they come from the Southern parts.'

Dilly grinned. 'I know, but my grandad didn't like it when my Auntie Maude married that Belgian chap, Uncle Emile, but he got over it in the end. And we'll only be talking.'

'Just the same, it'll be better if you talk in private,' insisted Ronnie. 'Believe me, you don't want to be caught at it in here. People have been drinking, and anything could happen. I'll sidle up to him as if I'm going to make a request and I'll tell him to meet you in a bit, outside the Regal. How about that? Have you two got a special tune I can ask for? Intrigues of a romantic nature should have a special tune. It's in the rules, ducky.'

Dilly smiled dreamily. 'He sometimes sings a song to me called "Honeysuckle Rose."'

Ronnie clapped in delight. '"Honeysuckle Rose" it is, then. I'll troll up to the bandstand now and wait for a break in the music. Ooh! I do love to meddle,' he said, and was gone. A few moments later he popped up beside the stage, where he waited politely for a pause before he approached Chester. Mission apparently accomplished, he jitterbugged back to our table with Molly; he'd snapped her up somewhere near the stage, when she'd found herself between dance partners for a fraction of a second. Molly was always a popular girl with the fellows. It had something to do with her sunny nature and impressive cleavage. The good thing was, women liked her too, so we were glad to get her back for a while. We brought her up to speed with Ronnie's plan. She was agog.

'So, that's the famous Chester. Well I never! If ever you get bored with him Dills, you just chuck him my direction, I'll be very happy to help you out.' Molly winked to show she was joking, but I wasn't so sure myself.

Poor Dilly had to wait almost an hour before she could keep her rendezvous with Chester. She was happy and anxious by turns, but in the end, terror won; Ronnie, Terry and I practically had to carry her the hundred yards or so down the hill towards the Regal. It was raining as we tumbled out into the street and I thanked God I wasn't wearing inky shoes and that Terry had thought to bring an umbrella.

The neon lights of the cinema reflected blood red off the wet pavements. White bulbs lit up the posters in their glass-fronted cases. Three marble steps led up to doors flung open on a foyer that glowed invitingly and the box office, which was closed. I checked my watch. The punters would be chucked out soon. I looked at the posters while we waited with Dilly. Humphrey Bogart and Lauren Bacall in *To Have and Have Not*. It was a wonderful picture. I'd been to see it twice already, in the West End and again in Hackney.

When we spied Chester walking towards us, we left Dilly, crossed the road and did our best to fade into the shadows. We didn't want to cramp the man's style.

Back at the town hall, we met Lenny sheltering in the entrance, enjoying a quiet fag and a bit of a breather in the night air. Then we heard a piercing scream. We turned: there was a scuffle outside the cinema. We all hurtled back down the hill, although I was trailing badly in my hand-me-down, over-large but very beautiful shoes. Seeing Ronnie and Lenny arrive at the scene, and haul a couple of GIs off a figure sprawled in the middle of a glowing puddle,

I stopped to take them off, along with my precious stockings. I loved old Dill like a sister, but I had plenty of sisters and only the one pair of intact stockings.

By the time I caught up, Terry was comforting Dilly next to a large picture of my beloved Humphrey and watching the end of a brief but vicious scrap between the two unknown soldiers and Ronnie, Lenny and Chester. The GIs staggered off, one of them clutching his privates and moaning loudly. As Ronnie said later, no sea queen survived for long without being able to grab a pair of balls when the need arose.

Chester swiped at the wet muck on his uniform with his left hand and used the right to shake with Ronnie, Lenny and Terry in turn. He proved to be a man of few words. 'Thanks guys, you were great,' he said.

'Pleasure,' they replied together.

Chester turned to Dilly. 'Are you OK, honey?'

Dilly nodded. I could feel her trembling next to me.

Chester turned back to the men. 'Who are you guys, anyway?'

'Dilly's friends,' I answered for one and all. 'My name's Zelda, by the way, and these here are Ronnie, Lenny and Terry.' There was a long silence as we all tried to think of something else to say. Ronnie saved the day once again.

'Ah good!' he said. 'A rattling cove, the very thing we need.' He stepped out into the road and hailed a passing taxi. 'Get in, you two. It's got to be safer than the streets round here, with all those GIs about.'

Dilly was about to step in, when Terry touched her arm. 'Here's my key,' he said. 'You and Chester can use my place to talk if you like. You won't want to disturb your mum. I'll stay with Lenny or Ronnie.'

Dilly nodded gratefully and took the key.

'Hang about,' I said quickly. 'You can drop me off back at the dance. My feet are killing me. You can collect your coat, Dilly, Chester can pick up his trumpet and the taxi can wait for you round the corner.' I wasn't about to take no for an answer. I had to get Dilly on her own and urge her to be careful. A man and a woman, alone in a flat at night, the world against them: it was asking for trouble, and I didn't want Dilly to run the risk of getting pregnant in the heat of the moment. The poor girl had enough problems as it was.

As soon as we were in the doors of the town hall I dragged her into the Ladies for a heart-to-heart. 'Now listen. I know you're mad for this bloke but you have got to keep your head screwed on, along with your drawers. It's important. Dilly, are you listening?' I sounded like her mum; worse, our old headmistress. 'Just hang on a tick. Don't go anywhere. Promise me. I'll be back.' She nodded. I think she was still in shock from the fight. I rushed outside to the cloakroom lady and begged six large safety pins from her. Minutes later I was back in the Ladies. 'Right, Dill. I want you to safety-pin your drawers to your petticoat. Here you are, here's the pins. I'll give you a hand.'

Dilly just stood there, looking at me as if I'd just escaped from the loony bin. 'Why would I want to do that?' she asked, 'And why *six* safety pins?'

'It's in case he tries anything,' I answered as patiently as I could. There were times, I thought, when Dilly could be a bit dim.

'And...?' She looked confused.

'Well, if he tries something, he'll have to undo the pins to get at the, you know, the important bits. I reckon you could get carried away, on account of you fancying him like mad, but by the time he's undone all six pins, you'll have come to your senses and you'll not want to ruin everything by running the risk,' I explained triumphantly.

It was a good plan. I liked it. I only wished I'd thought of it years before, when I'd gone to that dance with Charlie. Still, better late than never, if it saved old Dill from a fate only marginally better than death. She let me talk her into it—with much tutting and eye-rolling—but at least she'd stopped shivering and trembling and I'd made her laugh. I'd also made sure she wouldn't be caught by surprise. If she did decide to do the deed, well she would have *decided* to, and not been caught on the hop.

'Now remember,' I advised as we got ready to leave the safety of the khazi. 'Take a glass of water. Not before, not after, but instead. And here's a six-penny bit.'

'What's that for?' she asked.

'To clamp between your knees all the time you're alone together.'

She laughed and nudged me playfully in the ribs. 'I mean it, Dilly,' I said seriously. 'Don't get caught like I did. If you and Chester decide to try to make a go of it, have the baby a good nine months after the wedding. It's so much better that way. Then nobody can blame anybody and say they were forced up that aisle. If you must, you know…'—we both blushed furiously; thank God we were alone—'then use a French letter. Promise me.' She gave me a nod and a swift hug, and she was gone in a swish of taffeta and petticoats.

Naturally, all the talk at our table was of the fight, what had caused it and who had done what to who as a consequence. 'Dilly said the two soldiers had come out of the cinema with a couple of local girls,' Terry explained, 'but when the trouble started, the girls disappeared sharpish.'

'Yes, but who started it?' I asked.

'According to Dilly, one of the soldiers passed a remark to Chester, something about if he was at home, he'd find himself—let me remember this right—"swinging from a tree." Then he called Chester "Boy", which, according to Dilly, made Chester see red. The other GI called Dilly some terrible name she won't repeat, and Chester belted him one. Then the first bloke waded in, Dilly screamed, Chester went down and the rest you know.'

'Do you think they'll be all right?' I asked no-one in particular.

'What do you mean—right now or long term?' Ronnie asked.

'Both,' I said.

'Who knows, dolly? Who knows? The best we can hope for is that the dear things have some joy finding out.'

Chapter 32

'Auntie Zelda, Auntie Zelda.'

I heard the voice from far away and it took me several moments to line up behind my eyes. I was groggy, having just got to bed and flaked out. It had been the early hours when I'd finally staggered into the flat, knackered and more than a touch worse for wear. All in all, it had been an eventful night.

The journey home after the dance had been a long one, as transport in London was thin on the ground after midnight. Still, we were in good spirits and Lenny Hobbs had a half-bottle of whisky secreted about his person, which he'd generously shared as we trudged homewards. At some point in the evening he'd managed to win it off a sergeant with more booze than brains. According to the fellas, our Lenny was an ace poker player on account of his looks.

'You think he's a good-natured idiot, just off the farm, a bit of a sheepshagger and with hayseed between his ears, but he ain't,' Charlie told me once. 'He's a conniving cockney bastard who could definitely teach your average Monte Carlo cardsharp a thing or two.'

Lenny himself was modest about his gift. 'You try looking a queue of angry ladies in the eye and informing them they've missed the last of the meat ration this week, when you know for a fact that you've got two chops and half a pound of mince tucked under your counter. But you can't split that into thirty, and you know if you try to choose who deserves to get what's going, the rest'll tear you limb from limb. Bluffing comes easy then, I can tell you. A butcher's life ain't an easy one, what with this rationing lark,' he'd explained after a spectacular win over a cocky midshipman from Glasgow, 'but it can sharpen up your card playing a treat.'

So, what with the excitement, the long walk home, the whisky and all, it was a while before that urgent 'Auntie Zelda, Auntie Zelda' managed to penetrate the fug. I staggered to the flat door and there, huddled on the lino, leaning against the door, with his grubby knees drawn up to his chin, was Reggie.

'Good God! What's the matter?' I asked. 'What are you doing here? What time is it? Does your mum know where you are? Is she all right? The twins? How did you get in the street door? Is everyone all right?'

Poor Reggie did his best with the barrage of questions. 'I need to talk to you,' he gasped. 'It's about four o'clock I think, and no, I hope not, I hope she thinks I'm safely asleep in bed, and I wish I was, and Mum and the girls were all right last time I saw them. And getting in was easy, the door wasn't shut properly.' He spoke in a rush, between teeth I could have sworn were chattering, despite the warmth of the night and him having his pullover on. 'Can I come in?'

I stepped aside and my nephew got to his feet, headed for the kitchen and sat down again. I followed.

'Is everyone all right?' I asked again, groggily realizing it was the only one of my questions he hadn't answered. I put the kettle on. 'Do you fancy a cup of Ovaltine?' It was Reggie's favourite, and even in my state I could see he could do with a drop of comfort, poor lamb.

'Yes, everyone's OK, except...' He paused. 'I'd love a cup of Ovaltine, thanks.'

'Except what?' I asked. 'Do spit it out, whatever it is, there's a good boy. Your Auntie Zelda's not at her best after a night on the tiles and less than an hour's sleep under her eyelids. I could get tetchy fast if you keep me from my kip without a decent reason.'

At this point, he burst into tears and I snapped to attention. Big strong boys of twelve did not blub, and neither, in my experience, did this skinny, asthmatic, shortsighted one, not unless things were serious.

I put my arm around his heaving, bony shoulders and muttered such helpful things as, 'There, there'—whatever that's supposed to mean—and 'Oh sweetheart, whatever is the matter? Get it off your chest. I'm sure we can sort it out.' I was lying through my teeth, though, as it depended entirely on what the problem was.

'It's Tony,' he said at last, which was when my rattle finally flew out of my pram.

'I might have bloody known!' I shouted, surprising us both. Reggie jumped, slopping some precious Ovaltine on to his grey flannel shorts, and I calmed down. After all, it wasn't Reggie's fault that his cousin was such a liability. 'I'm sorry, petal. I know I shouldn't shout at you, you've done nothing wrong. But there are times when I think your grandad's got a point about Tony. What's the matter with the little toe-rag now?' I sighed.

'I think he's in bad trouble, Auntie,' he answered, then the rest came out in a rush. 'I was stopping over at Granny Ida's and Auntie Vi's with Tony and we was sound asleep when we heard someone tapping at the window. It was Bung'ole. He told Tony to get dressed and come along with him because he had something to show him. Tony didn't want to go, he kept arguing, but Brian wouldn't have it, just kept saying he had to come, over and over again.

'I was going to say something, but Tony kicked me to shut me up. Bung'ole couldn't see me and Tony didn't want him to know I was there. In the end, Tony got dressed and climbed out of the window and went with Brian.'

'How long ago was this?' I asked sharply, as I nipped into the bedroom to throw on some street clothes and shoes.

'An hour, almost,' Reggie answered. He was in tears again, I could tell by the catch in his voice.

'So what happened next?' I shouted from the wardrobe as I groped for a respectable skirt at the back. 'Did you go and get your grandad?'

'I didn't like to, not until I knew what was going on. I mean, you know how Grandad g-gets,' Reggie stammered, 'so I followed them.'

'You did *what?*' I shouted, head clear of clothes and mothballs at last, and a skirt clutched in my hand. 'So we've got three bad lads on the streets in the early hours? Well, two bad lads and one daft one,' I amended, in the interests of fairness.

'I only wanted to see what was happening before I got anybody out of bed.' He sounded sheepish.

'All right. Two bad lads and a brave and thoughtful one then. I'm sorry, Reggie, I'm tired and a bit squiffy. Well, you'd better tell me everything.' My panic was fast being replaced by a bad case of the hump. For Reggie's sake, I was trying hard to control it, but it wasn't easy.

'I came here 'cause I hoped you'd still be awake, after the dance,' he explained. 'Anyway, I followed them to Ma's shed on the allotments.'

'What on earth were they doing there in the dead of night? Gardening?'

Reggie rolled his eyes at me. 'No, not gardening, Auntie.' He sounded a little world-weary I thought, but then he was a weedy kid and it was way past both our bedtimes. 'If you let me finish, I'll tell you, won't I?'

'Yes, Reggie,' I said meekly.

'Brian does the allotment for his mum, right?' I nodded and he carried on. 'Well, he uses the shed as a sort of den, when he wants to get away from Ma.'

It made sense. Brian wouldn't be the first bloke to dive into his shed to get away from his womenfolk, or the last. 'So, you followed Tony and Brian to the shed...' I prompted. I was getting interested, despite myself.

'Yes,' he said, eyes growing enormous and his skin pale under the merciless, yellow glow of the electric light. He took a deep breath and began to stammer again. 'Th-they went in and I sort of hung about outside. They didn't b-bother to close the door, so I could hear everything.' He stopped abruptly and I waited, knowing that I had to let the boy get to it at his own pace. If I pushed him, his tongue'd get tied, his stammer would get worse and he'd be embarrassed.

'Auntie Zelda, Brian showed Tony a gun. I saw it. It was a real gun, Auntie! He's got ammo for it and everything, he showed Tony the box, I saw him. He said he got it off some bloke who works down the docks. Swapped it for some of the petrol he's been swiping lately.'

'What kind of gun?' I asked, stupidly, as if it mattered. Any sort of gun in the hands of the Holes was too awful to contemplate.

'He said it was a Luger.'

I nodded. Even I'd heard of them. It had obviously been taken off some German and brought back to Blighty as a souvenir. There were a lot of them about, and of course boys were naturally drawn to anything to do with war and weapons. They were always picking up bits of shrapnel for their collections. Anything German was highly prized and was swapped or sold for quite high prices. Every boy had a collection. So it was no surprise at all that Brian had managed to get hold of a gun, when I came to think about it. What made it really frightening was that he had the bullets to go with it.

Reggie broke into my thoughts. 'That's not all. He had a hand grenade as well.'

'A *hand grenade*!? What the…'

Reggie nodded. 'A live one, he said. He said he was going to get some more. His mate down the docks had a whole crate, he said. That's what he wanted Tony for,' he explained miserably. I thought he was going to cry again. 'He wants T-Tony to nick the Vicar's keys. He says he can swap the church candlesticks and that socking great silver plate for more grenades.'

'What the hell does Brian Hole want with hand grenades?' I'd no sooner asked it than I realized it was another silly question. He didn't necessarily want them *for* anything, he just wanted to possess them. At least, I hoped that was all he wanted. The thought of Brian Hole and Ma's 'boys' let loose with guns and hand grenades made every drop of blood an icicle. Bloody hell! 'What's Ma Hole planning now?' I wondered out loud.

'Nothink,' Reggie answered. 'At least, I don't think so. B-Brian threatened to give Tony a seeing-to if he mentioned it to anyone, 'specially Ma.'

So Brian was branching out, eh? Going solo, doing things that Ma knew nothing about? And his headquarters was their tool shed, the one place he was pretty sure Ma wasn't likely to disturb, because she made him do all the work on the allotment.

The thought of young Brian going into business for himself was a scary one. He wasn't the brightest spark in the tinderbox, let's face it. Ma discouraged thinking in others, as she preferred to do it for them, so Brian had never really developed the aptitude for thinking before he acted. Blundering about like an idiot was one thing; blundering about like an idiot armed to the teeth was quite another. I would have to do something, but I was blowed if my brain could wake up enough—or throw off the whisky enough—to work out what.

'You're a good boy, Reggie,' I said at last, 'and brave with it. What you've told me is very bad, as you know, but right now I'm too tired to think straight. We'll walk you round to Tony's and get you to bed again and I'll see you in the morning, after church. I'll be able to see things clearer then, with luck.'

'What if Tony's back in bed and wonders where I've been?' Reggie sounded scared.

'That's up to you, petal. You can lie like mad, if you can think of something he'd believe, or you can tell him the truth. The truth would be better, in my opinion, since lying would just make things more complicated, but you're the one who'll be on the spot.'

I walked Reggie back to the gardens and saw him slip safely through the basement window. He gave me the thumbs up, which I took to mean that the coast was clear and he had no explaining to do to Tony—which must have been a relief to him.

On my way back to my place, I noticed the light was on in Terry's flat above the shop. Dilly and Chester were still up, then. It really had been one hell of a night, one way and another. What was more, I had a strong feeling that Sunday would be a similar kind of day.

Why was life never simple? I wondered, as I sank back into my bed, fully clothed, even down to my shoes.

Chapter 33

'All things bright and beautiful,
All creatures great and small,
All things wise and wonderful,
The Lord God made them all.'

Tony's voice soared up to the rafters. His singing was as clear and as pure as Granny Smallbone's crystal wedding beads and he looked as innocent as a newborn chick, only not as fuzzy and yellow. Funny how deceptive appearances could be, I thought bitterly, as I listened. Tony was neither wise nor wonderful; I wondered if that made him the Devil's spawn instead? I wouldn't have been at all surprised that morning, I can tell you.

It seemed to me that I had only just closed my sore, prickly and exhausted eyes when I was called upon to prise them open again. Actually, it was the crack of eight, according to the clock. I'd had about three and a bit hours of kip, which was roughly four hours too few. My mouth felt as if someone had dumped a load of sand in it and my eyeballs felt pretty much the same, only hot with it. My arms and legs felt like lead. I sat up carefully and my head throbbed.

I was trying to work out what had woken me when I heard it again: knocking and wailing cries of 'Zelda, Zelda, open up—pleeease.' I crept painfully to the flat door, tottered down the stairs very gently and opened the street door to the blinding glare of daylight. All I could see was a figure in front of me;

whether it was male or female was a mystery. I couldn't make out any features.

'Come in,' I croaked and made my way slowly back up the stairs and across the kitchen to the kettle. I wasn't prepared, or indeed fit, to deal with anything until I poured tea on to my parched tonsils, and that was final. In fact, I was buggered if I'd even open my eyes until the first sip.

'Make the tea,' I ordered my visitor, as I sank into a chair and rested my head in my arms on the table.

I only came round again when I heard the chink of spoon on cup and the rattle of cup on a saucer a few inches from my left ear. 'Ta,' I whispered and took my first sip. Then, and only then, did I open my eyes. It was Vi, looking a little the worse for wear herself, but scrubbed up ready for church.

'I thought we could stroll to church together,' she said. 'I've had a chat with Reggie,' she added.

Ah! That explained her arrival at my door. I started to nod, then stopped abruptly in case my head fell off. I faintly remembered I had promised to meet Reggie after church, so getting there was the first order of my day. I tottered back to the bedroom for clean clothes, took off the ones I'd slept in, slipped on my dressing gown and returned to the kitchen sink to wash and clean my furry teeth.

I put my fresh, clean Sunday best on slowly. I felt like death warmed up, twice. Vi didn't say much, she seemed to be miles away. Her eyes had that glazed and inward look that could either be a deep, brown study or a hangover. I squinted at her a bit more closely; it looked like a bit of both. I knew the feeling all too well that sunny, Sunday morning.

Despite everything, we presented ourselves at church, ship-shape and Bristol fashion, on time and ready to sing and pray our hearts out. All the while I wondered how much Vi knew. I didn't want to put my foot in it by telling her too much before I had my wits about me. They'd been missing so far that morning, so I'd kept my mouth more or less shut, in the hope they'd come back before I had to talk to anyone, particularly Vi.

'Each little flower that opens,
Each little bird that sings…'

I took several deep, slow breaths and wished Zinnia was next to me with useful advice, but she wasn't. Some Sundays she travelled a considerable way to go to her own church, a 'watered-down' version of the Wee Free faith of her childhood. She didn't usually get back until around teatime or even later, Sunday transport being what it was.

To be absolutely honest, I wasn't at all sure I believed in God. I mean, if there was a God, why would He allow Hitler to be let loose on the world? Frankly, that 'free will' stuff seemed a handy get-out to me, very handy. For God, it would have been a simple matter to make sure Adolf had never been born—and He hadn't done it. Only He knew how many people had suffered and died because He hadn't made either Mrs. Hitler or Mr. Hitler senior sterile. It would have taken a matter of moments, one tiny adjustment at the planning stage, and Mr. Hitler could have been shooting blanks and that would have been the end of it. It beggared belief that any god worth his salt would have allowed Hitler to happen.

But I did like church. I liked the ritual. I liked the way the Reverend Cattermole's wayward hair was illuminated by the stained-glass windows on a sunny day. Sometimes when clouds passed by his barnet flashed on and off like neon, and with about as many colours. Blue was the Virgin's robe, red was one of the Apostles and yellow was the brilliant desert sun of the Holy Land shining down on Jesus.

Then Mrs. Cattermole would start thundering away on her organ, her back ramrod straight. The fruit, feathers or whole stuffed birds on her hat of the day would tremble and shake as she hit a note, yanked out a stop or pounded her plump little feet on the pedals. Mrs. Cattermole played the instrument with her entire body and soul, and you couldn't say fairer than that. Every now and then she'd turn her head and flash an enormous, white, porcelain grin at the congregation, like the organist on the

Mighty Wurlitzer at the pictures. Sometimes it was hard not to burst into rapturous applause at the end of a hymn—she seemed to expect it, and she certainly deserved it—but we sat on our hands. Clapping and God did not seem to mix, somehow.

The music and singing were always good at St Mary's—ever since the Cattermoles had taken over, anyway. Their enthusiasm spread to the choir and the congregation. We often found ourselves singing our way through the war, particularly when times were very hard; the singing got louder, somehow, and so did Mrs. Cattermole's organ. When the docks were copping it and you couldn't hear yourself think above the racket of aircraft and bombs and the ack-ack guns chattering incessantly, noisily but, in the end, uselessly over everything, we'd be down in the crypt, belting out 'Rock of Ages' for all we were worth and drowning it all out. It helped. It helped a lot.

Halfway through Mrs. Cattermole's 'winding-up piece'—she always played the same piece of Bach at the end of the service—the Vicar would come down from his pulpit and walk up the aisle to the great, oak, nail-studded doors. He and a few helpers would sling the doors open on whatever the English weather and London air could throw at us, and he'd stand beneath the porch smiling, shaking hands and exchanging a few words with his parishioners as we filed past. I loved it all. It was a comfort in its regularity and its sameness, week in, week out. The Vicar and Mrs. Cattermole were its musical centre, its beating heart, and I loved them too.

Without prior discussion, Vi and I tracked Tony down straight after the service. It wasn't hard. He was waiting in the churchyard and Reggie was with him. 'You two are going to help us water the beans,' I said. It was the only excuse I could think of for getting away from the rest of the family for a private chat. I still didn't know exactly what Vi knew, but judging by her grim expression, it was more than enough.

Tony was taking a deep interest in his boots on the way to the allotments and barely looked up in case he caught anyone's eye. We didn't speak at all until we felt the grass under our feet and knew we were out of earshot of everyone. That was the good thing about the allotments. There were few places to lurk and listen; you could see people coming long before they got within earshot, and shut up if necessary.

'So, what have you got to say for yourself?' Vi asked Tony, arms folded across her chest. 'And don't trouble to lie. Reggie had to tell me everything when I caught him creeping about in the early hours.'

To my utter astonishment, Tony burst into tears. Two sobbing nephews in one day—it had to be some kind of record. Nothing could have disarmed me more, except the sight of Vi putting her arms around her son and muttering, 'There, there,' into his thick, dark hair as she patted his back tenderly. Her fury had subsided and, I was surprised to discover, so had mine. 'There, there,' she murmured over and over until he hiccuped to a stop at last and was able to talk. He told us the same story as Reggie.

Apparently, Brian had told Tony that if he grassed him up to anybody, then he would make sure Tony went down with him. Tony had been involved in Brian's petrol thefts, he was involved in the warehouse robbery and there had been a good few other thefts along the way, a lot of them very recently. It was mainly small stuff, but it accumulated, and a stint in Borstal seemed certain if all of Tony's crimes were to catch up with him. On the other hand, he certainly didn't want to have anything to do with guns, hand grenades or nicking the church silver, which seemed to be the alternative.

'I don't want to do it, Mum, Auntie Zelda.' He sniffed hard. 'I don't want to do anything that will get the Rev. in trouble. He's my friend,' he wailed. I have to say, I was proud of the boy.

'You know,' said Vi, 'Borstal would be the death of Dad. He'd never get over the shame.' What surprised me was that she seemed to think she could, by the sound of things. She was right, though. Dad wouldn't see a stint in Borstal as anywhere near punishment enough for bringing shame on our spotless family. Mum and Gran would be more sorrowful than angry, and somehow, that would be worse than all the ranting Dad was likely to do. But being banged up was on the cards for Tony unless we could think of a plan.

In the end, we agreed on a plan that was no plan at all really. Tony should have nothing to do with Brian's schemes. He was to make himself as hard to get hold of as was humanly possible, to delay things while his mother and I thought some more. We needed to find a way to protect Tony from Brian, keep the church silver safe and keep Tony out of the hands of Lily Law. Nothing to it—and the band played 'Believe It If You Like,' I thought, but didn't say.

I was really surprised at how calm Vi had been throughout Tony's confession. Apart from the remark about Dad not surviving the shame of Borstal, she'd come out firmly on her son's side. There had been no weeping and wailing, no gnashing of teeth, just the simple desire to get her boy out of the terrible spot he found himself in.

It was Reggie who came up with the first concrete thing to be done. 'We've got to warn the Vicar,' he said quietly. 'Bung'ole's armed and he's after the church silver.'

Then Vi surprised me once more by coming up with an idea. 'We'll stop by Brian's shed and take the gun. That's where he keeps it, isn't it Tony?' He nodded. 'Well then, we're right here'—she looked around—'and there's no-one else about. I say we take the gun, then he can't hurt anyone with it.'

It was a good idea, but when we broke into the shed, with the help of a screwdriver taken from ours, there was no sign of any gun, hand grenade or box of bullets, just a strong smell of petrol.

'Where is it?' I hissed at Tony, who looked bewildered.

He shrugged and shook his head. 'I dunno, Auntie. Maybe he's taken it to show the other lads. I mean, not everyone's got a proper German Luger and the ammo to go with it, let alone a real live grenade.' Tony sounded awed, despite his fears. 'P'raps he wants to show them off.'

It made a half-witted kind of sense. Most villains would want to keep their personal arsenal quiet, but Brian didn't have the brains. By dinnertime, he'd probably have waved his grenade under a dozen youthful and envious noses, and then wonder why the whole neighbourhood knew all about it by teatime.

The fumes in the shed were beginning to give me a headache and I thought it best to beat a hasty retreat. Tony seemed to take ages to screw back the hasp, complete with an untouched padlock, but when he'd finished, you wouldn't have known we'd been there. Time was pressing. If Dad wasn't to have his suspicions and his temper raised, Tony had to be at the eleven o'clock service to sing again. We trudged back to church with Tony, not saying much. Nobody had mentioned it, but it had been silently agreed that he wouldn't be left alone for a single, solitary second that day, as the close company of witnesses was the best way to keep Brian at bay.

At the churchyard gate Reggie turned to go home to his mum and sisters, while Vi and I made our way to Paradise Gardens and what we hoped would be the relative quiet of Granny's basement. We should have known better.

Gran and Mum had arrived ahead of us, and were swigging tea before they went upstairs to get the dinner on. Gran eyed us shrewdly as we came in. 'Wotcha, gels,' she said. 'Who nicked your sixpence and gave you back a farthing?' We shrugged and tried to look carefree.

'Don't come that butter wouldn't melt lark with me. You two are keeping secrets. You've been like it all your lives: the minute you've got a secret you want to keep, you look as if you've swallowed the damned thing and you're about to burst at the seams with it. What's worrying you now? Something happen at the dance, did it?'

Vi and I looked at each other, then at Gran and Mum. We realized there was no point in not blurting it out, because they would find out sooner or later anyway. The Secret Service had nothing on them for information gathering. We told them everything we knew without the application of a single thumbscrew or electric shock.

Gran was firm. Reggie was right, we had to tell the Reverend Cattermole, and the sooner the better. 'Better still,' she said, 'Tony should tell him. The boy's got to take responsibility some time, and now's the time.'

Mum agreed. 'She's right, Vi. The Vicar must be told, the boy owes it to him.' For a moment, Vi looked as if she was going to argue but she gave it up the second she saw that there was no other way.

Gran looked closely at Vi, noting the lack of sopping hanky and wet cheeks. 'What's got into you, Vi? Why ain't you making more of a fuss? You've made enough racket over all his other pranks; how come you're so quiet and reasonable now it's serious?'

It was a good question. I'd been wondering that myself. After all, she had stood by and let Dad take charge of disciplining Tony ever since Fred had left. Why was she taking an interest all of a sudden?

Vi blushed. 'I s'pose I realize I've got to take charge. Make some kind of fist of bringing Tony up, now his dad's gone.' So that was it. Vi had finally accepted that she was a widowed mother with a job to do. 'I mean, we've done it Dad's way and it's not been working, has it? I reckon Zelda has the right idea, give him something else to think about. Anyway, he needs me.' Her voice was so quiet, I had to strain to hear her.

Gran didn't trouble, she simply grumbled, 'Speak up, gel! You know I'm getting a bit mutton in me old age.'

'I said, he needs me to stick by him,' Vi said, a bit louder. 'He needs to know that he's my boy, no matter what.'

There was a long, long silence as we three took in the full meaning of Vi's words. In the end, it was Gran's hanky that came out, and her cheeks were suspiciously damp. She had a good blow and, feeling better, became brisk.

'Right then, we're agreed. We'll keep our lips buttoned around Harry. Tony's not left alone for a minute until the Brian Hole business is sorted out. It's probably best if he kips somewhere different for the time being, in case there's any more midnight callers. He could sleep upstairs. We'll say we want his room decorated. It's time it had a good bottoming out anyway, there's probably *things* living under that bed.' She shuddered, then continued. 'Let's try and think of a plan, you lot. We can only hold the day of reckoning back. We can't keep it away for ever.'

It was my turn to shudder. While we were dithering, there was an armed idiot running loose in the neighbourhood.

Chapter 34

It was after Evensong by the time Vi, Tony and I were able to meet at the vicarage to see Reverend Cattermole. Mrs. Cattermole showed no surprise at all at seeing us on her doorstep at such an unusual hour.

'As the wife of a vicar,' she said, 'one must get used to irregular hours and a steady stream of callers. One would miss the excitement if one kept regular hours and the stream was dammed, so to speak. Come in. Come in, do.

'I'm afraid the Vicar has a young couple with him at the moment, but they shouldn't be long, they're just booking a christening. Do take a seat.' Mrs. Cattermole waved a large, capable-looking hand at some shabby chairs in the parlour.

The parlour was a homely room in a huge, draughty house originally built in the young Queen Victoria's day for a large family plus servants. The Vicar and his wife rattled around in the place, so most of the vicarage, I knew for a fact, was kept closed up and shrouded in dust sheets. They had chosen some of the smaller rooms as their own because they took less coal to heat in winter and less furniture to make them comfortable.

It was easy to imagine the Vicar and his wife enjoying quiet winter evenings in front of the parlour fire, her tinkling on her piano and him reading his Bible. Although, of course, it was rarely like that. As she said, theirs was a busy house with people tramping in at all hours for all sorts of reasons. It wasn't at all unusual to find Mrs. Cattermole sorting out a squabble between local ladies regarding the church cleaning rota in one room and the Vicar comforting the bereaved and arranging a funeral in another, while a small, orderly queue formed in the hallway. It was a stroke of good luck that we were the only ones waiting that evening.

Apparently, it hadn't been difficult for Vi to persuade Tony to tell all to the Vicar. 'I'd sort of rolled me sleeves up, in my mind like, ready to do battle with him,' explained Vi, 'and all he said was, "OK, Mum." He came as quiet as a lamb.'

'I knew there was no point in arguing, Auntie Zelda,' Tony piped up, 'with Mum, you, Gran and Granny Ida lined up against me. Let's face it, 'Itler would've won if he'd had you lot on his side, no question—and he wouldn't have needed no tanks neither.' Even when he was up to his ears in muck and bullets, my nephew could still find the neck to be a cheeky little sod.

'Would you care for some tea?' asked Mrs. Cattermole. Normally we would have jumped at it, but we turned it down; we were too fidgety with nerves to enjoy it. Poor Mrs. Cattermole tried to chat with us while we waited, but the jitters robbed us of small talk. In desperation, she turned to Tony and asked him about his singing lessons with Digby Burlap, but he didn't have much to say for himself, either. I expect he was too busy trying to stop his knees from knocking.

At last, the door to the Vicar's study creaked open and we heard his voice in the hallway. 'Good night to you then, good night.' The front door opened and closed. Mrs. Cattermole waited until we heard the Vicar's returning step on the hall tiles, then slipped out of the room. We heard the Vicar say, 'Really? Then send them in, dear, and perhaps some tea?'

We filed into the Vicar's study to be beamed at by an apparently delighted Reverend Cattermole. It showed the measure of the man. Sunday was his busiest day, he was at the church early and was kept hard at it, praying, preaching, singing and greeting all day, mostly on his feet; then, when he could reasonably expect to put his feet up with the lady wife and the wireless, an endless succession of callers banged on his door wanting his attention. And still he could beam at us as if we were just the people he wanted to see. And what's more, Mrs. Cattermole made the tea cheerfully. We could distinctly hear her singing along with her kettle.

We chatted about the morning service, then the weather. We had just got on to the continuing shortages, when the drinks arrived, along with a small glass of milk for Tony. Finally, the door closed once again behind Mrs. Cattermole's broad backside and Vi got straight to the point; the agony had been prolonged long enough.

'Tony's got something to tell you, Vicar.' She nodded to her son, who stood, his head bowed down so meekly that I'd have sworn he was taking the mickey, if it hadn't been for the knuckles of his tightly clasped hands gleaming white and sharp in the gloom.

It took a while, but at last Tony came to the end of his long and sorry tale. The Vicar had listened hard, kept his gaze on Tony and hadn't interrupted once, although Vi and I did, several times. Finally, when we'd all dried up, the Vicar said, 'I see,' in a thoughtful kind of a way. 'It must have been a very difficult thing for you to do, to own up as you have done, Tony, very difficult indeed. One must give credit where it is due; it took some considerable bravery, dear boy. You're a good chap at heart, I've always said so.

'Now, our three most pressing problems, as I see it'—it was such a relief to hear the 'our' in those words, as it meant the good Vicar was on Tony's side, and he could certainly do with him—'are first, to disarm that poor, misguided youth before he hurts someone, or himself. Secondly, we must secure the church silver until the threat to it is past. And last, but by no means least, we must ensure that Tony comes to no harm. It's a thorny thicket, there's no doubt about that, and we must think hard before we act—but act we must. The situation cannot be left as it is.' These were the family's thoughts entirely, to a woman, but not necessarily in that order or in quite those words.

'I think we can tell Lily L— er, the police about Brian being armed,' I suggested. 'He'll have shown his gun to so many people, anyone could've blabbed, it needn't be our Tony. 'Specially if we make sure the law doesn't associate Tony with the telling.'

I'd been thinking it through all day. There was no doubt in my mind that Tony wasn't the only boy Brian had shown off to, so if it was handled right, he might never suspect Tony of grassing, or at least never know for sure—which just might keep Tony out of the hospital. It didn't do to get a reputation as a grass around our way, unless of course you were a man of the cloth; then you'd probably get away with it, as long as you heard it as something you might call gossip and not a sacred confession. People expected that sort of righteousness from the clergy and didn't need to punish it, forgive it or overlook it. But if I ran to the law, it would be a very different matter.

As it happened, Reverend Cattermole was way ahead of me. 'That's not difficult, Zelda,' he assured me. 'I'll simply say that I have heard about the weapons from reliable sources that I am unwilling to name. I may not be a Catholic priest, but I do believe that George Grubb and, more importantly, his superiors, will respect the dog collar and allow me to have my way in this matter. It won't be the first time that I have felt it my duty to help the police with their inquiries, while protecting my sources. In the end, it works well for all parties concerned. Nobody will want to upset the status quo on this occasion. If I were a betting man, I'd place a modest wager on it.'

It was a massive relief. It got Vi, Tony and me off of that particular hook at least. That left protecting Tony and the silver; and the Vicar, bless him, had an answer for those knotty problems too.

'As to the silver, we'll pop it into the bank's safe until we're sure it's, er, *safe*. I'm sure the manager will oblige. He's a sound fellow, worships with us. And young Tony here; well, he did offer to help with repairs to the vicarage and the church in return for piano lessons. Perhaps it would facilitate matters if he stayed with us here at the vicarage for a while. Nobody will think to root him out in the dead of night and I doubt he'll have dubious callers even when they find out where he is. Which, of course, will be impossible to keep quiet after a few days, possibly a week or so if we're careful. You know how news travels. But at least there is a plausible reason for it. Even if Brian himself has his doubts, the rest of the neighbourhood will be happy enough. There is, after all, plenty of work to be done and you, young man, have much atoning to do.'

I could tell from his face that Tony didn't fancy the idea much, but then he probably didn't know what 'atoning' was. Vi and I did, though, and we agreed with the man wholeheartedly. It would also give Tony a place of safety, at least for a while, so the Vicar's idea was carried by a majority vote. We almost skipped home, the relief of having warned the Vicar was so great. The only thing we had to worry about now was how to keep Tony out of the hands of the law and well away from Borstal. That, and the rest of life's little wrinkles, of course.

That night, towards dawn, I had one of my dreams. All I can remember was a noose swinging gently in a dream breeze. I couldn't work out who it was for—Chester, Tony or Brian. I don't think it was a premonition, though. It was just that there'd simply been too much talk of hanging. At least, I hoped so.

Chapter 35

What with one thing and another, I took a while to notice that Mrs. Dunmore was in a filthy mood on the Monday morning. She hardly penetrated at all at first. Cook and Beryl were fed up, I could see that, but I just kept my head down, got on with the work and worried instead about Tony, not to mention Dilly and Chester, Zinnia's problems and, last but by no means least, Charlie. All my nearest and dearest seemed to be up to their eyebrows in it, and so was I; it seemed reasonable that Mrs. Dunmore came last in that particular field of runners, as far as I was concerned. Let her grumble, moan and find fault, I had other things on my mind. Life had seemed so much simpler, somehow, when all we had to worry about was survival; praying we'd dodge the next bomb, find a shilling for the gas and make a meal for two out of a minute lump of grey, unidentifiable fish, half a teaspoon of elderly Bisto and a dribble of Camp Coffee.

Mrs. Dunmore worked up a minor frenzy over the state of the gas oven, and I switched jobs from scrubbing tables to scrubbing cookers. All the while, I tried to reason myself out of my anxieties. Tony would either get out of trouble or not; only time would tell. The situation wasn't likely to sort itself on a Monday morning while I was slaving away, fighting grease armed only with a rag, scrubbing brush, soda and tepid water. So I should shove it to the back of my mind until I was in a position to do something—anything.

The same went for Dilly and Chester. Either they'd worked something out or they hadn't, but I wasn't going to find out about it while I was on my knees with my head in the oven. I would find out what had happened between them that night after work, and not a second before. I'd invited Dilly to my place for tea and I'd deliberately not asked Chester, so that we could have a proper chat between friends.

It was possible that she'd bring him anyway, love being what it is and parting being so painful, even for a few hours, but I hoped not. Men are a distraction when women want to talk. They always seem to want a cup of tea, a sandwich or to give us the benefit of their opinions. Either that, or the women are distracted, feeling it necessary to flirt if the men are single, even when they don't particularly fancy them.

So when Terry and Ronnie had angled to be invited as well, I was downright rude: 'Not on your nellies, gents. If she does bring Chester along, which I doubt, I want to get a good look at him without you two puffing your chests out and showing off. You blokes can't help it when there's a Yank about. And if he doesn't come, I want Dilly to myself, so that I get the inside story—which I won't get with you breathing down her neck, and demanding cups of tea while you're at it.' I brooked no argument. All their wheedling on the tube ride home from the dance had cut no ice with me.

The strange goings-on around Zinnia seemed to have come to an abrupt halt. The attacks had come out of nowhere and disappeared in the same direction. Of course, it was too early to breathe easy, but the fact remained, there had been nothing sinister for some days. Her cats seemed to be on the mend. Hepzibah was back to her normal sleek and glossy, tabby self, and Hallelujah had survived his stint in the oven. In fact, the warmth and quiet had brought him round a treat, as Zinnia had predicted. Although he limped very slightly, his wound was healing nicely. Zinnia reckoned the limp would go eventually.

Zinnia herself gave me more to worry about. She was unusually quiet and reflective and she'd made one or two mysterious journeys that she wouldn't discuss beyond saying that she was 'making provision for my future, hen.' Which alarmed me a bit, because I always thought her future would be pretty much like her present and her past thirty years; in other words, living and working in and around Paradise Gardens. But she wouldn't be drawn, just kept saying that when the time was right and some decisions had been made, she'd let me know what she planned. Zinnia was harder to crack than a Bank of Scotland vault, so I had to be content to wait and see.

That left Charlie. Once again, there was nothing to be done there and then but to carry on. I was trying to save some of my meagre wages, but it wasn't easy, what with my contribution to Tony's lessons every week and the fares to and from Soho to fork out. I often blew a few bob at the cafe as well, which wouldn't have been necessary if I'd taken sandwiches. But I enjoyed my trips to the cafe—they were my treat for the week—so my savings usually suffered. A few pennies would go in, only to come out again almost immediately. I suppose it would have helped if I knew what I was trying to save up for, but I didn't know; I just had the feeling it would be a good idea, 'against the day.' Against what day, I was blowed if I knew.

It was all so frustrating. I was stuck. I couldn't act. All I could do was fret and mark time by scrubbing the bloody gas cooker with Mrs. Dunmore's shrill voice nagging annoyingly in the background. I hated 'waiting and seeing' more than almost anything. I was a doer, not a waiter, and I was in the starting block, ready to dash off in four different directions at least. On and on I scrubbed. When Mrs. Dunmore finally left the room, Cook and Beryl started to grumble. Come the end of the day, it was all I could do not to scream.

I broke the land speed record getting ready to get off work that night, and was just at the door when Mrs. Dunmore asked, 'Where do you think you're going?'

'Home,' I said shortly, as if it was any of her business.

She took me by the elbow, led me away from the back door and blessed freedom and into the doorway of her office. She pointed at her desk. When I looked baffled, she said, 'Those crocks need clearing, washing up and putting away.'

Something snapped. I almost heard the 'ping' in my head, like knicker elastic giving way under too much stretching. 'Then clear them, wash them and put them away, you lazy, useless, good-for-nothing cow,' I said in ever such a reasonable voice. 'Me, I'm going home.' And I went, leaving her with her mouth open in disbelief.

I raced home that night, fuelled by fury, fear of what might happen to me at work the next day and an aching need to find out what had happened with Dilly and how Tony was doing. Dilly was on the doorstep as I panted to a stop, fumbled with my keys and explained why I was late.

'You never!' Dilly gasped as I finished my tale of woe.

'I did!' I answered, half defiant, half terrified.

'What'll you do if she gives you the order of the boot and with no references?' she asked, eyes wide.

It was an awful thought that I had been trying hard not to think all the way home. 'I dunno,' I admitted. 'I thought I'd cross that bridge when I got to it—or p'raps I could borrow some wellies,' I added hopefully. 'Let's not dwell, Dill. It'll do no good. I just have to wait and see, I suppose.

'Now tell me,' I begged as I put the kettle on, 'what happened with you and Chester?'

'Well,' she blushed, 'we got to Terry's and I made a cup of tea…'

'Dilly!' I yelled. 'Spare me the boring details. Move straight to the sordid ones.'

Dilly's blush deepened to beetroot and she laughed, slightly hysterically. 'I'll tell it in my own way, Zelda,' she huffed, 'or not at all.'

I rolled my eyes and sighed. 'All right, if you must. The boring details, if you please.'

She was all dreamy. 'It's not boring to me. It felt like being married. He's got a nice place, Terry has, cosy.' It seemed that they kicked off by getting Chester's uniform washed, dried and ironed, if you can believe it. I was staggered. Couldn't they think of anything *better* to do? Naturally, they didn't get the whole process done at once. Dilly washed his shirt and trousers and Chester made do with Terry's dressing gown while they waited for them to dry, and they talked while they waited. They'd talked for ages apparently, about how they felt about each other, which seemed remarkable to me. After all, when you boiled it all down, he felt 'crazy' about her and couldn't get her out of his mind. And Dilly was 'mad' about him and couldn't get him out of her mind, either. So why it took 'ages' was a mystery.

After a while I headed her off at the pass. The mushy stuff was making me feel embarrassed for some reason, and I wanted to get on to the really important bits. 'Yes, yes, but what did he say about marriage, him being sent home now the war is over and all that?' I asked. 'Were Terry and Ronnie right about how it is with him being coloured and you being a white woman?'

She didn't answer me for a long time, and her pretty blushes paled to a strained sort of colourlessness. 'I think it's worse, from what Chester says,' she answered at last, very softly. Tears welled up until they overflowed and dripped steadily down her cheeks, unchecked. I handed her a hanky from my handbag and waited while she mopped up, followed by a hefty and very unladylike nose-blow. At last she stopped crying, took a deep breath and carried on in a very small voice. 'I asked him what those GIs meant when they said he'd be swinging from a tree if he was at home and, oh Zeld…!' She choked up again and all I could do was pat her hand and wait. 'He said that in the Southern states of America Negroes are sometimes lynched for walking out with white women. Worse, a woman only has to accuse him of trying it on, even if it's not true, and he'd be a goner. No trial, nothing.'

'Bloody hell!' I whispered, awed by the enormity of it. Of course we hanged people for murder in England, but it was different, they had to be proved guilty and anyway, they'd killed someone themselves. I still wasn't sure about hanging though, guilty or not. Mistakes were too easy to make and the wrong person could get their neck stretched. Once it'd been stretched, there was no shrinking it back again and saying, 'Oops! Sorry, mate, our mistake,' now was there? Dad said that the courts didn't make those sorts of mistakes, but personally, I wasn't so sure.

What's more, I could imagine all sorts of situations where a person could murder someone almost by accident, in the heat of an argument, say, when both parties were off their trollies and not thinking straight. I could imagine taking a carving knife to Charlie, if he had me cornered and I was afraid enough. It didn't mean that I'd want him dead, but I could imagine doing it in a frenzy of fear.

The thought of people simply deciding a bloke had to be hanged, slinging a rope over a tree and hanging him, was too awful to think about without feeling sick. But we were having to think about it, especially poor old Dilly. I mean, how would she feel if Chester swung for her, for no better reason than they were walking out together?

'So,' I whispered—I don't know why, we were on our own— 'what have you and him decided?'

I didn't think she was going to answer but eventually she did. 'We haven't decided. We're both thinking about things.' Her chin came up and she looked defiant. 'We know we love each other and would like to get married. But we can't do that and stay in his home town, the neighbours would never stand for it and his family would suffer too.' I hadn't heard her sound so sad since we heard her brother was missing.

'Have you thought about living here, instead of over there?' I asked.

'We've talked about it.' This was all she said, and I gathered that Chester didn't fancy it much. Couldn't say I blamed him, England was so poor! Still, we didn't have lynch mobs. Well, none I'd ever heard of.

'Where does Chester come from, anyway?' I asked, suddenly realizing that I had forgotten. When places' names mean nothing to me, they don't stick in my mind, unless they're funny of course, like Timbuktu, or exotic, like Zanzibar.

'Memphis, which is a city in the state of Tennessee,' she answered as if she'd memorized it, which she probably had.

I shook my head. 'It means nothing to me,' I said, 'but then I don't suppose Aylesbury, Bucks, means much to most Americans neither. They'd probably think it had something to do with money and ask what the exchange rate was.'

'Well, it's not in what he calls the "Deep South," but it's south enough for us to have a lot of trouble if we tried to live there.' Dilly paused. 'They might even kill him for it.'

'God!' I exclaimed. 'What would they do to you?'

'Chester says they wouldn't kill me, on account that I'm white and that would be murder, but they'd make my life "a living hell," was the way he put it. But it'd be hell anyway, if someone lynched my husband, I'd've thought.'

I would have thought so too, even if that husband was Charlie—and that was saying something. I wouldn't want the bugger to swing, even though I could cheerfully give him away with a packet of tea. 'So what're you going to do?' I asked. I didn't really expect a reply, but I didn't know what else to say. Their situation was right outside my experience, but it did seem to me that if they married and moved to America, Dilly could find herself a widow in very short order. So, they were left with two choices: give it up, or marry and stay in England. I said as much.

'No, Zeld, that's not all. According to Chester, us being married would go down better in New York and some other northern places, like Chicago and Detroit. Or we could go to another country altogether, like Canada if they'll have us, or somewhere in Europe when things settle down a bit. He says Paris had a lot of American jazz musicians living there before the war and he thinks a lot of them'll drift back once the dust settles. Some of his mates in his regiment are talking about going. They're mostly musicians, but there's an artist and a writer too. So what we've decided is not to decide yet, but to muddle along as we are until a decision has to be made, then see what seems the best option. I quite fancy Paris,' she said. 'It's ever so romantic.'

It all seemed very hard to me. So I made things worse, by telling her about her nephew and his trouble. I had to, because I had to explain why I wanted to nip round to the Gardens to see how he was right in the middle of her visit. I had a niggling worry about him in the parts of my brain left over from taking in her news and the awful guilt at blowing my top at Mrs. Dunmore. Dilly's hand flew to her face and she swore, which was most unlike her. I put it down to strain. I knew the feeling all too well.

'Those bloody Holes!' she said. 'They ruin everyone they touch.' For Dilly, this was dead strong language. 'He'll have to tell the Vicar. It's the only thing he *can* do.'

I explained to her that it had been done already, and the outcome.

'Well, that's OK then. Still, it's a good idea to get round there just the same, to make sure the poor boy survived his day at school. I suppose there are plenty of people about in a school. That's something to be grateful for.'

Vi was home when we got there and so was Tony. It had been agreed that it'd be easier with his ration book if he ate at home as usual. It was such a palaver to swap and change when it came to shopping. This meant he'd sleep at the vicarage on school nights and work off his lessons at the weekends. He only lived around the corner, after all, so nipping home for meals wasn't too difficult, as long as Brian didn't catch him on his own in the streets.

We spent a pleasant enough half-hour talking over the dance, which seemed months ago, and drinking tea. Vi was jittery but bearing up. I noticed she was smoking more than usual and that her hand trembled slightly, but she kept shooting Tony fond and bracing looks, so she *was* trying. Dilly was amazed at the change in her and frankly, so was I, but grateful too. Tony really needed his mum.

Chapter 36

Sadly, Mrs. Dunmore hadn't had a bang on the head and a handy attack of amnesia. She remembered me swearing at her all too well. I'd slunk into her office the next morning, tail between my legs, to apologize for my terrible outburst of the day before. I just hoped like mad I could plead mitigation, as they say in the courts, and hang on to my job.

The interview was grim. She was working at her desk and her crisp, sharp voice cut through the woodwork as I knocked on the door. 'Come in.' I went in. She carried on with what she was doing, not troubling to look up. I waited and tried not to fidget. It wasn't easy. I felt as if I was standing on hot coals and it was all I could do not to run out of the room. It was just like being back at school and in trouble with the headmistress, only worse, a lot worse. Nobody had paid me to go to school and I hadn't had to pay my own rent then either.

At last she looked up. Her mouth was so pursed in disapproval it was wrinkled all round the edges, like a cat's bum. I had a sudden urge to giggle hysterically, but clamped my mouth shut on it, so that two cats' bums faced one another across the desk. Stalemate. Somebody had to say something. I tried to speak but the words got stuck. I coughed slightly and tried again. If Tony could face up to the Reverend Cattermole, I ought to be able to face up to La Dunmore, I thought to myself. I stiffened my backbone and my resolve.

A faint breeze from the window was stirring the papers on her noticeboard so that they fluttered like giant butterflies. All of them were from the Ministry, telling her to save slops for pigs, that uncooked scraps were to go in a separate bin, and that waste paper, cardboard, tins and bottles had to be sorted and saved for collection for the war effort. Even though there was no more war, the effort was still required. I suppose that's why she hadn't taken them down—or got someone else to do it, more like—because the shortages continued and the same rules still applied. It was a depressing thought. Would the dreary round of rationing, mending and making do and saving every little scrap never end? It was hard to see when.

I searched again for my voice and finally found it hiding somewhere in the pit of my stomach, all trembly and feeble. 'I'm sorry I was so rude yesterday, Mrs. Dunmore. I don't know what got into me.' This wasn't true, of course. I knew that the strain of all the troubles that had rained down on me and mine since the end of the official war had got into me, and had all built up such a head of steam, it was bursting to get out. But I wasn't going to tell her that. It was none of her business.

'I should dispense with your labours, Zelda. I can't have my girls speaking to me in such an appalling fashion. It's insubordination, that's what it is.' She sounded indignant all over again; her face was red with fury. But a lady did not rant and rave at her skivvies. It was coarse, and Mrs. Dunmore wasn't keen on coarse, naturally. 'Nobody has ever spoken to me in that way before. Not ever!

'However'—she could hardly get the words out but she had to go on—'Cook and Beryl have said that if I let you go'—plain sacking was too common for Mrs. Dunmore—'they will leave also. Obviously, I cannot run this establishment by myself, so I have to give in—this time. But it must never happen again, do you hear me? Never!' I heard her, and nodded. I felt so lucky to have hung on to my job I could have burst into loud cheers, but I didn't.

'Thank you, Mrs. Dunmore,' was all I could think of to say, although it was Cook and Beryl I should have been thanking. It was only once I'd got out of her office that I realized I hadn't promised it would never happen again.

I worked extra hard that morning and it wasn't until our tea break that I was able to thank my friends.

'That's our pleasure, love,' Cook said comfortably. 'We've all wanted to shove a boot up her jacksie more than once. It was nice that one of us managed to do it. We've got to stick up for our own, let's face it. No other bugger will.'

'Hear, hear,' grinned Beryl. 'So, tell us what happened *exactly*. La Dunmore only said you'd been rude and "insubordinate." Anybody'd think she was a ruddy general and you was a private, the way she carries on.'

So I told them, and they 'oohed' and 'aahed' in admiration, which quite bucked me up, because when I'd walked in that morning, I could have got under a snake's belly with a top hat on. Even so, I thought it best to keep my head down and work hard. So I did, not only that day, but for the rest of the week.

Mrs. Dunmore, however, seemed to wilt as the week wore on. She still drove everybody hard, but her heart wasn't in it, I could tell. There was an atmosphere too, one we couldn't pin down but which made us uneasy. It was almost better when the woman was everywhere, poking her sharp nose into things and making waspish comments. The unholy quiet didn't seem natural or right.

Away from work, things were pretty quiet, too, at least to begin with. Tony was managing to stay in one piece and so far, Hilda Handcuffs, in the form of PC Grubb, had not arrested him, or even questioned him. But the law *had* been seen poking around the Holes' shed and, once, stopping and searching Brian and a few of his pals. All George Grubb and his colleagues had found so far was a strong and deeply suspicious smell of petrol, but there had been no jerry cans full of the stuff and no guns, bullets or hand grenades.

And as he told the Vicar, 'You can't arrest somebody for a pong. You can't produce it as evidence in court, neither.' Which was true of course.

On that front, all we could do was carry on and wait. It was frustrating, but Tony was getting his piano lessons and the vicarage was getting a lick of paint, so it wasn't time wasted by any means. Besides, Tony was keeping his nose so clean, it almost shone and glowed in the dark. Gran was impressed.

'If Tony behaved any better, he'd be so clean he'd squeak when he walked. He only offered to carry the shopping for Mrs. Whitelock yesterday. You wouldn't know that only a week or so ago he was driving us all mental with worry about his wicked ways. Of course, it's very early days, but I do believe we might have turned a corner with that boy. It was the gun that did it, of course, not us. He's a funny bundle, that one.' She grew sombre. 'I s'pose with his dad and everything, he understands what death means and doesn't fancy it much. Poor little bugger.'

I thought we were coasting gently towards Saturday and our weekly trip into Soho when things warmed up once again. Thursday morning I got a letter. I recognized the handwriting and the postmark immediately: it was from Charlie. He told me that he expected to be home in eight days' time for a weekend leave, Friday night through to Sunday afternoon. 'So this time, make sure you get some proper food in,' he instructed.

I sank into a chair because my knees gave way. My heart hammered but, at the same time, seemed to want to plummet to the soles of my feet. I noticed that the hand holding his note trembled. I felt robbed. Then I thought about all those young widows who longed for their men to come home and I was stricken with a terrible sense of grief. For them, for me, for us all.

I could have wept. In fact, I think I did. I certainly had to mop up a bit before I went to work.

Chapter 37

It was a relief to get on the bus on Saturday morning, and to make a change, Reggie came with us. It was time the boy had a treat. After all, he had never wilfully given anyone a minute's trouble, although he couldn't help scaring us half to death with his asthma from time to time. Mr. Burlap had asked if he could hang on to Tony for a second hour that Saturday, as he wanted him to listen to another singer, and the extra time would give Reggie and me a bit of leeway to explore the area a little. So we were all in high spirits to be out and about and well away from home.

We dropped Tony off at Mr. Burlap's 'studio,' as he called it, arranging to meet him at the cafe after his lesson, then set off to have a look around. Mr. Burlap's place was in Greek Street, a mere hop, skip and jump from Soho Square, so that was our first stop. I knew Reggie would be interested by the little old house in the middle. We were just on our third lap around the outside of it, when someone called to me.

'Ah, the fascinating Zelda, gypsy palmist and interpreter of tea leaves. Hail, lady, and well met.' It was the lawyer chappie, Mr. Finn, Sharky to his pals.

I blushed. 'Hello, Mr. Finn,' I said, then got stuck. I didn't know what else to say to the bloke. Luckily, he had no such trouble.

'How fortunate our paths should cross again, the better to become acquainted, and it just so happens that I have a tiny commission you could undertake for me.' He smiled and, just for a moment, I could've sworn the sun dimmed.

I had no idea what he was talking about after the path crossing bit. I looked blank and then I felt a sharp elbow in my ribcage. What was it about our lot, I wondered, that they considered elbows an alternative to a polite 'Excuse me'? I turned to Reggie, whose eyebrows had shot up into his hairline in enquiry, and shook my head very slightly. His curiosity would have to wait. I turned my attention back to Mr. Finn. 'Ah?' I asked.

'A small commission, a little favour; it'll save me writing to her and she'll get the message all the sooner. It'll put her mind at rest,' he answered, with another flash of those teeth.

Her? Whose mind? I was thoroughly bewildered. 'Certainly,' I said stiffly, hoping enlightenment would come.

'Lovely. Tell her that Mrs. Joe has told Joe to put one of his boys on to it as soon as he can. When I asked Joe himself, he said it was as good as done. He's sending Frankie, you'll have seen him around. I imagine her problems will be solved very soon. Can you remember all that?'

I was a bit huffy. 'Of course I can remember it.' I repeated the message back to him, word for word. 'What I don't know is, who is supposed to get it?'

Mr. Finn slapped his forehead with the palm of his hand and laughed. 'Of course! What a fool I am! Miss Makepeace, your neighbour, Digby's good friend,' he explained.

'Right you are.' It was all I could think of to say.

'Fine. Cheerio then.'

'Who was he?' Reggie demanded as soon as Mr. Finn was out of earshot. I told him.

'He fancies you,' said Reggie confidently.

Despite myself, I blushed again. 'I've got a feeling that Mr. Finn fancies a lot of ladies, Reggie. I think he makes a bit of a habit of it.'

The streets of Soho are narrow, and most of the buildings are several storeys high with flats above and shops below. Many of the shops were empty, driven out of business by not being able to get stock during the war years. The ones that clung on were often real specialists, like a shoe shop especially for ballet and tap dancers, or an outfitters for chefs, waiters and kitchen workers. Of course, their window displays were a bit thin, but they had held out. There would always be dancers and the same went for restaurants and the men and women who staffed them. I tried to imagine Cook's round, merry face beneath a chef's hat and fell about laughing. Cook was all woman, and I had the feeling those tall chimneys were the sort of thing only a bloke would wear. Cook seemed quite happy in her wraparound pinny, with a snood to keep her hair out of the soup.

Down one dark little alleyway, too narrow to be called a street, we found a funny, crumpled-looking little shop, with low ceilings. Both its window and doorway showed a definite tendency to slant towards the middle, as if it had buckled under the weight of the building above. It sold model railways, and the reds, greens and gold of the various liveries glimmered in the gloom.

Next door was a hire shop, used by the theatres to supply costumes for their shows and plays. The window held a display of masks, some of them beautiful, with fake gems and winged shapes, while others were grotesque, with wounds, horns or hairy faces. There was an ass' head snuggled up to an ape, a devil beside a bear. Reggie wanted to go in and have a poke around, but when we got to the door a large CLOSED sign barred our way.

Another little street had a small row of food shops. There was one window that sported a proud Star of David—Caplin's it was called—and offered salt beef sandwiches, gefilte fish, pickles and latkes among other delicacies, but it too was closed, it being Saturday. I was partial to salt beef sandwiches. You could get 'em in the Whitechapel Road or Petticoat Lane, with a 'glass tea' for next to nothing, and they were absolutely delicious. There was a fish-monger and a butcher there, too. Both had small queues of women determined to stock up before the shops closed at one. A quick look in the windows told us that the meagre stocks were dwindling fast.

After many twists and turns, we arrived back in Soho Square with some time on our hands before we had to meet Tony. We made our way to Charing Cross Road, and began to poke about in the books left on the pavements outside many of the second-hand bookshops. It was there that I bumped into a second familiar face—and belly. Reggie had dived into a large box marked '6d' and I was looking vaguely at the passing pedestrians as I waited, when out of the shop next door popped Cassie.

'Oh hello,' she said. 'I know you, don't I?'

I explained that we'd met at the cafe. 'Of course,' she smiled. 'How are you? And this young man is…?'

'My nephew, Reggie,' I answered. 'How are you? How's the, you know…' I nodded towards her swollen middle. There was obviously no disguising it any more, she was well and truly preggers.

'Oh well, you know,' she answered vaguely, eyeing the book in Reggie's grubby paw. Wartime printer's ink could be filthy stuff. 'I say, Reggie, if you want *Swallows and Amazons*, nip next door to my friend Mr. Herbert and say I sent you and he'll let you have a copy cheaper.'

Reggie looked shyly at me and I nodded slightly. He dropped the book back in the box and nipped into the shop next door, pennies clutched hopefully in his sweaty palm. Cassie and I chatted awkwardly for a few moments; it seemed neither of us knew how to wind up so we could go our separate ways.

I was feeling more and more peculiar, sort of away with the fairies and barely able to keep up my end of the chitchat, when I was saved by Reggie's return. Cassie heaved a small sigh of relief and made her goodbyes, and Reggie's look of triumph turned to one of concern.

'Are you having a turn, Auntie Zelda?' he asked. I nodded. I blamed that swine Charlie for upsetting me and starting them up again. 'What is it?' Reggie asked. 'Something to do with the pretty lady?' I nodded again. I really was feeling most peculiar, all swimmy. 'Take my arm, Auntie, we'll go next door. Mr. Herbert will let you sit down, get you a glass of water.'

A few minutes later I was beginning to revive a bit and became aware of Father Christmas staring sympathetically down at me. 'Feeling a bit better now?' he asked in great concern.

'Yes, thank you. What happened?'

'You swooned, my dear, but Reginald here and I managed to catch you before you hit the floor. Would you care for a sip of water?'

I sipped, felt better and sat up. I had been stretched out in the aisle between towering bookcases and someone had put a rolled-up coat beneath my head. I sipped some more, and pretty soon I'd swigged the entire glass. Mr. Herbert trotted off to refill it.

'What's the time, Reggie?' I'd suddenly remembered Tony.

Reggie looked round and saw a clock above a till that was a work of art. It was silver-coloured, and every inch of it that wasn't the keys was covered in a bold design involving a great deal of fat, swollen fruit. 'A quarter to, Auntie,' said Reggie. It was time to pull myself together. I didn't know what had come over me; all I'd seen was a little girl with a lot of curls and big blue eyes skipping around the cafe. And I knew, don't ask me how, that the child I had just seen was Maggie and Bert's daughter. Maybe not their very own handiwork, but theirs just the same. It wasn't a sad vision, but a happy one, so why I should pass out cold, God only knew.

Kind Mr. Herbert wouldn't let me go until he was sure I could stand unaided, and this made us five minutes late in meeting Tony, who was waiting anxiously outside the cafe. He hadn't had the nerve to go inside by himself to wait for us. I pushed open the familiar door and just for a second, everything seemed to stop, as if frozen solid. There, sitting in the middle of the floor, was the little girl playing with a cardboard box, a tin cup and a large saucepan filled with several sorts of what looked like dried beans. She dipped the cup into the beans and dropped them into her box. Once she was satisfied she rattled her box for all she was worth and laughed with glee. Then she reversed the process and clattered her saucepan, which seemed to please her even more because she laughed harder.

Suddenly, 'Pop!' the vision vanished and it was the usual cafe, full of the hum of voices, the clatter of crockery—and no small girls.

Luckily, I was learning caution in my old age and I didn't blurt out to Maggie's smiling face that I'd seen her daughter. But I was sure that was who my phantom child was. It seemed logical that the two visions were connected, because it was definitely the same child in both. My feeling was that Maggie and Bert could wind up caring for Cassie's child for her. It would be a good solution to both sets of trouble.

Perhaps too good. Maybe Dad was right and my dreams and visions were simply down to an over-active imagination. In that case, getting people's hopes up on the basis of a fleeting hallucination or a funny feeling wasn't a good idea. Hope was too important to meddle with, to raise or to dash without very good reason and on the very best authority, so I kept schtum. But it was hard; I was so excited and happy for my new-found friends.

Chapter 38

Tony had caught glimpses of Brian in the distance, he told me, but not up close and hostile. Tony's removal to the vicarage, and the fact that he was in company of one sort or another every time he walked out into the streets or the school playground, had seen to that. It wasn't ideal, however, because there was a big question mark over how long we could keep the level of vigilance up. George Grubb and his colleagues had still to find Brian's arsenal and had given up going to check the shed after their third visit. I think they were beginning to wonder if their unnamed informant had lost some of his marbles and had begun to imagine dastardly deeds. Or so George told Dad in the King's Head during their Sunday dinnertime bevvy.

Naturally, our hearts stopped when Dad started to tell us PC Grubb's gossip during our family meal. We thought for a moment that Tony's name had surfaced in connection with the gun, and that all hell was about to break loose. But the Vicar had kept his word: his source remained anonymous and George Grubb hadn't mentioned the weapons at all, just that the police were acting on 'information received.' But not a word as to what the information was or where it came from, thank goodness; Dad might have twigged that Tony had something to do with it, seeing he was sleeping at the vicarage.

'Seems the law was all over the Holes' shed, but found nothing but the stink of petrol. Still, it shows that they've been behind all those petrol thefts, as if we didn't know that already. But they didn't find a drop, not a single drop.

'Ma's put in a complaint about her boy being picked on, and they've had to stop searching the shed now. I told George to have a look at that lockup down near the market. He said they'd been and found nothing much.'

'I heard they'd found something iffy down the docks,' said Gran, 'or so Iris was telling me at church this morning. Did George mention anything about that?' she asked innocently.

'He did, as it 'appens. Old George is having a big week. He was something to do with that an' all, even though it's way off his patch. It was crates of hand grenades, hidden under some sacks of imported dried beans.' From the way he told it, he obviously didn't realize the two stories were in any way connected.

The minute Dad mentioned dried beans, my mind flashed back to the image of the little girl and her saucepan full of rattling beans. It's a peculiar fact about dreams and visions that they're often stiff with hints and impressions but rarely give the straightforward story. It leaves me with the job of trying to work out what the hell they mean. To complicate matters still further, the threads get muddled until they are all tied up in knots, like washing coming out of a copper boiler. It could take ages to unravel the various bits and pieces.

I was suddenly so glad I hadn't told Maggie and Bert about the happy little girl, just in case my 'turn' was simply a way of telling me where the hand grenades were. Which, if that had been the case, had been a fat lot of good, because I had failed dismally to pick up the message. I thought it'd been about the child.

The main thing was, though, the grenades had been taken away and safely disposed of and Lily Law was actively seeking the blighter who had stowed them. At least they had managed to stop the swine from offloading any more on to a dangerously stupid boy. A stupid boy who had a mother like Ma. The blood froze! It was something to be grateful for but I, for one, wouldn't breathe easy until they had Brian's cache as well.

Gran made me jump. 'Zelda!' My head shot up. I'd been staring blindly at my plate. 'I said, you look like two penn'orth of Gawd 'elp us today, are you all right?'

'Sorry. I was miles away, wondering what anybody could want with crates of hand grenades. There's no accounting for folk. You'd think everyone would have had enough of all that.' I sighed hard. It was true, I did think we'd all had more than enough. 'I didn't sleep that well, Gran, I expect that's it.'

What I didn't mention was that I'd had a dream, vague and full of a nameless dread that hung around long after I woke up. I saw a thin figure stumbling through mist and felt the terrible fear. The way my mind was working it probably meant I was going to bump into a skinny bloke in a fog, or something. I could've clouted Charlie, if only I had the nerve, for upsetting me so that all the psychic business started up again. I hardly ever saw happy things; they were nearly always sad or grim. Even when I thought I'd had a 'good news flash,' it turned out to be about bloody grenades instead. It got me down, especially when it interfered with my beauty sleep and left me feeling like a wet rag.

'What's keeping you awake, love?' Mum asked.

'I got a letter from Charlie,' I told them. 'He's home on leave next weekend.'

'Ah!' said Mum, Gran and Vi together.

'I don't think you should stay there, then,' said Vi, shaking me and everyone else rigid. Vi noticed the shocked silence and added, 'Well, I don't. He really hurt our Zelda last time and he shouldn't get the chance to do it again. It's only for the weekend.'

Dad spluttered with indignation, enraged at the very idea. 'You can't come between a man and his wife! You know that, Vi. Anyway, I expect she asked for it,' he said, as if I wasn't there. I hated that. 'She can be a lippy beggar when she's got a strop on.'

'Nobody deserves what that man's done to her, Dad. I don't care what she did or what you say.' Vi was on her high horse, which was funny because I never knew she even *had* one. Something had definitely changed in our Vi.

'Now you watch your step, young lady,' Dad warned, not being used to defiance from his middle daughter. Me, yes, but not his precious Violet. 'And anyway, it ain't just for a weekend, is it? Our Enie's married to the man and he'll be home for good soon, won't he? She can't be away for ever, now can she? No, Enie made her bed and she can bloody well lie in it.'

Vi had her mouth open to answer him back when I stepped in. If Vi could show some backbone, then so could I. 'I expect, if it's all the same to you, Dad, I'll make my own decisions when the time comes. And my name's Zelda,' I added quietly.

I thought he'd burst. 'No, it's not all the same to me. There's no decision to be made. You're a married woman and you've got responsibilities, duties, and you will see to them. That's the way you've been brought up and that's the way you'll behave! And I ain't arguing with you about bleeding names either.'

I kept schtum but, at that moment, I knew he was wrong. I would do something about Charlie, whether Dad liked it or not. Suddenly, it really didn't matter to me what Dad thought. As he kept saying, I was a married woman, and my behaviour and the decisions I made were no longer any of his bloody business. I smiled a secret smile at Vi, who winked back. I really could not believe the change in my sister. It was miraculous.

When I asked her later what had got into her, she simply said, 'I dunno, really. I've been thinking, that's all. I saw what Charlie did to you, saw how scared you were and realized how lucky I'd been to have Fred. Even if he has been taken away from me, at least I've had him.' She paused for a moment, eyes glazed as she looked back to her time with Fred. She smiled sadly. 'You got lumbered with Charlie and that was never fair, not really. And Tony, well, he's missed his dad, too, and I've only just realized what it's meant to him. I feel bad, being so blind. I s'pose I was so wrapped up in my own feelings, I forgot about him and his feelings.' I listened to her in utter amazement and said not a word, but I did slip my arm round her waist and gave her a grateful squeeze. She was all right, my sister. Both my sisters were.

I went home that night in a very thoughtful mood. Everything seemed to be closing in. Charlie was looming, along with trouble for Tony, and work was awful, Mrs. Dunmore being an unforgiving sort. She might not have sacked me, but she made sure I really earned my crust. Likewise, she drove Cook and Beryl hard for their cheek; she hadn't forgotten that they'd threatened her, and I felt bad because they'd done it for me. If only I'd kept my mouth shut, everything would have been tickety-boo.

That night I had the brooding dream again: the thin man, the mist, the dread. Perhaps Charlie was the thin man and the dread was mine—I mean, I *was* afraid of him, there was no denying that. But they felt separate. My fear of Charlie felt like mine, but the nameless dread felt more general. The thin man's? Perhaps Charlie dreaded coming home. It was possible. Ours was hardly a marriage made in heaven, and I expect he felt as stuck with it as I did.

I woke up with the dread hanging around like a bad smell. When I sniffed, I got Evening in Paris. The air was drenched with it, and then it was gone. I blinked hard, shook myself slightly and got up. No point in hanging about in bed worrying and dreaming. I washed my face in cold water, had a cup of tea and then lay down again, hoping for another couple of hours' sleep before work, bright and early on Monday morning.

Chapter 39

Zinnia didn't answer her back door when I knocked that Monday after work. So, as was my custom—and indeed, everyone else's—I simply walked into the kitchen when I found the door wasn't locked. It meant she wasn't far away. Halfway between the door and the centre of the room, I stopped in my tracks: there in the middle of her kitchen table lay a tabby cat, stretched out and stiff and looking distinctly dead.

I couldn't bring myself to examine it more closely, to see which one it was. I had thought Hallelujah was mending nicely, almost back in mid-season form. I backed away. Then I noticed a note beside it, in red. It looked as if it had been written with a forefinger, dipped in blood.

> This time your cat, next time it could be you. Fuck
> off, your not wanted here. You have been told. A
> Friend

I think I had my mouth open to scream, but nothing came out. The breath had caught in my gullet when I'd heard a sound from the other side of the door that led from the kitchen to the hallway and the rest of the house. The shiny brass knob turned and I stared at it, heart in my mouth. 'Zin?' I squeaked. Then, a little louder, 'Zin?'

Nothing happened for what felt like three days, but was more likely thirty seconds. Finally the door knob was released with a quiet 'click.' I waited for the door to swing open but I distinctly heard retreating footsteps heading for the front door. I tried to move my feet, but I must have had lead shoes on, because they wouldn't leave the flagstones. I had to shuffle across the room, past the table and its grisly burden.

Zinnia could have been hurt, she could even be dead somewhere in the house. I had to get to her. She might need help, if she wasn't beyond it. I took another scared look at the cat and tried harder. Despite feeling sick and shaky with fear, I made it to the door and yanked it open just in time to see a dim figure disappear out of the front of the house. Suddenly, my leaden heels had wings and I fair flew across the hallway, out of the swinging front door and into the open air.

All I can remember is falling, blackness and stars, lots and lots of stars, and thinking that stars couldn't be right, it was still daytime. I woke up to find Zinnia peering down at me. Her dear, familiar and, what's more, still living face was full of anxiety.

'Are you all right, hen?' she asked, which struck me as a silly question. Of course I wasn't all right. For the second time in just a few days, I'd found myself coming round from being sparko. It had to stop. I sat up gingerly, rubbed my head and found a bump the size of half a lemon on the back of it. It throbbed and I had a mighty headache.

'I think I'd better get you into the parlour. You can lie on the sofa. If I put my arm around you, can you stand up, hen?' I nodded, then wished I hadn't; I saw more stars than the Milky Way and felt the ground heaving like a heavy sea. I was definitely about to lose my dinner. Zinnia was on top of the situation and whipped a plant out of its fancy jardinière in one deft movement. I chucked my socks up into that.

I don't remember getting there, but we must have made it to the parlour because that's where I woke up next. I sat up again and felt better this time; groggy, but better. I took a while to work out where I was, but got it in the end. I must have been at Zinnia's for a while, though, because it was daylight when I last looked and it was getting dark when I woke up.

I was thirsty. I swung my legs to the floor but found I had jelly knees that didn't feel at all safe to walk with. I gave it a few moments, then had another go. It was better; I managed to stand and, by hanging on to the furniture and then the wall, I made it to the door and out into the hallway, where I paused before feeling my way to the kitchen door. I was parched and the tap was my distant oasis.

When I pushed open the door, I saw a man sitting in Zinnia's kitchen. He looked very faintly familiar, but I couldn't place him. He looked up and grinned at me. My heart almost stopped. Who was he? What did he want? Where was Zinnia?

'Wotcha. How're you?' he asked. It wasn't the sort of question or grin you expected from a murderer, but I was cautious. Things had turned very nasty round at Zinnia's, one way and another.

I didn't answer straight away, but just gawped at him. Who *was* this geezer anyway? He looked a bit foreign to me, but he didn't sound it. There was one way to find out.

'Who are you?' I asked rudely.

'I'm staying here for a few days, guest of the lady of the house, and you're her mate what got coshed,' he told me. So that's what happened. I *had* wondered. The last thing I remembered was a dead cat...

'Hallelujah?' I croaked.

'Nah, Frankie. I'm a mate of Maltese Joe. I'm from up West.'

I had a vague memory of someone called Joe and a message for Zinnia, but I couldn't quite recall it all. The bloke *was* cleaning his fingernails with the tip of a vicious-looking knife, which was a bit off-putting, but on the other hand, that's all he was doing, and he was familiar. If he was dangerous, surely I'd remember who he was. I decided I ought to be thorough, though. 'If you're her guest, you should know her name. What's this lady called?' I asked.

He grinned even wider and was about to answer me when the lady in question breezed in from the garden with a handful of herbs. 'Oh, I see you two have met. Sit down, hen, before you fall down. I'll pop the kettle on. I've got some fennel here, it might help your poor stomach. How're you feeling?'

I told her and she nodded sombrely and got me a glass of water while we waited for the kettle to boil. 'Take small sips, in case you're sick again. I think it's only a minor concussion, but I'd like to keep an eye on you all the same. Looks like whoever coshed you didn't quite have the aim; it was a glancing blow.' I felt my bump with tender fingers. If this was 'glancing,' I thought, I'd hate it if the bugger really meant it.

'Do you know what happened, hen?' she asked.

I explained about hearing footsteps and the lights going out, as it were. 'I'm sorry about Hallelujah,' I told her. My eyes filled with tears. I must've been weakened by the blow. But I had grown fond of the moggies, especially since we'd rescued them from the cellar.

'Ach, that wasn't Hallelujah,' Zinnia reassured me. 'He's away out chasing moths, I've just seen him. No, that was a puir wee stray that's been hanging about lately. I've been trying to tempt it in but it's been awfy shy for a starving cat, so I've had to leave its food on the step. If it's any comfort, hen, I think it died of natural causes. It was never right, that one.' She handed me a clean hanky and I had a good blow.

'So how did it wind up on your kitchen table?' I asked. 'And the note, what about the note?' I paused. 'And who bashed me over the head?'

Zinnia laughed softly. 'One question at a time, there's a dear. You've always been a great one for the questions. It's why we get on: I like an inquisitive mind, and yours has always been that all right, from a wee bairn.' She smiled at me and carried on.

'We don't know who hit you—the one who left the puir moggy on my table, doubtless, and the note. But who the miscreant is, we still have no idea. George Grubb was here. He'll be wanting to speak to you when you feel up to it. We all seem to have made educated guesses, yes, but certainties, no. I think whoever it is, found themselves in possession of a dead cat and took advantage of that fact. It was already dead, I'm sure; it was stiff as a board when we found it, and rigor mortis takes a wee while to set in.' That was a sort of comfort, anyway, that no-one had actually killed the poor, wretched thing.

Another question sprang to mind, this one for Frankie. 'So why are you here?'

'I'm here to find out who has got it in for Miss Makepeace,' he replied. 'Like I said, Joe sent me—well, Mrs. Joe really. I told you, I'm from up West.'

'Who is Joe?' I asked. 'And this Mrs. Joe, is she his wife?'

'Joe's my boss, and Mrs. Joe's his mum.'

'What's he got to do with Zinnia?'

'You're a nosy little piece, aren't you?'

'Who are you calling a "piece"?' I demanded shirtily.

'You, egghead,' said Frankie, who laughed heartily at his own wit.

'Children, children. Behave, do,' pleaded Zinnia, vegetable knife in one hand and a tomato in the other. 'I can see you'll do fine, Zelda, if you're fit to argue with the man, but I think you'd better stay the night just the same, to be on the safe side.

'Maltese Joe is an acquaintance of mine. I have treated his mother for more than thirty years. She gets headaches and I give her feverfew, among other things. She's inclined to be a touch liverish,' she told me, as if that explained everything.

I insisted I had to be at work the next day, because I was still in the doghouse for my insubordination. Frankie found that hugely amusing, and mentioned that my mouth obviously matched my nose for size. Cheeky bleeder! Zinnia thought about work for a while, then grudgingly said it would be all right as long as I didn't feel either sick or dizzy in the morning or during the day.

'If you do, you must arrange to be brought back here or to the hospital straight away. Is that understood?' She had her schoolmistress voice on, so I knew she was serious. According to her, concussion, however mild, had to be watched for twenty-four hours, 'just in case.' In case of what, she didn't say, and I preferred not to ask. But I agreed to do as she asked.

'Good, that's settled then. Now, how about a game of cards?'

Zinnia, Frankie and I played pontoon for the rest of the evening and, despite the cat, the note and the undoubted fear they'd brought up for Zinnia and for me, I thoroughly enjoyed myself. I could see that Zinnia was anxious about me and her invisible enemy, but she did her best to hide it. She was not one to display her feelings: she was a Scot, after all. Stoical types, the Scots. I put it down to the salty porridge, that and their climate. According to Zinnia, a Scottish winter is not for the faint-hearted. The Germans called the Highland regiments 'the ladies from hell' in the Great War, on account of the kilts, their bloodcurdling war cries, the eerie wail of the bagpipes and the fact that they would not stop coming, once they charged over the top of a trench. Hebridean seamen were viewed in pretty much the same way by their fellow Jack Tars. Ronnie reckoned they were the best sailors in the world, but it didn't do to cross one.

'They close ranks, dolly, and they even have their own language. There is no more chilling sight than a bunch of Highlanders lined up against you. I've even seen the Russkies quail, and they usually think they're armour plated after a couple of swigs of vodka, but they won't take on those Scotties, not if they can help it.'

So, Zinnia was being a Scot and not showing how worried she was, but I could tell anyway. However, I felt safe with Frankie there. He turned out to be a good laugh and a nice enough bloke—for a henchman that is, because I reckon that was definitely what he was.

Just as I was settling down for the night, Zinnia came into my room and sat on a chair beside the bed. She had a good look at my eyes and asked me if I felt sick, dizzy, disorientated, anything like that? I said no, just a bit scared. Not for our safety that night—I had every confidence in Frankie—but scared in general. I could feel things coming to a head, all sorts of things. Exactly *what* things, was harder to pin down.

'I've been dreaming again, Zin,' I told her, 'ever since I heard Charlie was coming home for another leave. I can feel this awful dread, but I'm not sure what about. Charlie, yes, it's about him

I'm sure, at least in part. But there's this dead cat business—I thought whoever was out to get you had given it up, but they haven't, have they? What are you going to do, Zin?'

I didn't think she was going to answer me, she took so long about it, but in the end she said, 'Well, to begin with, I shall put some trust in that young man in my kitchen. He swears to me he'll harm no-one, just "put the frighteners on," as he so graphically puts it. Sure enough, we have to do something, and the police have made no headway in their investigations at all. I think they're more worried about guns and grenades at the minute.' She sighed, eyes far away, seeing something beyond the little bedroom.

'However, the cat was several steps too far.' She spoke firmly, but I could tell that she was almost as shaken as I was, underneath her calm exterior. 'And you hen, how are you—really?'

'I've decided that my future doesn't lie with Charlie,' I said. You could've knocked me down with a feather. I hadn't realized I'd come to a decision. It must have been the bash on the head; it had finally knocked some sense into me. I knew now that I could not spend the rest of my life living with a man who frightened me. We didn't even like each other that much, and I was sure that we could both do better if we gave it up. All it took was for one of us to stand on their hind legs and say so, and that someone might as well be me. It was time I took control. I was sick of being pushed around: by Charlie, by Dad and by Mrs. Dunmore.

Zinnia nodded slowly. 'Aye, I thought you'd come to it in the end. Where do you see your future?'

'I dunno. But not with Charlie and probably not round here. If I go, then it's best if I make a new start in a new place.' I hadn't known I'd been thinking that, either; it just popped out as I was talking with Zinnia. It seemed my brains had been busy without me, planning, deciding and moving right along.

'You're probably right, hen. I think it's difficult to see too far ahead, with all the general upheaval, but the world *is* changing. Soon, we'll not recognize it. I'll be out of a job, if there's anything in this idea of a National Health Service Digby's been telling me about. If it comes to pass, I think it'll be a good thing, even if I do end up in the scrap.' She sighed heavily. 'I'll be the last Makepeace in Paradise Gardens, that's for certain.'

Then she laughed gently to herself. 'But I've got a good few years in me yet, to make a nuisance of myself. Time to sleep now, hen. You'll sleep without dreams this night, Zelda,' she told me, and passed her hand in front of my eyes, once, twice and three times.

And I was gone, out like a light, sparko. When I woke in the morning, I was refreshed and almost full of beans. As I was getting washed and dressed, I thought about the night before and it crossed my mind to wonder when Mr. Burlap had had the opportunity to talk to Zinnia about the Labour Party's ideas. I had been so busy worrying about everything else, I had quite forgotten about the little mystery of Zinnia and Mr. Burlap.

I made up my mind to grill Frankie for information while he was handy and I had the chance. He'd be an easier nut to crack than Zinnia herself, because I got the feeling he'd taken a bit of a shine to me and, as he said, I was a 'nosy little piece.' A very nosy little piece, as it happens. I love other people's business; it takes my mind off mine, and anyway, it's usually more interesting.

Chapter 40

George Grubb made me late for work. He'd arrived bright and early and just in time to join Zinnia, Frankie and me for breakfast. PC Grubb wasn't called 'Nosher' Grubb for nothing, as his huge, belted belly testified. George had a beat that passed several tea stands, caffs and friendly widows, and he did not stint himself when it came to being 'sociable.'

George's sociability was a double-edged sword. It could be hard on a person's rations, but on the other hand, there were few faces on his manor that George didn't know. Faces gossiped. It was in their nature; that's why God gave 'em mouths, according to George. He raised his head from his steaming cup and took a bite of the thick hunk of bread and jam he held in his plump, red fingers. Everything about George was plump and red, except for the top of his head. When his helmet came off, it revealed a bald and shiny dome. All the Grubbs lost their hair early; his brothers were just the same.

'So, Mrs. Fluck,' he said round a mouthful of bread, 'would you recognize him again, the bloke you saw leaving via…'—he paused and glanced at his notebook—'the front door?' He took another swig of tea.

I said I didn't think so, but that wasn't entirely true. I kept getting flashbacks, like little snippets of film, or a photograph, of that back against the light flooding through the door. There was something very familiar about it. It was definitely someone I knew, but I couldn't think who. It was like seeing the girl from the Odeon on the street, away from her ticket booth: you know you know the face well but can't quite place it. Well, I knew I knew that back, but the name of its owner just wouldn't come.

George turned to Zinnia. 'So let me get this straight. First, someone broke in and swapped your furniture around, but you didn't trouble to report it because you thought it was a practical joke. Then your shed was set alight, which you did report, arson being no joke. Then your cats went missing; again, no report because there was nothing to report, they could've just wandered. But when you found one of them with an airgun pellet in it, you did report that. And now, a nasty note, a dead cat—not yours—and a friend bashed over the noggin on your doorstep. Have I got it all?'

Zinnia nodded. George then turned to Frankie, who was eating an egg sandwich while trying not to draw too much attention to himself and failing dismally. 'And your friend here?' he asked innocently, chomping the last of his jammy wedge.

'Is my nephew, Francis. He's here to look after his old aunt,' lied Zinnia, barefaced and as if to the manner born. I could quite see why Frankie's origins were best kept from George Grubb, but Zinnia telling whoppers was new to me.

'I never knew you had a nephew. Funny he's never thought to visit before…' began George Grubb.

'Aye, well,' Zinnia cut him short. 'Things happen in families, fallings-out, you know how it is. But still, the least said, soonest mended, eh? Another jeely piece, George?'

'A what?' George looked bewildered and 'Francis' tried hard not to laugh. I looked from one to another, so completely absorbed in the goings-on that I didn't notice the time.

'Bread and jam. What you call a "doorstep" we call a "piece," north of the border,' Zinnia explained kindly. 'Another cuppa to go with it?'

George allowed himself to be persuaded and spent the time between mouthfuls trying to find out more about Frankie. He didn't get very far, but that didn't mean he wasn't going to. As soon as Frankie started the rounds of the boozers, snooker halls and clubs, news of his reputation, connections and credentials would go ahead of him. That was what he was there for, after all. He'd been sent to let the swine know that Zinnia had heavyweight help behind her, should the need continue to arise.

What fascinated me was how a middle-aged woman, who had spent her life caring for and healing others, had connections with West End villains. Also, how could a woman I had known all my life have this whole other side to her that I knew nothing about? What's more, neither did Mum or Gran, I'd put money on it. I decided, there and then, to do some detecting of my own. It'd take my mind off Charlie's impending leave and the sinister bugger who went round coshing people. I felt my lump. It was smaller, but for some reason it reminded me about the time and getting to work. I glanced at the clock and let out a small shriek—I was running very late. Seeing my panic, Frankie very kindly offered me a lift in his motor. It also handily got him away from George Grubb and his questions.

It was just as well I always kept my keys all together in my handbag, because when I arrived like Lady Muck in a real live car, I found Cook and Beryl tapping their feet on the doorstep. As I had worked there the longest, I kept the spare keys. Which wasn't much of an honour, it just meant I had to open up if Mrs. Dunmore was late or away ill. Mind you, it had hardly ever happened. She was normally a stickler for punctuality, in herself and in others.

'Who's your friend?' Beryl mouthed as I fumbled with the keys. Her eyes glinted and her arched, pencilled eyebrows danced up and down in enquiry.

'Mind your own,' I mouthed back as I finally got the key in. I heard a clatter from the other side of the door. 'Funny,' I said out loud. 'I think there was a key in the lock. The door was locked from the inside.' I shoved the door, but it snagged on the fallen key.

Frankie pushed me and Beryl aside gently and said, 'Allow me, ladies,' before giving it a giant heave with his shoulder. The door crashed inwards and Frankie stumbled in after it.

I saw a pair of feet first, pointing at me from across the room. My first thought was that the bloody woman was inspecting the ovens yet again, ready to issue sarcastic comments, soda and a scrubbing brush. But then I smelt gas.

'Stay out here a sec,' I told Cook and Beryl, then followed Frankie into the room and hurried over to the feet. I turned the gas tap widdershins and the ominous hissing stopped. Frankie stooped and tugged gently at the legs attached to the feet. I recognized the shoes: it was definitely Mrs. Dunmore. Out she slid, her back moving effortlessly along the glossy lino. Even in that grim moment, I thought it was good to know that my ceaseless scrubbing and polishing hadn't been for nothing. All my life, in moments of stress, I have thought of silly things like that. I suppose it's nerves, like laughing hysterically at a funeral.

The next thing I noticed was the distinctive whiff of gin, and lots of it. Mrs. Dunmore reeked of the stuff, despite the hour. She must've been at it all night. Her eyes were closed and her face was a funny colour, sort of pale, with a touch of green around the gills. For a moment, I thought she was dead, then I saw her eyes flicker.

I thanked the God I wasn't sure existed with sincere gusto. I might not have liked Mrs. Dunmore much, but I didn't wish the old bag dead. None of us did. Then the flickering stopped and her eyes opened and she stared up at a perfectly strange man bending over her. Bewildered, she turned to me. She tried to speak, but before the words could make it to the outside world, she was violently sick. Frankie stepped back smartly but I was a little slower and copped the lot.

'Bloody hell!' I squeaked. It was disgusting.

Frankie took charge. 'Right, let's get her out of here. You've turned the gas off, so open all the windows and leave the door open and it'll clear pretty quick.' He bent down and scooped Mrs. Dunmore up as if she was as light as an empty paper bag. I looked down at my filthy, smelly clothes and realized that empty was what she was. I could testify to that. I followed Frankie and his burden out into the blessedly fresh air.

'Phew!' Beryl held her nose. 'You honk of second-hand gin,' she told me, as if I didn't know. 'What's the matter with her?' She nodded at Frankie's back as he helped Mrs. Dunmore into the back of his motor.

'She's been hitting the gin, it's made her ill,' I said shortly. I turned to Cook.

'Can you two manage while I nip home and change my clobber? I can't work in this state. Frankie and me'll see to Mrs. Dunmore. If you can see to this place, I'll get back as quick as I can.'

Cook nodded. 'Take your time, Zelda. We'll manage. We'll just give the blokes less grub to choose from, it'll cut the work down. You go and sort yourself out. We'll see to this lot.' She moved towards the door.

'Oh, and Cook, don't light a fag for a while,' I warned her. I was rewarded by a long stare as Cook worked it out, and then she nodded slightly. It was as well that Beryl didn't find out too much about what had just happened; she'd blab to anyone with a set of ears, and attempted suicide, if that's what it was, was a criminal offence. So the less said, the better.

Nobody spoke much on the way back to Zinnia's. Frankie and I agreed that Zinnia should have a look at Mrs. Dunmore and we left it at that. Every now and then, we heard a snivel from the back seat, but diplomatically pretended we hadn't. It's hard to know what to do or say when it's your boss who's in a bad way. Mrs. Dunmore wasn't the sort you put an arm round, somehow.

At last, we arrived at Zinnia's. Frankie nipped in to make sure George Grubb had left. He had, so we helped Mrs. Dunmore in. She had revived a good deal in the air, and sobered up considerably since she'd dumped her load of gin all over me, but she still looked a sorry sight. So did I.

Having left Mrs. Dunmore in Zinnia's capable hands, Frankie took me home to change my clothes before going about the business he'd come to Paradise Gardens to do.

'I gotta start asking some questions, getting some answers. Joe's gonna want to see some progress,' he explained as he dropped me off on my doorstep. 'So I can't give you a lift back to work or nothing, but if you're quick, I can drop you back at Miss M.'s.'

He had a deal. I was anxious to know what had got into Mrs. Dunmore, besides gin that is. She might not have been the friendliest person, but for all her sharp, slave-driving and sarcastic ways, she wasn't all bad. And I always thought she seemed lonely and a bit sad.

I changed my smelly clothes, dumped the soiled set in a sink full of water and was back at the kerb in seven minutes flat. I was about to climb into the motor when someone called my name. 'Zelda, yoo-hoo!' I turned, and even in the open air the wave of Evening in Paris almost knocked me over. I swear it made my eyes water at ten paces.

'Oh, wotcha, Mavis. Can't stop, got to get to work.'

Mavis smirked and raised her sandy eyebrows until they almost disappeared into the long roll of hair above her forehead. 'I see…' she said, voice so slimy with suggestion that I realized how it must look to her, what with me diving into a strange car with a strange man, very late for work and with Mavis having a dirty mind and putting two and two together and coming up with ninety-eight. But I didn't have time to argue the toss.

'No you don't…' I managed to say, but then a masculine voice came from behind us.

'Hurry up, Zelda, I haven't got all day.'

'I'll see you later, Mavis. I'll tell you then,' I said hastily and climbed in beside Frankie.

'I bet you will!' She grinned, rather nastily I thought.

Frankie dropped me off at the mouth of the Gardens and drove away. I hurried to Zinnia's. I wanted to know how Mrs. Dunmore was. I had almost forgotten my own sore head, which probably meant I was on the mend. If tearing around like a blue-arsed fly all morning had made me neither sick nor dizzy, I reckoned I'd do.

'I've given her a wee sedative and popped her into bed, hen. She'll do for now,' Zinnia told me. 'It wasn't a serious attempt anyhow. She'd hardly had any gas at all; it was mostly gin, I believe. Had she really meant to do away with herself, she'd not have done it in a kitchen where she was expecting the workers to arrive at any moment. No, hen, she'd have done it in the privacy of her own kitchen, well away from everyone. She lives alone, I understand.'

After a brief discussion with Zinnia, I felt reassured enough to get back to work. Zinnia promised that Mrs. Dunmore would be safe enough with her for the day and that she would do her best to get to the bottom of what had led to Mrs. Dunmore's drunken act.

Cook and Beryl were all ears when I got back to work, but I wasn't able to tell them anything beyond what they already knew. Naturally, I left out all mention of the word 'suicide,' although Cook had her suspicions. They oohed and aahed over my encounter with Mavis, agreeing with me that it could be seen as very iffy by those unacquainted with the facts.

'Who was the bloke with the motor, anyway?' demanded Beryl.

I decided to go with Zinnia's story. It seemed best in the circumstances, what with Beryl and her gob. 'He's my mum's mate Zinnia's long-lost nephew, Francis,' I told her. 'He's come to stay with his auntie,' I added.

'Yes. If you say so. But what were you doing coming to work with him in the morning? That's what we'd like to know.' Beryl was like a terrier with a bone, and if that was the way her mind was working, I could see that Mavis' mind would definitely be going along the same route. It didn't do for married women to be seen in strange blokes' motors first thing in the morning, I could see that now, but it was too late. I'd been too worried about being late for work, when I was already in my boss' bad books, to think how it would look if I was seen. Then of course, when I was worried about Mrs. Dunmore, appearances hadn't crossed my mind. Bugger!

I explained about my clonk on the head, let them feel the bump to prove it, and hoped like mad the counter-rumour would run round the manor as fast as the first one was bound to. Everybody liked a scandal—except the object of it, that is. The last thing I needed was for Charlie to hear that I had been playing fast and loose, especially when I hadn't.

I turned the subject to speculation as to why Mrs. Dunmore was drunk on duty. We were all agreed—Percy Robinson!

'Stands to reason,' Cook assured us. 'We haven't seen him in a while: she's been bad-tempered and running us ragged for ages: it's got to be him. He's given her the old heave-ho. Or his missus has cottoned on and given Mrs. D. a piece of her mind. That's enough to send anyone on a bender, a mouthful from her. She can be ferocious about her Percy.

'His last bit of sly, Lily Matthews, told me his wife can be very firm, very firm indeed. She says Percy's bleeding terrified of her, and dumps his lady friends as soon as she finds out about them. Of course, her dad is his boss, so she's got him tied up in both places, home and work.'

I made the last few customers bolt their food, skimped on the tidying up and closed the door bang on closing time. I was in a hurry to get back to Zinnia's and check on Mrs. Dunmore, and while I was at it, I thought I'd pop in on Vi and Tony too, to see how the land lay with them. Also, I could tell her the story of my previous evening and my morning, in the hope she'd pass it on to Mavis. I was praying it would stop the rumours before they started. Charlie was due home and I was a nervous wreck.

I burst in Zinnia's back door to find Mrs. Dunmore sipping tea at the kitchen table. I won't say she actually looked rosy, but she certainly looked heaps better. She smiled a wan smile at me and I was stuck for words. How do you behave when your boss is sitting in your 'second mum's' kitchen, where she has no place to be? What do you talk about when you're dodging tricky subjects like toe-rags called Percy Robinson, suicide and gin? What do you do when someone's already given her a cup of tea, so you can't even break the ice with questions like, 'Tea?' 'Milk?' 'Sugar?' and 'How many?' and you can't break the tension by buggering about with a kettle, a tea caddy and a teapot?

You talk about the weather—what else? That's why we have so much of it in England, to provide a subject for small talk to cover those awkward situations and the pauses between cups of tea.

'It's a nice day out,' I said lamely.

Mrs. Dunmore smiled a pale smile and inclined her head slightly. 'Is it? I've been asleep for most of it.'

I took the plunge. 'How're you feeling now?' I asked, half hoping she wouldn't tell me.

'A lot better, thank you.' She took another sip of tea. 'I understand from, er…Zinnia'—she thought for a moment—'I understand…'—she faltered again—'that it was you that saved me.'

'Not really. Well, it was me and Frankie,' I said. 'He's Zinnia's nephew.' I might as well keep the myth up. 'Nobody knows. Well, not Beryl anyway. I think Cook's probably guessed, but she won't say anything.'

God, it was difficult. I was trying to let her know that it was more or less OK, that everyone understood a bit of drunken hysteria now and then, even in one as snooty as Mrs. Dunmore, but I didn't say it. Without mentioning words like 'oven,' 'gas,' or 'topping yourself,' it was really hard to reassure her that she could go back to work, head held high and nose in the air as usual.

To my horror, a large fat tear started up in her right eye, the one I could see, then spilled over and began a long, slow journey down to her chin. I watched it, rather than look into her stricken face. Bosses aren't supposed to be stricken. The tear clung to her sharp chin for a moment, then splashed on to her navy blue cardigan, which was done up to the neck, as if she was cold. Where was Zinnia when I needed her? I patted the skinny hand that lay trembling on the table. She *was* cold. Her hand was icy.

'I'll get us a fresh pot of tea,' I said. Tea and the weather, every Englishwoman's twin social saviours.

She started to talk as soon as I sat down again, steaming cups in front of us. 'It's Mr. Robinson, of course.'

I nodded. 'I guessed.'

'His wife…' she said faintly.

I nodded again. 'She always does. Percy's terrified of her, they say.'

'Who says?' For the first time, her face took on some colour and stopped looking quite so pinched.

'People. Everyone knows Percy Robinson. I've never met his wife, but I hear she's got a gob, er, a mouth on her.'

Where the hell was Zinnia?

'Oh,' said Mrs. Dunmore in a very small voice.

Just then, Zinnia walked in from the garden holding a trug with some tender, new runner beans laid in it, the first of the season. They weren't very big, but way ahead of anyone else's.

'Wotcha, Zin,' I said, voice hearty with relief.

'How's your bump, hen?'

'Fine, fine,' I told her. I got to my feet. 'I'm just nipping over to see how Vi and Tony are doing.'

'Will you be back for your tea?' she asked.

I thought about it. I couldn't really leave her lumbered with my boss. 'If you'll have me,' I answered.

'Aye, I'll have ye. You can keep Sylvia here company until Frankie gets back. He'll take her home. I've some folk coming for their remedies. Be back here in an hour,' she instructed.

Sylvia? The penny dropped. Mrs. Dunmore! I shot out into the fresh air like a drowning woman.

Chapter 41

Vi and Tony were all right, but the skulking around was beginning to tell on them. They both looked strained and tired. I told an open-mouthed Vi all about the previous couple of days and urged her to tell Mavis as soon as possible, because I didn't want Charlie to hear anything about Frankie to set him off. After all, we were as pure as untrod snow and it wasn't our fault that Mavis' mind ran on grubby tracks. Vi promised me that she'd do her best.

'But I hardly ever see her any more,' she added. 'She always stops in at night to save money for her wedding. It wouldn't cost her nothing to come here for a visit of an evening, but she's been scarce all the same. We still haven't heard a word about who she's supposed to be marrying and when. I'm beginning to think she bought her own ring in Woolworth's. I could've sworn it left a green mark on her finger the other day, but she said she'd been painting the lino in her mum's kitchen.'

The piano upstairs suddenly burst into life with a fairly good rendering of 'Chopsticks.' Vi grinned. 'Tony,' she told me proudly. 'Mrs. Cattermole says he's got a good ear. He's having a practice while Dad's out. You know how he does carry on so.'

'You stopping for your tea?' she asked. I told her that I was expected back at Zinnia's. 'Oh well, never mind, another day.'

'How about you and me going up West together when Tony has his lesson?' I suggested. 'We could look around the shops—not that they've got much, but there's the market, that's worth a look. We could have a bit of dinner at the caff I go to and you could meet Mr. Burlap. I'm sure he'd love to meet Tony's proud mum.' I was rewarded by one of the sunniest smiles I had ever seen on our Vi's face.

I went back to number 23 just in time for tea, which was boiled ham, new spuds and the precious runner beans. The plates had just landed on the table when Frankie appeared. Another place was set while he washed his hands, and we started tucking in. I noticed 'Sylvia'—I couldn't get used to the fact that Mrs. Dunmore had an actual name—was pushing her grub around her plate, and I vowed to get first dibs on the leftovers. She hadn't touched hers with anything other than a clean fork.

'Well,' Frankie told us, 'looks as if I've narrowed the source of the trouble down to three faces, probably linked, according to one helpful bloke. There's Ma Hole: we all thought she'd be in there somewhere. Joe warned me about her. Nasty piece of work by all accounts. There's this geezer from down the docks, and last but not least…'—Frankie paused and turned to me—'there's your old man, Charlie.'

I almost choked. Zinnia had to pound me on the back. 'Charlie!' I managed to splutter at last. 'Charlie? How could he be plaguing the life out of Zinnia? He's in Catterick most of the time.'

'Seems he was shooting his mouth off last time he was home,' Frankie explained. 'It was something about you interfering in his family business once too often, Miss Makepeace.'

There was a gasp from my left. Sylvia muttered, 'Miss Make-peace?' under her breath. I had almost forgotten about her, she'd been so quiet.

'Charlie reckons that you're a snooty bitch who thinks she's better than everyone else,' Frankie continued. 'What's more, Ma Hole agrees with him, according to some spotty tyke who was listening in at the King's Head.'

'That still doesn't explain how Charlie managed to pull all those tricks, does it?' I had no trouble believing Charlie could be that vengeful and stupid; I just couldn't see how he had done it.

'Did you say Makepeace?' Sylvia Dunmore asked suddenly.

'That's Zinnia's name,' I told her, answering for the lady in question. 'Zinnia Makepeace.'

'Good Lord!' Mrs. Dunmore said faintly. 'I've heard about you from Percy. Makepeace is the sort of name you remember.' She turned to me, face pale, eyes wide. 'I didn't realize his friend Charlie was your husband, Zelda. Why should I? I've never even met your husband, or at least, I thought I hadn't.'

We were mystified. What *was* she talking about? I asked her outright.

'Percy said he was helping his friend, Charlie, to, er, "tease" a woman called Makepeace who had upset him. I didn't think it was nice at the time, and said so, but he said it was a harmless prank. He and a few lads swapped the furniture around in two of her rooms. He thought it was hilarious. A practical joke, nothing more, he said. But I thought that if I came home and found that, I'd be really frightened. I wouldn't want to think just anyone could simply walk into my home and fiddle with my things. Especially as I live alone and I understood the lady in question did too. I told Percy so, as well, but he just laughed at me and said women had no sense of humour.

'And it was you, was it, Zinnia, the one he was tricking?'

I didn't give poor Zinnia a chance to get a word in edgeways. 'I'll say it was! And the bastard didn't stop at that.' I was about to give her chapter and verse when Zinnia finally managed to butt in.

'That's enough, Zelda. You mustn't shoot the messenger, they're invariably innocent. Let's just say that things took a wee bit of a nastier turn and leave it at that, shall we? Sylvia is not responsible for that man's actions any more than you are responsible for Charlie's. They're both grown men who make their own decisions.'

She had me there. It was true, so I kept my lip buttoned.

'Do you know of anything besides the one incident, Sylvia?' Zinnia asked. Mrs. Dunmore was a shadow of her former self. Her face was pasty and, if possible, even sharper with her hangover—which must have been a blinder—and all the strain she'd been under. I was sorry for her, which meant that I didn't feel in the least bit scared of her any more.

'No, not really,' she said. 'I'm sorry. I'm sure it was only meant as a joke. It was about the time things began to go wrong between us. He kept telling me that someone was pressurizing him, "putting the squeeze on" as he put it. He seemed very nervous, anxious all the time. That was why he kept getting into tempers, he said. He suddenly found fault with everything I said and did. He even struck me once.' Her hand went absentmindedly to her cheek, as if she could still feel the sting. Perhaps she could.

'And then he stopped coming to see me altogether. And then, his wife called on me. I hadn't known about his wife, although I was beginning to suspect…' Tears were welling up, so we tactfully turned our attention back to Frankie, who had taken the opportunity to clear his plate. I patted her hand vaguely. The poor duck. Percy's missus was famous for the short shrift she gave his floozies. Charlie used to say that they were a double act. When Percy got fed up with his bit of sly, he made sure his wife found out and she saw them off for him. It must've been mortifying for Mrs. D. I patted a bit harder, but made sure I didn't catch her eye. I didn't think she'd want to see pity in my face, somehow.

Frankie wiped up the last of his gravy with a hunk of bread and grinned at us. 'Sounds about right. Geezer by the name of Percy Robinson, a mate of your Charlie and, of course, an acquaintance of Charlie's close relative, Ma Hole.

'Seems introductions were made before Charlie joined up, and after that, Ma often used Percy in her quest to liberate certain items from warehouses, docks and even ships. He was the middle man. Ma'd tell him what was wanted and when it came in, and he'd organize handily placed geezers to do the liberating. Dockers, warehousemen and sailors, blokes like that. So, of course, Ma had something on Percy boy, didn't she?'

We agreed that she certainly did. Frankie grinned evilly. 'And, of course Ma, being Ma, and totally without a single, solitary scruple, did not hesitate to use her man from the docks when the need arose. She's not above a spot of blackmail, that one. A real charmer. Anyway, she was aware of Charlie's grievances and his plans and she decided to up the ante. She was behind the fire, the cats, all of it.'

Zinnia looked bewildered. 'I can believe it. There's never been any love lost between us. But why now? I've been here more than thirty years: why has she become so hostile all of a sudden? She's always restricted herself to being generally nasty in the past.'

It was a good question and one that had been nagging away at me.

'She's taken a fancy to your gaff,' Frankie told Zinnia. 'She wants your house and land, 'specially the land. Envy, simple as that. My man on the inside says she always has been green with it, but it's only now that she could see her way clear to do anything about it.

'She saw a way to drive you out, get your house and, more important, your plot. She reckons she could make a packet developing it. Homes for our homecoming heroes; you get the idea. She could probably stick a good few prefabs on the site, even a block of flats. So she jumped on Charlie and Percy's little bandwagon and turned it into a socking great campaign. She's had Percy working on persecuting you, Miss Makepeace, her own boy Brian's been at it and so have some of her lads. It was a combined effort, to kill two birds with one stone, kinda thing. Get Charlie's job done and her own at the same time.'

We talked for a long time about what we'd learned. What it boiled down to was that Charlie was a resentful swine who had the needle to Zinnia for taking me in and shaming him when he'd beaten me up. That had led to a chain reaction of other nasty business involving Ma Hole. She'd seen an opportunity to make a fortune and milked Charlie's spiteful vendetta for her own ends. And there you had it—mayhem. Any lesser woman than Zinnia would have been terror-stricken by recent events and even she had shown signs of mounting fear. The bastards! All of them.

The big question, of course, was what to do about it? Zinnia and my family were all beset with troubles and it all went back to the Hole clan and those bloody offshoots, Charlie and Brian. Right there and then, I could've swung for Charlie, I was so angry with him. How dare he set Ma Hole loose on Zinnia? How dare he? Even if he hadn't meant to, it was him that started the whole thing.

I was hopping mad, but also, funnily enough, eerily calm. The decision I'd made to leave my husband had hardened into a firm resolve to do it as soon as possible. Nothing on the face of this Earth was going to stop me, and once Frankie had escorted Mrs. Dunmore home, I was free to talk about it. We talked until late, too late for me to go home.

But first we talked about what to do about Ma Hole and Percy Robinson.

'It's probably gonna take a slap or two to convince the parties concerned there's no future in it,' Frankie observed.

I brought up a point that had been slowly dawning on me. 'And Brian's armed. The law hasn't found the gun or the grenade yet. There's no telling what that idiot would do if he was cornered, Frankie.'

'I'll have to make sure I don't corner the little bugger then, won't I?' He smiled at me, and winked.

'The blood runs cold to think of his mother in possession of an armoury,' Zinnia warned him. It was true, too. Ma was very definitely a loose cannon.

'It bears some thinking about and planning,' said Frankie. 'I won't rush into anything. I can always send for reinforcements if it looks like I'll need them. Never seen no point in being a dead hero.' He turned to me. 'What's this about you and your old man? You planning on doing a runner?'

I nodded. 'I can't stop with him any more. I want to strike out on my own. The only thing is, I'll have to move right away. You can see what a vindictive so-and-so Charlie is by what he's done to Zinnia. Can you imagine how he'd be if his wife dared to walk out on him? He'd make my life hell if I was handy. The only good thing is, he's a lazy sod. I don't suppose he'd travel far to make me miserable.

'Then there's my dad. He won't want me bringing shame on the family. The only thing that worries me is that I'll have to move away from everyone I know.'

'If Charlie's as idle as he sounds, it's not as if you've got to leave town. You can stay in the Smoke, near your folks. It don't have to be Timbuktu, does it? You know people in Soho. You know Mr. Burlap, Sharky Finn, Maggie and Bert, and now me.' Frankie flashed a blinding smile. 'Why not try there? I reckon Joe'd find he had a spare gaff for you somewhere. He owns a lot of places round and about.'

It was an idea, certainly. I started to get quite excited the more I thought about it. I liked Soho, and if I could find a place there, it'd suit me fine. I wouldn't be too far from home, I could see my family, my mates. Of course, I'd have to find work, I'd have rent to pay, food to buy. I said as much, and Frankie had ideas about that too. The man was firing on all cylinders all right.

'You've done catering. There's lots of nosheries in Soho and more'll be opening now the war's over, you can bet your life. There's waitressing in the clubs as well. Miss Makepeace mentioned you're a dab hand with the sewing; lots of theatres and costumiers in the area. You might find something to suit you there. Wardrobe mistress or something like that. You won't know until you try.

'I'll tell you who to ask: Maggie and Bert. They know everybody and pretty much everything that goes on in the manor. Ask them, they'll set you straight.'

I looked at Zinnia. She was smiling so hard, I thought her face would split in half. She thought he had a point, that it was a good idea. Suddenly my heart was racing and I was truly, wildly excited. For the first time in years, I could see a future I could live with, that didn't fill me with dread.

I wanted to rush off there and then and get started straight away. But I didn't. I'd be in Soho soon enough, on Saturday morning with Vi and Tony. I'd start then. The thought even held the terror of seeing Charlie at bay. I had a plan, a concrete plan at last!

Chapter 42

Tony was still trying to stay out of trouble, but the strain was beginning to tell on us all. The poor kid was looking haunted as well as hunted. He'd lost weight, too.

I happened to be with Gran when pent-up feelings finally boiled over into a slanging match in the street. We were outside the King's Head, having just bought a couple of jugs of stout to take home for Mum, Gran, Vi, Zinnia and me. Mum was convinced that stout was the thing to perk me up after the gruelling few days I'd just had. It wasn't surprising that Mrs. Dunmore hadn't turned up for work on Wednesday, but she didn't turn up on Thursday either, which was. I was worried about her, and had decided to call in during work the next day if she still hadn't shown up in the morning. Apart from anything else, Friday was pay day; we all needed our money, and I couldn't draw it from the bank.

Also, despite my secret plan, I was beginning to get nervous about seeing Charlie the next night. I had been trying to make up my mind whether or not to tell him I was leaving him while he was home on leave. Part of me felt it'd be best simply not to be there when he came home for good, to just melt away and disappear. I doubted that he'd take the trouble to look for me, in case he found me; I didn't think he really wanted that.

Another part of me felt I owed it to him to tell him I was off, but then masculine pride might rear up if I was actually there with my suitcase. I could imagine Charlie being so determined that no woman was going to leave *him*, that he'd stop at nothing to bar the exit. But if I was actually gone, the same pride would stop him from hunting me down, on the grounds that Charlie Fluck didn't run after women. It was all so confusing.

To add to my worries, Frankie seemed to be taking more than a passing interest in me and I found I quite liked it. Apart from Percy Robinson, there'd been nothing like that for a while, and let's face it, having a pulse was enough for old Percy, so he didn't count. But Frankie taking an interest was flattering. Being flattered was better than being flattened any day, and that had been my lot for far too long.

I didn't think a swig of stout was likely to sort that little lot out, but it might just take my mind off it all. That was my reasoning, and that was why I was stepping out of the King's Head with a large jug of bevvy in one hand and my handbag in the other. Gran was right behind me, also with a jug in her hand.

'Birds can't fly on one wing and if we're going to have a sip of stout, we might as well make it a good one,' was Gran's notion, and it happened to match Mum's sentiments exactly. Vi and me were more cautious. It was a week-night, and three of us had to be hard at work in the morning. Zinnia would have a steady stream of boils, scraped knees, asthmatics, rheumatics, women's troubles, bad backs and rashes to deal with, and had to be on the ball, but she was a whisky drinker and a little stout wouldn't cramp her style. Vi, though, sweated it out in a laundry down Dalston Junction way and, like me, had to have her wits about her if she wasn't to be steamed, scalded or boiled.

Anyway, I just stepped out of the King's Head and right into the path of Ma Hole, who crashed into me, slopping the precious stout. Gran walked straight into my back, and spilled some of her jug too, so I was sopping wet and reeking of stout, front and back. Which made Ma's words all the more infuriating.

'Watch where you're going, you stupid mare,' she spat.

'I could say the same to you,' I answered. I was feeling full of myself, now I'd come to a decision.

'Watch who you're speaking to, Zelda Fluck, or I'll tell young Charlie to teach you your manners when he gets home. He's a good boy is Charlie, does as he's told.'

At this point Gran stepped from behind me and glowered at Gladys Hole. '*You* watch who you're speaking to. You barged into us *and* you slopped our drink.' Gran's face was red and her specs glittered in the last rays of the sun, giving the appearance of flames sparking from her eyes.

'Daft old women shouldn't hit the booze. Their brains is addled enough already, if you ask me.' Ma sounded amused.

'Ah! But we didn't ask you. And talking about addled, what are you doing letting your Brian run around with guns and bloody hand grenades? That's what I want to know.'

I saw a brief look of utter bewilderment cross Ma's face. She had no idea what Gran was on about! Her mouth was open to speak, but Gran's own gob was running away with her, and nothing was going to stop it except lack of steam. I just hoped like hell that she wouldn't drop Tony further in it. I stood ready to jump on her foot if I sensed it heading towards her gob.

'I'm sick and tired of you lot thinking you can just walk all over everybody, take what you want, scare people half to death and get away with it. The law's on to your Brian, and you as well, I'm sure. It's only a matter of time, Mrs. Hole; it's only a matter of time before you get your just deserts.'

Ma had gathered her wits, and wasn't about to let on that she hadn't got control of her own son. She hadn't, though. I saw it in her face. Brian's personal arsenal was a complete surprise to her.

'I told you'—Ma ran her index finger round her temple in a circle and rolled her eyes—'off your trolley. Senile, completely doolally, bats in the belfry. I've long thought it and now I know. You'd better not go spreading your lies about my boy, Ida Smallbone, or you'll have me to answer to, you evil old cow.'

She turned to me. 'You ought to keep her off the streets. She's a bleeding liability, the state she's in.' Her voice took on an edge of menace. 'Talking of off the streets, I haven't seen your Tony lately. I know my Brian's been looking for him. P'raps I'll keep an eye out for him an' all. I'll tell Brian to bring him home for his tea.'

She made it sound as if Tony was on the menu, or maybe I was just overwrought. But in a state or not, I knew what I had seen. Ma hadn't known about Brian; but she did know now. It'd be a good idea to keep Tony very, very close, I thought, and I watched Ma's large back disappearing down the road with Gran's final insults apparently bouncing off it.

'You and your lot have always been wrong'uns, Gladys Hole, always. You bring down everything you touch. You corrupt people, you do, even your own offspring.' Judging by a slight stiffening of Ma's backbone, Gran had hit home with that one.

Since he'd been driving poor Sylvia Dunmore mad by not coming to the canteen for his dinner, Percy Robinson had been very scarce generally. Frankie was chafing at the bit, trying to track the man down, but Percy kept managing to dodge him at the docks and Zinnia wouldn't let Frankie corner him at home. She thought that Mrs. Robinson had enough to contend with, being married to Percy, without being mixed up in his messes.

As Frankie said in an aside to me, 'And one less witness is always welcome, should there be any necessary violence to make Percy boy see the error of his ways. It ain't nice to frighten old ladies.'

Zinnia heard the 'old ladies' and thought he meant her. 'Less of the "old" lady, young man. I'll have you know I'm in my prime.'

Frankie laughed. 'True enough, Miss Makepeace, true enough. I'm sure Mr. Burlap can vouch for that. But I was talking about Percy's old lady as it happens.'

I could hardly believe my eyes, but Zinnia blushed almost as deep as a ripe Victoria plum. I thought at least her barnet must catch fire with the heat, but it didn't. Did Frankie mean what I thought he meant? Surely not. Not Zinnia and Mr. Burlap! I tried to imagine the two of them together. No, surely not!

But then, Zinnia was secretive about him. We'd known her for donkey's years and only very recently heard Mr. Burlap's name, let alone got to meet him. Yet she'd known him more than thirty years, and they kept in such close touch that she was dispensing her remedies to some of his cronies. People in Soho had seen enough of her to grow fond of her and to want to look out for her welfare. Bert had mentioned it, Sharky had too, and Mrs. Joe had seen to it that something was done, via her boy, Maltese Joe.

What's more, Frankie obviously respected her, judging by the way he'd never call her 'Zinnia.' So perhaps her many mysterious trips and days away over the years had been assignations with her lover, Mr. Burlap...No. I couldn't see it, not Zinnia. Not Mr. Burlap. But then, she *was* the colour of plum jam. It certainly gave me something to think about, but it was like trying to imagine my mum and dad on the job. I mean, they had to have done it, at least six times, but I didn't want to have to think about it. And when I did, it made me squirm with embarrassment.

I'd always thought of Zinnia as a maiden lady, like so many who had come through the Great War. So many millions of eligible young men had either wound up dead on the battlefields, or of influenza or so badly maimed, gassed or shell-shocked that they were incapable of taking up normal life again when they got back from the front. It made for an awful lot of spinsters. And naturally, to us younger women, middle-aged spinsters were automatically suffering from in-growing virginity, and quite right too. Sex was for the young, any fool knew that. But I was beginning to think that nobody had bothered to mention it to Zinnia and Mr. Burlap.

Chapter 43

Mrs. Dunmore was late, but at least she did turn up at work that Friday morning, much to the relief of her workers. It meant we'd get paid. She still looked pale and drawn, but her tongue had been blunted by her troubles and she wasn't sharp or critical. If anything, she was depressed and withdrawn and crept about as if she didn't want to be noticed. Her manner was *so* different, we almost—but not quite—longed for the old Mrs. D. back.

'What's the matter with *her?*' Beryl wanted to know. 'I mean, if it's Percy that's got to her, p'raps we should tell her he spends his dinnertimes in the boozer, nowadays. He's there most nights too, keeping out of his missus' way. Her ladyship could nip along there and give him a piece of her mind. You never know, a good old slanging match might make her feel better.'

'It might,' I said, 'but then again, she might do better just to ignore the bugger. Which boozer is he going to anyway?' I asked innocently. I wanted to be certain that it was the Star and Garter before I passed the news along to Frankie.

'Don't tell me you fancy him yourself,' scoffed Beryl cheekily. I didn't trouble to answer. She knew what I thought of Percy Robinson, so I simply glared at her.

'Don't be daft,' said Cook. 'If any female between nineteen and ninety wanted Percy, she wouldn't have to track him down, he'd find her. He can smell a bitch on heat from miles away,' she pointed out—rather unkindly I thought, seeing he'd found Mrs. Dunmore.

What none of us realized was that Mrs. Dunmore had been listening. The first we knew of it was when Molly Squires came in the back door a few hours later, with a very distressed Mrs. Dunmore under her wing. She'd taken her dinner hour in the snug of the pub, and instead of giving Percy what for, as Beryl had suggested, she'd begged to be taken back. While I was plying Mrs. D. with a cup of tea and several hankies in her office, Molly was telling Cook and Beryl what had happened. I was brought up to date later, once I'd seen Mrs. Dunmore home for a nice lie down—via the bank for our wages, naturally.

'Molly said he was cruel, really wicked,' Beryl told me with relish. 'Said she was a dried-up old bag and he'd only been having his bit of fun, that she should never have taken him serious.'

'The bastard!' I breathed. Well, he was!

'We've always known that, ducky,' Ronnie piped up. He'd popped in for his dinner and, sensing scandal, had waited for me to come back.

'It's true enough. She's not the first and she won't be the last,' Cook said sagely. 'It's his wife you've got to feel sorry for. What must it do to her?'

I nodded. Talk of unhappy marriages made me think of Charlie. He'd probably be in soon after I got home from work. My heart felt like lead as I doled out our wages on the large kitchen table. Ronnie watched as I carefully counted out our measly pounds, shillings and pence. It didn't seem much for the week I'd had, or any of my weeks, for that matter. I think Ronnie noticed that I was in the doldrums, because he offered to stroll home with me. Charlie couldn't object to Ronnie being my escort, if anyone reported seeing us together, him being a confirmed bachelor and all. I decided to close the canteen early. I was due the bonus of an hour or two of Charlie-free time, if only for being sicked up on by the boss.

'You're on,' I told Ronnie, and let the others know we were getting off early. They took it in their stride; in fact, I almost got trampled in the rush for the door.

On the walk home, I brought Ronnie up to date with what had been happening and what decisions I'd made.

'Well, dolly, you certainly live in exciting times! All that in one week! We can't let you out on your own, can we?' Ronnie gave me a reassuring squeeze. He realized that I was badly rattled by all the events: the clonk on the head, Mrs. Dunmore, Tony, and now Charlie.

'I won't say I'm surprised you're leaving Charlie. It's been a long time coming and you'll be better off without him. You'll manage. You're a tough little palone, dolly. You just don't know it yet. But look at the stock you come from: your gran, your mum—they're not shrinking violets, either of 'em.

'And I think Soho will suit you down to the ground.' He smiled widely and squeezed again. 'Yep, down to the ground.'

Ronnie was a poppet. Seeing my dread, he climbed the stairs and waited while I turned my key in the flat door, saying he'd have a cup of tea with me. We heard scuffling noises from inside and knew that Charlie was home early, too. Ronnie took the lead. 'Yoo-hoo, Charles, look who's come for tea.' And he minced into the flat like a drag queen, flapping a limp wrist in greeting.

I was bringing up his considerable rear when I heard him squeal, 'Ooh! I say!' And he stopped dead so that I barged into him. Once I was free of Ronnie's back, the first thing I noticed was the reek of Evening in Paris. The second thing I noticed was Mavis standing next to Charlie in the middle of my kitchen, and the third thing was that they both looked guilty and flustered. Even so, it took a moment for the penny to drop.

'What do you say, Ronnie?' I asked, innocently, though my heart was racing. What *had* I almost seen?

'I say, WHAT'S going on here?' Ronnie answered. 'Or I would if I was you. I think some delecto is being flagranted right in the middle of your very own kitchen, dolly.'

I tried not to laugh, but suddenly my heart was as light as a Granny Smallbone sponge cake. 'I think you could be right, Ronnie. They certainly look like a pair of startled rabbits. What's the matter, Charlie, Mavis still got your tongue? You've certainly got her lipstick, almost up to your eyebrows.'

Charlie found his bluster. 'It ain't what it looks like.'

I laughed. 'Oh yes it is, Charlie. Oh yes it is. I think I'll be leaving you now. I'll just pick up some things and I'll be back for the rest when you're tucked up in Catterick. Can you wait for me, Ronnie?'

'Until hell melts and heaven dies of boredom, dolly, or at least until opening time, when I'm meeting a man about a…Well, never you mind about that. Until then, I'm all yours.'

Charlie followed me into the bedroom with Mavis close behind. Piccadilly Circus in the rush hour had nothing on that room: we were so squeezed in, there was barely room to swing a corset. Ronnie, not to be left out, hovered at the threshold, grinning. I started throwing clothes into a canvas bag as Charlie began to pull himself together.

'You're my wife,' he told me. 'You ain't leaving.'

I had my mouth open to tell him that I was, when something rammed him hard in the kidneys, shooting him forward a few steps. It was a red-faced Mavis. 'And I'm your fiancée, Charlie Fluck, and I've got the ring to prove it, so don't you forget it. If she wants to go, let her go. You've got me now.'

I stopped packing. Of course! Mavis' mystery fiancé. I'd forgotten him in the heat of the moment. 'Seems you've neglected a little formality there, Charlie,' I sneered. 'Aren't you supposed to be single before you get engaged to someone?'

I continued to pack. Just enough for a few days; that should do it. I was ever so calm and methodical. Three pairs of drawers, brassière, clean blouse, clean skirt, cardigan, nightie, dressing gown, toothbrush, hairbrush and comb. In it all went, and the years of misery and fear were left behind, along with my wedding ring, which I placed in the very middle of my marriage bed. I checked my handbag for my purse, ration books, keys, compact, lipstick, mascara, nub of eyebrow pencil and clean hanky. It was all there.

'Right, that'll do for now. I'll be back for the rest in a day or two, when I find my feet a bit.' When I moved towards the door with my bag, Charlie stepped into my path, face white and pinched. I knew that look. My heart lurched and then began to beat faster. I ducked instinctively but Ronnie stepped forward too, showing he was ready to intervene should things turn ugly. He was much bigger than Charlie, and much more powerful from heaving socking great wet ropes about. He had the arms of an all-in wrestler—which is why he looked a little odd when he wore anything strapless, with evening gloves. However, he was in his civvies that day and he just looked awfully big.

'You ain't going nowhere, I told you,' Charlie hissed and grabbed my arm. His fingers dug into me until I winced and let out a little squeal under my breath.

'That'll do, Charlie.' Ronnie heaved Charlie's spare arm up his back until he was forced to let me go. Ronnie didn't let go, though; he dragged Charlie back into the kitchen and threw him at the wall opposite the flat door, then stood between Charlie and my way out. All the while, Mavis just stood there, hands up to her mouth as if stifling a scream. Perhaps she was; after all, it didn't do to alert the neighbours to your domestics. They had to be carried out behind closed doors, even if you died for it. But not me. I was off. I turned to her.

'Good luck, Mavis. I really do wish you luck.' And I was out on the landing and almost tripping down the stairs in my rush to get out of there. I virtually skipped round to Zinnia's, I felt so relieved. All that dread, all that terror, all those rehearsals of what I was going to say, all for nothing. In the end, it had been so easy I could hardly believe my luck. I could've blessed Mavis, made her a saint there and then.

The thought stopped me in my tracks. The trouble was, all the saints were dead, and I hoped fervently that that wouldn't happen to my cousin. She might have been sneaking around with my old geezer behind my back, and she didn't know she was doing me a favour, she must've thought she was betraying me—but even so, she still didn't deserve to be lumbered with Charlie.

'I'll have to warn her,' I said out loud.

'What? Warn who, dolly?'

'Mavis.'

'Why? She's your old man's bit of sly and a blood relative who did the dirty on you. Warn her about what, anyway? My plus is nonned, dolly.'

'I must warn her that Charlie's violent when he's on the bevvy,' I answered.

Ronnie's face fell. 'I s'pose you're right. She should at least know. What she does about it is up to her. Still, you don't have to do it now. Wait till Charlie's safely behind barbed wire at his camp and tell her then, before you take off for pastures new—or even after. It might be safer after. Drop her a postcard or something.'

I nodded. A postcard would do. 'Dear Mavis, Charlie beats his wives, 'specially when he's tanked up. Thanks for everything, Zelda.' That should do it. I smiled at the thought and carried on up the road.

We bumped into Terry outside the King's Head and regaled him with my news.

'*Mavis?*' was all he could say, then, 'I must tell Dilly. I expect you'll see her straight after work tomorrow night. She'll want it from the nag's mouth.'

'Who are you calling a nag?' I demanded, eyes sparking; the cheeky sod.

'Nag as in old horse,' explained Terry hastily, as if that made it any better. 'Shall I tell her to nip round your mum's, seeing you'll not be at home?'

I shook my head. 'No, Dad won't have me. I'm supposed to put up with anything Charlie sees fit to dish out. It's my duty. So Dad'll be shirty. No, I'll be round at Zinnia's.'

'What've you two got on tonight? Fancy a drink somewhere?' Terry asked.

Ronnie declined graciously. 'Not me, sweetie. I've got a date with a Yank, one of Chester's friends.'

'Gawd! You're a quick worker. When've you had the chance to chat up any of Chester's pals?' I wanted to know. 'How come I haven't heard about this before?' I hated to miss anything.

'Keep your wig on, dolly. You have been a bit busy yourself, remember. Nobody's seen you to keep you abreast of affairs, now have they? I bumped into Dilly and Chester in a jazz place off Wardour Street and Chester introduced me to some of his chums. Marlon and I just hit it off, that's all. I don't s'pose it'll lead to anything of interest, but a girl never knows.' Ronnie fluttered his eyelashes, but they were his own and therefore not up to much.

I turned back to Terry, who was laughing gently to himself. 'Why don't you pop round Zinnia's after your tea?' I suggested. 'I've got loads to tell you that you haven't heard yet. P'raps we can go out for a drink later.' Terry agreed and hurried off towards his shop.

Ronnie and I carried on towards Paradise Gardens. I have to admit, I was in a daze. It was like being threatened with having your leg cut off and then getting a reprieve right on the operating table, only better. I had never expected to get away from Charlie so easily, or to be so firmly 'in the right' while I was doing it. Fancy old Charlie and Mavis being at it. I never saw it coming.

Then I remembered the phantom whiffs of Evening in Paris I had had over the last few weeks. My hooter had been trying to tell me all along, I had just failed to understand the message. What was the point of being sent messages if they were in a code I couldn't crack? It was bloody annoying.

Chapter 44

Vi, Tony and I were in high spirits on the bus up West. Vi was agog to hear about our cousin and my husband, and that kept us amused all the way to town. Tony was just pleased to get away from hostile territory and not to have to keep looking over his shoulder.

'I like it all right at the Rev.'s, Auntie Zelda. It's just that it's not where all my stuff is,' he confided as we got off the bus in Oxford Street.

'Well, neither's your bedroom until we've got those walls distempered,' his mum told him. 'What's more, Granny Smallbone was right, there are *things* under that bed of yours.' She ruffled his hair and he leaned away from her, blushing.

'Geroff,' he said, but I could tell that he liked it.

We arrived at Digby Burlap's door, and climbed the stairs to his studio. 'Ah, dear lady,' he boomed at the sight of me. 'Enter, enter do.'

We traipsed in in single file as Mr. Burlap beamed down at us. I introduced Vi, and Mr. Burlap solemnly kissed her hand, much to her surprise. I had warned her that Tony's teacher was a touch colourful, but she hadn't realized the man was a complete rainbow.

'Your son is very gifted, madam, I do hope you realize that. He is very musical, which might sound obvious, but not all musicians are, you know. And, of course, he has the gift of perfect pitch, which helps enormously. I understand his pianoforte studies are going well too?'

Vi nodded proudly. 'So Mrs. Cattermole says. Of course, he's very new to it, but she thinks he's picking it up a treat.'

'Oh excellent, dear lady, excellent.' Mr. Burlap clapped his hands together. 'Right, are you two ladies staying or going?'

'Going,' I said. 'But first, a message from Zinnia. She says to tell you that Frankie is looking after her and there has been no new outbreak of nastiness. She also said that her mind is made up. But she didn't say what it was made up about.'

'I can guess, dear lady, I can guess.' Mr. Burlap looked serious for the first time, and perhaps even a little nervous. 'Did she say when she intended to enlighten me as to her decision?'

'She said she'd be over to see you tomorrow, around dinnertime.'

Mr. Burlap nodded and said, 'Ah.' Then he waved a plump hand at us as Vi and I left.

'Do you want to look round the shops?' I asked half-heartedly. I was itching to get round to Maggie's and ask about the possibilities of finding a place to live and a job to pay for it. Luckily, Vi agreed with my sense of urgency and was all for sitting down with a cup of tea and a mine of useful information in the ample form of Maggie.

'Hello, Zelda,' Maggie said cheerfully. 'Tea for two, is it?'

'Hello, Maggie. This is my sister, Vi. Can you make it tea for three if you've got time? I'd like to talk to you about something.'

'Right you are. Take a seat at that table in the corner by the window and I'll be over in two shakes of me tea strainer.' She laughed. 'Make that three shakes.

'Bert, I'm going to have a break now. Can you cover?' she called into the kitchen.

'OK, love, out in a tick,' came the answer.

Vi and I made our way to the table, and Maggie busied herself with cups and saucers and a plate of digestive biscuits.

Such luxury! The place was very quiet and nobody interrupted us as I explained my situation to Maggie.

'Do you know,' she said, 'I've got a feeling that there's a place next door falling vacant soon. I don't know if Maltese Joe has anyone for it or not. Leave it with me, love, I'll ask him. He's a mate of my Bert.'

'Did someone just use my name in vain?' asked Bert, coming up behind me.

I heard my sister gasp quietly. 'Has anyone ever told you you look a bit like Humphrey Bogart?' she asked, before she could remember her manners.

I kicked her under the table and smiled up at him. 'Sorry about my sister, Vi, Bert. She can't help it.' I turned to Vi, who was laughing. 'Vi, this is Maggie's husband, Bert.'

'Pleased to meet you, I'm sure.' Vi was still stifling a giggle.

Luckily, Bert was laughing too. 'As it happens, Vi, they have, but me and Maggie can't see it ourselves. Can we, love?'

'No,' Maggie twinkled. 'Humphrey Bogart looks a bit like my Bert to me. Zelda here is looking for a place round here, Bert, and a job. Was I right in thinking that the flat above Sharky could be empty soon?'

'I dunno, Maggie, but I can find out for you.' Bert turned to me, 'How soon do you need it?'

'As soon as possible,' I answered. My heart was hammering so hard in my chest that I thought it must burst out into the open. It was all becoming real to me, bit by bit. I was still reeling from being let off the hook by Charlie and Mavis the afternoon before, and now these people were listening to me calmly, taking me seriously and offering to help. I was on my way.

'As to work, am I right in thinking you work in catering?' Bert asked.

'Well, yes. I don't do the actual cooking, I keep the place clean and tidy and serve the men at dinner-time,' I answered, heart still going like the clappers.

'It's just that Maggie and me could do with a bit of a hand since we rejigged the place and got more tables in.' He turned to Maggie. 'What do you think, love? We've been talking about it long enough.'

'I think it's a good idea, if Zelda fancies it. It'll be a start, won't it?' Maggie smiled at me.

It would be a start indeed. We shook hands on it and talked about wages and when I could begin. 'When you're ready, love,' Maggie told me. 'We'll still be here. We've managed this long, we can manage till you're ready. It'll be the same sort of thing as you're doing now. Mucking in with the cleaning, taking orders, serving meals and teas. There's not a lot to it, really.'

Not to Maggie, maybe, but to me it was a means to a whole new beginning and I suddenly felt overwhelmed with gratitude to this lovely couple, as well as the unlovely couple that I'd surprised in my kitchen.

The doorbell tinkled and a large belly came through the door, followed by Cassie. We moved chairs around so she could join us, and she sank gratefully into one of them.

'Darlings, if I don't drop this little blighter soon, I shall go stark, staring bonkers,' she declared and we all laughed. I introduced Cassie to Vi and they smiled at each other. I could tell that Vi was a little intimidated by the very pregnant glamour-puss before her. Cassie was everything that Vi had always wanted to be: blonde, beautiful and posh. I wondered if she wanted those things still, or whether that had changed along with her newly revised attitude to life.

'Tea, Cassie?' Maggie asked, heaving herself to her feet. 'Everyone else fancy a top-up?'

There were cries of 'Yes please,' and Maggie went to the counter to make it. I joined her to help carry the teapot, while she loaded a tray with cups for Bert and Cassie, a slop basin and strainer, a jug of milk and a bowl of precious sugar with two fresh spoons. She added another plate of digestives. Where *did* they get their sugar and biscuits? I was going to like working here, I just knew it. And no-one could be more different from Mrs. Dunmore than Maggie and Bert, that was certain. I thought my face would split with the grin that spread across it.

'Thank you, Maggie,' I said, tears of gratitude in my eyes. 'I can't tell you what it means to me.'

'Thank Bert. It was his idea. I just agreed that it was a good one. And it's true, we've been talking about getting help in for ages. It's a bonus that we're getting experienced help, believe me. Welcome aboard, Zelda.' Maggie's beam could've directed shipping safely into harbour. In a funny sort of way, I suppose it had.

We rejoined the others and Cassie smiled at me. 'I hear you're joining this happy little band. Bert was asking me about the top flat next door and as far as I know, Joe's in the process of evicting the tenants for non-payment. He's very cross, hopping mad in fact.' She laughed, as if delighted with the notion of a hopping Maltese.

Bert joined in. 'They're related to Joe. He reckons they should know better than to try to take the mickey like that,' he chortled.

'I should imagine it'll come free soon. Mind you,' Cassie warned me, 'he's said it before and they've mollified him with some rent. But if Bert puts in a word for you and, what's more, assures Joe you'll be paying rent on a regular basis, I'm sure that would swing it. They are *very* distant relatives, after all. Second cousins twice removed or something.'

'You'll have to make it clear to Joe, Bert,' Maggie warned in a serious tone, 'that Zelda here is a respectable girl. She's not going to be working for him, she's going to be working here, with us. We don't want any mistakes or misunderstandings, Bert Featherby.'

Bert held his hands up like a boxer defending his face. 'All right, old girl. Keep your hair on. I'll make a point of it.'

'Right, I'd better get me dinners on. You lot staying? It's macaroni cheese or shepherd's pie.'

I plumped for the macaroni cheese, Vi had the shepherd's pie, and Cassie had another cup of tea and her third fag. The girl was a chain-smoker in a time when that wasn't easy, due to shortage of supply. Somebody kept this lot amazingly well supplied with all of life's little luxuries.

I began to think I had fallen on my feet—stockinged feet at that. I'd never seen either of these women in anything other than real, ladder-, hole- and darn-free stockings. They didn't even have little dabs of wet soap on them, to stop snags from spreading. Of course, in times of plenty we used nail polish—it worked better than wet soap. But I had never seen the tell-tale splodges on either set of legs.

As I sat there, idly thinking about things and eating my macaroni, I felt an unfamiliar glow spread outwards from my chest. I think it was happiness.

Chapter 45

'Leaving?' Dad asked into the silence. 'Leaving? Did you say you was leaving?'

I nodded, hardly daring to breathe, let alone speak. I'd shot my bolt bringing the subject up at all. But it seemed best to tell the whole family at once, while they were sitting at the Sunday dinner table. It saved repeating myself over and over.

Dad turned to Mum, face purple with beer and fury. 'Did you know about this?'

Mum shook her head. 'Although I'm not surprised—that Charlie of hers is a pig.'

'I don't care if he's the whole fucking farm! She married him, she can bleeding well stick it out like any other married woman.' Dad was beside himself with a mixture of disbelief and rage. His females did not defy him; even his sons didn't, until they got old enough to clout him back, that is.

'Watch your language, Harry,' Gran warned him. 'There's kids present.'

'What am I supposed to do about Mavis?' I asked, reasonably enough, when I'd got my second wind.

'See her off. It shouldn't be beyond you. She can't go around getting engaged to other people's husbands. There's laws about that sort of thing.'

'But Zelda doesn't want to see her off, Dad,' Vi pointed out. 'She reckons they deserve each other. And I agree with her. I reckon they do, too.'

'What you reckon is beside the bloody point, Vi. She's a married woman,' Dad said, as if talking to a lunatic. The words 'married woman' seemed to cover everything as far as he was concerned.

'We know that, Harry,' Gran piped up patiently, having got over the initial shock. 'But nowadays, she doesn't have to stay married if she doesn't want to. He's a married *man*, but that hasn't stopped him and Mavis having it off, has it? It shouldn't be too hard to prove there's been adultery. There's laws about that kind of thing, too,' Gran pointed out sneakily. 'That's why they have divorce.'

The word hung in the air, like the smell from a gaping sewer that had taken a direct hit. 'Times have changed, Harry, and it's about time you caught on to that fact. If I can, you ought to be able to, you being younger and all. Not that anyone would notice, the way you carry on. Anyone would think the old Queen was still on the throne if they listened to you. You're halfway through the twentieth century, for Gawd's sake, not the nineteenth.'

'And what about Charlie?' I asked, still managing to sound reasonable, although I was rapidly losing patience with Dad's point of view.

'What *about* Charlie?' Dad demanded, not giving an inch. 'Men was made to put it about a bit. It can be hard not to stray. Of course, a man should *try*,' he added hastily, seeing the glint in Mum's eye, then ruined it by muttering, 'even if it is against nature.'

'No,' I said, boiling over, 'I'm sorry, Dad, but what's sauce for the goose is also sauce for the bloody gander. If I have to stick to my marriage vows, then so does Charlie. It never said in any vows I heard that he should start having it off with my cousin and worse, as far as I'm concerned, knock me about while he's at it. If you're so keen on Charlie, you bloody live with him.'

I realized that everyone was staring at me. 'What?' I asked, bewildered.

Gran grinned a grin big enough to berth the *Queen Mary*. 'It's you, Zelda. You're beginning to remind me of me.'

'It's true, love. You even remind *me* of your gran,' agreed Mum, looking proud. 'For what it's worth, I think you should take this chance. Ignore your dad. He's a silly old fool anyway.'

Dad spluttered, showering gravy and Yorkshire pudding all over Reggie and the twins. I noticed that Doris quietly wiped them down with a tea towel while listening to every word.

'Who are you calling a silly old fool? You're my old woman, you're supposed to be on my side, not calling me names.' Dad simply couldn't believe such wholesale insurrection in the ranks.

'Give it a rest, Dad, do,' Doris backed our mum up. 'We're all grown women here, and you've had it your way for far too long.'

Dad tried to butt in, but Doris wasn't having it. 'Times have changed. We've had jobs, we've dug for victory along with the blokes, we've made bombs, planes, ships, tanks, the bloody lot—we're not going to go back to our kitchens. And we're not going to keep our mouths shut any longer neither, just to keep the peace and the wage packet coming in to feed the kids. You'd better keep up, Dad, because you're in danger of being left way behind.

'And as to our Zelda, I say good luck to her. She's paid her dues. She's got no kids to worry about and her husband's a bully who's betrayed her—with a relative, no less. I say that Zelda has a right to say "Good riddance to bad rubbish." So there!' Doris finished triumphantly, then burst into tears. It had been a brave speech for my big sister and we were all proud of her, including her son.

'You tell him, Mum,' I heard Reggie mutter quietly.

'I'm lucky,' Doris continued in a choked voice. 'I love Ern and I know he loves me. But it were never like that for Zelda, and so she should cut her losses and leg it, I reckon. You can't make do and mend for ever, Dad, 'specially if what you're trying to mend started out a mess, like our Zelda's marriage.'

Dad looked around at us all. 'How many of you think like that?' he asked, incredulously. Everyone in the room put up a hand, even the twins, who had no idea what was going on—a situation they shared with their grandad.

'Well then,' he said heavily, 'I suppose there's nothing I can do. I won't wish you luck, Enid, but I'll do nothing to stop you neither. But I don't think that Soho is a fit place for any daughter of mine all the same, even you.'

'And you'll be welcome home any time, dear, for a visit,' said Mum. 'You will come and visit, won't you?' She sounded anxious.

I laughed, relief at breaking my news flooding through me. 'Of course, Mum, and you'll come and see me. It's only a bus ride away.'

'I can show you how to get there, Granny Flo,' Tony said proudly. 'I know my way about up there.'

'Bloody hell! What is the world coming to? My daughter and my grandson swanning about in bleeding Soho? It's a den of vice, stiff with bloody whores and spivs. It's disgusting,' Dad roared.

'That's enough, Harold Marriott!' Mum shouted back. 'I dunno about Soho, but my grandchildren are learning all about bad language and vice at my own dinner table. Now shut up, for goodness sake, and eat your rhubarb crumble.'

Frankie and Zinnia were still out when I got back to 23 Paradise Gardens. Frankie had given Zinnia a lift to Soho to see Mr. Burlap while he was reporting to his boss, Maltese Joe. He'd promised to put a word in about accommodation for me. The poor man would have it coming at him from all directions. Frankie was to bring Zinnia back when both their bits of business were satisfactorily concluded.

Meanwhile, I repacked my belongings ready to head home again. Charlie'd be on his way back to Catterick and I could do my washing and decide what things to take to my new life.

I had jumped two huge hurdles already in telling Charlie and my family my plans. It looked as if the third and fourth hurdles weren't going to be as hard as I feared, either. It seemed that a job and a new home wouldn't prove too difficult to come by with my new friends to help me. Without them, it would have been really hard. So many women were leaving work to get back into their kitchens. Well, perhaps not so much 'leaving' as being pushed, in a lot of cases.

Good old Hitler had made it his mission to ensure that houses were in chronically short supply, too. He had not only flattened loads of them, but had also made sure the blokes who would have built new ones were either in the army or kept busy repairing the old ones blasted by shrapnel or shock waves. Supplies of bricks, cement and wood—most of all wood—had been used in the war effort and to make essential repairs. There was nothing left over for new houses, so lots of people were crammed into what was left of the old ones.

When my brothers got back, they would doubtless have to live in Arcadia Buildings along with Mum, Dad, Gran, Vi and Tony. So I knew I was very, very lucky to even get a sniff of a place to live and a job. I was counting my blessings even as I walked through the flat door.

'At last!' a voice said.

I peered into the gloom—I had just come in from bright daylight and my eyes hadn't caught up—and made out a figure slumped in an armchair. 'Charlie?' I asked, disbelievingly. Then the stink of stale booze hit me. It was Charlie all right, and the worse for wear by the smell of things.

'You've finally decided to turn up, have you?' he sneered. He was struggling to stand, but the chair was low and his legs were unstable. He was unshaven, his hair stood up in spikes and he'd obviously been sick at some point. I don't know if it was the sight or the smell of him that made my own stomach heave. Maybe it was just fear.

'What are you doing here?' I asked. 'You're s'posed to be on the train back by now.'

'Well I ain't, am I? I've gone AWOL,' Charlie answered, finally staggering towards me.

I took a few steps backwards. 'I can see that.' Going AWOL was a serious business. The army took a dim view of it and men wound up doing time in the glasshouse for less.

'I reckon they'll understand. When a man's wife has the sauce to walk out on him, he's bound to get a bit upset. They'll go easy on me, I reckon, if I bother to go back at all.' Charlie took some more steps and so did I. My back was against the door of the flat. I moved away and tried to inch it open a tiny fraction. I knew that I mustn't allow myself to be locked in with him, even for a second.

'Desertion's a very serious offence, Charlie. You'll be for it if they catch you, and if you hang about here, they'll catch you for sure. You live here. It'll be the first place the military coppers'll check. Then they'll try your mum's.'

I was playing for time. I needed the flat door open. I inched it a bit further, just far enough so that I could sling it open in one movement, should the need arise.

The need arose immediately. Charlie lunged for me. I dodged out of his reach, threw the door wide and scuttled onto the little landing. I tried to pull the door closed after me, but Charlie had a hold on it. I stepped backwards down a couple of steps, not wanting to take my eye off him for a moment. Then Charlie wrenched the door open and lunged again. I dodged quickly to one side and he plunged past me head first down the stairs, the very same flight that he'd thrown me and our unborn baby down.

I watched him tumble and land at the bottom in a shabby, grubby heap. I wondered if he'd broken his neck, but then I saw him move and heard a groan. My heart sank. He was between me, the street door and freedom. If I wanted to get out, I'd have to step over him, and I wasn't at all sure how hurt he was. He was very drunk, and I'd noticed before that drunks seemed to bounce better than the sober.

He groaned again and whispered, 'Help me, Zeld.'

I walked gingerly down the stairs to help him. Talk about stupid! No sooner did I bend over him, checking to see that he wasn't badly hurt, than he had his hands round my throat. He began to squeeze for all he was worth. Luckily, he was too drunk and in no physical position to be worth much, and I managed to wrench myself away and step over him to the front door. I yanked at it. It flew open with such force that it smashed into Charlie's face as he got to his knees and lunged towards me for a third and last time. He went down again, clutching his nose. There was blood everywhere.

'Oh well done, dolly.' Ronnie's hand was raised to knock. Terry was standing right behind him. The pair of them assessed the situation and then sat on Charlie while I gathered up my bags and found a clean set of clothes.

I half ran back to Zinnia's. A mix of fear and excitement would not let me walk. By the time I got there, she and Frankie had got back from Soho and were sitting at the kitchen table sipping scalding hot tea. They heard me out without interruption. When I'd finished my tale of woe, Frankie rose purposefully to his feet.

'I'd better head round there,' he said. 'I want a word with Charlie boy about the way he likes to lay into the ladies. I'll be back.'

Once I'd calmed down enough, I was able to grill Zinnia about her meeting with Digby Burlap. She wasn't very forthcoming at first, being a secretive sort when it came to her own business, but she did open up a tiny bit when I pointed out that she knew everything about my life and it was only fair that she put me out of my misery.

'It's driving me potty, when I have the time, wondering about you and Mr. Burlap,' I told her.

She smiled and, just for a moment, looked and sounded like a young girl. I had never noticed before, but Zinnia was a striking looking woman; not beautiful, but striking.

'You have a point, lassie. I'll not deny I'm secretive. I suppose it comes from being brought up on an island, where your neighbours know when a body last sneezed and how regularly you change your underwear. They know almost as soon as you do, and the rest of the island knows by dinnertime. Anyway, a tale will take our minds off what's happening round at your place, which is probably the best thing for us both.

'Where to begin…?'

I listened until I thought my ears must drop off. I heard all about her childhood on the remote island and how, after seagulls and seals, the traffic and the rush and bustle of London had come as a tremendous shock to her.

'And the heathenism. Ach! You English are terrible heathens,' she laughed. 'Where I come from, Sundays are for kirk and that is all. No washing, cooking, cleaning; just praying, and walking to and from the kirk. I could not believe it when I found I could walk just for pleasure on the sabbath day. It was never so at home.

'Anyway, I was training for a nurse at the Middlesex Hospital and living in the nurses' quarters. I was very happy. Then, one Sunday in Regent's Park, I met Digby.'

Zinnia's vivid grey eyes looked back across the years and her face softened. 'We met up on most Sundays after that. I felt so wicked, to be walking out with a young man on the Sabbath; so wicked and so free. I loved my new life—and I loved Digby.'

Eventually, they became engaged, against her family's wishes. He was, after all, an entertainer, which was the next best thing to the Devil himself, according to Zinnia's lot. There was little they could do about it, them being hundreds of miles away, but her father never spoke to her again before he died, and her mother was little better. Singing was sinful. They didn't even sing in church, and that was that.

'Of course, we had no money, so we were forced to wait. I wanted to finish my training too. Married women weren't taken into nursing, and I would have had to leave the hospital. So we waited for better times, and I think I secretly hoped my parents would come round. But better times were slow in coming and my parents were obstinate.'

Zinnia sighed. 'Then Digby began to tour all over the place and we drifted apart.' She faltered to a stop. 'I eventually came here and Digby married someone else. We lost touch.'

But they had met up again by accident, at a concert at the Albert Hall. Digby's wife had run off with an acrobat and he'd settled in Soho, giving lessons to hopefuls and making a tidy living.

'The rest you know,' Zinnia concluded.

'Oh no I don't,' I wailed. 'His wife ran off with an acrobat and…?'

Zinnia blushed to the roots of her hair. 'And Digby and I kept in touch. That's all you need to know, young lady. We have kept in touch for many years now, and recently…' she paused—'recently, Digby heard that his wife had died. He heard it from a mutual acquaintance who had been there when it happened. She fell from her trapeze just before the war. She broke her neck. It was very sad and Digby was most distressed to hear of it. However, it did mean that he was free. So, after a decent interval, he proposed marriage to me once again.'

'So that's what the message was about,' I breathed. 'You went there today to give him your answer.'

Zinnia nodded. I waited. The baggage let me wait. In the end, I had to beg. 'So?' I prompted. 'What did you tell him?'

'I told him yes.' She smiled a radiant smile, like a cat with a whole cow full of cream. 'As long as we live here.'

'Oh, congratulations, Zinnia!' I yelled, and launched myself across the table to give her a big hug, which shook us both rigid. Zinnia was not one of nature's huggers. It was like grabbing a plank. But she did her best. Then we broke out her whisky to celebrate.

I have to admit, it never occurred to me that Zinnia would ever tie the knot. She seemed content as she was. And she was, she assured me.

'But my work here will soon be over, hen. This here National Health Service everyone's talking about will see to that. And I always intended to marry Digby, when we were engaged the first time, but I just let things drift. I didn't want to hurt my parents, I suppose. So now's as good a time as any, hen, when there's already so much change in the air.'

Chapter 46

Ronnie and Terry had cleaned Charlie up after I left. They had just got him on his feet when Frankie arrived. Frankie explained his mission and what he wanted with Charlie.

'So we stepped back smartish, dolly, and let the nice man take over,' Ronnie told me at work the next day.

When he'd got back to Zinnia's the night before, Frankie had simply mumbled that he thought Charlie had got the message about leaving Zinnia alone in future. He'd also mentioned he'd dumped Charlie on a train for Penzance, the opposite end of the country from where he needed to be, 'To keep the little bastard busy.' Then he went to bed. It was most unsatisfactory; I wanted more details. So I was glad to see Ronnie at dinnertime.

'Then what happened?' Beryl asked for me.

We were all agog, even Mrs. Dunmore, 'whose gog, dolly, has been missing for some time, let's face it,' as Ronnie observed later.

'Well, the nice man explained to Charlie how Zinnia was a good friend to his boss' mum and how his boss had been urged to intervene in Zinnia's spot of bother. He went on to explain just exactly how it wouldn't be in Charlie's interests to force his boss to make a personal appearance. He told Charlie that if he got too cocky, the likelihood of Charlie ever walking again was slim and that breathing itself might prove tricky. He said that, now and in the future, it was probably best if Charlie kept himself to himself.'

I could tell that Ronnie had been impressed, by the relish with which he told us the story. I was pretty impressed myself, and I hadn't even had the pleasure of witnessing it.

'Then,' Ronnie continued, 'the nice man got on to you, dolly.' He looked at me hard, but with a merry glint in his eye. 'He said that if Charlie ever laid a finger on you again, he would personally see to it that Charlie ran out of fingers and possibly arms as well; working ones, anyway.'

I didn't know what to say. What did it mean? Was Frankie sweet on me? Or was he, like Ronnie said, simply a nice man? I really couldn't say, but either way, I was glad he'd had a word with Charlie.

'Did he give Charlie a slap or what?' Cook wanted to know.

Ronnie had to disappoint her. 'No, ducky. The only slap he got was from the front door smacking him in the hooter. Claret everywhere, if that brings you any satisfaction. But it wasn't that little toe-rag that swabbed the decks, it was Terence and me.

'No, the nice man didn't hit him. Didn't need to: he was very hot on the *menacing* tone and the rippling muscles. Charlie might be a fool but he knows genuine menace when he sees it. After all, he's related to Ma: he's familiar with it.'

'So he's safely off the manor?' I said, wanting to make absolutely sure.

'Oh, yes, dolly, take my word. And in no hurry to come back, either. I doubt even Mavis' allure will tempt him back until he's sure that nice man has left us.'

'Will you stop calling him "that nice man"?' I said. 'His name is Frankie.'

'Ah!' said Ronnie.

Frankie, having seen Charlie off, was left with Ma Hole and Percy Robinson to deal with, and of course it was Ma that gave him the most concern. He'd taken advice from Maltese Joe, who had said she was a 'vicious bitch' without a single saving grace or a conscience. Worse, she wasn't stupid, either.

'It's a nasty combination that: ruthless, intelligent and armed. Joe says she's the brains behind at least half a dozen smash and grabs at jewellers all over the Smoke. He even thinks she organized the big fur blag from Goldsteins, the furriers that supply Selfridges, Harrods, the lot. Now that's on our turf, and the boss takes a dim view. So he wants her hurt bad,' Frankie reported to us at teatime. I'd been at work all day and Frankie had been on what he called a 'reccy' of Ma's manor and her 'firm.'

Zinnia was not happy. 'I can't condone serious violence, young man,' she said, sounding appalled at the notion. 'I'm a healer, not a killer.'

I must admit, I found Frankie's attitude a bit chilling. Normally, he was such a sunny character, but he was solemn when he told us what he was up to. I could quite see how he could be frightening when he chose to be.

'He don't mean hurt bad in the limb department, Miss Makepeace,' Frankie assured her hastily, then hedged his bets. 'Well, not necessarily, anyway. He says it'd be easier to threaten her lads, get them to rethink their career prospects, than to try and frighten Ma Hole. He says to offer them the option of joining another firm, like ours, if they're up to it, or moving right out of the way. That'd leave her isolated and easier to pick off.'

'And how're you planning to persuade her young men to desert the rat,' asked Zinnia, 'without using violence?'

'Don't you mean something about rats deserting a sinking ship?' Frankie asked, bewildered for a second.

'I know what I mean, young man.' Zinnia's voice was sharp. 'That woman is a pestilence upon the land, she always has been. If I call her a verminous rodent, it's what I mean.' Zinnia was getting all biblical again; it proved you could get the girl off the island, but not get the island out of the girl. As Zinnia always said, 'The Wee Free Kirk has a lot to answer for, hen. So much intolerance of other ways of thinking and doing.'

'Well, there's money and better working conditions,' offered Frankie, 'and of course becoming part of a West End outfit's gotta be a leg up from being part of an East End one.' Frankie grinned, knowing he was getting right up my East End nose. 'And don't you go getting shirty, neither. You're heading West yourself,' he pointed out.

It was true, I couldn't deny it.

'Then there's the body parts,' Frankie said quietly, trying hard not to catch Zinnia's eye.

'What do you mean, "body parts"? I said that I'll have no serious violence. What's this about parts?'

'It's like this. Ma has got to be shown, in no uncertain terms, that she has to stick to her own patch. Other faces may get notions if she ain't stopped from poaching. But she's a stubborn and dangerous woman, according to Joe, who does not say such things lightly. Even he thinks twice about taking her on. It makes no sense for him to waste time, money and men on a war, when he could be using his resources in a more gainful way. But she still has to be stopped, right?'

We nodded, and Frankie carried on. 'So, he's decided that if he can't persuade her troops to leave her voluntarily, he'll use the body parts.'

'Wha—' Zinnia began but Frankie held up a hand to silence her. She shut her mouth and waited for the explanation.

'He reckons if you leave the odd hand, ear, finger, even an arm or a leg, in the right spot, it will give her lads something to contemplate when they are considering their next move,' Frankie explained to a stony-faced Zinnia and a green-around-the-gills me. 'And it don't do Joe's reputation any harm neither. Other faces are bound to get to hear about it. Don't panic! The bits don't come from anyone living, they come from the dissecting rooms at the medical school. The Prof there owes Joe big: bloody hundreds.'

'What for?' I asked. 'How do they even know each other?' Somehow a West End crook and a medical professor didn't seem like natural chums to me.

'Gambling, what do you think? Joe owns a few spielers and the Prof's obsessed with blackjack. Anyway, Joe'll wipe the Prof's slate clean for enough parts to do the job. He doesn't think it'll take that many. It'll save manpower, bloodshed and mayhem and,' he finished triumphantly, 'the stiffs don't belong to anyone who's gonna miss 'em.'

Zinnia and I sat there, dumbfounded by the simplicity of the plan, as well as its gruesomeness. We were both sure that there were some serious moral objections to be made, about the sanctity of the dead and so on, but Frankie asked us what about the sanctity of the living? And there was no real answer to that.

'Ladies, think about it. Hitler or the Prof's students have done the dismem—er, taking apart, half the time at least. Nobody knows what belongs to who. They ain't going to be buried by their families, with a name on their graves or anything. The hospital sees to it and they ain't sentimental. It's just bits to them, what have outstayed their usefulness. Joe's used them before. Works a treat. No-one gets hurt, but it concentrates the mind.'

'He has a point there, hen. Hospitals mainly throw those, er…items in the furnace and incinerate them. Sometimes they're buried in a mass grave.' Zinnia wasn't sentimental about bodies either, having laid out so many.

'I see your point,' I said, 'but it still strikes me as revolting.'

'Not half as revolting as having your head blown off by some snotty kid with a hand grenade,' said Frankie with feeling. 'And it would most likely be *my* head that copped it.' He was right. Ma had to be stopped, and if the departed could help save lives, then there was no point in objecting.

'You could say they're gonna be performing a public service,' Frankie pointed out. 'Saving lives, 'specially mine.'

So it was finally agreed. Not that it mattered whether Zinnia and I agreed or not. Maltese Joe said it was a plan, therefore it was a plan as far as Frankie was concerned.

'But for starters, there's old Percy to see to. Fancy a drink down the Star and Garter tonight, Zelda? You can point the bugger out to me.'

It didn't take me long to get ready, because most of my clothes were still back at the flat. A lick and a promise had to do. It was a nice evening, so we decided to walk to the pub.

'I forgot to tell you, Zelda,' Frankie said on the way. 'Joe says the flat's yours. Bert had already spoken to him about it when I brought it up. He's evicting his present tenants'—he looked at his watch—'even as we speak.'

I could have skipped! In fact, I think I did; I certainly shrieked. Then I gave it a little more thought. 'I'm not putting anyone on the street, am I? I wouldn't want that,' I said, not quite truthfully. If there were kids involved I wouldn't want it, or even a lone female, but I thought a grown bloke could probably take care of himself and I did need the flat.

'Keep your hair on,' Frankie smiled. 'They're just a couple of geezers who are getting on Joe's nerves, that's all. They're always slipping up when it comes to paying rent. If they weren't some sort of cousin, they'd've been out on the pavements months ago. He reckons they should piss off back to Malta, because he ain't running a bleeding charity, family or no family.'

'When do you reckon I can move in?' I asked.

'Joe says to leave it till the weekend, in case it takes a day or two for reason to sink in with his cousins. Bert'll have the keys for you on Saturday and Maggie says you can start work at the cafe on Monday if you like.'

I could hardly believe my luck. The weekend suddenly seemed a year away, instead of a few days. I was so happy I could have burst into a song and dance right there in the street. I didn't, but I just couldn't wipe the silly grin off my face as I walked into the pub.

Chapter 47

The Star and Garter was quite busy for a week-night. I saw Dilly and Chester sitting with Ronnie.

'Cooee!' Ronnie sang out as he waved across the saloon bar when he saw us come through the door. 'All aboard! We're celebrating.'

'Celebrating what?' I asked as soon as we came alongside.

'I'm not going to tell you, dolly, until you introduce me to this nice man.' Ronnie simpered and gave Frankie his most winning smile. 'I know we met over Charlie, but we were never formally introduced.'

I laughed and rolled my eyes at Ronnie. The man was incorrigible; you only had to show him a handsome face and a few muscles. I made the introductions. 'Frankie, this is my friend Ronnie, my friend Dilly and her friend, Chester.'

'Ah!' Dilly laughed, her face alight with an almost unearthly glow. 'Zelda's mysterious admirer, according to Mavis that is. She's told half the world about you and a strange man coming out of your place in the early hours of the morning—and Charlie's told the other half. He needs an excuse for you leaving him, Zeld, to save face. He says he slung you out because of your fancy man.'

I blushed. Of course, nothing was going on between me and Frankie, but I was beginning to have quiet hopes. I liked the man.

'Well, there's no truth to it. Frankie's just a friend,' I told her. 'He's been helping Zinnia out,' I added, as if that explained everything.

While all this was going on, Chester quietly stood up, held out his hand and shook Frankie's. 'How do you do, can I get you a drink? And you, Zelda? As the man said, we're celebrating. What can I get you two?'

'What are you celebrating?' I looked into Dilly's eyes and she smiled so wide, I swear that Gibraltar would've fitted with room to spare. She held up her left hand to show a rock considerably smaller than the famed one, but a respectable size none the less. It was an antique, she informed me—new rings were in very short supply, thanks to bloody Hitler.

'Second-hand,' Chester corrected softly. 'The guy at the store said it was second-hand.'

'Antique, second-hand, either way it's a dazzler,' I assured my friend and was rewarded by the wattage on her glow going up still further. Her face outshone her ring, and that was saying something.

'Molly. Champagne for the happy couple,' Ronnie sang out.

Molly guffawed. 'On yer bike, Ronnie. We don't have bubbly here, but I can do you a nice shandy.'

In the end, the men settled for beer and Dilly and I had shandy.

I raised my glass in a toast. 'To the happy couple.'

'To the happy couple,' came a pleasing response from every customer in the place—even Percy Robinson and Mrs. Dunmore.

I goggled. What was Sylvia Dunmore doing with Percy Robinson? I nudged Frankie and nodded very slightly towards the snug end of the bar. Frankie glanced over nonchalantly, then winked at me. 'Get Sylvia away from him, Zelda. Take her to the Ladies or something, the way you women do. What is it about women that they never seem to go to the khazi by themselves?' He seemed genuinely interested. I couldn't tell him offhand, because I'd never given it any thought. But it was true, we often did go mob-handed.

'What's she doing here with Percy anyway?' I said, bewildered by the turn of events. 'I thought he told her he was only messing about.'

Molly laughed. 'Well, Mrs. D. says that having sent her away, old Percy realized he couldn't live without her. But the truth is, Percy's old woman's slung him out at last, and he's got nowhere else to go.'

I tried to shift her, I really did, but Sylvia Dunmore had spotted Frankie and had correctly guessed that Percy was in for some bother. She would not budge. In the end, Frankie simply presented himself in front of the quaking couple, with Ronnie and Chester standing behind him, in case Percy made a run for it. Personally, I don't think the man's legs would have carried him. I could almost hear his knees knocking.

He'd heard about Charlie from somewhere, but then news travelled along with the wind in our neck of the woods, although the details were often wrong. Charlie's squashed nose had assumed the proportions of a thorough pasting, leaving him barely recognizable and unable to stand, and Frankie was identified as the one who had delivered the pasting. There was no mention of any front door smacking Charlie in the chops.

I was learning, though. When I'd heard the story, I knew Frankie would appreciate the publicity. In his game, any publicity was good as long as it involved gore. So I left the story uncorrected. Gossip had done Frankie's job for him. Percy needed no persuasion to leave Zinnia alone. He practically begged for the privilege of ignoring her completely, but that wasn't enough for Frankie.

'Nah,' he said. 'I still think I ought to give you a slap. Scaring an old lady like that, it definitely deserves a slap. And how do I know that once I'm gone, you'll keep your word? I mean, you're not known for your trustworthiness, are you? You can see my problem, I'm sure.'

Mrs. Dunmore saw it straight away. 'What if I told you we were going away?' she asked—pleaded, more like. What was *wrong* with the woman? I mean, he'd humiliated her publicly and here she was, back in his lap, practically.

'Going away, eh? When? Where?' His eyes narrowed. I saw what Ronnie meant about menacing. Good old Frankie suddenly looked really frightening. I shivered slightly and backed away a step.

'Brighton,' Mrs. Dunmore said. 'We'll go on Friday. I have a little money. We're going to open a boarding-house,' she said, grabbing Percy's reluctant arm and hanging on to it like grim death. Her knuckles were white as she dug her fingers into his sleeve, willing him to tell Frankie it was true.

Frankie turned his pitiless gaze on Percy, as if he was a specimen in a bottle. Percy nodded hastily and hard.

'Right then. You can piss off now, because I'm sick of looking at you. Don't let me see your ugly mush again, and believe me, come Saturday, I'll be looking.' As he spoke, Frankie poked Percy Robinson in the chest several times with a rigid finger to emphasize his words. Even that was too much violence for Percy, who whimpered slightly and backed away.

Frankie turned to Mrs. Dunmore. 'I'm warning you, Sylvia. This bit of rough'll see you wrong every time, but I don't s'pose you'll listen. Make sure you get him out of here, that's all, just make sure.' He allowed them to finish their drinks, then escorted them to the door and watched them slink down the dark street.

Ronnie clapped his hands together and shrieked, 'Ooh dolly, I do love a forceful omie,' as Frankie walked across the room. ''Specially if he's got a bona vardering eek, bod—and have you clocked the corybungus in those lally drags? Fantabulosa!'

I exploded, showering Chester with the last of my shandy. I couldn't even apologize, because I was choking. Chester kindly thumped me on the back.

'Ronnie!' wailed Dilly, 'I hardly ever understand a word you say and I'm certain Chester doesn't.'

Frankie had come back to our table by then. Ronnie had the grace to blush, but Frankie grinned and translated for him,

'He said, "I do love a forceful man, 'specially if he's got a good-looking face, body and have you noticed the bum in those trousers? Fabulous!" and I'm not sure…'—Frankie paused and looked round the bar carefully, to see if there was anyone else wandering about who fitted the description—'but I think he was talking about me.'

I choked all over again and Ronnie blushed harder.

'Unless he was referring to Percy boy; but I doubt it, his eek is anything but bona vardering and anyway, he's got nanty riah. But then I didn't vada his corybungus. That might've made up for it,' Frankie laughed.

'What's "nanty riah"?' Dilly asked, but she was ignored because I was staring at Frankie with my mouth wide open. Frankie was looking at Ronnie, and Ronnie was staring right back at him, face blank with utter astonishment. I heard a faint, far-off crash and tinkle as my hopes concerning Frankie were dashed.

I thought about it for a moment and decided it really didn't matter. It was enough that I was on the brink of freedom. I didn't need to clutter myself up with another bloke before the sheets were even changed after Charlie—metaphorically speaking, of course. I pulled myself together and heard Dilly's voice still plaintively asking, 'What's "nanty riah"?'

'No hair,' I answered absentmindedly. I was thinking how nice it was that Ronnie had found a new friend. 'So,' I said cheerfully. 'Where will you live when you're married, you two? London? New York? Paris?'

'Paris,' Dilly and Chester chorused, faces wreathed in happy smiles.

Chapter 48

There was panic stations at work the next day. Mrs. Dunmore had disappeared. No Mrs. D., no wages. I was going to need my wages if I was to pay the first week's rent in Soho. It wasn't easy telling Beryl and Cook that I was leaving on the Friday. But on the whole, they were pleased for me, knowing my situation with Charlie as they did. It left them in a spot, with no Mrs. Dunmore and no me either, but Cook took her courage in both hands and telephoned the man in charge, Mr. Frobisher, known to one and all as Old Misery Guts.

'He carried on about the lack of moral fibre nowadays,' Cook told us afterwards. 'And had a good moan, but Old Misery Guts promised to have our wages in our hands by Friday and someone in to help us out by Monday.'

I was going to miss Cook and Beryl, too. We even got weepy about it, until we cheered ourselves up by saying that Soho was only a bus ride away. We celebrated by raiding Mrs. Dunmore's drawers for her cache of Rich Tea biscuits and scoffed them all with a nice cup of tea and a good gossip about our ex-boss. None of us could understand her throwing in her lot with Percy Robinson, but as Cook said, there was no accounting for tastes.

Each night towards the end of that last week in Hackney, I went back to the flat and packed up a few more things. It really didn't amount to much. I took the pots and pans, the crockery and the cutlery on the grounds that Charlie couldn't cook. I took all my clothes, my camel-skin pouffe, some bedding and, after much thought, the gramophone and records. I'd earned them, I reckoned. Charlie could always get new ones with all the money he'd saved by not paying any rent on the flat for six long years.

By Friday night it was all done. I was ready to go. I had promised to meet Zinnia, Mum and Gran at the allotments because the judges were coming round to judge the plots and vegetables. As usual, some of Reverend Cattermole's honey was up for grabs, and so was Dobbin Whitelock's manure. Terry had put up two packets of Typhoo Tea and a bottle of Camp Coffee as further prizes, but the big one that year was forty Player's Navy Cut. Everyone was after those. Even if they didn't smoke, they could swap them with someone who did for all sorts of luxuries, such as chocolate, stockings, setting lotion or a pound of stewing steak.

The judging took place on the Friday evening, while the prize-giving was on Saturday afternoon at the grand picnic. All the interested parties and their hangers-on were gathered. I looked around for my lot and saw them camped out, adults on their Lloyd Loom chairs and kids sprawled on the grass, outside Zinnia's back gate. I thought my heart would break as I looked at them: Mum in her battered straw hat and Dad in his cap; Gran also in a straw hat, trimmed with faded pink roses; Doris with her hair neatly rolled into a blue headscarf and a clean wraparound pinny tied tight round her plump figure; Reggie, the twins, Vi, Tony and Zinnia—they were all there. I wondered when, if ever, I'd see them like that again. I wiped my eyes, blew my nose and went to join them.

As soon as I was within earshot I heard Gran hiss, 'There's been dirty dealings on the allotments. Some swine's gorn and nobbled Zinnia's beans.'

'Pardon?' I said.

'Somebody's gorn and nobbled Zinnia's beans,' repeated Gran, swivelling her eyes. 'Naming no names, but follow me eyes.' I followed her gaze and there, just on the other side of Zinnia's patch, stood the squat figure of Ma Hole and the stringy outline of her Brian, both grinning malevolently in our direction.

Rumour had it that there had been violent rows between mother and son over the previous week or two. Brian had been seen slamming out of their house on more than one occasion, with Ma screeching obscenities and threats and waving her fist after him, but they seemed united as they came to witness the judging. Ma stared down at the tangle of runner bean vines, blood-red blooms and velvety young beans crushed and battered into the soil, and smiled. Even the bean canes had been snapped and scattered around.

'I don't think much of your beans this year, Zinnia Makepeace,' she jeered. 'Looks like someone else'll have a chance for once. Can't see them making any kind of prize, can you, Brian?'

Brian shook his head. 'Don't reckon so, Mum. You always said she fixed the voting. Well, let's see her fix it now. They can't pretend a pile of rubbish like that's anything to write home about, can they?' And they walked back to their own plot, talking and laughing as if they hadn't a care in the world. We all watched them go in silence.

A few moments later, Reverend Cattermole, Mrs. Cattermole and several other worthies from the Allotment Committee came to judge our group of allotments. They tutted sympathetically at Zinnia's obviously sabotaged plot. 'Oh, Miss Makepeace, we are so sorry,' the Vicar told her. 'It's such a dreadful thing to do. I can't imagine who would do such a thing.'

'Well you must be the only bug…er, person who can't,' muttered Gran into her buttered scone. The Vicar and his party moved hastily on. He knew a disgruntled Gran when he saw one.

'What are you going to do?' I asked.

'Take it philosophically,' said Zinnia, placidly. 'There's nothing else I *can* do, hen. At least we know who did it. There's been no mystery about this particular act, and that makes it easier on my puir nervous system.'

'I dunno,' grumbled Gran. 'They didn't ought to get away with it.'

'Ach, well. Forget it now, Ida,' suggested Zinnia, 'and enjoy the cool of the evening and the spectacle of the judging.'

I looked about me, and thought that a load of shabby allotment owners plus our Vicar and his chums didn't make much of a spectacle. The judges plodded round, looking solemnly and carefully at each plot and making their deliberations. The Vicar carefully noted all comments on his clipboard before they moved on to the next one. Every face there was at least known to me, and quite a few were very dear. The event had become an important part of our social calendar. I realized with another pang that I was going to miss each and every one of my old neighbours: even the Holes, in a peculiar sort of way. Having a common enemy came in handy: they stopped you turning on each other.

I made up my mind there and then to come back the next day, after moving my stuff over to my new home and delivering Tony for his lesson. Suddenly, I wanted desperately to be at the Allotmenteers' annual picnic and prize-giving, in case it was the last time I ever got the chance. Anyway, a body never knew, we might even get our hands on that honey—or possibly the fags.

I was up bright and early the next morning. I had the urge to walk around, to say goodbye to familiar places while the streets were quiet. I was torn between excitement at a new beginning, sadness at leaving all that was familiar and relief that I was getting away from Charlie. I think excitement and relief had the edge, although the sadness did threaten to overwhelm those feelings at times, especially when it came to the nooks and crannies around Paradise Gardens. It was only the thought of tube trains and buses running east to west and west to east that stopped me blubbing my heart out.

Frankie was giving Tony and me a lift up West in his car, with all my household goods crammed in the spaces between bodies. It wasn't a comfortable ride, but we did get everything in the motor, which saved making two trips. It was arranged that Frankie would help me carry my stuff up the stairs to my new home while Tony was at his lesson. Once his lesson was over, Tony would hotfoot round to the flat and help where he could. Then, after a bite to eat at the cafe, all three of us would head back to Paradise Gardens in time for the picnic and prize-giving.

I hadn't yet made up my mind whether to spend Saturday night at my new place, or to troll over there after church and Sunday dinner. I was leaning towards the Sunday option, suddenly unwilling to give up all my rituals at once. All those months and years yearning to get away, yet when the moment came, I was reluctant to go!

'Ach hen, it's only natural,' Zinnia assured me when I got back to number 23. 'But you forget, you'll be seeing me quite often until Digby and I actually marry—and we're in no rush. And of course, Vi and Tony will be up to see you every Saturday, and I dare say your mother and grandmother will get in on the act too. You don't think they'll be able to control their curiosity, do you?'

I had to admit it was impossible to imagine Mum and Gran not being nosy. Of course they'd want to visit, to give unasked-for advice and even to meddle in my new life. The thought perked me up immediately.

The trip to Soho went smoothly, and Maggie was smiling widely as she handed over the keys to my new place. 'You'll want to nip up and have a look,' she told me. 'Frankie'll have a cup of tea with us. You better go on your own to begin with. You'll want to take it all in. I whipped round yesterday for you and gave it a bit of a clean. Joe's cousins left some mess, but I think Mrs. Joe threatened them with losing vital bits if they were too squalid. It comes with a bed, a cooker, table, chairs, stuff like that, but if you need anything, you've only to ask. I reckon we can rustle most things up between us.'

My hand was shaking as I stuck the key in the lock of the brown street door next to the cafe. A glossy brass plate announced that Peter R. D. Finn, Solicitor and Commissioner of Oaths, had his offices there. Even though he was a randy, flirtatious devil, I found the thought of Sharky being on the premises vaguely reassuring.

I pushed the door open and found myself in a narrow, dark hallway with a heavy locked door to the left and a set of painted stairs ahead of me. Maggie had told me that Sharky's offices were on the first floor and my flat was at the very top. I climbed the stairs with shaky legs. My heart was thundering as if I had just climbed Everest. It was ridiculous.

At the top was a tiny landing with one door leading off it, and another flight of stairs heading up to the roof. I turned the second key in the lock and pushed the door inwards to a small kitchen, with a window looking out on to a patch of weedy concrete entirely surrounded by other buildings. The air above the concrete patch was crisscrossed with washing lines and, sure enough, I also had a rope and pulley arrangement for my washing. A tiny table and two chairs were placed in front of the sash window. There was a larder, a cooker and a butler's sink with a cupboard under it. Everything sparkled with Maggie's elbow grease. I smiled to myself as I imagined eating my meals at that little table. I'd be able to wave at my neighbours while I was at it.

There was a bedroom next to the kitchen. It looked out over the roof of next door's extension, which had filled up their patch of concrete. The flat roof had a small table, some chairs and, arranged around the edges, large tin cans stuffed full of bright red geraniums. There was a coffee pot, a cup and a plate on the table. Somebody had had their breakfast out there.

I took stock of the room. It wasn't large, but it did have a cupboard, a bed, a dressing table with three drawers beneath and the window. All I was likely to need. I was going to have to replace the curtains, which were dark and shabby, and the brown lino on the floor had also seen better days. Still, all in good time.

The living room was a lovely room. It faced out on to the street, and at the moment I walked in, the sun was pouring in one of the two windows. There was a fireplace, with a mantel over it, and a sideboard with a mirror hanging on the wall above it. There were two comfortable-looking chairs upholstered in a ghastly brown fabric that would have to go, and an understuffed sofa that didn't match them. The curtains were a mustard shade, with a pattern of overblown brown roses, also nasty. Thank goodness for my trusty Singer.

I knew I was going to love this room. Despite the drab furniture, it had a warmth and a cosiness about it that promised much.

There was also a small spare room, just big enough for a narrow, single bed and a chest of drawers. It had a tiny fireplace with shelves set into the recess on one side of the chimney breast, and a cupboard set into the other. It may have been small, but I reckoned it'd take the odd nephew or niece now and then. It was good to know that I had room for them to stay when they wanted. It lessened the awful sadness at leaving them behind. And the long school holidays were about to start!

I thought I would burst with joy when I pushed open the last door in the flat. It was a bathroom! A bathroom of my very own, complete with a proper bath, a basin and an indoor khazi. I had never, in my life, had a plumbed-in bath and an indoor toilet, let alone one all to myself. I thought I must be in heaven, or the Ritz at the very least. I gazed lovingly at that bathroom for what felt like a week, but was only minutes. I was in love. As well as being besotted with my bathroom, I loved every inch of my new flat; I could hardly wait to start making it my home.

I spent the rest of the morning happily puttering about putting things away as Frankie and Tony ferried bags and boxes up the stairs. It didn't take long, because I didn't have a lot, and it was noon when I finished. Just time for dinner at the cafe and then back to Paradise Gardens for the picnic. The prizes were to be announced and given at three, and the bunfight was scheduled for straight after that.

'So, what do you think? Suit you, will it?' Maggie asked as soon as I stood in front of her.

'I love it. I just love it. Thanks for cleaning it for me, it's spotless. It was very kind of you and I appreciate it.' I felt awkward. I wasn't used to people skivvying for me.

'That's all right, love. Mamma Campanini and her girls helped me. They live the other side of you and run the delicatessen. I'll introduce you later. Lovely people. Now, what can I get you? There's liver and bacon with mashed spuds and onion gravy or, as a special treat, there's some of Mamma Campanini's ravioli with a tomato sauce—but don't tell anyone because there's only a few portions of that.'

I had no idea what ravioli was, but suddenly I felt adventurous. 'Ravioli please,' I said firmly, a huge smile plastered across my face.

'Liver and bacon, please,' said Tony, equally firmly, and we all laughed.

'One ravioli and one liver it is. Drinks?'

Pretty soon we were seated at what had rapidly become 'our' table and tucking in for all we were worth. The ravioli was delicious! Maybe I did have Italian blood after all.

Chapter 49

Everyone was there for the prize-giving, because nobody wanted to miss the picnic. It was the nearest we got to a holiday. That and hop picking in Kent.

'Ladies, gentlemen and children,' sang out Reverend Cattermole, 'it is my great pleasure to announce the winners of the Annual Vegetable and Allotment Competition.' He always did the announcements on account of him being used to public speaking, what with church services and everything. He had a good, strong voice that carried right across the allotments—unless there was a train passing, in which case even he was drowned out.

'As usual, we'll start with the smaller prizes. The first prize for a magnificent marrow goes to young Arthur Whitelock. Well done, young man. May I present you with a packet of refreshing Typhoo Tea, kindly donated by Rainbird's the grocers.' The Vicar did the honours and young Arthur grinned in triumph. How keen he was on tea was anybody's guess, but I was pretty sure his parents wouldn't grumble.

Molly Squires' mum got the other packet of tea for her carrots. The Camp Coffee went to the Whitelocks again, for the best beetroots; they had Dobbin to thank for that. I listened to the Vicar's voice rising and falling above the hum of the spectators' talk and the buzz of his very own bees. The warm sun, the gentle murmuring and contentment were making me drowsy. I lay flat on my back staring up at fluffy clouds and blue sky, happy in the knowledge that there would be no doodlebugs or enemy aircraft, and that the only things likely to dive-bomb us were the sparrows, starlings and pigeons.

'This year, the best runner bean award has been won by Florence Marriott. Congratulations, Mrs. Marriott.' I sat up. With Zinnia out of the running, Mum had won the beans! I jumped to my feet and flung my arms around her dear neck.

'Mum! You won the beans!' I yelled, as if she didn't know.

Mum laughed; her face looked so young, suddenly. 'No, lovey, I didn't win the beans. It might be my allotment, but this year, you did all the work. *You* won the beans, Zelda.' She turned and shouted across the plots. 'Did you hear that, Vicar? Zelda grew the beans, she should get the honey.'

'Right you are, Florence. It is my proud pleasure, then, to present a pot of honey donated by my own dear bees to the winner of the best beans section, Mrs. Zelda Fluck!' I didn't know what to say. My cup ran over: new home, new life *and* a pot of honey. It was just hard that I'd won because Zinnia's runners had been nobbled; but looking at her happy, smiling face I thought she didn't seem to mind, so I decided not to mind either.

I accepted the honey gratefully. It was only on my way back to my mob that I noticed Ma Hole and Brian. Ma's expression would have curdled milk. Brian's face was harder to read: he looked nervous, if anything. I passed close by them and heard Ma hissing at her son, 'You useless little sod. I can't even trust you to grow a decent row of beans, but you spend bleeding hours on the allotment if you're to be believed. What have you been doing down here, if you haven't been growing prize sodding veg?' She landed him a hefty clip round the ear. I thought it was no wonder he was so dim, the way she rattled his poor brains—such as they were.

I had just arrived back and settled down on the grass with my precious honey, when the Vicar coughed and announced that we had come to the first prize, the one awarded to the best overall plot.

'I feel a few words of explanation may be due here, ladies, gentlemen and children,' the dear man told us. 'As you may know, a most heinous act of vandalism took place here recently. Miss Makepeace's runner beans were quite deliberately destroyed by a person or persons unknown'—he looked hard towards Ma and Brian, letting us know that he, for one, had his suspicions—'before the official judging could take place. However, the Committee is unanimous in the opinion that Miss Makepeace still deserves a prize. We all garden here and see her efforts regularly, and we are agreed that, before the thugs trampled her beans, hers was by far and away the best-kept plot, with the healthiest vegetables. Therefore it is with great pleasure that we award the first prize to Miss Zinnia Makepeace.'

The allotments erupted in clapping, cheering and yells of 'Speech, speech!' It seemed the good people of Paradise Gardens didn't like bean-nobbling cheats either. I looked at the crowd and saw Brian and Ma shove their way to the front.

Ma's face was purple with rage. She pointed at Zinnia but spoke to the Vicar. 'You rigged it!' she screamed, spittle flying in all directions. 'You rigged it so that miserable Scottish hag could win. Those fags are mine by rights, and you know it.' It was ridiculous; the woman was apoplectic with fury, yet she could get cigarettes any time she liked. After all, she had supplied the local black market with them for years. It made no sense. Whatever it was that was getting on Ma's top note, it wasn't the forty Player's Navy Cut.

'We was born and bred round here,' Ma said bitterly, 'but that don't count for nothing when you fucking outsiders come along and take things over. You divvy up all the best houses, the best allotments and the best prizes between you, year in and year fucking out.'

She turned to the sea of listening faces. 'And you lot ain't no better. You let them. And if it ain't the outsiders, then it's the bleeding Marriotts and Smallbones, thinking they're better than the rest of us. Look at when our Charlie got trapped into marrying one of them. You'd think they couldn't sink any lower the way they bleeding carried on...' Ma took a breath and would have continued but for Gran's interruption.

'That's enough of that, Gladys Hole. There's kids present and even one or two ladies'—we all sniggered at that—'and we don't want none of your filthy language, thank you very much. Has it ever occurred to you that we might think we're a cut above you because we *are* a cut above?'

Gran appealed to the listening crowd. 'You don't hear any of us carrying on, effing and blinding and being bad sports, now do you?'

'No!' they all roared as one.

'No,' repeated Gran with enormous satisfaction. 'See? That's why people treat you different, Gladys Hole. We don't like you. We don't like the way you carry on. We don't like the thieving and the bullying, and we 'specially didn't like it in the war, when the rest of us was trying to pull together. And you're still at it now, when we all want to rebuild our lives the best way we can.

'Only yesterday Terry Rainbird said someone had the petrol out of his motor. Broke the padlock on his garage to get at it. Of course, that meant he couldn't collect his stock, which meant no sugar ration for the rest of us. Now, I wonder who had that away? He gets that petrol ration on account of his ticker, but you don't give a monkey's about that, do you? You or your use-less thieving toe-rag of a son.' Gran took a breath and the Vicar grabbed the opportunity to butt in.

'Ladies, ladies, I'm sure the good people here don't want to listen to this…' he began, only to be drowned out by the good people yelling, 'Oh yes we do.'

'We wouldn't miss it for the world,' rang out one voice, I don't know whose. 'It's time someone told her.'

It was then that Zinnia stuck her oar in. 'Well, I for one would like my tea. So, Mrs. Hole, if it'll keep the peace, you can have the cigarettes. I dinna smoke the things anyway.'

Mum, Gran, Vi and Dad all spluttered in outrage. *They* had a use for those fags and we all knew some poor sods would be paying top whack for them on the black market by suppertime. Ma would sell most of them, one or two at a time, for maximum profit and smoke the rest. We were all appalled, but Zinnia was unrepentant.

'Ach, it's supposed to be fun and there's no fun if there's arguments over the prizes. I know I'm a good gardener. I've had my fair share of prizes and I know that I won this one fair and square. I don't need the cigarettes to prove it.'

The Vicar beamed his approval. 'A fine Christian attitude, Miss Makepeace, I must say.' His smile dropped as he turned to Ma. 'Here, Mrs. Hole, with the compliments of the gracious winner.'

I thought Ma would snatch his hand off as she grabbed the fags and moved away through the murmuring, hissing and, in places nowhere near Ma, actually booing crowd.

The Vicar clapped his hands together. 'Right you are. Tea, I think. Let the eating and drinking commence.'

We didn't need telling twice. As one, we moved towards the trestle tables set up by the boundary wall. We'd all contributed to the feast and I must say we did ourselves proud. Not only was there plenty to eat and drink, but we had Ma Hole's performance to talk about too. Good food, good company and good gossip on a sunny afternoon in peacetime. What could be better?

I finished my Spam sandwich and looked around me. The food had settled everyone down. It was hard to believe there had been an ugly scene at all. Even Ma and Brian weren't fighting with anyone, but then it's difficult to pick a quarrel with people who have turned their backs on you and are pretending you're not there. Virtually everyone had moved away from the pair and joined the throng at the other end of the allotments, as near as they could get to the tables and the food.

However, being the Holes, it was against their nature for peace to reign indefinitely in their vicinity. As soon as the food was finished, we heard raised voices coming from their direction.

'I said, get me another cup of tea, you ungrateful little bastard,' Ma shouted, raising her hand to give her beloved boy's ear another clip. This time, though, he blocked the move with his forearm and jumped to his feet. By this time, they had the attention of everyone present.

'Leave me alone, Mum, I mean it,' said Brian, as clear as anything.

'And what are you going to do if I don't?' Ma sneered. 'I said, get your arse over there and get me another cup of tea,' she repeated, only louder.

'No. I ain't going in among that lot. They hate us and I ain't doing it. Get your own sodding tea!' Brian's face was red, his fists balled and his arms were rigid by his side. I thought he was going to punch his mother for a moment, but then he thought better of it and turned and ran, barging past Frankie, who was on his way in, having been at the pub suggesting alternative employment to some of Ma Hole's other 'boys.' Everyone, including Ma, was watching Brian's back as he raced down the alley and out of sight. It was only when he was gone that we let out our breath in one giant sigh.

'What was that all about?' Frankie asked as he arrived at our little group. Zinnia had her mouth open to tell him when there was an enormous WHOOSH, followed by a rapid rat-a-tat-tat sound. '*Down!*' shouted Frankie above the noise. 'Get down! That's gunfire.'

We all hit the deck and covered our heads with our arms as clods of earth, bits of flowerpot and sundry pieces of garden tools rained down upon us. Young Arthur Whitelock missed being impaled by a flying gardening fork by inches—although it got his marrow fair and square—and I looked up just in time to see a trowel whizzing through the air. The air above us was thick with black smoke and cries of 'What happened?,' 'Was it a doodlebug?' and 'Is 'Itler at it again?'

Eventually, I heard Frankie say, 'Sounds like that's the lot, but stay down till I've had a shufty.' A few moments later he was back. 'It's all clear. You can get up now.'

'What happened?' asked Mum.

'Looks like one of the sheds blew up,' Frankie answered. 'There's a bloody great crater over there and it's still smoking.'

Gingerly, we made our way through the throng towards a puff of smoke that was rising like a genie from the hole in the ground and the ruins of a shed. I took my bearings. 'It's Ma Hole's shed,' I said. 'Or at least it was. Where's Ma?'

'I think she went up with it,' a shaky voice answered. It was Mr. Whitelock, looking shocked and pale. He had one arm round his Arthur, who was trembling from his narrow squeak, and the other round Mrs. Whitelock, who had gathered the rest of their brood around them and was busy counting heads to make sure they were all there.

'Did you see what happened?' Frankie asked him.

'Yes. Well, sort of. After Brian run away, Ma seemed fine, just sat there and lit a fag as if nothing had happened and she didn't have a care in the world. Then she must've decided to go home because she started packing their stuff up. She went into the shed with their deckchairs and that's when it blew.'

We edged closer to the crater and looked in, but there was nothing much to see besides a blackened hole, bits of shed smouldering in the grass and the remains of garden tools, beanpoles and crops scattered about. Frankie paced about a bit, looking hard at certain items he found in the grass, but he simply nudged them with his foot, making no attempt to touch them. Ronnie appeared beside him, having left his mum in the capable hands of Molly and her mum, and they paced the area between them, urging the rest of us to step back.

'Watch out, here comes Hilda Handcuffs,' Ronnie said and Frankie glanced up in time to see George Grubb approaching the scene, still holding a meat paste sandwich in one hand and a cup of tea in the other.

'Any idea what happened?' he asked.

'It looks like Gladys Hole has blown herself up,' Ronnie answered.

'She just walked into her shed to put a deckchair away and BOOM!' Mr. Whitelock added.

Frankie beckoned George Grubb over and pointed to something in the grass. 'Looks like we've found the boy's gun,' he said. 'And his box of ammunition went up, judging by the bullets that were flying about after the shed exploded.'

'Any idea what caused it to blow?' George Grubb asked.

'There's bits of jerry can scattered about all over the place,' answered Ronnie. 'At a guess, I'd say petrol.'

'It could be petrol what done it, Mr. Grubb,' Tony piped up. 'Brian sometimes puts what he swipes in the shed until he sells it or swaps it.'

'And Ma did have a fag on,' added Mr. Whitelock. 'I saw her light up.'

'And somebody has been nicking petrol lately.' Terry put in his two penn'orth. 'They drained my van last night. Couldn't get to the suppliers because of it.'

'Hmm,' said George Grubb, putting two and two together slowly. 'Doesn't sound like foul play. A nasty accident, on the face of it. Still, I'd better get the proper authorities to take a look as soon as possible. Keep everyone away from the site, will you? But don't anyone leave until they've been questioned.

'I'll nip along to the station and get things in motion,' concluded George, who had never nipped anywhere in his life.

Everyone was too stunned to argue. We all simply drifted away, back to our picnic spots, and settled down to wait for the men in blue. Soon, the unholy, shocked silence gave way to quiet murmuring as people talked among themselves.

'Funny,' Mum said. 'All those years of war when nothing hit Paradise Gardens and we have to dodge bullets and flying sheds in peacetime. It goes to show you something—I just ain't sure what.'

All Dad could think of to say, over and over again in an awed voice, was, 'Fancy Ma Hole copping it.' It was a shocker all right.

'It seems like divine retribution, somehow,' Zinnia observed, 'when you consider the havoc that woman has wreaked in her time.'

'I wonder where Brian is,' Tony said in a shaky voice. 'I mean, he won't know about his mum, will he?'

'It'll certainly go hard on the boy,' Reverend Cattermole observed. 'In a way, you could say he's responsible for his mother's, er, demise.'

'But are we sure the old bat's dead?' Gran voiced the question the rest of us were too polite to ask. 'I mean, are we absolutely certain that she went up with it?'

'Oh, I think so, Mrs. Smallbone,' Mr. Whitelock reassured her. 'I saw her walk into the shed and then up it went. She certainly didn't step out again. Even if she had, she wouldn't have had time to escape the blast.'

Chapter 50

When I started work in Soho on the Monday morning, I had plenty of news to tell my new employers. The breakfast rush was over and we were taking a breather over our own mid-morning tea and toast. The Featherbys didn't stint on food for the staff; I'd already had bacon and egg at six.

'No,' breathed Maggie as I explained how the police had finally found Ma Hole's body, with hardly a scratch on it, up a tree.

'Yes,' I said. 'Blown straight up in the air and landed on top of this conker tree. Hanging over a branch, she was. She still had her hat on and everything.'

Bert laughed. 'I bet Maltese Joe'll get some mileage out of that, what with his man being on the spot. It won't be an act of God by the time he's finished with the story; it'll be an act of Joe. That'll show any other would-be scallywags: they better lay off his manor, or else be blown into another one down kingdom come way.'

I have to say that, although I missed Cook and Beryl, I didn't miss Mrs. Dunmore one little bit. Maggie was a much easier person to work for. She never asked me to do anything she wouldn't do herself, she was always friendly about it and seemed to really appreciate my efforts. She even showed a pride in my work, and wouldn't hesitate to tell customers how I'd been slaving away on the oven and that she could see her face in it when I'd finished.

'She does a better job than I ever did, I can tell you that,' she'd confide to regulars. 'Remind me not to take advantage of her, otherwise she'll be off, and then where would I be?' she'd chuckle. At the same time as singing my praises, she was, of course, introducing me to the locals in my new neighbourhood. It didn't take me long to begin to feel at home.

After work I'd concentrate on my lovely new flat. The first thing to do was track down some distemper. It wasn't hard. I asked Bert, who mentioned it to Frankie, who sent a skinny bloke round with some cans of it two days later. By the end of the week, the trusty treadle on my Singer was rocking away on curtains, a bedspread and some cushions, using fabric supplied by yet more 'friends' in the schmutter trade. It seemed that nothing was impossible to come by: sometimes difficult, but never impossible. Bert usually knew a bloke, and if he didn't, Frankie did, or Maggie did, or someone else knew a bloke who knew a bloke.

Maggie insisted I took a day off for Ma Hole's funeral.

'But I didn't even like her,' I pointed out.

'I know, but you must show respect all the same. It'll be expected,' she reminded me.

It was true, it would. So I went, not at all sure what I was walking into. What I wasn't expecting was to be one of only a dozen or so people there. Usually everyone turned out for one of our own. 'Even the heathens, agnostics and downright atheists,' as Gran pointed out in a loud whisper, only to be shushed by Mum.

It was sad; there was just a small group of 'mourners' huddling in that big, old church, and not one of us actually mourning. There was Reverend Cattermole, of course, and Mrs. Cattermole on her organ. Zinnia was there in a severe black hat that did nothing for her, just made her look washed-out. Mum and Dad had made the effort, and Vi and Tony had turned up, too. Doris had decided it was no place for the twins, while Reggie's asthma had taken a convenient turn for the worse. George Grubb represented the Law. There was no sign of Brian. No-one had seen him since he'd fled from the allotments just before his mother had been blown up to meet her Maker.

Once the service was over, we all traipsed out into the sunny churchyard and gathered round the recently dug grave. We spread out a bit, to make it look more populated. 'I know I shouldn't speak ill of the dead,' Gran said quietly, 'but Gladys Hole's no great loss, no great loss at all. It's good riddance to bad rubbish. The woman only got her comeuppance, if you think about it. In fact, you could say that life's bound to be better round here, with one more Hole in the ground.' She cackled, pleased with her joke.

Mum shushed her again. 'Everyone deserves to have someone who's sorry they're dead at their own funeral. It seems only right and proper,' she said, but there was no getting away from it: we all agreed with Gran's sentiment, but were too polite to say so.

Chapter 51

I was settling in very nicely and very quickly, so all my worries about that had been for nothing. I'd transformed my flat and taken to my new job as if I was born there. It was wonderful. I had expected to feel lonely, but I wasn't, thanks to Maggie introducing me to every regular who walked through her doors. Pretty soon I was being hailed on the street by familiar faces, addressed by name in shops and at the market and chatted to by the customers.

'Nice day for it, ain't it, Zelda?' some bloke'd say with a friendly leer. Things stay the same wherever you are.

'Nice day for what? You cheeky beggar,' I'd reply. We'd both laugh and a funny kind of friendship would be struck up. It oiled the wheels and helped my face to fit. It also made for an extra carrot or spud in my veg shopping, if I saw the joker at his stall, but nobody ever tried to take advantage. It was understood: I worked in the cafe with the Featherbys and I was a local 'face.' What's more, I was a friend of Frankie, which did no harm at all.

I also got to know the women pretty quickly. That was down to Maggie too. Almost as soon as they met me, she would tell them I could read the tea leaves and was 'ever so good.' It wasn't long before I had a steady stream of girls and boys from the local theatres coming to have their fortunes told.

That was how I worked up a sideline in running up costumes: or altering them, to be more precise. There was rarely enough fancy fabric to make something completely new, but I was good at unpicking and resewing, mending and making do. So I made a little extra money doing just that. Money or sugar or chocolate, I wasn't fussy. I'd outfit a cast of thousands for a whole large bar of chocolate all to myself. Well, a cast of several, anyway.

Truth to tell, I liked hanging around with the theatrical types, and my working knowledge of Polari didn't hurt in Theatreland either. I also found I had a whole host of people ready, willing, able and, indeed, eager to part with multi dinarly, in hard cash, for my clairvoyant skills with tea leaves, palms and eventually, once I'd boned up on them, astrology and Tarot cards too. Theatricals are very keen on the Tarot, in my experience. Packs of the special cards have travelled all over the globe with them for hundreds of years.

Still, all that came later. Right then, though, when I first arrived, I worked for Maggie and Bert and I loved it. If I hadn't had my lovely flat to go to, I wouldn't have left the cafe at all, I'm sure. I didn't even get the chance to miss my family Sunday dinners, because Maggie and Bert often entertained their friends on Sundays. Rations were pooled in just the same way, only without the added family fights, and black market nosh was also readily available.

In Soho, you were just as likely to get an Italian Sunday dinner or a Maltese one, depending on who was doing the cooking and what was around. So I not only got to know a wide circle of people, but I experienced different sorts of food too. The whole thing was one big adventure.

I'd been there just a couple of weeks when Sunday dinner was cooked by the Campaninis, my neighbours with the roof garden, geraniums and delicatessen. We'd eaten and drunk far more than was good for us and were all feeling bloated and sleepy. The Campaninis went home for an afternoon nap, leaving just Cassie, Maggie, Bert and me.

Maggie and I were in the kitchen tackling a mountain of washing-up, just to make a change, when we heard a cry come from the cafe. We ignored it, thinking it was part of some story that Cassie was telling Bert. Then there was another cry, followed by an urgent, 'Maggie, come here, quick,' from Bert.

We dropped what we were doing and rushed into the cafe to find poor Cassie groaning and doubled over in pain and Bert looking stricken.

'What on earth's the matter?' Maggie asked.

'It's Cassie,' Bert said, unnecessarily as it happened, because we could see and hear that. There was a large puddle on the floor. When I noticed that, I was certain of what was going on. Years of trailing around after Zinnia had taught me a thing or two.

'Her waters have broken. She's in labour,' I told them.

'What do we do?' Bert asked in a panic. It was amazing. Here was a man who would face down an armed spiv if the need arose, but he flew into a panic at the thought of childbirth—a far more natural event, in my opinion.

'We should get her to hospital if we've got time, or call a doctor at least,' I said. 'How often are the contractions coming?' I sounded as if I knew what I was talking about, which quelled some of the rising fear I could sense around—and inside—me.

Maggie looked relieved. 'I'll go and find a phone and call an ambulance, shall I? Or would the local quack be better?'

'No. You stay with me, Maggie. We'll send Bert. Who do you think is likely to get here quicker, the doctor or the ambulance? I don't think there's going to be a lot of time to spare, judging by the way Cassie's panting. I've got a feeling that this baby is the impatient type and not likely to wait around for too long.' If I was any judge, the baby was well on its way.

'Try Doc Goodbone first, Bert. He's just round the corner. If he's not there, call an ambulance. Sharky's got the nearest telephone.' Maggie's initial panic was settling down to solid common sense. 'Oh, and Bert, if all that fails, Miss Makepeace might be at Digby's place. She'll know what to do.' Bert nodded at his wife and headed for the door, relief set in every line of his body.

'Maggie, help me get Cassie to a more comfortable spot. We don't want her giving birth in front of those windows. The poor girl deserves her privacy. Then, can you put some water on to boil, and plenty of it?'

Maggie and I were only able to get Cassie as far as the counter before another huge contraction doubled her up again. Maggie ran upstairs and came back with some pillows, towels, sheets and a blanket. We made Cassie as comfortable as we could behind the counter, out of sight of the street.

We were crouched down beside her, hanging on to a hand each, when there was a loud knocking at the cafe door. Maggie hurried to answer it. It was Mamma Campanini. Bert had banged on their door as he galloped past, rightly thinking that Mamma had lots of experience of childbirth.

There was no doubt that the baby was well on the way. The chances of medical help before it was born were slim. We would have to manage between us. Mamma and I took up our stations each side of the screaming, panting and writhing Cassie, while Maggie boiled water, and while she was at it, sterilized a sharp kitchen knife and a set of scissors.

Cassie didn't think much of giving birth. You could tell by the wild-eyed screams and curses that accompanied every contraction. She used language that would have made a sailor colour up, if we'd had one handy. I was too busy to blush and Mamma showed no signs that she'd even heard the effing and blinding. I must admit, Anglo-Saxon screamed in a posh, plummy accent sounded a tad out of place. Maggie tried to moderate things a bit by telling Cassie that a lady didn't swear like that.

'On the contrary, Maggie, only a fucking lady can,' was Cassie's reply, yelled between earth-shattering screams. 'Now for Christ's sake, get this bloody thing out of me.'

At last, after what seemed like days but was probably less than an hour, I saw the crown of a small and very hairy head appear between Cassie's legs. 'Right, love,' I said. 'Push now, push hard.' A few moments and an eardrum-bursting scream later and a bloody, squirming little bundle entered the world.

'It's a girl!' I cried and burst into tears of relief. Both mother and baby were still alive, despite my ministrations!

'Congratulations, Cassie love, you have a beautiful baby girl,' said Maggie, mopping up her tears on her pinny.

Only Mamma, smiling from ear to ear, gold teeth flashing, seemed to be on top of the situation at that moment. She deftly wiped the baby down with a wet flannel and gave her a smack on her tiny little rump. Right on cue, the baby let out her first cry. Mamma laid the baby on Cassie's belly and I got ready to cut the umbilical cord. I took a deep breath as I tried to decide between the kitchen knife and the scissors to do the job.

I was shaking like a leaf. I'd never had to actually cut a cord before and I was very frightened that I'd hurt the baby or her mother. I'd just decided that the scissors were the thing to use, when I heard the bell of an ambulance and a screech of brakes. Thank God! I dropped the scissors and the knife. Bert had arrived with an ambulance in the nick of time. I was saved!

There was a spontaneous party that night. Once we'd all been made to leave mother and baby in peace at the hospital, we'd hurried back to the cafe to find a party already in full swing. When I finally fell into bed, slightly drunk and almost numb with all the excitement and the praise heaped upon my undeserving head, it was well into the early hours of Monday morning. I don't know if it was the drama, the booze or sheer high spirits, but despite my exhaustion, I tossed and turned all night, dreaming dreams that mostly made no sense—except for one.

It was Christmas in my dream, and there was a party at the cafe. Everyone was there: the Campaninis, Maltese Joe, Mrs. Joe, Frankie and my friends and family from Paradise Gardens too. Gran was dancing with Papa Campanini and laughing so hard that I thought her teeth must fly out, while Zinnia and Digby Burlap were sitting quietly in a corner, talking about something I couldn't quite hear, however hard I flapped my dream ears—and believe me, they *were* flapping; I'm nosy even in my sleep. Terry and Vi were at another table, listening to Tony singing, their faces rapt.

There was a Christmas tree in the corner and a table groaning with the remains of a turkey dinner with all the trimmings. Bits of home-made crackers littered the table, making bright splashes of colour against the white tablecloth. On the counter, several Christmas puddings and two large jugs of custard waited to be served, but Maggie and Bert were busy bending over what looked like a sideboard drawer placed on a table in the corner. In my dream, I sort of peered over their shoulders. There, waving her arms about, was Cassie's baby.

Maggie picked the little girl up and cradled her in her arms, rocking her gently and smiling tenderly. In the background, Tony's voice soared above the now hushed crowd. 'Silent night, holy night…'

Maggie turned towards me, her face alight with joy. 'Her name's Rosie,' she told me, as Bert stood close beside her, his large finger clutched in Rosie's tiny hand, 'and she's ours.'